About the Authors

From as far back as she can remember, Michelle Conder dreamed of being a writer. She penned the opening pages of a romance novel just after she finished university, but much study, many (varied) jobs, one adorable husband, and three gorgeous children before she finally sat down to turn that dream into a reality. Michelle lives in Australia, and when she isn't busy plotting she loves to read, ride horses, travel and practice yoga. Visit Michelle: michelleconder.com

Melanie Milburne read her first Mills and Boon at age seventeen, in between studying for her final exams. After completing a Masters Degree in Education she decided to write a novel, and thus her career as a romance author was born. Melanie is an ambassador for the Australian Childhood Foundation, a keen dog lover and trainer, and enjoys long walks in the Tasmanian bush. In 2015 Melanie won the HOLT Medallion, a prestigious award honouring outstanding literary talent.

Tara Pammi can't remember a moment when she wasn't lost in a book, especially a romance which, as a teenager, was much more exciting than mathematics textbook. Years later, Tara's wild imagination and love for the written word revealed what she really wanted to do: write! She lives in Colorado with the most co-operative man on the planet and two daughters. Tara loves to hear from readers and can be reached at tara.pammi@gmail.com or her website tarapammi.com

Sins and Seduction

December 2022
Terms of Surrender

January 2023
The Ruthless Rival

February 2023
Wicked Games

March 2023
Her Every Fantasy

April 2023
Tempting the Boss

May 2023
A Deal in Passion

Sins and Seduction: Wicked Games

MICHELLE CONDER

MELANIE MILBURNE

TARA PAMMI

MILLS & BOON

First Published in Great Britain 2023
by Mills & Boon, an imprint of HarperCollins*Publishers* Ltd,
1 London Bridge Street, London, SE1 9GF

www.harpercollins.co.uk

HarperCollins*Publishers*
Macken House, 39/40 Mayor Street Upper,
Dublin 1, D01 C9W8, Ireland

SINS AND SEDUCTION: WICKED GAMES © 2023 Harlequin Enterprises ULC.

The Italian's Virgin Acquisition © 2017 Michelle Conder
Blackmailed into the Marriage Bed © 2018 Melanie Milburne
An Innocent to Tame the Italian © 2019 Tara Pammi

ISBN: 978-0-263-31866-1

MIX
Paper | Supporting
responsible forestry
FSC™ C007454

THE ITALIAN'S
VIRGIN
ACQUISITION

MICHELLE CONDER

Thank you to Laura, my beautiful editor, who deserves amazing things to happen in her life.

CHAPTER ONE

SEBASTIANO CHECKED HIS Rolex as he strode into SJC Towers, his London office building, completely oblivious to the wintry rain landing like icy pellets on his face. From the moment he'd woken up he'd known it was going to be an interesting day. Interesting as in the Chinese curse 'interesting'—not 'it's going to be great' interesting. Not that he held much with curses or proverbs.

But he wasn't going to let noisy workmen, an unexpected early-morning visit from his now ex-mistress or a flat tyre derail him. He had been waiting for over two years for this day and finally his crusty old grandfather was going to give up on his stubbornness and hand over the reins of the family dynasty. And not before time!

Bert, his weekend security chief, gave him a nod as he approached the reception desk, not at all perplexed to see his boss arriving for work on a Sunday morning.

'Catch the game yesterday, boss?' Bert asked with a flashing grin.

'Don't gloat,' Sebastiano advised. 'It's a very unattractive quality.'

Bert's grin widened. 'Yes sir!'

Their friendly rivalry was a source of great amusement to Sebastiano. Too often those around him hid behind a mask of eager deference to get on his good side all because he had been born into a life of wealth and privilege. It was irritating to say the least.

He caught a glimpse of the newspaper Bert had spread out on the desk showing a picture of Sebastiano leaving a posh, and utterly boring, cocktail party the night before. Evidently his now ex-mistress had seen the same photos on the Internet which was why she had decided to ambush him outside his Park Lane home after his early-morning run, wanting to know why he hadn't invited her to attend with him.

In hindsight, *'because it didn't occur to me'* hadn't been his best answer. Things had rapidly deteriorated after that, ending when she'd issued him with an ultimatum: either move their relationship forward or end it. Not that he could blame her for being frustrated. He'd pursued her a month ago with the ruthless determination that had seen him rise to the top of the *Forbes 500* list by the age of thirty-one and he'd yet to sleep with her more than once.

Which wasn't like him. He normally had a very healthy libido but he'd been off stride lately. Probably only this damned situation with his grandfather. Not to mention the twenty-hour days he had been putting in at the office to finalise a deal that would see him take over as industry leader in the hotel construction market.

Of course, he'd apologised to the world-renowned ballerina, but she hadn't been impressed, blowing him a kiss over one elegant shoulder and purring that it was his loss as she had gracefully exited his life. Thinking about it now, he might suggest she give break-up lessons to some of his past involvements. She'd make a small fortune teaching basic relationship-exiting etiquette to others, particularly to the Spanish model who had thrown her hair brush at him when he'd suggested they part ways some months back.

'Better luck next time, eh, boss?' Bert chortled, feigning contrition. Sebastiano grunted. He knew Bert was referring to yesterday's football match, in which his team had annihilated Sebastiano's, but equally he could have applied the sentiment to his stalled sex life.

'Your team wins again,' Sebastiano said as he headed for the bank of elevators. 'I'll dock your wages by half.'

'Yes sir!' Bert's grin widened as he checked the security monitors on his desk.

Stepping into the lift, Sebastiano stabbed the button for his floor and hoped that his adroit EA had found time to collate the reports he wanted to present to his grandfather this morning as part of his winning pitch. Ordinarily he'd never ask Paula to come in on a Sunday, but his grandfather had landed this visit on him at the last minute and he hadn't wanted to leave anything to chance.

Not that his business acumen was the reason behind his grandfather's reticence to hand him control of the company. No, what he wanted was to see Sebastiano settled down with a lovely *donna* who would one day become the mother of his multiple *bambini*. His grandfather wanted him to have something other than work to sustain him. Something called work-life balance. A modern-day catch cry if ever Sebastiano had heard one, and one he suspected his grandfather had acquired from his cherished wife. Whatever Nonna wanted, Nonna got.

'How can I expect you to take on another demanding role when you already have so little time to relax?' his grandfather had said over the phone a month ago. 'Your grandmother and I just want to see you happy, Bastian. You know how we worry. I can't die if I don't know you will be taken care of.'

'You know I can take care of myself,' Sebastiano had growled. 'And you're not dying. At least, not right now.'

But his grandparents were old-world Italian. If there wasn't a good woman cooking in his kitchen and warming his bed at night, they considered him to be living a lonely, substandard existence. And apparently having a house-keeper providing those hot meals, and as many women as a man could want offering to warm his bed, wasn't what they were talking about.

More's the pity.

Because for Sebastiano being busy *was* his work-life balance. He thrived on it. There wasn't a day went by he didn't wake up wanting to conquer some new business opportunity or some new corporate challenge. Love? Marriage? Both required a level of intimacy he didn't have it in him to give.

Being a little removed from those around him had served him well over the years and he couldn't see a reason to change that. And if some nights he had a lonely, late-night aperitif by himself, overlooking the glittering lights of whichever city he happened to be in at the time... well, so be it.

Right now he was in the prime of his life, and as he had just bought Britain's largest steel and concrete supply company there was no better time to take over as head of Castiglione Europa. The two businesses dovetailed so beautifully that Sebastiano had already asked his marketing and sales team to work up a plan to move into the hotel refurbishment industry across Eastern Europe.

He just had to convince his hard-headed *nonno* to retire and see out his twilight years with the wife he adored in the family's Amalfi coast villa. Then, and only then, could Sebastiano make up for the hardship he had caused his family fifteen years ago.

Deep in thought, he flicked on the lights to the executive floor and heard a text come through on his phone. Switching on the coffee machine on his way to his office, he opened the text and pulled up short.

He read it twice. Apparently Paula was in Accident and Emergency with her husband who had a suspected broken ankle. The report he required was still on her computer.

His frown turned into a scowl. With his grandfather due any minute, he didn't need this kind of delay.

Texting back that he hoped her husband was okay, he retrieved her laptop from her desk and carried it into his office. Glancing at the screen festooned with multi-coloured icons that made his eyes cross, he couldn't find any folder that looked like it held the report he needed.

Great. That was just great.

Poppy checked the Mickey Mouse watch on her wrist and groaned. She had to get out of here. Her brother Simon would be waiting and he always became agitated when she was late. On top of that Maryann, her wonderful neighbour who had been more of a mother to both of them than anyone else they had ever known, had just been diagnosed with MS. It was a cruel blow for a woman who was beautiful both inside and out and Poppy wanted to do something nice for her today.

Trying not to dwell on the awful news, Poppy tightened her haphazard ponytail and skimmed over the legal brief she wanted to present to her boss tomorrow morning. She only had one week left of her internship at SJC International and she wanted to make sure she sparkled. Who knew, once her law degree was finished she might even be offered a job here if she impressed the powers that be enough. The ultimate power being her boss's boss, Sebastiano Castiglione. She hadn't had anything to do with him directly, but she had seen him stalking through the halls, his long stride indicating a man who was always on a mission, his wide shoulders denoting that likely he would succeed at that mission.

Catching herself daydreaming about his dark bad-boy good looks, and reminding herself that he had a bad-boy reputation to match, she stacked the files she had been using back in the cabinet and switched off the computer.

Not being a morning person, she would have liked to work from home this morning, but the laptop she used for university was a thousand years old and wouldn't run the program she needed to use. On top of which intern privileges didn't extend to downloading company files on her private device, even if she was doing company business.

Stretching the kinks out of her neck, she was about to leave when she noticed the legal book she had borrowed from Paula a week earlier. Tomorrow was going to be a hectic day so it made sense to return it on her way out today.

Ordinarily she wouldn't have access to the big boss's hallowed ground, but since her boss had lent her his access pass she did. Still, she hesitated for a second. She didn't want to get Mr Adams into trouble by doing something she shouldn't, but she also didn't want to risk the chance she would return the book late and look sloppy. One of the best ways to stand out as an intern was to be as efficient as possible and Poppy took her job very seriously. And, since no one else was around this morning, who would know?

Making her mind up, she grabbed the book and headed for the lift. After having been raised in the foster care system since she was twelve, and having to take care of a brother ten years younger who had been born deaf, she knew the only way out of her current poverty-riddled existence was to focus on bettering herself. She'd been given a second chance when Maryann had found them both huddled up to a heater at Paddington Station eight years ago and she intended to use every second of that chance to make sure that they both had a future to look forward to.

Swiping the access card and pressing the button for the executive floor, she waited patiently for the lift to open out onto the stylish elegance that denoted that one had truly arrived in the world. Crossing the softly carpeted floor into Mr Castiglione's outer office, Poppy paused to take in the sweeping views of London she so rarely got to see. Despite the pale grey sky the city looked picture-perfect with its seamless blend of new-and old-world architecture. It was as if nothing could touch a person from way up here, but Poppy knew that, once you got down to ground level, things could not only touch you; they could destroy you if you let them.

Caught up as she was by dark, unwanted memories, she jumped when a deep male voice cursed loudly, shattering the stillness.

Heart thumping, Poppy turned to find who it was, but no one was about. Then another curse coloured the air and she realised it was coming from inside her boss's office.

Always too curious for her own good, she stepped forward on light feet and paused at the open doorway to Mr Castiglione's internal space. She sucked in a sharp breath as she saw the man himself standing, legs braced wide, in front of the plate glass windows.

She'd recognise him anywhere, of course. Powerful. Untamed. Stunningly good-looking. He raked a hand through his hair, mussing it into untidy black waves. He was tall for an Italian, and muscular, as if he worked out every day and then some. Since he was reputed to work about twenty hours a day, Poppy didn't know where he found the time, but she was glad he did. He was eye-candy extraordinaire. Or 'sex on a stick', as Maryann was wont to say.

As if he sensed her silent perusal, he shot round from studying the phone in his hand, his brilliant green eyes piercing her straight to her core. For a moment Poppy forgot to breathe. Then he spoke, his aggravated gaze sweeping over her and lighting tiny spot fires of sensation in its wake.

'Who the hell are you?'

'I'm an intern.' Poppy cleared the frog from her throat. 'Poppy. Poppy Connolly. I work for you.'

His frown deepened as he looked her up and down again.

'Since when have jeans and a sweater been considered appropriate office attire?'

Poppy flushed at the dressing down. 'It's a Sunday,' she explained, forcing herself not to tuck thick strands of her untidy brown hair behind her ear. 'And I wasn't expecting anyone else to be in.' Which wasn't really much of an explanation when he stood before her in a snowy-white dress shirt, red tie and dark trousers that did little to hide his powerful thighs.

'Yes, it is a Sunday. So why are you here?'

'I have a week left and I wanted to finish up a presentation for Mr Adams. He said it would be fine if I came in.'

One dark eyebrow rose. 'Taking dedication a bit far, isn't it?'

'Not if you want to get ahead,' she said simply. 'And I'd love to work here when I graduate. Being flexible and committed are just two of the things interns can do to stand out.'

Sure that he was about to toss her out of his office, maybe via one of those plate glass windows, she was surprised when instead he asked, 'What are the others?'

'Be punctual, treat the position like a job and dress for success.' She ticked off each item on her fingers.

His gaze fell to her ancient skinny jeans and Poppy tried not to cringe. When she had first started at SJC five weeks ago she had imagined one day meeting this man, who was reported to be some sort of corporate god, but in her imaginings it hadn't quite gone like this.

'Broke that one, I see,' he said sardonically.

Poppy felt heat creep into her cheeks and realised that her heart was beating at double its normal rate. Probably 'finding your boss attractive' wasn't on that special intern's list either, and she tried to crank up the wheels of her sluggish brain to think of a way to salvage the rapidly deteriorating situation.

When the phone rang on his desk it broke the taught

silence between them and also threw Poppy a welcome lifeline.

'Let me get that,' she said in her most businesslike manner.

Before he could respond, she had made it to his desk and snatched up the phone. She smiled widely at him as she chirped, 'Mr Castiglione's office,' in her most professional voice.

Her smile dimmed as she strained to listen to the teary sound of a woman on the other end of the line. She had a heavily accented voice and, coupled with her distress, Poppy could just make out, 'Sorry to interrupt,' and, 'Is Sebastiano in?'

'Yes, he is here,' Poppy said, all too aware that the man they were discussing had not taken his eyes off her. 'Yes, of course. Just a moment.' Not knowing which button on the handset was the mute, she held out the phone. 'It's for you,' she half-whispered.

Once more his eyebrow climbed his forehead. 'What a surprise.'

Feeling as if she had mucked up again, she stepped back from his radiating warmth as he moved closer and took the phone.

'Yes?' he barked into it.

Seeing his scowl instantly deepen, Poppy decided to take the initiative and make him a coffee. She had noticed the red light glowing on the coffee machine in his outer office and, since there was no cup on his desk, it stood to reason that he'd intended to make one but hadn't had the time.

Well, she would fix that and earn herself some Brownie points in the process. Maybe some of the ones she had lost handing him a call that, now that she thought about, was most likely from his current girlfriend. Or ex, given that the woman was crying. His short-term conquests were the stuff of legend around the office. As was the expensive break-up-and-move-on jewellery he supposedly got Paula to buy for them at the end.

Eager to get home and check on Simon, and give Maryann a hug and a cup of tea, she hurried to the coffee machine, surprised to find her boss still on the call when she set the cup down beside him. He passed a weary hand through his hair and she was inordinately pleased with herself for thinking of the coffee when he suddenly reached out and manacled her wrist with his large hand, preventing her from leaving.

Poppy instantly stilled, staring down at his darkly tanned fingers that were now idly stroking the soft skin on the inside of her wrist. Her breath hitched as darts of wicked pleasure shot up her arm. Her eyes shot to his and she could tell by the way his brilliant green eyes narrowed that he had registered her heated reaction.

Lust turned her knees to water. Lust and disbelief because, not only was this man her current boss, but he was listening to a woman—who she was now pretty certain was his girlfriend—sobbing on the end of the phone while caressing her!

Louse!

Annoyed that she had felt such pleasure given the circumstances, Poppy jerked her hand back, knocking over the coffee mug she had only moments ago set so carefully in front of him. Before either of them could react, the contents of the mug went flying over the desk, dark liquid splattering all over the front of her boss's pristine white shirt.

Sebastiano let out an explosive round of Italian curse words that made Poppy blush even though she didn't understand a single one of them.

She stared open-mouthed as he hung up his call, holding his sopping wet shirt away from his chest.

'What the hell was that?' he ground out, fury splitting the air between them.

'I… You…' Glancing around wildly, Poppy grabbed a wad of tissues from a side cabinet and started dabbing at his chest. When he held his hand up for her to stop, she noticed that drops had splashed down onto his crotch and, without thinking, she dabbed at the offending liquid only to have that hand manacle her wrist again. This time without the light stroking.

'There's a shirt hanging in the closet behind you. Get it.'

Glancing up into his irritated gaze, Poppy felt a fresh wave of heat fill her cheeks. The air seemed to thicken and crackle between them like heat shimmering off concrete on a hot day. 'Yes, sorry. I…'

'Any time today would be good,' he growled.

'Right,' she stammered.

Even more annoyed with herself, she reached into his closet and ripped the clear plastic from a fresh shirt, not at all ready to turn around and find her boss shirtless and wiping his ripped, tanned abdomen with another wad of tissues.

Good God, the man had sheets of muscles layered on top of more muscles, and all of that bronzed, fit perfection was covered in a pelt of healthy dark hair that arrowed down…

'I— You—' She pointed to the vicinity of his torso. 'You have a red mark on your chest. Do you want me to get some salve for it?'

'No, I do not want you to do anything else,' he bit out.

'Okay.' Poppy thrust the shirt at him, turning her burning face away, hoping he couldn't hear her thundering heartbeat. 'I—I'm sorry,' she stammered, her throat tight with embarrassment. 'I don't know what happened. I'm not usually so clumsy—really I'm not—but when you… I just… I'm really sorry.'

'I'm sure you are,' he bit out tersely.

Hearing the rustle of fabric, Poppy turned back to find him shoving the ends of his shirt into his trousers and swallowed hard. She wished she didn't know what lay beneath that shirt because she couldn't get the image of his toned torso out of her head. She watched, mute, as he straightened his cuffs and wound his red tie around his neck.

'At least the coffee missed your tie,' she offered.

His cutting glance told her more than words how little he thought of her comment. 'Is that supposed to make up for you dousing me with coffee?'

'I didn't *douse* you,' she said with a touch of asperity. 'You were rubbing my wrist while breaking up with your girlfriend.'

'And that made you spill coffee all over me?'

'I didn't do it deliberately,' she said, secretly thinking that actually he deserved it. 'Maybe you should be thankful it wasn't hot.'

His implacable gaze held hers. 'It was hot.'

Poppy bit her lip and watched with interest as he tussled with his tie. Cursing, he yanked it off and started over. Her lips twitched as her annoyance dissipated. There was something completely disarming about a man of his size and capability wrangling with an innocent strip of fabric. 'Do you want me to help you with that?'

Once more he flicked her with his green gaze. 'I think you've done enough, don't you?'

She held her hands up in front of her. 'Look—no coffee.'

Not even the trace of a smile crossed his sinful lips and she thought it such a shame that a man who was so good-looking should have no sense of humour.

Wondering if now might be the best moment for her to cut her losses she paused when he indicated to the computer open on his desk.

'Can you use a Mac?'

Hesitating only briefly she marshalled her usually sunny nature and smiled at him. 'Yes.'

'I need a report printed off before my grandfather arrives for a meeting. Think you can handle it?'

Poppy moistened her dry lips. 'Of course.' She sat down in his chair and set her fingers on the keyboard. 'What's the name of the file?'

He leaned forward and she got a delicious whiff of sandalwood cologne. 'If I knew that, intern, I'd already have it done, wouldn't I?'

'Oh, well, yes...' When she realised how close he was behind her Poppy's voice trailed off, her lips drying up again faster than a trickle of water in the Mojave Desert.

'It'll be something to do with Castiglione Europa, or CE for short,' he growled.

Ignoring the butterflies in her stomach Poppy scanned the folders on the screen and didn't see anything related to either of those. Then her eyes fell on an interesting one.

'Are you getting married?' she queried, peeking up at him.

'No.' He scowled. 'Why would you ask that?'

'No reason. Except Paula's got a file called "Operation Marriage" but that's probably got to do with the bet and not what you're looking for.'

'The *what*?'

Poppy told herself to shut up but knew by his thunderous expression that she was going to have to explain herself. 'The bet,' she said in an upbeat manner. 'Even I've heard that your grandfather is encouraging you to settle down— and, well... some of the legal department have dubbed it "Operation Marriage".'

His gaze turned flinty. 'I see the office grapevine is alive and well, then. Why have I not heard it?'

'Well, because the gossip is about you—obviously. But don't worry. Nobody thinks you'll do it.'

'Good to know my staff know me well at least.'

Poppy shrugged, relieved that he didn't seem annoyed by her revelation. 'I take it by your reaction you can't imagine anything worse than marriage?'

'Death.'

Poppy's smile grew at his grim tone. 'Right. But I think it's kind of sweet, actually. Your grandfather wanting you to find love.'

'I'm glad you think so.' He leaned over her. 'Click on the folder. Now open that file.' He pointed at the screen and Poppy had to force herself to focus on his instructions and not his steely arm brushing the outside of hers. 'There. Send that report to print.' He straightened away from the chair and cursed again.

Poppy glanced up to find him yanking his tie open again.

'I do know how to tie a tie,' she murmured.

His gaze told her he'd rather set his hair on fire than have her help him again.

'Fine.' His hands dropped to his sides and the two ends of the tie dangled down his lean body like twin arrows signalling paradise. 'I'm all yours.'

Sure that her face must look as hot as it felt Poppy reminded herself of the last man she had found attractive, and how that had ended for her and her brother.

Fortified by that particularly humiliating memory, she gripped the tie and reached up, doing her best to ignore the dark stubble that lined his hard jaw. He was tall, well over six feet, and she had to rise onto her toes to position the knot in the centre of his throat. This close, she could feel his heat, and smell his potently male scent. It made her want to lean in and nuzzle against him, to breath it in more deeply.

Not that she would. She wasn't a fool.

She noticed his tanned throat working as her fingers grazed his skin and she steadfastly refused to look at his face. 'What kind of knot do you want?' she asked, her voice husky and unlike the way it usually sounded.

'What kind of knots can you do?' His seemed deeper too, rougher.

'All of them.'

'All of them?'

Braving a quick glance upwards, she found that his eyes were heavy lidded as they met hers.

'Just how many are there?' he asked.

'Eighteen that I know of.'

'Eighteen.' His eyes glittered down into hers. 'Can you name them?'

'Yes. Do you want me to?'

'No.' He gave a short laugh. 'You've obviously done this before. Lucky guy.'

'Mannequin.' She adjusted the length of the tie and created a loop. 'I dressed in-store mannequins part-time during high school.'

His lips twisted into a small smirk. 'Lucky in-store mannequins.'

Poppy's hand flattened against his chest as the tie slipped. She could feel his heart beating heavy and strong beneath his breastbone... Was that a shudder that just went through his big body?

All of a sudden she felt surrounded by his warmth, his deliciously male smell, and she had to swallow hard before speaking. 'So, which one do you want?' she asked thickly.

'Just do a Windsor knot.' The words seemed to rumble out of his chest.

'That's the one most men prefer,' she said.

'Are you calling me common, Miss Connolly?'

'No.' Poppy tugged a length of the tie through another loop, her heart beating twice as fast as usual. 'It's just that it's the largest, and most men who wear neckties like to have a large knot.'

'Most women probably like them to have a large knot as well.' His voice was deep, his chest rising and falling evenly beneath her suddenly clumsy fingers. 'Wouldn't you agree?'

Deciding not to take this conversation any further for fear that he might actually be flirting with her, and it was the last thing she wanted, she concentrated on finishing the knot. 'I wouldn't know, Mr Castiglione. I don't date men who wear ties.' In fact she didn't date period.

'No?'

'No.'

'Then what do they wear?'

'Nothing. That is they…' Blushing furiously she folded his collar into place. 'There. All done.'

'A word of advice, Miss Connolly,' he began, waiting for her to look up at him before continuing. 'If you do happen to get a job here, don't ever hand me a call without first finding out who it is.'

Remembering how upset the woman on the end of the phone had been, Poppy pursed her lips. 'Not even if the person is crying?'

'*Especially* if the person is crying.'

Shaking her head Poppy wondered if he was really as ruthless and heartless as he was reputed to be. Of their own accord her eyes drifted to his mouth. His lips were firm and chiselled without seeming hard. Rumour also had it that he knew how to make a woman go wild in bed, and she wondered if his mouth would be rough or soft if she reached up and kissed him.

Instantly another fierce blush suffused her face as she registered the insanely inappropriate impulse, making her flustered. 'Why were you holding my wrist before anyway?' she asked belligerently. 'When you were on the phone?' He'd been stroking her skin so tenderly she could still feel the impression of his fingers against her skin.

'I don't really know.' His gaze flitted over her face, his green eyes hot and hungry. Poppy blinked, unable to look away. She was used to men noticing her, finding her attractive even, but she wasn't used to this answering heat rise up inside of her. She wasn't used to this overwhelming urge to…

'*Scusa, Sebastiano, sono in anticipo?*'

A deep, croaky voice intruded on the moment, startling Poppy out of her sensual haze.

CHAPTER TWO

HER BOSS WAS the first to step back and a floodgate of embarrassment rushed into Poppy's face. For a moment she had forgotten they were boss and employee. Forgotten that she was now late to meet Simon, who would be starting to fret when she didn't return when she said she would—a leftover issue from their childhood.

'No, you're not early, Nonno—in fact, you're late,' Sebastiano murmured, his eyes still on her. 'Miss Connolly was just helping me fix my tie.'

Feeling as if she'd just had her hand caught in the cookie jar, Poppy turned to face a much older version of her handsome boss and tried to smile.

His dark-green eyes were warm and encompassing as they swept over her.

'Nonno, this is Poppy Connolly. Poppy, this is my *nonno*, otherwise known as Signor Castiglione, or Giuseppe.'

'*Buongiorno, come stai?* Pleased to meet you.' His grandfather smiled broadly.

Still reeling from the shock of imagining how it would feel to kiss her boss—the owner of the company she at least needed a great reference from—Poppy murmured a greeting and wondered how rude it would be just to cut and run out the door.

About to suggest she do exactly that, her words were cut off when Sebastiano's mobile phone rang.

Glancing at the screen, he scowled. '*Nonno, scusa un momento.*'

Poppy wondered if it was his teary ex-girlfriend again,

but then realised that the poor woman probably didn't have his private mobile number or she would have rung it earlier instead of his office phone. It probably demonstrated her level of importance in the scheme of his life. Which was low. She wondered what a temporary girlfriend warranted at the end of an affair with the virile Sebastiano Castiglione? Diamonds or sapphires?

Shaking herself out of such senseless ruminating about a man who no doubt intended to put her on the black list with HR, Poppy smiled at his grandfather and once more tried to salvage something of the situation. 'Would you like a drink? Some coffee?' She tried not to cringe as she offered that. 'Or sparkling water?' That would be much better. No stains from sparkling water.

'No, no.' Signor Castiglione smiled. 'You relax.' He took a seat in one of the bucket chairs opposite the large oak desk. 'So, how long you know my grandson?'

'Oh, not long. About five weeks.' Or really, under an hour, if you counted face-to-face time.

'Ah, *va bene*. He is very demanding, no? He needs a firm hand.'

The image of someone handling Sebastiano Castiglione with a firm hand made Poppy want to laugh. But she fully agreed. 'Oh, absolutely.'

'But you handle him, *si*?'

Ah, definitely not *si*! She might have tied his tie before, but just being that close to him had completely tied her insides up in knots. 'I wouldn't say that exactly,' she hedged. 'Your grandson is his own boss.'

'Don't let him get his own way all the time. It is not good for him.'

He was telling her!

Poppy grinned at the lovely old man. 'I'll keep that in mind,' she murmured, thinking that there was little chance she'd even see her boss again after next week. If she even made it to next week. Especially after the way she'd just been caught staring at his mouth.

Mortified all over again, she stole a quick glance in Sebastiano's direction. Despite his less than stellar reputation with women, he was the most superb specimen of a man she had ever come across. Tall, broad-shouldered and with that air of power that was like an invisible warning to those who might dare to take him on.

Which would not be her. She was more a 'steer well clear of overpowering men' sort of girl. In fact, she was a steer well clear of *any* kind of men sort of girl. She had definite plans for the future, and they included climbing the corporate ladder, not falling for some good-looking, over-confident business mogul!

Unfortunately, before she could drag her gaze away from him, his eyes connected with hers and something hot and shivery jolted inside her. Once again sensing the effect he'd had on her, his eyes turned darker, his gaze telling her that he could read her most secret thoughts. The ones that said that he was so hot, she thought she might combust on the spot.

'*Sei la persone giusta,*' the old man said, nodding and smiling at her.

'What? Oh…yes.' Poppy turned to face him, relieved to have the unwanted spell of his grandson broken. 'Okay, well…' She moistened her lips and turned just as Sebastiano stepped forward, bringing them almost nose to chest. 'Sorry.' She stepped back quickly. 'I'll…uh…let you have your meeting. It was nice to meet you, Signor Castiglione.'

'What? No coffee?' Sebastiano mocked.

Poppy's eyes widened. *Was he making a joke?*

'Yes. It was a joke. Seems I'm a bit rusty. Thank you for tying my tie,' he said softly. Intimately.

'You're welcome.'

Cut and run! her common sense shouted at her. 'Have—

er—have a good meeting,' she said, finally kicking her brain into gear and hurrying through the office door. She didn't take another breath until the lift doors had closed around her and she could put that surreal experience behind her. Then she slumped against the wall and wondered if any of that had really happened.

As soon as she closed his office door, Sebastiano turned back to his grandfather. 'How was your flight?'

'Good. This woman.' He nodded slowly. 'I approve.'

An image of his intern's nimble fingers skating over his chest as she fixed his tie jumped into Sebastiano's consciousness.

He approved as well, or at least his body did.

From the first moment he'd looked round and seen her standing in his doorway he'd felt as if he'd been punched in the gut. It was why he had sounded so rude about her clothing. Of course she could wear casual clothing to the office on a weekend if she wanted. He wasn't a tyrant. He'd just been thrown by those velvet-blue eyes staring squarely back at him with no artifice in them at all.

The rest of her wasn't bad either. *Understatement*, he acknowledged wryly. Her figure was glorious: slim hips, rounded breasts pushing against her thin sweater and a thick pile of ash-brown hair pulled into a high ponytail, revealing a slender neck below sweet rosebud lips. She wasn't his usual type by a long shot but there was something about her that was at once innocent and impish. And hot. The way she had looked at him…an intelligent sparkle lighting those blue eyes as if she could see right through him.

When she had turned pink and asked him why he had been holding her wrist, he'd had an inexplicable desire to know what it would be like to wake up beside her, her face that colour from his love-making.

The memory pulled him up short. She was an intern in

his office so she was automatically off limits—no matter how tempting—and, even if she wasn't, he kept his relationships light and uncomplicated. Something about the way she hadn't turned coy or giggly to attract his attention told him that she was neither light nor uncomplicated. Which was why he intended to forget that he had even met her.

'I'm glad you approve,' he said to his grandfather. 'But it's your approval for me to take over as CEO of Castiglione Europa that I want. You can't keep travelling to Rome every other day to bark at everyone, and you know it. You also know that Nonna wants you to retire,' he added, playing his trump card. 'It's time.'

'Time to do what?' his grandfather grouched. 'Play *boules*? Pick grapes? Spend time with my grandchildren? Now there—' he pointed a knotted finger at Sebastiano '—there would be a reason to retire.'

And here were go, Sebastiano thought. *Operation Marriage.* It was a clever name for it but he'd still give Paula grief about not informing him of the office betting pool when she came in tomorrow morning. 'Yes, yes, I know what you want,' he said. 'And I'm working on it.'

'So what is the hold-up?' his grandfather asked. 'You are having trouble making her say yes, is that it?' His grandfather grinned, seeming to like that idea. But having a woman say yes wasn't a problem Sebastiano had ever encountered. Quite the opposite, in fact, but regardless of that he understood that he was too much of a loner to make any relationship work in the long term. A fact many of his women would be more than happy to attest to.

Realising that his grandfather was waxing lyrical about how nice Poppy seemed, Sebastiano shrugged off his uncharacteristic lapse in concentration. 'Forget all that,' he dismissed, not wanting to let his mind wander back to his sassy little intern. 'Tell me what I want to hear. You need to retire, and now, with this new deal I just finalised, the timing couldn't be better to merge SJC with the family business. You know it as well as I do.'

His grandfather steepled his hands beneath his chin, taking his time answering, as he was wont to do. When he was a child Sebastiano had grown fidgety under that steady regard—now he just used it himself when it suited him.

'I'll tell you right now, I'm impressed with what I just saw,' his grandfather said slowly. 'You should have mentioned Poppy sooner.'

Poppy? Were they still talking about his intern? 'Why would I mention her sooner?' he rasped, his brain prodding him that he was missing something important.

'Ah, I see, you want me to hand over the family company on your terms and not mine. That pride of yours will not do you any good in the long run, I've always told you that.'

'Nonno—'

'You always were a good boy, and now you have grown into a fine man. But seriously, Sebastiano, sometimes you cannot see what is in front of your face. Fortunately for you I am here to point out the obvious.'

Sebastiano frowned. 'Wait, do you...?'

His grandfather reached across the desk and laid a hand over his. His *nonno*'s skin was old and leathery, almost papery in its frailty, his fingers vibrating slightly as they gripped onto him. 'We have been waiting for you to ditch all those party girls and choose a nice girl to settle down with. And this girl is good.'

Sebastiano went perfectly still. His grandfather thought he and Poppy were an item—it was written all over his craggy features—which was ironic, when in fact they had only just met. But he supposed he could see how his grandfather had got that impression. For one, she had turned up in the office looking as much like an intern as he looked like a monk. And, two, he had very nearly lost his head and kissed her when she'd finished tying his tie.

'She is the one for you, and when your grandmother sees you together she will be so proud that we did right by you after all.'

Hold on—what? 'The one?'

'*Si.* And she said she knows how to handle you.' His grandfather chuckled. 'You need a strong woman like that.'

Sebastiano knew his grandmother ruled their *casa* but, hell, had Poppy—Miss Connolly—truly said she had him under the thumb?

His frown deepened; no wonder his grandfather had jumped to all the wrong conclusions. But why would she say that? And more importantly what was he going to do about it?

He recalled the slumberous way her eyes had moved over him when she'd been tying his tie. It had been from desire; he would have put money on it because his own body had sent the same message to his brain.

I want her, it had said, *right now.*

Sebastiano didn't want to think about his grandfather's reaction when he told him that, far from being his latest girlfriend, Poppy Connolly was nothing more than a temporary employee. But, instead of wasting his breath to try and convince the old man he was wrong, Sebastiano tried again to direct him away from his love life. 'Let's get down to business.'

'No. Let's save it for your trip to Italy.'

Sebastiano went as still as a stone. As a general rule he limited his trips to his home country as much as possible. Especially to the family *casa* where his memories were so strong. 'What trip to Italy?'

'For your grandmother and my sixtieth wedding anniversary. We are having a party. Bring your lovely Miss Connolly.'

Sebastiano couldn't move as his grandfather stood up. A look of sorrow briefly clouded his *nonno*'s eyes, his voice quiet when he broke the lengthening silence between them.

'We need to put the past to bed, *nipote mio*, and we want you to come. No more excuses. No more putting work first. It is time to move forward.' He cleared the emotion from his throat. 'After I tell Evelina about Miss Connolly she will want to meet her. In fact, I will text her now.'

Sebastiano blinked. 'Since when do you and Nonna text?'

'Since I bought her a smart phone for her birthday.'

His grandfather pulled his own phone out of his pocket and pressed the keys with the agility of someone half his age.

Sebastiano watched him, brooding. He would do a lot of things for his grandparents—he would even cast aside his deeply buried memories of the past to attend their anniversary—but pretend he had a relationship with a woman he barely knew and who might have just set herself up to become the next Mrs Castiglione?

Not a chance in hell.

CHAPTER THREE

'Two HUNDRED AND fifty thousand pounds?' Poppy stared at Sebastiano, who sat behind his desk like a leanly muscled King Tut with a pot of gold in front of him.

When he had requested to see her in his office she'd been convinced she was about to be fired. Instead he had offered her enough money to make her heart stop beating, in exchange for her pretending to be 'the light of his life', as he had condescendingly put it.

'As in two hundred and fifty thousand pounds *cash*?'

'You want more? Fine. Make it five hundred.'

Poppy's mouth was so dry it was arid. The man was insane. Or drunk. She narrowed her gaze, scanning his face for signs she was right. 'Have you been drinking?'

'Not since last night, and unfortunately the effects have worn off by now.'

She glanced around, waiting for a camera crew to jump out from behind his Chesterfield and yell, 'Surprise!' Only they didn't. All that happened was her heart thumped so fast she felt faint. 'I don't think this is very funny.'

'I never joke about money. And you only have yourself to blame.'

'Excuse me?'

'Something you said to my grandfather suggested that we were a couple. Something about handling me.' His dark brows rose mockingly. 'Which I can assure you, Miss Connolly, no woman will ever do.'

Poppy's throat felt tight and uncomfortable. 'I didn't say I could handle you.' She frowned. 'Your grandfather said something about you needing a firm hand and I agreed. Then he said something in Italian that I didn't get.'

'Do you remember what it was?'

She gave him a look. 'I grew up in the outskirts of Leeds, Mr Castiglione. My Italian starts with *si* and ends with *ciao*.'

'Well, thanks to my grandfather mistaking you for my latest mistress, it's about to extend to a few days on the Amalfi coast. So, what's your price?'

Poppy was so shocked at the thought that anyone could mistake her for this man's anything that she couldn't take any of this seriously. 'You're so desperate to impress him you're prepared to lie?'

'I like to think of it as taking advantage of an opportunity when it arises. And, believe me, I spent most of those wasted hours last night trying to come up with an alternative plan. I failed.' His sculpted mouth quirked at one corner. 'Something I don't admit to easily.'

Poppy let the subtle insult that he would rather do anything else than pretend he was in a relationship with her slide. She felt a little drunk herself at the thought of all that money. Five hundred thousand pounds? That kind of offer only happened in the movies, didn't it?

She stood up. 'I... I can't take your money.'

'Really? You'll do it for free?'

She heard the mockery in his tone and frowned. 'No, of course not, I—'

'Which is as I suspected. So, what is your price?'

'I'm not a prostitute,' she informed him sharply, those early schoolyard taunts about her biological mother coming back to haunt her.

'There's no reason to get in a temper,' he said calmly. 'I'm not suggesting we sleep together.'

Poppy scowled. 'Your arrogance knows no bounds, does it?'

'I'm a businessman, Miss Connolly, and I have a problem. Like it or not, you're my solution.'

'You're out of your mind.' Poppy shook her head. 'I won't do it.'

He regarded her steadily, making her feel hot in her navy suit. 'You're knocking back half a million pounds?' His toned was loaded with arrogant disbelief and it only made Poppy more determined to deny him. 'In *cash*.'

'I just…' She frowned. Growing up poor and without a proper family made a half a million pounds seem like a dream come true. 'It doesn't feel right.'

'It doesn't *feel* right?' She had no doubt that if he'd been a car he would have blown a head gasket by now. 'Are you seriously turning me down because it doesn't *feel* right?'

'I don't expect you to understand,' she shot at him, thinking of the devastated woman on the end of the phone the day before. 'You'd need to have *feelings* for that.'

'I have feelings,' he shot at her.

Poppy might have debated that but she still had a week left of her internship and she wanted to get a good reference—and, frankly, she felt a little dizzy. Five hundred thousand pounds was a lot of money. What she could do with it was mind-boggling.

Buy Simon new trainers, for one. The poor kid had been wearing hand-me-downs for as long as she had. But he was fifteen and the right trainers were integral to a teenager's self-esteem. With five hundred thousand pounds he would never have to go without anything again!

And five hundred thousand would be enough to help Maryann, whom she'd spent the rest of Sunday visiting. She'd also been researching MS on the computer to see if there was something she could do to help. Unfortunately the information had been depressing. Once the effects of the disease set in, Maryann would need a flat on the ground floor and, with no family or funds at her disposal, moving was going to be difficult. Poppy had already thought of asking Maryann to move in with her and Simon, but Maryann was as fiercely independent as Poppy was herself, so she knew she wouldn't take to that idea easily.

But with half a million pounds Poppy might be able to buy her a flat rather than have her continue to rent. She could pay Maryann back for all the help she had given her over the last eight years. Or could she? She had no idea how far half a million pounds would stretch.

For a moment she was tempted to take the money, oh, so tempted, but she knew there was no such thing as a free lunch. Taking money for nefarious reasons would always come back to haunt her. It would make her feel as cheap as her beginnings.

'Well?'

Poppy felt a jolt go through her as Sebastiano impatiently advanced into her personal space with the lazy grace of a man who had it all.

'Well, what?' she asked, wishing she didn't sound so breathless.

A muscle ticked in his jaw. 'Your answer?' he said in his rich bedroom voice.

Holding her ground against his intimidating force, Poppy shook her head. 'I'm not for sale, Mr Castiglione.'

'I know that.' He ran a hand through his hair. 'I'm not asking for this to be real. It's a few days of your time. A trip to Italy.' He pinned her to the spot with his stare alone. 'I'll even throw in a new wardrobe. No budget. It's every woman's dream. Not to mention you could buy yourself jeans that aren't about to fall apart.'

The fact that he had noticed her unfashionably worn jeans made Poppy feel unclean. The fact that he was so arrogant, and thought he could buy anyone with his money, made her even more resolved to hold her own against him.

'No.' Poppy stepped back from him, feeling immediately

cold without his body heat radiating close to hers. 'You'll have to find someone else.'

'Admit it,' he demanded quietly, his voice preventing her from turning around and walking out. 'You're tempted.'

'Of course I'm tempted,' she shot at him. He was *so* sure of himself. So sure of *her*. 'I wouldn't be human if I wasn't tempted, but…' She smoothed her already neat hair into place and noticed her hand was shaking. Turning it into a fist at her side, she raised her chin. 'I don't think I would like myself very much if I agreed to take your money to pretend to be something I'm not.'

Sebastiano blew out a beleaguered breath. '*Dio*, save me from martyrs.'

'I'm not a martyr.' She tilted her head back to glare up at him, wishing he wasn't quite so tall. 'I just have principles.'

He nodded and she felt that finally she'd penetrated his shallow exterior. It should have only taken the flick of her nail, given his lack of depth. Somehow finding out that he really wasn't a man of substance, but a self-absorbed rat like the rest of his ilk, had seriously disappointed her.

'Will that be all?' she asked stiffly, a picture of five hundred thousand pounds flashing like a neon sign inside her head.

Sebastiano stuck his hands in his pockets, his thunderstruck expression priceless. 'You're really turning me down?'

'Yes.' She tilted her chin higher, wondering if she wasn't being an idiot to do so. But then she thought about what she would have to do to get that money. Pretend to be this man's girlfriend. There was no way she could carry that off. Not for a million pounds!

His eyes gleamed predator-like as he watched her, and Poppy had the distinct impression she was in danger. *Run*, her inner voiced urged. So she did, reversing out of his office with the pace of a teenager texting on a phone.

When she was safely on the other side of the door she blew out a breath and walked on unsteady legs towards the lift. Since Paula's husband had indeed broken his ankle, she wasn't in the office, and Poppy was glad she didn't have to face the older woman's knowing gaze. Various employees had already warned her that every woman who came into contact with Sebastiano fell in love with him, and Poppy didn't want anyone to think that she had joined their adoring ranks when she hadn't.

Taking her phone from her handbag, she decided to duck into the ladies powder room before heading downstairs and facing her colleagues. She was tempted to call Maryann— Lord knew she could use the pep talk, and Maryann had been there for her right from the start. Well, not the start, exactly. Maryann had found her and Simon after Poppy had made the mistake of trusting a man that she shouldn't have. She had met him on the long train ride to London and somehow he had wheedled out of her that she was underage and that she and Simon were runaways with no place to stay.

At first Poppy had thought him a knight in shining armour. And he had been for two weeks. He'd been everything she could have asked for: complimenting her at every turn, giving them a place to stay and buying Simon little gifts. Then one night he'd come to her bedroom to extract payment for his many kindnesses, and when she'd refused he'd grown angry. He'd made her wake Simon and had turfed them both out into the wintry night, shouting that there was no one who would take her on anyway. Not with her 'idiot brother' in tow.

Finding out that he had stolen all her hard-earned savings was the lowest point and had shattered her trust altogether. Unable to go to the police for fear they would take Simon from her, they had been forced to slum it, sleeping in train stations and eating out of rubbish bins. Simon had only been seven at the time, to Poppy's seventeen, and she had cried silent tears every night, praying to God that an angel would come down and rescue them.

And one had. Without batting an eyelid, Maryann had taken them in, fed them, clothed them and given them the kind of affection they had missed out on for most of their early life. Through Maryann Poppy had learned real kindness and respectability and that was what she wanted for herself. For Simon.

But Maryann, who had lost her dear husband many years earlier, was a proponent of true love and would most likely ask Poppy all sorts of probing questions about her boss's offer that she'd rather not answer. Questions such as: *Is this the sexy boss whose photo you showed me? The one with more women than hot dinners? The one who makes you blush every time his name is mentioned?*

To which Poppy would have to answer yes, yes, and double yes.

She stared down at her phone and screwed up her nose. Probably best not to call her.

'Miss Connolly, are you in here?'

Poppy gave a small yelp when her boss's voice broke the heavy silence.

'Maybe.' She gripped her phone in both hands as if it were a sword, making no attempt to open the door.

'Are you planning to come out any time soon?'

Poppy rolled her eyes. Was it too much to ask to have a moment of privacy? 'Do I have to?'

'I prefer having conversations face-to-face. So, yes.'

'I thought we were done.'

'No.' He narrowed his eyes on her as she reluctantly opened the stall door. 'It ends when you say yes.'

'God, you're relentless. You should have been a barrister.'

He leaned his perfect butt against the basin, a killer grin

on his face, his muscular arms braced either side of his lean hips as if he was totally relaxed. *Yeah, right.*

'If that was supposed to be an insult, it failed,' he drawled. 'I respect people who go after what they want and succeed.'

'In other words, you're pushy.'

'Determined.'

Poppy rolled her eyes. 'You know you're in the ladies' loo right?'

His grin widened. 'I'm aware.'

'Well, I was having a private moment, and I'd like to go back to it.'

'It looks like you were about to have a meltdown. But you shouldn't. In my world women know what they want and go after it. It's nothing to be ashamed of.'

A shiver snaked down her spine. 'Why does that sound so cold?'

His half-smile turned mocking. 'I don't have a problem with it and I won't think badly of you for taking my offer.'

'You're all heart.'

'Actually, I'm all business.'

'Yes, well, it's an awful lot of money.'

'It isn't to me.'

Poppy shook her head. 'You could sound a little humble when you say that,' she said, a touch of exasperation in her tone.

'Why? It's the truth. I'm a wealthy man. That brings with it certain perks.'

'Like buying fake girlfriends.'

His green eyes glittered down into hers. He was too tall for her. His grandparents would notice that right away. 'I think I might have insulted you when I offered you five hundred thousand pounds,' he said.

Poppy blinked, hearing that figure again. Five hundred thousand was an amount of money she had never thought to see in one lump sum in her lifetime. The temptation to take it was wicked, and she finally understood those fairy tales where the hapless princess was lured to her doom by the evil villain. 'Yes, you did,' she murmured, holding firm to her flagging principles. 'Because I—'

'So I'm willing to up it to a million.'

'I am not— Did you just say a million pounds?'

He smiled at her smugly, victory lighting his green eyes. 'I did.'

Poppy stared at him blankly. She was sure that what he was offering must be immoral, and if she said yes she'd be looking over her shoulder for the rest of her life, expecting to see someone pointing a finger and accusing her of coming by the money unethically. It would be like being back at school all over again, when kids had whispered behind her back and called her 'Poor Poopy Poppy'. The memory put some much-needed steel in her voice. 'Stop. I already told you that I'm not for sale.'

His smiled dimmed and he stared at her for a long, tense minute before releasing a harsh breath. 'But you are exactly what I need. Okay, what do you want, then? What's your end goal?'

Poppy's head was spinning with so many pound signs she doubted she could even spell 'end goal' right now. She frowned. Did merely surviving each day count as an end goal? 'I don't really think in terms of end goals,' she said.

'Then you should start.' He paced away from her and glared at his reflection in the mirror with distaste. Or was that her reflection he was glaring at? 'Can we take this back to my office?' He held the door open for her, automatically expecting her to obey his request, his commanding demeanour suggesting that if she didn't he'd be happy to make her. 'The ladies' bathroom is hardly the place to have this conversation.'

Poppy stopped beside him. 'I'd rather not have this conversation at all.'

'I can see that. Be careful you don't knock yourself on the door.'

He steered her around the door she'd nearly walked into and Poppy found herself reluctantly seated on the opposite side of his desk before she thought better of it.

'So, if a lump sum is too difficult a concept for you to grasp, let's get to what it is that you do want.'

Too many things to count, Poppy thought, but none she would share with him. Especially not the number of wakeful hours she had spent last night reliving every hard angle of his torso. Sheesh! She had even imagined what it would have felt like if she had stretched up onto her toes and kissed him. 'I don't want anything.'

Sebastiano snorted at her prim response. 'That's patently untrue. Everyone wants something.' He glared at her. 'Even me. In fact, I find myself in the rare position of being a desperate man. So, what is it going to take, *bella*, to get you to give me one weekend out of your life to help an old man?'

Poppy's gaze sharpened. 'Is your grandfather unwell?'

'Would that influence your decision?'

Her frown deepened at the way he pounced on her unconscious show of sympathy. 'You would really use that as a bargaining tool?'

Sebastiano shrugged. 'If it would work.'

'You are such a shark!' Poppy exclaimed, both awed and shocked by his ruthlessness.

'Probably.' He sat forward, his green eyes intense on hers. Poppy's heart thumped heavily behind her breastbone. 'But my grandfather is old and I really don't know how much time he has left.' His lips firmed, as if that thought made him truly uncomfortable. 'And the old goat is far too stoic and proud to admit it if he were ill.'

Poppy heard the deep caring in those terse words. Perhaps it was Maryann being sick, and the dread Poppy felt at possibly losing her some time in the near future, but in that moment she felt an unexpected connection with her big, bad boss. Caring deeply, she knew, was an avenue for pain and she didn't wish that on anyone.

About to tell him that she understood how he felt, he undermined that feeling of accord with his next words.

'How about I grant you three wishes? Would that be more palatable to those prized principles of yours?'

'What are you, a genie now?' She snorted. The thought of seeing him wearing a turban and harem pants softened her irritation at his superior tone. 'Or my fairy godmother?'

'I'm hardly nice enough to be anyone's fairy godmother.'

'You got that right,' she agreed. 'You're a ruthless wolf.'

'I thought I was a shark.'

Poppy's lips twitched again. 'Shark... Wolf...' She swallowed as his gaze lingered on her lips. 'Anything with big teeth, really.'

The air between them suddenly pulled taut, and Poppy's mouth went dry as his smile kicked up at one corner. The man was devastating. Devastatingly attractive and devastatingly persistent.

'Think about it, Poppy,' he said, his soft tone and the use of her first name lending the moment an intimacy she didn't want to feel. 'Three wishes. Anything you want. If they are within my power to grant them, they are yours.'

She blinked in an attempt to shake off the spell he was subtly weaving around her. Three wishes did seem strangely more palatable than a cold, hard lump of cash, though she didn't know why it should, because in the end it would amount to the same thing.

He leaned forward, his gaze unwavering, a predator sensing weakness and homing in on the kill. 'People marry for money and status all the time. This is merely a weekend away. Nothing more.'

But it felt like more to her. She had never thought of herself as someone who could be bought. Not when so many of her foster families had taken her and Simon in for the government grants they would collect, rather than wanting to offer them a secure home.

'Come on, Poppy,' he urged. 'Tell me something you've longed for lately.'

Love. Companionship.

She frowned. *Where had that come from?* She had her career to work towards. That was more important than a transitory state such as love.

'New shoes.' Distracted as she was by her own thoughts and his persuasive tone, she said the first thing that came into her head.

'New shoes?' A sexy grin crept across his face. 'Done. Name the designer and you can have a wardrobe full.'

'Nike, I think.'

'Nike?'

'Size ten.'

'You're serious?'

'Yes. Do you have a problem with that?'

'Okay, okay. Fine. Nike trainers. What else?'

'I don't know…' Suddenly her thoughts veered to Maryann. In particular to the issue of her needing a ground-floor flat. Like Poppy, she lived hand to mouth, and Poppy knew her lovely neighbour was scared about what the future held for her now.

'A new apartment,' she said, waiting for her boss to laugh and tell her she was dreaming.

'Now you're speaking my language,' he said, confidence oozing from every pore. 'A penthouse, no doubt. How many bedrooms?'

'It can't be a penthouse, they're on the top floor.'

'I'm well aware of where a penthouse is located,' he said. 'I own several.'

Poppy was so deep in thought she barely heard him. 'It has to be on the ground floor. And near Brixton.'

'Brixton?'

'Yes. Maryann is really attached to Brixton.'

'Maryann?'

'My neighbour.' The more she thought about it, the more she warmed to the idea. 'And it should be near a park and the tube. Maryann likes to go into Stratford most Saturday afternoons. Her husband is buried there.'

'Right.' He pinched the bridge of his nose. 'I'm getting a headache just thinking about it. Give the details to HR.'

'I'm not giving the details to HR!' Poppy exclaimed. 'It will completely ruin my professional reputation before I've even got one.'

'Fine, send me an email. But what does your neighbour have to do with this anyway?'

'The apartment is for her.'

'I thought it was for you.'

'She needs it more than I do.'

He looked at her as if she'd suddenly grown two heads. 'Okay, fine, whatever. And the last one?'

Poppy stared at him, realising too late that in negotiating with him she was entering into a deal she wasn't at all sure she wanted to make. A deal with the devil. 'I...eh... I don't have a third.' Mostly because her brain had now turned to mush.

'Nothing for yourself?'

Those first two *were* for her. For her peace of mind. She shook her head, trying to clear her thinking. What was she doing even considering this?

'No need to stress,' he said, once more reading her correctly. 'When you think of it, you let me know. In the meantime we will leave for Italy at the end of the week.'

'I don't have a passport!'

'I'll take care of it. And Poppy?'

She raised troubled eyes to his. 'Yes?'

He came around his desk all lean, hard, muscular grace. 'Thank you.'

He held out his hand and guided her to her feet. Poppy felt a tingling sensation light up her arm at his touch, distracting her. 'Wait!' she cried. 'The end of the week? That's too soon. I can't get organised by then.' Meaning that she couldn't organise care for Simon by then.

'You'll have to. That's when my grandparents are holding their anniversary party.'

'Anniversary party?' Her stomach pitched alarmingly. 'This gig just gets better and better.'

'My grandparents are very important to me. Please remember that.'

'So how can you lie to them so easily?' she asked, hoping to see some faint trace of humanity in him.

He shrugged, giving her nothing. 'I see this more as an opportunity to get an outcome that is long overdue.'

'You running your family business.' Him making even more money.

'Yes.'

He really was a shark, Poppy thought, a shark who swam around in shallow waters. What was she doing getting mixed up in this? 'Can't you tell them we broke up and take one of those breathtaking blondes you apparently date instead?'

'No.' His jaw hardened. 'My grandfather has it in his head that you are "the one" for me, and no blonde, no matter how breathtaking, will cut it.'

What didn't cut it for Poppy was how attracted she was to him. He was a shining example of how little taste her hormones truly had when it came to choosing men. 'Don't you find this all a bit deceptive?' she pleaded.

Sebastiano's lids came down to shutter his gaze. 'Your point?'

'My point is that you don't seem to care.'

She wasn't sure she'd kept the distaste from her voice when he scowled. 'What I care about right now is taking over CE.'

'So you believe that the end justifies the means?'

'When it fits.'

Just like the well-dressed louse who had picked her up. But this wasn't the same thing, was it? She had her wits about her this time. And this man was granting her three wishes, not trying to take something from her.

'Poppy?'

She bit her bottom lip, and, when her eye finally lifted to his, his were softer. 'I can see this is not as easy for you as I thought it would be—but my grandfather needs to re-tire. If him believing I am in love with you achieves that, then I'm willing to bend the truth a little.'

Poppy's eyebrows rose. 'A little?'

He smiled. 'A lot.'

Something in his tone told her that the deception wasn't as easy for him as he made out. Maybe it was that, or maybe it was just the fact that she could already see the expression on Simon's face when he received his new trainers—not to mention Maryann's delight when she learned she would be moving into a ground-floor flat beside a park—but Poppy found herself oddly compelled to agree. 'Okay.' She re-leased a long, drawn-out breath. 'I'll do it.'

He gave her a faintly mocking smile. 'That face is not going to convince anyone you think I'm the love of your life.'

'That's because I feel sick,' she said.

As sick as she used to feel whenever the social worker would turn up and tell her that she and Simon were moving on to yet another family. She had that same dreadful sense that her life was headed over a cliff and she had no idea if the landing would be soft or hard, experience warning her to prepare for the worst.

Sebastiano shook his head. 'I'm not sure you're actually real.'

Poppy grimaced. 'Well, that makes two of us, because I'm not sure you are either. Now, if you'll excuse me, I have to get my head around a presentation for Mr Adams. Oh, and feel free to change your mind about all this. I won't be sorry.'

'I won't change my mind.'

Long after the building had emptied for the day, Sebastiano sat in his office, staring across at Big Ben but not really seeing it. He couldn't quite believe he had just coerced a woman into posing as his fake lover, or how difficult it had been to get her to agree.

Honestly, he'd expected the whole process to take no more than five minutes. Offer her a large sum of money and count the seconds until she said yes. When Poppy had baulked he had initially believed she'd been holding out for more money. No surprise there. What *had* been a surprise was how hard he'd had to work to convince her, and how heated his blood had become in the process. He knew it was just ego, but still the whole time she had been resisting him that voice in his head had said, *Take her!* and *Now!* with predictable consistency.

A voice he would not be listening to next weekend. Sebastiano had met enough women on the make to encourage a lifetime of bachelorhood. Women who would do and say just about anything to marry up in society. Since he was from a centuries-old Italian dynasty with all the trappings that entailed, he'd been a target for avaricious types ever since he'd reached puberty.

But he wouldn't be caught. And not just because he distrusted most of the women he met, but because his life was perfect as it was. Why interfere with that?

A pair of bold velvet-blue eyes slid into his consciousness. Was Poppy Connolly for real? He didn't think so, but he wasn't going to waste time wondering about it. She had agreed to go with him and that was all there was to it.

He blew out a breath and pushed to his feet.

In truth he didn't need to take her to Italy with him. Yes, it would be easier to present the package his grandfather believed to get what he wanted, but it wasn't essential. He hadn't even confirmed that his grandfather was right in his assumptions.

He could easily turn up to the villa alone and they could laugh at the mistake over a *negroni* or two. Sebastiano could then assure his grandfather that he was perfectly fine as he was, and wear the old man down without having to revert to a lie.

The problem was that he still remembered how soft the skin was on the inside of Poppy's wrist, and he'd enjoyed meeting a woman who hadn't behaved as if he was the best thing since sliced bread.

His lips twisted into a self-mocking smile. Was it just the novelty of having a woman say no to him? Surely he hadn't become that arrogant, or full of himself?

Or was it the thought of returning to his family home at this time of the year, alone?

Yes, that made his stomach knot, but it had been fifteen years since the accident. And, while he might still live with the guilt and loss, it didn't govern his actions any more. He'd mastered that years ago. Hadn't he?

Perhaps it was nothing more than simple lust. He'd felt it straight away, an edgy hunger to feel her against him. Feel her against him and under him and over him. Feel every soft, satiny, naked inch of her as he buried himself deep inside her. Just the thought of it aroused him to a burning point of hardness. Which was ridiculous in the extreme. His libido did not control him. He controlled his libido.

Regardless, this relationship was fake, he reminded himself, one-hundred-percent fake. And that made Poppy Connolly one-hundred-percent off limits.

CHAPTER FOUR

'WHERE DID YOU say you were going?'

'I didn't,' Poppy signed back to her brother, debating between packing black linen dress trousers that had seen better days or a navy skirt that was a little on the short side. 'But it's somewhere in Italy. I was planning to text you the details after I arrived.'

Black trousers definitely. She didn't want to give Sebastiano Castiglione any ideas that this relationship was anything other than phony.

'Italy!' Her fifteen-year-old brother signed excitedly, bouncing up and down on the bed as if he'd just been stung by a wasp. 'I want to come.'

'You can't,' she signed. 'I already told you, it's a work thing, and I deliberately didn't tell you where I was going because I knew you'd want to come.' She went to smooth his fringe back from his face like she'd used to when he was little but he moved back out of range. 'You know I'd love to take you. Don't make me feel guilty.'

'I won't if you at least let me stay in the flat by myself.'

Poppy pressed her two fingers to her thumb to signal no. 'You have to stay with Maryann. And make sure you heat up the Bolognaise I prepared for dinner tomorrow night. I don't want her having to do any cooking this weekend.'

Her brother gave her a belligerent stare. 'I'm old enough to stay by myself.'

'You're fifteen.'

'Exactly.'

Poppy sighed. 'If you don't leave now you'll be late for

school,' she signed to him. 'And stay off your phone this weekend. You need to read a real book instead of playing games all the time.'

'I tell you what...' He uncoiled his lanky frame from the bed, signing rapidly. 'I'll read a real book if I can stay here by myself.'

Poppy grabbed a couple of tops that went with the black trousers. 'Go to school.' She pulled him in for a kiss. 'I love you.'

He gave her the shorthand sign for 'love you' in return before blowing out of the door like a dervish in his new trainers. Or one of the ten pairs of new Nike trainers! They had arrived the day after she had struck her devil's pact with Sebastiano and Poppy had been forced to say she had won them in a work raffle to explain the extravagance.

She didn't know if Sebastiano's generosity was a sign of the man himself, or just his desperation to get his own way. Somehow she suspected the latter.

Straightening her bed, she padded into the bathroom and took a shower. It was still a few hours until Sebastiano was due to arrive, but she felt jittery.

Around noon she received a phone call from her brother. Usually they used messaging, but due to a new hearing app she was able to speak into the phone and have her words converted to text. Simon wanted to know if he could go to the movies that afternoon with some friends he had made at his new school and Poppy's heart swelled. Because her brother had been born deaf he'd had many developmental delays and those, combined with their volatile childhood, had seen him become a shy and insecure kid. Lately, though, he seemed to be coming out of his shell and it made Poppy's heart sing to see it.

Telling him it was fine with her, she jumped when a decisive knock sounded at her front door. Knowing who it would be, she told Simon she loved him before opening the door wide, all her nerves from earlier returning full force at the sight of her boss standing in her dank hallway.

He was so tall, dark and utterly male he took her breath away. It just wasn't fair that a man should look this good and yet have no decent moral fibre about him. The reminder of his poor character had her determined that she would not let him walk all over her.

'Are you early, or am I late?' she asked, raising her chin in an unconscious challenge.

'I'm on time,' he drawled. 'But if you're like every other woman I know, you'll be late.'

Poppy's eyes narrowed. 'For the sake of our very fake relationship I'm going to pretend you didn't say that.'

Sebastiano laughed. 'Are you going to invite me in or are we going to conduct this conversation in the hallway?'

'Better than the ladies' toilets.'

A small smile tugged at the corner of his mouth. *'Touché.'*

He brushed past her as he entered her tiny hallway and Poppy's eyes unconsciously drifted to the shape of his butt in the denim jeans he wore. Combined with the effect of the thick navy sweater and black boots, he looked good enough to eat. Not that she was hungry.

'Coffee?' she offered pleasantly.

His gaze, that had been scanning her shabby living room with laser like intent, swung back to hers. 'Cute, but I think we should skip the refreshments. Who were you on the phone to just then?'

He asked the question as if he had every right to know and Poppy's hackles immediately rose. It was instinctive for her to shield her brother from prying, ridiculing eyes and a deep sense of self-preservation told her that the less this man knew about her life, the better.

'Nobody,' she said.

'It didn't sound like nobody.'

Knowing he wouldn't let up until he had the information he wanted she relented. 'It was Simon, if you must know.' And she wasn't revealing any more than that.

His mouth firmed as he noted her belligerent expression but he didn't push. 'Are you ready to go? My plane is waiting.'

His plane was waiting?

She already felt incredibly inept standing before him in a cheap corduroy skirt, an even cheaper blouse and second-hand boots. 'Hold up a minute, my lady's maid is still packing my trunk.'

His lips quirked. 'Do I sense some hostility, Miss Connolly?'

Poppy huffed out a breath. 'Not really. More a change of heart.'

He glanced at her feet. 'What, the trainers didn't fit?' He scrunched his brows together. 'I have to confess I'm struggling to picture size-ten trainers on those feet. Or is it that your neighbour wasn't happy with the apartment she was shown yesterday. Is that the problem?'

Poppy shoved her hands on her hips and glared at him. Maryann had come to her late last night in a whirlwind of excitement with news that, out of so many MS patients, she had been singled out to receive a grant to cover all her medical expenses, as well as assistance to move to a ground-floor apartment beside a park. She had kept pinching herself the whole time and didn't know how she could have been the recipient of such good luck.

Poppy had told her that of course she deserved every ounce of that luck, and more, to which Maryann had said that Poppy's luck was changing as well.

'I can feel it.' Maryann had hugged her tight. 'It started when you got that coveted internship. You're such a smart, wonderful girl, Poppy, and a beautiful sister to Simon.'

Poppy's eyes had welled up and she now thought it completely heartless of Sebastiano to remind her of that part of their deal right when she was trying to figure out how to back out of it.

'She loved it,' she informed him with a sigh. 'And thank you for arranging to have her put on the special list for the new drug trials. That was…thoughtful.'

'You're welcome.'

'But I still think this is a bad idea, Mr Castiglione.'

'You cut a deal,' he said with ironclad resolve. 'And the name is Sebastiano, or Bastian. I answer to both.'

But which did he answer to in bed?

Horrified by that rogue thought, Poppy pressed her sweaty palms together. Therein lay one of the reasons this was a bad idea: she hadn't been able to stop thinking about Sebastiano all week. In particular, his impressive naked chest! It made her feel less in control to be at the whim of someone else and she didn't like it. And she hadn't felt like that for a long time.

Not since she'd picked herself up as a lost seventeen-year-old and decided she would never be at another person's mercy again. And it wasn't so much that she felt out of control right now, it was more that she felt…okay *out of control*. Totally out of control. And inferior, if she was being completely honest with herself. Lacking, in some way. It would take his family two seconds at most to re-alise she was an imposter.

Especially when his family was descended from centuries-old Italian royalty. 'They'll see right through me,' she implored. 'They'll know we're a sham.'

'Just relax, Poppy, I have this.'

'But how can you?' she asked.

'I arrange multi-billion-dollar business deals all the time. Pretending that we're a couple will be a walk in the park by comparison.'

She wished she agreed, but she did not arrange multi-billion-dollar deals at all, so for her this was much worse.

'You'll really do anything to get control of this company won't you?' she said.

'Yes.'

'Surely your grandfather knows that.'

'In my experience people see what they want to see. My grandfather wants me to fall in love. Since that's his focus, that's what he believes has happened.' He paced around her small living room. 'Sometimes I think I should have just bitten the bullet—isn't that what you English would say?— and taken a wife already.'

His cavalier attitude to something Poppy had romantically believed—hoped—led to happy ever after for some people appalled her. 'It's not too late,' she drawled. 'Perhaps you could send Paula out to Fortnum and Mason's to pick one up for you this afternoon. Who knows, you might even find one on sale.'

Sebastiano cast her an amused glance. 'There's that latent hostility again, Miss Connolly.'

'What you just said was completely outrageous,' she snapped. 'One doesn't just bite the bullet and get married. But why haven't you, out of interest? Is it that you don't believe in love or because no woman would have you?'

Sebastiano gave her a mocking smile. 'I'm not married because I don't care to be married. But I'm sure love exists. In fact, I know it does, because I've seen it. I just don't want it or need it for myself. My life is perfect as it is.'

'Your grandfather doesn't think so.'

'My grandfather is old-world Italian. To him, family is life.'

'And what about your parents? Are they happily married?'

A muscle ticked in his jaw. 'My parents are dead and

therefore off limits as a topic for discussion. Any other questions?'

Immediately contrite by the wealth of hurt she picked up in his aggravated tone, Poppy's own irritation fell away. What did she care what he thought about love and marriage? It wasn't as if this was real. Surreal, maybe. But definitely not real.

'Now I just feel bad,' she said. 'But if this is supposed to look legitimate then we would know certain things about each other. Like how they died.'

His green eyes turned as murky as the waters at Loch Ness on a stormy day. 'They died in a car accident. I was fifteen.' He paced her small room like an angry caged tiger. Or panther. He was more panther, with his dark good looks and green, green eyes. He swung those eyes to her now and once more she felt the jolt of a strange connection in her chest. For a minute neither of them spoke, then his lips twisted in a wry grimace. 'Satisfied?'

No, she wasn't satisfied. He had been around the same age as Simon when his parents had died and she knew how devastated Simon would be if something were to happen to her. The realisation made her want to go to Sebastiano, wrap her arms around him and keep him safe from the harsh realities of the world. Which was absurd. Not only would he not welcome her efforts, but if there was anyone who could take care of themselves in this world it was this man.

She felt a little sick at having pried into his life. Lord knew there were things she didn't want him knowing about her life. 'I'm sorry for your loss,' she said. 'I didn't mean to upset you.'

'You didn't,' he bit out, running his hand through his hair and giving it that sexily mussed look she didn't want to find attractive. 'You've worked for my company for six weeks, so you already know everything you need to know about me. If you want my favourite colour or my favourite food, the answer is blue and *pesto alla genovese*.'

'You're that complex, huh?'

His grin was slow. 'I do have a voracious sexual appetite, but I doubt my grandparents will quiz you about that.'

Poppy shook her head. 'TMI,' she said, making him laugh softly.

'So, what about you?' he asked.

The simple question made her instantly wary. 'No, I do not have a voracious sexual appetite.'

Her cheeks stung with embarrassment, worsening when his lips kicked up at one side. 'Are you sure?'

'Yes!'

'Pity,' he drawled meaningfully. 'But I was referring to you as a person. You drilled me about my life: turnabout is fair play.'

Poppy swallowed heavily, even more embarrassed than before. 'Red and rice pudding,' she said stiffly.

Sebastiano shook his head slowly. 'You're going to have to do better than that, *bella*.'

Noting her red face Sebastiano decided to cut her a break and moved to the roughly sanded sideboard against the cracked wall, studying the meagre number of photos on display. There was one of Poppy a few years younger, with a young boy and an older woman, and various others that were a variation on the same theme.

'Who's the boy?'

'My brother.'

Sebastiano cast her a glance over his shoulder, noting her stiff shoulders and pursed lips. So Little Miss Intrusive didn't like being on the receiving end of probing questions. How interesting.

Not that he really cared. He already knew her impressive academic credentials and he had no wish to learn more about a woman he found himself unwittingly attracted to and would never see again after the weekend.

But she did have a point. If this were a legitimate relationship they would know certain things about each other. Things his grandfather, in particular, would expect him to know.

'So this woman would be your mother, yes?' He pointed to a framed photograph, curious despite his intentions to remain detached from her.

'No.' She came to stand beside him and he could smell the faint trace of flowers clinging to her skin. He doubted it was perfume, because she didn't seem the type, so it had to be soap. And her. He inhaled deeply, his gaze drifting to her straight hair hanging past her shoulders in a thick, lustrous curtain. It looked soft to the touch and he had to shove his hands inside his pockets to stop himself from finding out for sure.

When she didn't elaborate on her answer about the woman in the photo, he raised an eyebrow. 'Just "no"?'

She sighed. 'That's Maryann. My neighbour with MS.'

'And your parents?'

'They're not around.'

'Where are they?'

'I don't think it's fair that you get to ask me all sorts of probing questions,' she complained, 'when you gave me such clear back-off signals before.'

'I answered your questions, didn't I? Now you answer mine.' He scowled down at her. 'Anyway, you were right, my grandfather will expect me to know everything about you.'

Her eyebrows climbed her forehead. 'Everything?'

'Yes. The Castiglione men are very protective of what is theirs. If I was truly in love with you, I would know everything about you.'

Even as he said the words, Sebastiano knew he was

being unfair but he didn't care. This was just strategising to achieve the best outcome. And he was a master strategist.

He wasn't sure she was going to answer, but then she said, 'My mother died of a drug overdose when I was twelve and I—I don't remember my father.'

Shocked by her matter-of-fact revelation, Sebastiano stared down at the top of her glossy head. 'Who raised you and your brother?'

'We lived in the foster care system until I was seventeen.'

Foster care?

'It wasn't as bad as you probably imagine,' she said, reading him correctly, and Sebastiano knew by her off-handed tone, and the way she avoided eye contact, that it had probably been very much worse than anything he could imagine. 'So we're both orphans,' he mused.

She gave him a look. 'So it seems. Hell of a thing to have in common.'

He paused, noting the way her chin jutted forward, as if she dared him to feel sorry for her. 'You're a tough little thing, aren't you, Poppy?'

Her small chin jutted even further forward in a stubborn tilt. 'I thought your plane was ready to go, Mr Castiglione?'

For a moment there was something naked on her face—pride? Determination? Vulnerability?—before she quickly masked it. Sebastiano felt a stab of admiration for her. This place she lived in might be small and run-down, but she'd made it a home, and it struck him that for all its negatives it was probably far more welcoming than any one of the show pieces he lived in. And why that bothered him he didn't know.

'It's Sebastiano,' he reminded her, watching as she crossed the room and disappeared through a door. She returned a moment later carrying a worn duffle bag.

His eyes narrowed on the bag. 'That's all the luggage you're taking?'

'Afraid so,' she said. 'Justina broke the trunk.'

'Justina?'

'My lady's maid.'

'Ah…' He shook his head. His grandfather was right; this woman had a rod of steel running through her. And yet she looked as delicate and as untouched as a hothouse flower. 'It's hard to get good help nowadays,' he agreed.

Her soft lips curled into a reluctant smile, as if she hadn't expected him to play along with her joke. 'You're telling me.'

Then her gaze drifted from his and she looked so lost and alone he felt an inexplicable need to comfort her. An inexplicable need to take her into his arms, stroke her hair back from her face and tell her that whatever, or whoever, had dimmed the brightness in her beautiful blue eyes would find themselves on the wrong side of his wrath. Then he wanted to do what he'd wanted to do since he'd walked in and kiss the breath from her body.

He didn't know what it was about her that drew him but there was no denying it existed. Or that he would have to control it. What was between them was business, not pleasure.

'Are you ready?' he asked, clearing the gruffness from his voice.

'Ready as I'll ever be. Bring on the weekend!' She picked up her bag and pasted a wide smile on her face.

Sebastiano walked over and took the bag from her. It barely weighed enough to be holding socks. 'Try not to look like you're going to the gallows, *bella*; I promise you, everything will be fine.'

'You know, you shouldn't make promises you can't keep.'

'Who said I can't keep this one?'

She gave him a superior look. 'Sorry, I forgot, you eat billion-dollar business deals for breakfast.'

Sebastiano couldn't hold back a laugh, inexplicably delighted by this prickly female he just couldn't get a bead on. 'I don't eat them, *cara*, I make them.'

She rolled her eyes, something no woman had ever done to him before, and grabbed her winter coat. She shrugged into it, the fabric of her shirt pulling tight across her small, high breasts. His groin hardened and he immediately tamped down on the reaction before following her to the door. A sense of foreboding warned him that the weekend might not go as easily as he had first hoped.

CHAPTER FIVE

POPPY STARED OUT of the window as Sebastiano's private jet levelled out above puffy white clouds floating in a perfect blue sky. The tranquillity of the view did not at all reflect the myriad of troubled emotions swirling around inside her.

She couldn't quite put her finger on what was bothering her but Sebastiano's words—that if he were in love with her he'd know everything about her—had unfurled something deep inside her.

Nursing a cup of coffee the stewardess had just handed her, the words played over and over in her mind. She had never had anyone other than Maryann take a genuine interest in her, and in many ways that had been a good thing. Having had a mother who had either been borderline unconscious or just plain absent, it had fallen to Poppy to care for her infant brother and the experience had taught her how to take care of herself. How to take care of her own.

Unfortunately it hadn't taught her how to pretend to be in love with a man she hardly knew. A man who until today had been her boss. She screwed up her nose. Not only had she never seen a healthy adult relationship, she had never been particularly good at pretending. It was partly why she and Simon had been shipped around between so many families on a semi-regular basis.

'There's just something about her,' she had overheard one of her foster mothers say. 'We can't explain it.'

'She looks at you with them big, innocent blue eyes of hers…makes a person feel guilty,' another had said. 'And that brother of hers? I didn't know he was retarded when I agreed to take them on.'

'Now you listen, girl,' a particularly obnoxious foster father had warned, pointing a finger in her face. 'When that effing social worker turns up, you make like everything is sweet. You do that and it will work out real good for you and your baby brother.'

Poppy felt that old tightness grip behind her breastbone. She knew now that the social worker had done her a huge favour in removing her and Simon from that particular family, but it didn't diminish that old sense of failure she struggled to shake off. That old sense that the world was a harsh place and it was every man for himself.

And now she had to pretend she was in love with a man she was stupidly attracted to, but one who was a virtual stranger. At least on a personal level. And what if she failed? Would Sebastiano withdraw the help he had already started to give Maryann? Would he take back Simon's new trainers?

It was hard for Poppy to trust anyone, let alone a man known for his ruthless exploits, and she knew that part of her anxiety about the weekend was in knowing that she was putting herself in the way of a man who could make an unguarded woman do stupid things. Stupid things such as fall in love with him and cry over the telephone when he ended their relationship.

Not that she was in any danger of falling in love with him—that kind of thing didn't happen after only meeting someone a week ago—but she couldn't deny that a part of her was intrigued by him. And not just because he was the sexiest man she had ever seen. It was his self-confidence and, yes, as much as she didn't like to admit it, his arrogance. He was just so sure of himself, it automatically made her feel safe in a way she never had before. Then there was the way he looked at a woman. As if he knew all the ways to touch her and give her more pleasure than she could ever dream about. And that he'd enjoy doing it. Now, *that* was definitely appealing!

Poppy had never experienced any sort of passion, hence her virgin status, but when Sebastiano looked at her with those knowing emerald-green eyes she wanted him to do things to her. She wanted him to reach for her and put his hands on her, as she had imagined him doing the other day in his office. She wanted to run her hands through the mat of hair on his manly chest and press her aching body against his until she couldn't think of anything else.

She shifted in the soft leather seat, an uncomfortable heat flaring between her thighs.

Even if he saw her in a remotely similar light, she wouldn't want anything to happen between them. Unfortunately, to a man like Sebastiano she would just be another fish swimming in his very large ocean, one he would cast off as soon as he'd had his fill of her. Anyway she couldn't afford to be distracted from her goals by a man who was only out for a good time.

She glanced at him working in the seat near the front of the plane. She should also be going over study notes for an exam she had to sit in a couple of weeks, so she pulled her ancient laptop out of her satchel even though she doubted she'd take in a word.

The problem was that she had responsibilities. A teenaged brother to take care of, and a plan to be top of her class so that she could get any job she wanted straight out of university. She didn't need a man to derail her or, worse, weaken her. That had been her mother's plight and it wouldn't be hers.

And yet here she was, mooning over a man who broke hearts like they were china at a Greek wedding. She scowled at her notes. She wasn't mooning, exactly, she was… She was… She sighed, her mind turning to the three wishes he had promised her. Accepting his deal came too close to relying on someone else for her liking, though at the same time she couldn't deny that he had thrown her a lifeline. That was if he kept his word—and so far it certainly seemed as if he would. And that was another thing. She wasn't used to that kind of follow-through from anyone other than Maryann and it made her feel jittery because deep down she knew it was most likely too good to be true.

She sighed. If only she didn't feel so conflicted when she was around him. On the one hand, she wanted to push against all that dominant male energy to find the flaws in his armour, and on the other she wanted to lean into it and hope that there were no flaws. She wanted to lean into it, soak him up and learn what it felt like to be cherished by someone who would love her enough that he would want to know everything about her.

The latter being the most dangerous inclination of all, and one she could never afford to give in to.

'Poppy?'

Startled out of her reverie, Poppy glanced up, not realising that Sebastiano had come to sit beside her. Immediately her nerves tightened and the blood fizzed in her veins. Forcing out a slow, relaxed breath, she collected herself. 'Yes?' she queried mildly.

'I have something for you.'

Poppy stared at the oblong-shaped blue velvet box. 'What is it?'

'A gift to show you my appreciation,' he drawled. 'Open it.'

Reluctantly she did and gaped at him when she saw a stunning, luminous pearl surrounded by diamonds. 'This is the most beautiful thing I've ever seen.'

Pleased, glittering green eyes stared down at her. 'I'm glad you like it. I think it will look perfect against your skin.'

Poppy stared at the jewels that twinkled under the plane's halogen lights, her heart beating too fast. No wonder women fell for him hook, line and sinker. Rich, good-looking, generous and *entitled*, she reminded herself.

'Please tell me these are fake.'

Sebastiano smiled. 'I don't do fake.'

Her eyebrows hit her hairline and she saw that he had immediately picked up on her train of thought.

'Jewellery. I don't do fake jewellery,' he amended.

Poppy closed the box before she became too dazzled to give the precious jewels back. 'If I wore these, I'd be mugged.'

'You will if you continue to live in the neighbourhood you're in now.' He frowned. 'I hope that third wish you're holding on to includes a new home somewhere more salubrious.'

He hadn't tried to keep the contempt out of his voice and it raised her hackles. 'Not everyone can be born rich.'

'I know that. But I'm giving you a chance to improve yourself.'

'Oh, really?' It was all Poppy could do not to tell him what he could do with his chance. 'Why thank you, kind sir.'

He sighed and ran a hand through his hair. 'That wasn't what I meant and you know it.'

He suddenly looked tired and Poppy suspected he was as tired as she felt. She knew from the legal team that he'd had back-to-back meetings all week and maybe their current situation had played on his mind more than he let on. Or maybe that was just her imagination going wild, and the dark circles beneath his eyes were because he'd followed back-to-back meetings with back-to-back sex.

'I admit my neighbourhood isn't brilliant,' she said, forcing herself to be conciliatory. 'But it's not that bad either.'

'I suspect you know how to make the best of a bad situation, *bella*. But I saw a group of teenage boys working the corner of your apartment block and they weren't selling lemonade.' He smiled once more, as if everything was right with his world, and no doubt it was. It was just hers that had become topsy-turvy.

'They're okay if you leave them alone.' She handed back the velvet box. 'Thank you, but I can't take this.' She sounded ungracious, and she hadn't intended to, but she was a little disconcerted at his insight into her personality. She usually did try to make the best of bad situations.

'Why can't you take it?'

'Well, for a start I believe this is usually the kind of thing you give *after* the relationship has ended; and for another it won't suit my complexion.'

'I bought it to suit your complexion.'

He had bought it? Not Paula?

'Well, there you go.' Her throat felt tight. 'You do fall short on some things. I'll alert the press. I can see the caption now: *Sebastiano Castiglione, megalomaniac, human after all*. It'd sell a few papers, don't you think?'

'What I think is that you have a very smart mouth and need to be put over someone's knee.'

A hot flush flooded Poppy's face as he glared at her. 'Not yours,' she murmured huskily, fighting the urge to squirm in her seat.

'You are turning out to be one of the most exasperating women I have ever met,' he muttered. 'Anyone would think I was handing you tinted marbles tied together with string.'

'That would be better. It would at least match my outfit.'

Without responding to her pithy comment, Sebastiano clamped his hand around her wrist. Before Poppy could take exception he'd propelled her to her feet and frog-marched her down the plane in front of him.

His touch sent tingles up and down her arm and she frowned. 'You have to stop doing that.'

He pushed open a door and ushered her through it. 'Doing what?'

Taking charge of her body. 'Grabbing me as if I'm yours to push around.'

'I'm not pushing you around.'

Poppy held up her hand and his came with it. 'Exhibit A, Your Honour.'

Sebastiano scowled and released her wrist. 'Exhibit B would be you being contrary. But at some point you have to get used to my touch. It might as well be before we land.'

'Get used to your touch?'

Just the thought of it sent her senses into an alarmed spin. She had an image of him stripping the clothes from her body, and then his from his own, and it wasn't a bad image.

Poppy took a step back and rubbed at her wrist, her eyes riveted to the enormous silk-covered bed that dominated the luxurious room. Before she could prevent herself, her eyes flew to his with apprehension. If he touched her now, if he kissed her as she had dreamt of him doing all week, would she have the wherewithal to deny him?

'No need to look at me like that,' he rasped. 'I meant in public. It will look a little odd if you flinch or cover me in coffee every time I get too close to you.'

Poppy took a minute to think about where her head was at, reminding herself that she was here not because he *wanted* her here, but because he *needed* her here. Which didn't mean she had to give into his every demand. Especially if she wanted to maintain her sense of self. 'Then don't get too close to me,' she said matter-of-factly.

As if he was completely exasperated with her, he shook his head. 'I brought you in here because I've organised some things for you, and you might as well sort through what you want here rather than cause a scene at the villa.'

Poppy followed his line of sight and noticed a row of glossy carrier bags with couture names stacked neatly along the wall. She frowned. 'What things?'

'Clothes. Shoes. Handbags.' He waved his hand dismissively. 'Things women need.' He frowned. 'I texted Paula on the way to the airport. She took care of it.'

Heated embarrassment filled Poppy's cheeks. So that was the reason their take-off had been delayed. He couldn't have made it any plainer that she was beneath him and she couldn't deny the ripple of hurt that passed through her. 'Really?' She strolled over to the first bag and opened it up. Could a girl feel any more inept than she did already?

Carelessly pulling the first item she touched out of one of the shiny bags, she unwrapped the tissue paper and held up an exquisite blue skirt. 'A skirt. Thanks. I never would have thought to pack one.'

'I had to guess your size,' he said, a little discomfited. 'I hope it fits.'

Poppy smiled serenely. She intended to make him feel more than discomfited by the time she finished with him.

'I'm sure Paula is exemplary at her job.' Then a horrible thought struck her. 'Oh God, you didn't tell her they were for me, did you?'

His eyes narrowed at her panic. 'No, I didn't tell her that. And actually I've never asked Paula to buy a woman clothing before so yes, I hope she did a good job.'

'Really?' Poppy put a hand to her chest. 'That makes me feel so special.' She unwrapped another, smaller parcel of tissue. This time a demi-cup bra fell out of it. *Perfect.*

She let a soft smile touch her lips as she dangled it in front of him, gratified when his eyes darkened. 'And underwear. I never would have thought to pack underwear either. It's so lucky you're around, Mr Castiglione. What would a girl do without you?'

A muscle ticked in his jaw as he registered her sarcasm.

'It's Sebastiano,' he said, frowning. 'And I take it from your tone that you don't approve?'

'Smart,' she said, dropping the offending items back in the bag and slapping her hands on her hips. 'But I packed my own clothes and shoes and *women's* things, thank you very much.'

'Damn it, Poppy.' He rubbed the back of his neck in frustration. 'Stop being so stubborn about this. That duffle bag of yours was half-empty.'

Affronted, Poppy glared at him. 'My duffle bag is none of your concern.'

A low-level growl emanated from his throat as if he had reached the end of his tether. 'Any other woman would be more than pleased with what I'm offering. No-strings-attached jewels and designer clothes. An all-expenses-paid holiday in Italy.'

'Then ask those women to Italy.'

'I don't want to ask those women to Italy!' he all but bellowed.

'Then you'll have to put up with me.' She whirled around to stalk out of the room but his hands descended on her shoulders.

'Okay, what's wrong?'

Poppy stared up at him. *The man had to ask!*

'I don't want your designer clothes,' she said, her temper and insecurities sparking in equal measure. 'And as for the holiday? I have to spend time impressing people I've never met and pretending to be in love with a man I hardly know. I don't know any woman who would want to do that.'

'Unfortunately I know plenty.'

'Like I said—invite them.'

'You know I can't.'

'So says the man who makes trillion-dollar deals every day.'

He had the grace to look contrite. 'You don't like me

very much, do you?' His voice was low and packed with an emotion she couldn't identify.

Poppy's chin came up. 'It's not that I don't like you. It's more that you're not my type.'

He looked startled for a moment. 'You're into women?'

Poppy rolled her eyes. 'It's a testament to your enormous ego that you would think the only reason I wouldn't find you attractive is because I'm gay. But I'm not. The truth is, you're entitled, and you have no sense of humour.'

A muscle ticked in his jaw again. 'I have a sense of humour. It might not extend to wearing Mickey Mouse watches, but I have one.'

Poppy gaped at him, affronted. 'What's wrong with my watch?'

'Nothing,' he said levelly. 'I just wouldn't date a woman who wore one.'

Poppy's lips pursed. 'Well, you do this weekend, because I never take it off.'

His eyes narrowed. 'It's special to you?'

'Very.'

'Did Simon give it to you?'

'Yes. As a matter of fact, he did. Do you have a problem with that?'

'Take it from me,' he said with lethal softness. 'You're selling yourself too cheap.'

Poppy made a choking sound in the back of her throat. 'I can't believe you just said that.'

'Dio!' He stalked away from her and then back, frustration vibrating through his big body. 'You know, you would try the patience of a saint.'

'I would!'

He towered over her, all six-foot-four of outraged male, and for one heart-stopping moment Poppy thought he was going to pull her into his arms and kiss her. And she wanted him to kiss her. So desperately it made her knees tremble.

'I did not mean to insult you,' he said stiffly.

Poppy's chin jerked up. 'Well, you did. But unfortunately for you, your grandfather thought you'd date someone who would wear this watch, so you'll just have to deal with it.'

His mouth flattened into a grim line. 'I doubt my grandfather made it past your dazzling smile to even notice the watch,' he growled. 'Wear the clothes, don't wear the clothes; I don't care. Just make this look real.'

He stared at her as if he had a lot more to say on the subject but thought better of it, stalking out of the room and leaving a vacuum of deflated air in his wake.

Poppy sank down onto the edge of the bed. She was stunned by the argument they had just had. She never argued. Never. Easygoing by nature, she was the kind of person who got along with everyone, both men and women. So he had bought her clothes for the weekend, so what? It wasn't as if she wanted him to like her for herself. She didn't care what he thought of her. It was unlikely that she'd ever get to work for SJC in the future anyway so…what was her problem?

Sexual frustration, a small voice said. Sexual frustration for a man who was using her, just like every other person she had ever got close to other than Maryann.

She sighed. She was going to have to get over the fact that she disliked that he was using her too and figure out how to play the game. Because she had agreed to this deal and, if he wanted some besotted girlfriend to convince his grandparents that he was a reformed rake, then that was exactly what he was damned well going to get!

CHAPTER SIX

'POPPY, THIS IS my grandmother, Evelina. Nonna, this is Poppy Connolly.'

'*Buongiorno*, Poppy, *come stai*? It is lovely to finally meet you. Giuseppe spoke so highly of you.'

Poppy beamed at the beautifully coiffed Italian woman and wound her arm through Sebastiano's, leaning against his side to give the impression of the picture-perfect girl-friend. 'It's nice to meet you too. You have a beautiful home.' Which was an understatement. The pale pink mansion that was built on a rugged bluff in the heart of the Amalfi coast, and surrounded by palatial gardens, was a place mere mortals only got to see in *Vogue Living*. Or Bond films. And she should know. Simon had made her sit through enough of those of late.

'Thank you. Now, please, you must come inside. It is a sunny day but winter still has us in its grip.'

As they made their way up the stone steps to the portico entrance, Poppy gazed up at Sebastiano adoringly. 'Thank you for bringing me, darling.'

His eyes glittered down into hers. 'My pleasure, *pumpkin*,' he murmured, his eyes conveying a warning that he was unhappy, though why that should be was beyond her. This whole charade made her nervous, and he was the one who had told her to make it look real between them.

'Come through to the living room,' Evelina bade them. 'I've organised refreshments.'

Stepping into a lavish room straight out of a bygone century, Poppy headed straight for the large picture windows that showcased the deep-blue sea and rugged coast-line beyond. Magnificent candy-coloured houses perched along the hillside while sleek-hulled yachts bobbed in the harbour. 'Oh, wow,' she murmured. 'I'd heard the Italian Riviera was beautiful but this is something else.'

'Is this your first time in Italy, Poppy?'

'Yes.' She smiled at Evelina. 'It's my first time out of England.' She moved to stand beside Sebastiano and didn't have to look at him to know he was on edge. 'I was so surprised when Sebastiano invited me, wasn't I, honey?'

She smiled up at him, trying to coax an answering smile from him, but when it came it was more of a snarl. 'You certainly were.'

'Then you must make sure you show Poppy some of our wonderful country, Sebastiano. Do you take cream in your coffee, Poppy?'

'Yes, thank you.' She took the dainty cup Evelina offered and sipped at the rich brew. 'Oh, this is heavenly.' She breathed, closing her eyes to better savour the taste. 'I'd heard that Italy does the best coffee.'

'Where is Nonno?' Sebastiano barked impatiently, his eyes blazing down at her as if she was somehow responsible for his grandfather's absence.

'He is still at the office,' his grandmother murmured. 'He was delayed but said to tell you he would be back in time for dinner.'

Catching Sebastiano's irritated glance at his watch, Poppy hunted around for a distraction and found it in the form of a cluster of framed photos on the far wall. So far she was doing all the work in making their relationship look authentic and she was fast running out of ideas on how to keep it up. 'Are these family photos?' she asked, feeling Sebastiano stiffen beside her.

'Si,' Evelina confirmed softly. 'This is our beautiful family.'

Intrigued, Poppy strolled over to the wall. Her eyes skimmed over the twenty or so frames, stopping on one of a boy holding on to the stern of a yacht. 'Is this you as a boy?' she asked Sebastiano, smiling at the carefree look on his face as the breeze caught his dark hair, the potential of his wide shoulders already evident even though he must have been about ten in the shot.

Sebastiano stopped beside her. 'Yes,' he said curtly.

Poppy glanced at him curiously, unsure as to why he wouldn't be happy that she was looking at the photos. She glanced at the other frames that showed a very normal, happy family. For some reason she had expected that Sebastiano's family would be snobbish and distant but, seeing this wall of coveted memories, she could already tell that they were the type of family she admired the most. Close. Supportive. *Loving*. It made her heart ache for something she had always wanted but had never been able to find.

'And this?' She pointed to a photo of a young girl in a ballet costume.

'My cousin.' He leant close and she instinctively stilled. 'What are you doing?' he murmured gruffly, his hand firm on her shoulder. To his grandmother it might look like a loving gesture, but there was so much tension radiating off him Poppy knew it was the exact opposite.

'I'm looking at photos,' she murmured, risking a glance into his stormy gaze. 'Just as you did at my place. Why are you so tense all of a sudden?'

'I'm not tense.'

Before she could check herself, she ran a hand over one corded shoulder and felt the muscles bunch beneath her fingertips. Fire flitted along her nerve endings and she did her best to ignore it. 'You certainly feel tense. You just jumped six foot in the air.'

'Listen, I—'

'*Sebastiano, come stai tesoro mio?*'

Poppy turned to see a willowy blonde woman heading towards them, a wide smile on her face.

Embracing Sebastiano, she gave him a traditional kiss on each cheek. *'E così bello vederti.'*

'It's good to see you too,' Sebastiano murmured.

Poppy swallowed heavily, a sick feeling invading her stomach. Was she about to meet one of Sebastiano's ex-girlfriends?

'I'm sorry, I shouldn't be speaking in Italian.' The woman smiled at her warmly, her brown eyes alight with interest. 'I'm Nicolette, Sebastiano's cousin—and you must be Poppy. Welcome. You can call me Nicole, like everyone else does.'

His cousin! Poppy was disconcerted to find that she didn't have to pretend her sense of relief. She smiled in greeting and had no choice but to accept a warm kiss on each cheek as well. Unused to being welcomed into a family so wholeheartedly, she felt something inside her clench in reaction. She had always been openly affectionate with Simon, replacing the mother he'd never known from an early age, but she wasn't so used to being embraced herself.

As if sensing her unease, Sebastiano ran his hand down her arm, as if he were gentling a startled animal. The gesture of comfort was so unusual, she felt instantly overwhelmed.

'Please don't tell me Nonna invited the whole family over tonight?' he drawled to his cousin.

Nicolette laughed. 'We invited ourselves.' Then she turned to Poppy. 'Giulietta and I are dying to hear all about how you landed our elusive cousin. We think it's fantastic, by the way.'

'Oh, well, thank you. I think.' Now that she'd had a moment to take stock, Poppy couldn't help liking this woman and she gave Sebastiano an amused look. 'It wasn't easy.

What with all the supermodels he always has hanging off him.'

Nicolette laughed and Sebastiano scowled. 'Okay, I can already see you two are going to be trouble together. I think I'll take Poppy upstairs to rest before dinner.'

'Rest?' Nicolette gave him an impish wink. 'Is that what they call it nowadays, cousin?'

'Don't embarrass Sebastiano and his guest, Nicole,' Evelina scolded, her eyes shining with happiness. 'I don't want to scare him away when he has not been home in so long.'

Poppy felt Sebastiano tense again and wondered what had put that distant look in his eyes. Then he put his hand in the small of her back and she couldn't think at all.

'No fun, Nonna,' Nicole complained. 'We've been waiting for Sebastiano to fall in love for a long time. At least let me enjoy the moment.'

'Just wait till it's your turn, cousin,' Sebastiano drawled, ushering Poppy ahead of him.

'*Pah*, it's never going to happen!' Nicole lamented. 'I'm going to die an old virgin.'

'Nicolette!'

'Sorry, Nonna.' Nicole giggled, clearly not sorry at all. 'Okay, I'll be quiet now. You two run along and *rest*.'

Poppy threw Nicole a bemused smile. She'd never had a girlfriend growing up but, if she had, she would have wanted one as bubbly and lively as Nicolette.

Trailing Sebastiano up the moulded stone staircase, she was out of breath by the time he ushered her through a solid wooden door.

'*Dio,*' he muttered. 'What made me ever think this weekend was going to be easy?'

Poppy blinked up at him. 'Those long billionaire breakfasts?'

'I never said billionaire breakfasts,' he growled, dragging a hand through his hair. 'And what was with all the touching downstairs?'

'You told me to make it look real between us so I was playing my part.' Poppy glanced around the beautifully appointed sitting room and across to another set of French doors that overlooked the sea. 'I'm a pretty affectionate person so…if this was a real relationship, I'd probably touch you.' *A lot*, she silently added.

'Well, I'm not overly affectionate, so you can cut that out right now.' His eyes narrowed as they swept over her. 'Unless of course you're looking to make this real.'

Poppy frowned, hearing the edge in his voice. 'Of course I'm not looking to make this real. Why would you even think that?'

'Never mind, just…follow my lead in this.'

Poppy shrugged. 'Whatever you say, boss.' She walked over to the French windows. 'Your home is like something out of a fairy tale,' she murmured, taking in the quaint coloured houses nestled around the harbour town. 'You're so lucky to live here.'

'I don't live here any more.' He shrugged out of his jacket and tossed it on the edge of a white sofa. 'When I visit Italy, I stay in Rome.'

Poppy felt her curiosity pique at his offhand comment. 'So where do you call home?'

'I have houses in London and Boston. I spend my time where I'm needed the most.'

'Don't you get sick of packing a suitcase?' she asked, trying not to ogle his body in his fitted sweater. 'When you go from home to home.'

'I don't pack a suitcase. I have a wardrobe in each house.'

'Oh, right.' Could the gap between their two worlds be any wider? 'Me too.'

A reluctant grin flashed across his face. 'I apologise for

my cousin ambushing you before. I wasn't expecting to see my extended family until tomorrow night.'

'It's fine.' She shrugged. 'At first I thought she was an old girlfriend, but of course, what would an old girlfriend be doing here? But she was so nice it was hard not to like her. Is she always so bubbly?'

'Will you accuse me of having no sense of humour if I say "unfortunately"?'

Poppy laughed. 'Probably. But you love her anyway, right?' she asked softly.

'She's family. Of course I love her.'

A dark cloud settled over Poppy just as the wintry sun ducked behind a grey cloud, casting the lovely vista in shadows. She instinctively wrapped her arms around her torso. There was no 'of course' about it; being family did not guarantee anybody actual love.

Realising that Sebastiano was watching her with those keen, intelligent eyes, she moved away from the window. 'Nicole said that there would be others at dinner tonight. How many more of you are there?'

'Nicole's older sister, Giulietta, and her partner, Giancarlo. As well as my uncle Andrea and my aunt Elena. My uncle will most likely drink too much wine before the first course is served and fall asleep on the sofa, and my aunt will reprimand him to no end.'

'It sounds lovely.' She found herself envious of his closeness with his family. 'Is there anything else I should know?'

'Not really. We are a very small lot by Italian standards, which is one of the reasons I suspect my grandfather wants me to hurry up and settle down.'

'And holding the family business over your head to get you to do it.'

'Something like that.'

'It sounds a bit Machiavellian,' she commented.

'My grandfather doesn't mean it to be. He just has a bee in his bonnet over my single status.'

'Because you're the last Castiglione male.'

'Exactly.'

'Well, that's a relief, because he seemed really nice when I met him.' She frowned. 'But what about one of your other relatives? Can't they run the company?'

'Giulietta is in fashion, Giancarlo is a flourishing wine maker and Nicolette is in engineering. Since my uncle is an artist and my aunt a homemaker, they were never contenders.'

'So that leaves only you.'

'Yes.' His tone was curt. 'My father would have taken over but... Anyway, my grandfather means well. He just thinks I work too hard.'

'Everyone thinks you work too hard,' Poppy said lightly. 'It's admirable on one hand and a bit scary on the other. Even your social engagements are usually for work.'

'I run six miles a day. Sometimes more.'

She made a face. 'Running? Seems like more work to me. Not that I don't admire the results.'

Realising what she had just revealed, she blushed, and his eyes gleamed with interest. 'Did you just tell me you found me attractive, Poppy?'

'No.'

His smile told her he knew she was lying. 'That's a relief because I'm not your type, remember?'

'Well, you're not if we're talking boyfriend material, but as a boss you're pretty sensational.'

'So what is *boyfriend* material for you?'

'Um, I don't know.' She smoothed her hair back behind her ears. 'Someone kind and considerate. Someone with a sense of humour and who is interested in making a difference in the world.' Someone who would love her for herself and understand that she would always put her brother's needs first. 'You know, the usual suspects.'

'You didn't mention money.'

'I'd rather find someone who was trustworthy than someone with a large bank account. And anyway, I intend to make my own money so I don't have to rely on someone else for the rest of my life.'

He shook his head. 'I find that hard to believe.'

Poppy blinked at him. 'Why?'

'My experience of women is that they're all looking for a man to pay the bills. Are you telling me you're the exception to the rule?'

'Since I pay my own bills and am happy to do so, I suppose I am.'

Uncomfortable with the way he was studying her, Poppy cleared her throat. 'Maybe you should tell me where I'll be sleeping so I can get ready for dinner.'

With me, was Sebastiano's first thought.

Don't be an idiot, was his second.

He wasn't sure if this beautiful, guileless woman was for real but some deep-seated part of him wanted her to be. She'd been surprising him ever since he'd collected her from her flat, and he'd only realised when she had opened her front door how much he had been looking forward to seeing her. He had even made an excuse to visit the legal department during the week, and that impulse had irritated him so much he'd filled the rest of his week with back-to-back meetings.

He didn't know what it was about her, but she got to him. Those bold blue eyes that could spark with both humour and fire and held a wealth of secrets; that mouth that was inviting even when it was pressed into a taut line; her body... *Dio*, her bones were so delicate, her figure so slender, he'd have to go easy on her at least the first time.

The first time?

Dio!

There would be no first time between them. No matter that her sweet scent filled the space between them and made him salivate; no matter that she turned him on to the point that the women in his past became faceless names whenever she touched him. She had made it more than clear that she wasn't interested in him—that he wasn't her type. And that was for the best. Even if it grated.

What had she said on the plane? That he was *entitled*? And with *no sense of humour*? By God, when she had said that he'd had an overwhelming urge to toss her onto the bed and show her just what he did have to offer. And downstairs, when she had clung to him like a barnacle on a rock, it was all he'd been able to do to stop himself from hauling her into a dark corner and pulling her skirt up to her waist. Unused to feeling so caught up over a woman, Sebastiano scowled when he realised that he still hadn't answered her question about the sleeping arrangements.

'You'll be sleeping in my bed,' he said gruffly, irritation warring with arousal as her gorgeous eyes flew to his.

'Your bed?'

'Relax, Poppy, I won't be in it.'

'Well, I didn't expect that you would but—where will you sleep?'

Sebastiano glanced at the white sofa against the window that was designed for high tea rather than sleep.

Her eyes followed his gaze and she frowned. 'You can't sleep there. It's not long enough.'

'It will do.'

'No.' She shook her head. 'I can bunk down on the sofa. Believe me, I've had worse.'

Sebastiano frowned, remembering that she had been brought up in the foster care system. The knowledge had played on his mind all the way to Italy. 'How much worse?'

She crinkled her nose. 'Oh, you know—*worse*.' She

glanced around his luxuriously appointed room. 'Or perhaps you don't. Anyway—I'll take the sofa.'

'Actually, I do know,' he said, affronted by her belief that he was some spoilt, rich ingrate. 'I did a year in the army when I was younger, and no matter which country you're in the ground is always hard.'

'Okay, I stand corrected,' she said, waving off his irritation as if she was completely unperturbed by his scowl. 'But I'm still taking the sofa.'

A muscle ticked in Sebastiano's jaw. 'You're my guest. You get the bed.' And, so saying, he moved to the door to his old bedroom and pushed it open.

Poppy followed reluctantly and glanced inside. 'Big,' she murmured as she took in his king-sized bed, her husky tone forcing Sebastiano to grip the doorframe a little harder.

'What did you expect?' he asked, his voice deeper than usual.

She looked up at him, her blue eyes wide, and he cursed himself for his provocative question. She wasn't here for sex so best he get his mind back on track.

'Perhaps I could use a spare room,' she murmured.

Sebastiano stepped away from her and poured himself a glass of water from the pitcher standing on the sideboard. 'And how would that look to my family?'

'I don't know. I had imagined your grandparents would be old-fashioned about sex before marriage and give us separate rooms anyway.'

'I'm a grown man, *bella*. They would think it strange if I wasn't sleeping with you. And my grandparents have moved with the times. Apparently my grandmother even has a smart phone.'

Her soft mouth curved into a delightful smile. 'You sound put out.'

Sebastiano dragged a hand through his hair. 'This whole weekend has put me out.'

'Because you have to be here with me?'

'Because I have to be here at all.'

She frowned. 'I thought you loved your family.'

'I do love my family. This…' He waved his hand around and had no idea what he was doing. The last thing he wanted to do was open up to a woman he barely knew and tell her that this villa brought back too many painful memories he'd rather bury deep than think about. 'Never mind.' He took a deep, steadying breath. 'Usually we don't dress for dinner, but since the tribe has been invited you might want to make it semi-formal.'

'Thanks. Oh—and one other thing.'

Intending to plunge himself into work, Sebastiano paused with his hand on his laptop. 'What is it?' he asked curtly.

'Even though you don't seem to want to be here you might want to be a little less obvious about the whole work thing. A man in love would take some time to enjoy himself with his girlfriend while he was here.'

Sebastiano frowned. 'What are you talking about?'

'Before, when you found out your grandfather wasn't available, you kind of looked like you wanted to kick something.'

'That's because I did want to kick something.'

Her sparkling eyes disarmed him completely. 'Like I said, you might want to tone that down a little. I mean, isn't the whole purpose of me being here to show you in a new light?'

Unaccustomed to having his actions questioned, Sebastiano frowned. 'The reason you're here is to do whatever I say.' He noted the way her eyebrows hit her hairline and it only aggravated him more. 'Trust me, Poppy. I know what I'm doing.'

'Oh, right, because you—'

'Don't you dare say it,' he growled, secretly astonished at

her temerity when he realised the direction of her comment. He'd been a superior ass when he'd told her he could handle anything, because he closed billion-dollar deals every day and he didn't even think his impish cousin would tease him about it as openly as Poppy did.

She laughed softly and held her hands up in mock surrender. 'I wasn't going to.'

But they both knew that she was and something pulled tight in Sebastiano's chest when he realised that her light teasing had been to pull him out of the mood he'd been about to spiral into.

He stared at the closed bedroom door long after she had disappeared through it. Usually the women he dated thought more about themselves than anyone else, and he wasn't completely comfortable to think that Poppy wasn't one of them.

CHAPTER SEVEN

POPPY CLOSED THE door on Sebastiano's scowling face and leant back against it, waiting for the butterflies to resettle in her stomach. She didn't know why she felt the need to tease him; she just couldn't seem to help herself. He was so serious most of the time, so controlled, and she couldn't help but wonder what had made him that way, and whether he allowed anyone to penetrate beneath his aloof exterior.

Let it go, Poppy, she urged her curious side. *You're not here to fix the guy.*

Sighing, she spied the bed and the row of shopping bags that must have been delivered to her room while she had been downstairs. Right now she longed for more than a shower and a change of clothing. She longed to go home, the instinctive need to protect herself riding her hard.

She checked her phone for any further messages from Simon but he must still be in the movie. She smiled as she remembered snapping a heap of photos on her phone on the drive from Naples to the house and sending them to him. He had replied with a playfully annoyed face after he'd received them, telling her that he should be there with her.

Next time she'd love to bring him. Not that next time would be any time soon. Once Poppy finished her degree, she would be working hard to give them both a better standard of living, not holidaying in exotic locations such as this.

Glad for that reality check, she headed for the bathroom, sighing at her pale complexion. The weekend had barely started and already she felt like a fish out of water.

After washing and drying her hair with the luxurious products set out on the marble bench top, Poppy padded back into the bedroom and paused in front of a walk-in closet as big as a shipping container. Someone—most likely one of the discreet white-coated servants she had noticed earlier—must have unpacked her duffle bag because her measly amount of clothing hung in a forlorn row as if the wearer had needed to escape in a hurry and had left the dregs of their wardrobe behind.

An image of Nicole in her svelte purple dress slid into Poppy's mind. She knew she could never pull off Nicole's polished poise if she spent a century getting ready, but she guessed that whatever was in those bags beside the bed would get her closer to the mark than what was currently hanging limply in front of her.

Was she being silly in her insistence that she wasn't going to wear any of them?

Probably, and she recalled the vow she had made back on the plane to make their relationship look real. A pretence that would require a lot of acting, and well, what was an actor without a costume? Or a knight without armour? What was a person without integrity?

The thought stayed her. She was already compromising hers by fabricating this relationship with Sebastiano so that he could take control of his family's company; she wasn't going to expound that by pretending she was someone she wasn't.

It was probably only pride driving her decision to ignore the shiny bags, but it was all she had to hold her head up high, and she wouldn't compromise that.

Sighing deeply, she once again scanned her clothes and pulled a green jersey dress from the hanger. She had found it at a vintage shop and Maryann liked it on her.

'It shows off your legs,' she'd said. 'Especially when

you team it with those sexy black heels with the little strap around the ankle.'

Dressing quickly, she tied her hair back in a stylish pony-tail and slid her feet into said sexy black heels. She rarely had a chance to dress up in her day-to-day life, and a fizz of excitement invaded her belly as she stared at herself in the mirror.

Would Sebastiano admire her in the dress, or would he be angry that she was not wearing one of his offerings?

Poppy's lips flattened as she realised where her thoughts were leading her.

She didn't want Sebastiano to like her or approve of her; she just needed to convince his family she was someone he could fall in love with. Her gaze fell to her Mickey Mouse watch. So far she'd never had any cause to take it off and, since it was more playful than garish, she stubbornly decided that she wasn't going to now. No matter that Sebastiano would not date a woman who wore it. As she'd said to him, he could invite someone more sophisticated to Italy if image was so important to him!

Hearing a text come in on her phone, she smiled as she opened Simon's message telling her all about the movie he had just seen. Texting back made her feel more like her usual self, and she was so absorbed she didn't even hear Sebastiano until he bit out a terse. 'Let me know when you're done.'

Whirling around, her heart skipped a beat when she saw him standing in the open doorway.

'I did knock, but you were too busy on your phone to hear it.'

Poppy took in his black trousers and matching shirt that was rolled to his elbows. He looked every inch the arrogant bad boy that he was and she warned her heart to settle down. A woman would have to be mad—or incredibly sure of herself—to take on a man like him. And she was neither.

Still, she was only human, and an unwilling awareness flared inside her, along with that old feeling of wanting to desperately hold on to something but knowing it would never be yours to keep.

'Right.' She moistened her dry lips. 'I take it it's show time?'

His eyes fell on the unopened bags by the bed and his lips tightened. 'Like I said, follow my lead and everything will be fine.'

Poppy smoothed down the skirt of her dress and walked towards him. 'What does "follow your lead" mean, exactly?'

'It means stop fretting.' He glanced at her fingers that were pleating a fold into her skirt.

'I'm not fretting,' she said, feeling uncomfortably exposed by the fact that he had picked up on her nervous habit. 'Okay, maybe I am a little, but—' A wave of panic assailed her and she grabbed on to his forearm without meaning to. 'But I really don't think—'

'This will work?'

He raised a brow and Poppy scowled.

'Well, I don't see how it can,' she said hotly, annoyed that he wasn't taking her concerns seriously. 'We're from different worlds, Sebastiano, and I feel badly about lying to your family. They're really nice and I'm not that great an actress. They've probably already seen through me.'

'So, if they were fire-breathing dragons, that would make it easier?'

She glared at him. 'I'm being serious.'

'So am I.' He sighed and raked a hand through his hair. 'To address your first concern about us being from different worlds, my *nonna* worked in my *nonno*'s kitchen when they met so, believe me, you working for me will just seem romantic to them. As to your second concern…' He shrugged. 'We won't lie.'

Poppy blinked as she absorbed his words. 'I think you might have to clarify what you mean,' she said warily. 'Your cousin already said she couldn't wait to hear the details of how I *landed* you!'

'All you need to do is pretend that we're in a relationship but as to the details…we stick to the truth as much as possible. We met six weeks ago when you came to work for me—'

'Technically we met a week ago.'

'A minor detail.' He shrugged. 'We can say we only got together recently—which is true—so our relationship is still new.'

She frowned. 'I thought you wanted me to pretend that you're the light of my life?'

Sebastiano's lip curled sardonically. 'Since seeing Nicole's unbounded enthusiasm, I think it's too difficult to pull off the whole "desperately in love" angle. It will have to be enough that my family thinks we are a couple. If my grandfather interprets that as a lifetime commitment, that's his problem, not mine.'

Poppy bit her bottom lip, expecting to feel relief at his words, but somehow feeling slightly deflated instead. Why she should, though, she didn't know. Of course a man like Sebastiano would find it difficult to pretend to be desperately in love with a woman like her. Hadn't he already said as much?

'Fine,' she managed in a falsetto voice. 'But what if that's not enough for him to hand you the CEO position?'

It was a good reminder of why they were both here and Sebastiano grabbed on to it so that he wasn't tempted to grab onto her and show her all the reasons it would be a good idea for them to forget dinner and share his very comfortable, very *big* bed behind them. 'I'll cross that bridge when I come to it.'

'Okay,' she said, grabbing a brightly coloured shawl from the back of a chair. 'It's your show.'

Sebastiano looked down at her as she came to stand beside him. It was his show, so why didn't he feel like he was running things?

Frowning, he deliberately invaded her space, fascinated by the tiny pulse point that started fluttering in her creamy throat. 'It is my show, and what I need from you is no unnecessary touching, no inquisitive questions and no elaborating on our story. Do you think you can do that, intern?'

The pulse at the base of her throat jumped before speeding up even more. 'Of course I can do that.' She gave him a smile that didn't quite reach her eyes. 'One ready-made, non-adoring, fake girlfriend to go.'

'Good.' He let out a calming breath and ignored the tightness in his chest.

Of course she couldn't do that, Sebastiano thought two hours later as frustration turned his muscles hard. The woman was a law unto herself and she didn't even seem to know it. A human wrecking ball. Not that she had spilt anything on him this time. No, she was just playing havoc with his senses: brushing up against him every time she shifted in her seat; stroking her fingers across his forearm every time she needed something. Water. Salt. Sugar. The last time she'd leant into him, he'd nearly dumped the entire contents of the table in front of her so she wouldn't have to ask for anything else.

And all the while she was completely charming, regaling his family with stories about working for his company, and how she had accidentally thrown coffee over him when they had met—leading Giulietta to ask if it had been love at first sight.

Poppy had thrown to him for that one, nibbling on her

plump lower lip as if she wasn't sure how to respond. And how was he supposed to answer, other than to say yes?

Che palle! His family would have him setting a wedding date if he wasn't careful!

She had also talked about how she wanted to help those less fortunate than she was when she finished law, and all the while she hadn't revealed any real details about her past, always managing to draw his family's interest back onto more present day issues. She was slick, he'd give her that, but little did she realise that, the less she revealed about herself, the more he wanted to know.

Who was he kidding? he thought as she murmured another apology after her leg brushed his; the only thing he wanted to know about her was how she would taste if he kissed her.

Right now she'd taste of Riesling, heat and passion. A passion he suspected she would try to deny before it even bloomed, but one he was starting to crave to draw out of her.

His hands clenched into fists at his sides. His body ached to find out if he was right, if she was as responsive as he'd imagined she would be that morning she had knotted his tie.

He warned himself to give it a rest because the more he thought about her in that way the more he wanted her. And, apart from the fact that he didn't want to lead her on, there was something about her that was dangerous to his equilibrium. Something that warned all his instincts to back away and keep going.

'Sebastiano,' she murmured beside him. 'Is everything okay?'

And that was another annoying habit she had. She seemed to be able to read him better than anyone else he knew. 'Of course, *bella*,' he said smoothly. 'Why do you ask?'

'Well…' She gave him a worried sideways look. 'You're very tense again.'

'I'm tired,' he excused. Which wasn't an actual lie; it just wasn't whole truth.

Before she could rebuke his assertion, her mobile phone started ringing. He had noticed her texting on it throughout the day, and again when she'd been waiting on him to bring her downstairs. The damned thing never seemed to be far from her side, and for some reason that annoyed him about her too.

'Excuse me,' she murmured softly, sliding her chair back. 'I have to take this.'

Va bene, va bene,' his grandfather said indulgently, even though he was a tough old bird who banned mobile phones from his dinner table.

Scowling, Sebastiano watched a tender smile flit across Poppy's lips before she stepped outside the French doors onto the balcony that led to the pool pavilion and beach beyond.

Who was she talking to? Simon?

He had no idea who the man was but it grated that he'd overheard her tell him that she loved him when he'd arrived to collect her. It might not have mattered if she hadn't been so evasive when he'd asked about it, but she had been, piquing his interest even more.

'Sebastiano?'

Was he a boyfriend? A lover? And if so what did he think of her coming to Italy with him? Did the poor sod even know?

'Sebastiano, dove hai la testa?' his grandfather asked with a soft chuckle.

Where was his head? Good question. Not where it should be. About to shove back his chair and go after Poppy, he was foiled when Nicolette did it first. 'It's cute to see you worrying about your new girlfriend,' she said, completely misinterpreting his distractedness. 'But you relax. I'll go find her and make sure she doesn't get lost.'

Foiled by yet another irritating female, Sebastiano subsided back in his chair and wondered if he would look too 'focused' if he started talking business with his grandfather...

A smiling Nicole came over to join Poppy, who noticed Sebastiano had come outside and was speaking with his grandfather. Hopefully they were finalising the business Sebastiano had come here to do so that they could leave early. It would be much better for her strained nerves if he did. Though even as she had the thought she knew there was no way Sebastiano could miss his grandparents' wedding anniversary tomorrow night.

'Gorgeous view, no?'

Poppy stared out at the twinkling lights dotted around the majestic coastline and nodded. 'Unbelievable.'

'I meant the man, not the backdrop,' Nicole teased with a soft laugh.

'Oh!' Poppy smiled, or she tried to. 'Yes to both.'

'I'm really glad you're with my cousin,' she said. 'I've never seen him look at a woman the way he looks at you.'

As far as Poppy could tell, he looked at her as if he wanted to strangle her most of the time, especially when she had inadvertently cornered him into saying that he loved her. Which hadn't been entirely her fault. His terse instructions upstairs, and her worry over making their relationship look normal when she really had no idea what a normal relationship looked like, had made her fidgety. It hadn't helped that he'd sat so close to her at dinner she'd felt the press of his powerful thigh against hers every time he moved. The man just took up too much space!

'I'm sure your cousin has looked at many women the way he looks at me,' Poppy commented, wanting to down play the lie she didn't enjoy telling. She'd heard so many lies in her life so far, she'd vowed to not tell any herself, and here she was pretending to be involved with this lovely woman's cousin.

'Not that I've seen,' Nicole said. 'In fact, he's never brought a woman home to meet *la famiglia* before. It means you're important.'

Poppy frowned. 'No one?'

'No,' Nicole confirmed. 'That's how we know you're the real deal. Apart from the fact that he looks at you as if he wants to gobble you up whole.'

Poppy felt her whole face flush and Nicole was immediately contrite. '*Mi dispiace.* I'm sorry, Poppy. I didn't mean to embarrass you. It's just that I'm jealous.' She gave a dramatic sigh. 'I want a man to look at me like that one day.'

'Like what?' Sebastiano asked as he came to stand beside Poppy.

Poppy's heart kicked up at the sound of his voice, her body going on high alert. He was so close she could feel the heat of him driving out the chill of the night air.

'Like he wants to eat me up,' Nicole said.

Poppy groaned; the only thing she wanted eating her up right now was the ground.

'You're too young.' Sebastiano was deadpan. 'If any man looked at you that way, he'd have me to contend with.'

'*Pah!* I am twenty-four,' Nicole retorted hotly. 'One year younger than Poppy!'

'Like I said,' Sebastiano smiled down at her. 'Too young.'

Nicole pulled a face and Sebastiano tweaked her nose as if she were ten years old. It reminded Poppy of how she liked to fool around with Simon, and a sense of warmth invaded her heart. Initially she had thought Sebastiano just a corporate shark with no feelings but seeing his more playful side come out with his family made him more human than she would like him to be. It made him more of a man she could grow to like if she wasn't careful.

'Be warned, Poppy,' Nicolette advised her loftily. 'The Castiglione men think they own the world sometimes.'

Sebastiano laughed as his cousin wandered back inside.

'Don't listen to her,' he said, looking down at Poppy. 'We Castiglione men *know* that we own the world.'

Poppy couldn't contain a grin and shook her head. 'You are so full of yourself.'

'*Si.*'

His smile took her breath away and she shivered. He wasn't even trying to be charming and yet he was. What would happen if he actually tried to win her over?

'Are you cold?'

'No… I mean, yes. A little, but…' She paused as he draped his jacket over her shoulders. His clean scent and warmth instantly enveloped her and she breathed in deeply, warning herself to put some distance between them because she was already feeling overwhelmed by him. 'I'm sorry about earlier,' she murmured. 'That whole "love at first sight" thing at the dinner table. I didn't mean to trap you like that.'

'Didn't you?'

'Of course not.' His suspicion was as thick as a pea-souper and, frankly, insulting. 'You really have mixed with the wrong women, haven't you?'

'So my grandfather would have me believe.'

'Look, Sebastiano, I'm not likely to forget that this whole thing is phony and I'm under no illusions as to why I'm here. The problem is, I'm not used to being the centre of attention, and I don't like it.'

'What are you used to?'

His unexpected question caught her off-guard and dashed her indignation. 'What do you mean?'

'I mean, what do you do with yourself when you're not studying or working as my intern?'

Poppy shrugged. 'I work, like anyone else.' And she

ran around after her brother during those brief moments she had off.

'Work where?'

'I clean offices during the night.'

His eyes narrowed. 'During the night? Why?'

Uncomfortable to be talking about herself, Poppy made to shrug out of his jacket. 'Look, you're cold now, so—'

Sebastiano grabbed the lapels and kept the jacket in place. 'I'm not cold. Why do you clean offices at night?'

She gave a short laugh. 'For the love of it. Why do you think?'

'Okay, I deserve that,' he acknowledged impatiently. 'But why night in particular? Is it to fit in around your lecture times?'

'No, it's to fit in around my brother. I like to be there when he gets home from school.'

'I assumed your brother was still in the foster-care system.'

'No way.' She shuddered. 'I would never leave him in foster care when I'm perfectly capable of taking care of him myself.' *Well, she was now.*

She didn't like the way Sebastiano was studying her and made to put some distance between them.

Frustrated, Sebastiano gripped the lapels of her jacket more firmly, and didn't realise he had drawn her closer until her sweet scent caught on his senses, making him burn.

For some reason the idea of Poppy working hard and lugging heavy cleaning equipment around during the night while he slept bothered him immensely.

Previously he had always been coolly indifferent to a woman's needs outside of the bedroom, not wanting to encourage them to think he wanted anything more from them than the physical. Previously, until Poppy.

He scowled. He couldn't even put his interest down to the fact that he had made her off limits, because he'd felt the pull of her right from the start. No, this wasn't about his ego, it was about heat and desire and, while he might not be able to explain this compulsion to have her, he knew the only way to get rid of it *was* to have her. Have her naked, spread out and on fire for him, as he was for her. And he damned well knew she wanted him too. He'd seen the way she'd stared at his naked torso last Sunday morning, and felt the way she stiffened with awareness whenever he got too close.

Not her type?

He was more her type than whomever that Simon was who had given her the Mickey Mouse watch she treasured so dearly.

'Who's Simon?' he asked curtly. The man had been a burr in his side since he'd heard her tell him she loved him and it had become imperative that he find out more about him. So much easier to shoot an adversary down in flames when you knew who you were firing at.

Adversary?

He was getting in way over his head and he knew it.

Poppy blinked up at him. 'Simon?'

'*Si,*' he said gruffly. 'The one who gave you the watch. You were on the phone to him when I arrived at your apartment, and every time his name flashes on your damned phone you jump to respond, as if it's a fire you need to put out.'

Poppy frowned. 'You seem surprised by that.'

'I have to confess that I am.'

'I don't know why. You're obviously close to your own family. Would you not respond to a text if Nicole or Giulietta sent one?'

'We're talking about Simon, not my damned cousins.'

'I know that, but I don't see the difference.'

Sebastiano stared into her luminous blue eyes, made even bluer by the reflected light glowing from the infinity pool nearby. Something in her guileless gaze finally registered in his usually agile brain. 'Right,' he said, feeling like a fool. 'Simon is your brother.'

'Yes. Who did you...? Oh!' She clapped her hand over her mouth as if to stifle a laugh. 'You thought he was...?' She shook her head. 'Who? My lover?'

At his silence her grin widened and that only made him scowl harder. 'Of course I thought he was your lover. You told him you loved him.'

Her glee was evident in her mischievously sparkling eyes. 'Is that why you glower at me every time I use my phone?'

'You need to stop laughing.'

'You have to admit, it's kind of funny,' she said, making a meagre attempt to stifle her mirth.

Sebastiano drew her even closer, releasing the lapels of his jacket to slide his hands into the wisps of hair either side of her face. She stopped laughing instantly then, her eyes suddenly as wide as saucers. Her hair felt like silk against his fingers, her skin even softer. His eyes drifted from her mouth to the tiny pulse point flickering in the base of her throat, a sense of victory he couldn't explain coursing through him. 'Kind of funny, you think?'

'Sebastiano?' Her voice was soft and her hands came up to grip his thick wrists. 'What are you doing?'

'I'm going to give you a lesson in what *I* would do if this relationship was real.'

Only it's one-hundred-percent fake, he reminded himself right before he bent to her and covered her mouth with his. Her petal-soft lips parted on a gasp of surprise, her body stiffening beneath his touch.

Sebastiano gathered her closer, feeling her rigidity give way to a trembling need as old as time.

He groaned, pressing his lips harder over hers, seeking access to the warm recesses of her mouth. 'Open for me,

Poppy,' he growled. 'Kiss me as I've imagined you doing this past week. Let me taste you, *bella*. Let me—' Another groan escaped his lips as she did as he requested, willingly parting her mouth for him, a tiny whimper escaping her lips as his tongue swept inside.

He tilted her head back further, seeking even deeper contact with her, one hand leaving her face to skim down her body and curve around her waist, bringing her into firmer contact with his hardness. His other hand fisted her sleek ponytail, holding her steady beneath the onslaught of his hunger.

Dio, but she tasted sweet. Tasted sweet and felt sweeter. He wasn't sure he'd ever experienced a kiss like it, her hot, unguarded response making his body throb heavily.

Mine, a voice in his head chanted. *Take her.*

Some part of him questioned the desperate yearning behind that notion, but she was like a living flame in his arms, driving out rational thought, her hands gripping his shoulders, her tongue curling around his in a delicious imitation of what his was doing to hers. Hot need poured through him. He'd never experienced hunger like it and he wanted to drive her back against the nearest hard surface and take everything she had to offer.

A spear of blue fire flamed through him as she rubbed against him and he raised a hand to cup her breast, dragging his thumb across her distended nipple.

She gave a soft whimper and wrenched her mouth from his, her hands braced against his chest.

'Poppy...' He groaned, dragging her mouth back to his.

'Sebastiano, wait!'

Her cry of panic infiltrated his sluggish brain and he stilled, suddenly aware that they were standing by the pool at his family home in full view of anyone who might be watching.

Dio!

He eased his arms from around her, insanely gratified to find that she wasn't any more composed than he was.

She gazed up at him, her blue eyes blank with unsated lust. Her tongue snuck out to touch her reddened lips, and he saw the moment she came back into herself.

'Oh, God. I… We… Was somebody watching us?'

He had no idea. Really, the Pope could have been performing a holy communion and he wouldn't have noticed. 'It's possible.'

'It's possible?' Her hand went to her hair, smoothing the strands he had just dislodged, her breathing as hard as his. She stepped back, grabbing at his jacket before it slipped from her shoulders. 'Then why did you kiss me like that?'

He had no idea. 'Insurance,' he clipped out. 'If one of my family members *were* watching us, they would have no doubt that we're the real deal now.'

'Wow.' She blinked up at him. 'You're totally ruthless.'

Sebastiano took a deep breath. He couldn't remember the last time he had kissed a woman with so little self-control. And self-control was something he prided himself on. 'Not so ruthless,' he growled. 'If I was completely ruthless, I'd already have you upstairs. Naked.'

CHAPTER EIGHT

'IF I WAS *completely ruthless, I'd already have you upstairs. Naked.'*

Poppy's heart thudded inside her chest as those growly words once more replayed inside her head. She rolled over for the hundredth time and punched her pillow into a new shape, hoping that might help propel her towards sleep. Five minutes later, she gave up and again listened for signs that Sebastiano was having similar trouble sleeping.

Of course there was nothing but silence coming from the other room. And why would he have trouble sleeping? He probably kissed women like that for breakfast, while she—she truly understood for the first time how a woman could become stupid over a man. Something she had arrogantly assumed would never happen to her. Well, it just had. And her insides still felt quivery at the memory.

What she would like to know was how this had happened. Sure, he was sensationally good-looking and loved his family, but he was the ultimate megalomaniac bad boy who treated women poorly and whom she shouldn't feel anything for.

But she did feel something. She felt…she felt… God, she didn't know how she felt other than completely shaken by the memory of that powerful kiss. She shivered as she mentally replayed the scene moment by moment—the feel of his fingers in her hair, his tongue filling her mouth, his hand on her breast! Her own hand rose to her still sensitive flesh and she pressed her fingers against herself as he had done.

Stop! she ordered herself sharply; reliving something that shouldn't have happened in the first place wasn't going to get her to sleep any quicker. But her brain wouldn't listen. Which was just annoying. Poppy might have an inherently sunny disposition but she had always been a sensible person, even as a child. Her own mother had lamented that side of her nature and none of her foster families had liked it any better. But it had worked for her. It allowed her to compartmentalise the things that happened in her life, and it allowed her to pick herself up and move on when bad things happened.

Not that kissing Sebastiano had been bad. Quite the contrary. It had been heavenly. Earth-shattering… Poppy punched her pillow again. The truth was she had never kissed a man like that in her life. Had never felt the inclination before; too aware of her mother's under-age pregnancy and the devastation it had caused. But for those brief, wild moments in Sebastiano's arms she would have happily thrown all her cautious principles to the wind. She would have happily slaked the wild hunger he had induced in her and that still made her knees feel weak without any thought to her heart, or to Simon's welfare.

Which was completely incomprehensible and was an indication of how tired she was, and how much pretending to be his girlfriend this weekend had stressed her. In her desire not to fail at the role she was playing and displease him, she'd thrown herself into the part a little too enthusiastically. That surely helped explain her absolute abandon when he'd kissed her?

Didn't it?

Sighing heavily she closed her eyes against the faint night shadows. The thing to do was to banish the incident from her mind and make sure they were never in a position where it was likely to happen again.

* * *

For the first time in fifteen years Sebastiano woke up on the anniversary of his parents' deaths and they weren't the first thing on his mind.

Poppy Connolly was.

He didn't know whether to be pleased about that or put out.

What he did know was that somewhere between two and four am he had reached a decision to treat Poppy as if she was still one of his employees. Sebastiano never mixed business with pleasure and if he thought of her in a professional capacity he was unlikely to be tempted to kiss her again.

And pigs might fly. Backwards.

Ignoring the mocking voice in his head, he pushed to a sitting position and stretched the stiffness out of his neck. He'd lied to Poppy the day before when he'd said he'd slept on worse than this sofa. Nothing could be worse than this sofa.

Hearing that Poppy was already up and in the shower, Sebastiano beat back the urge to join her and grabbed his running shorts.

Work was usually his go-to panacea when this day dawned. Work and Scotch. Unfortunately Poppy would no doubt interrupt his work, and his grandparents would frown if he downed a bottle of Scotch before breakfast. So exercise it was.

Taking the back stairs to avoid any nosy family members he set off, grimly setting himself a challenging pace along the narrow, winding path that ran along the outskirts of the harbour village and wove in and around ancient vineyards until his lungs were heaving. It was fifteen years since he had been home at this time of the year. After today he'd make it another fifteen and send his grandparents an enormous anniversary present as compensation.

Grimacing at a twinge in his calf, he pushed himself harder, hoping that physical exertion would keep the demons at bay just as easily as alcohol.

Sex would, his unhelpful brain informed him.

Yeah, well, sex wasn't on the cards. Erotic dreams about plucky interns notwithstanding.

Another grimace shot across his face. He hadn't had a dream about a woman he couldn't have since he was a teenager. The image of Poppy coming over the top of him in a pale pink slip that slithered over her ripe breasts, her hair unbound and falling around her face as she lowered herself over him and took him deep, was now front and centre in his mind.

'Damn!' He stumbled as his foot twisted on a pebble, but at least it had jerked him out of his X-rated fantasy. Turning back, he pushed himself even harder until he came to a halt at the edge of the terraced gardens that skirted the villa. Pausing, he stretched out his calf. He had to stop thinking about Poppy. He hadn't brought her here this weekend to have sex with her. He'd brought her here to convince his grandfather that he was a changed man who deserved to take over the family company.

Deserved?

If anyone deserved it less, it was Sebastiano but, as Poppy had made him realise, he was the only one who could take over, and his grandfather needed to retire. He'd have been retired already if Sebastiano hadn't taken his eldest son from him: Sebastiano's own father.

He clenched his jaw as anger and self-loathing twisted like a tight, bitter knot inside him, threatening to pull him under. He'd been a snivelling little brat the night of the accident that had led to his parents' deaths, and he'd never let himself forget it.

Maledizione.

What had made him think that it would be okay to be

back here? On this day? He'd mistakenly thought it would prove that he had put the guilt of his past behind him, but it had only proved the opposite. He just thanked God that there were no photos of him and his parents on his *nonna*'s photo wall. Was that for his benefit, or for theirs?

He shook the sweat from his eyes and forced himself to sprint up the last steep incline towards the villa. But still the memories of that fateful day intruded into his consciousness like a jackhammer smashing through a slab of concrete.

In the days after his parents' accident when none of it had seemed real he'd walked along these hilltops until he was falling over with exhaustion, his grandparents' old Retriever keeping him company and licking away the tears he'd been unable to suppress. He'd unburdened himself on that poor old dog and a month later she too had died. No doubt from all the misery he had heaped on her. It was the only time he had let himself wallow.

Since then he'd kept to himself, working for his grandfather and branching out on his own, growing SJC into a global concern. It was something to be proud of, and he was. The company employed thousands of people around the world, but still something nagged at him. Some hollow sensation he knew would only be satisfied when he took control of CE.

Firmly resolved to focus only on his end goal, and not what sex with Poppy Connolly would be like, Sebastiano rounded the corner of the villa and spotted his grandparents, Nicolette and Poppy breakfasting on the sheltered outdoor terrace. They didn't notice him at first, their eyes focused on a gift his grandmother was unwrapping. Poppy tucked a strand of ash-brown hair behind her ear and bit into her bottom lip, and immediately the painful memories that had assailed him on his run were replaced with a much more pleasurable sort. The feel of her lips against his. Her breast in his hand.

He immediately wanted to drag her upstairs, strip the bulky sweater and jeans from her body and turn his midnight fantasies into reality.

Dio mio, Castiglione, did that run sort nothing out in your head?

'Bastian? Come join us,' his grandfather said, finally noticing him. 'Poppy has just given us a beautiful gift for our anniversary.'

Sebastiano's gut clenched. She had brought his grandparents a gift?

'It's exquisite,' Nicolette said. 'Who's the designer?'

A becoming flush highlighted Poppy's cheeks. Sebastiano glanced at the delicate glass-blown figurine his grandmother was carefully inspecting. It was of a horse with wings—at once whimsical and evocative. 'It's not from any particular design house; Simon did it.'

'Your brother? He's so talented,' Nicolette gushed.

'That's nice of you to say,' Poppy commented. 'I think he is too, but it's just a hobby at this stage. I took him to a glass works exhibition at the Tate Modern last year and he's become obsessed.'

Casting a cursory glance at the piece his family was admiring, Sebastiano stepped closer to Poppy. Immediately her eyes cut to his, a blush staining her cheeks. She went still and all his senses homed in on her. He'd bet that she was remembering their explosive connection the night before and he wasn't traditionally a betting man. *'Buongiorno, Poppy,'* he said, barely stopping himself from reaching for her to find out. 'You're up early.'

'I… I couldn't sleep,' she admitted, then, realising that they had a rapt audience, added, 'After you left.'

He lightly gripped the nape of her neck beneath the fall of her hair and felt her body quiver. A swift, answering response made his throb. 'I didn't want to disturb you,' he murmured as if he really had just left her bed.

'The coffee has just been poured,' his grandmother pointed out. 'Let me get you a cup.'

'That's fine, Nonna.' Sebastiano stayed her. 'I have to take a shower before I sweat all over Poppy. Nonno, what time do you want to meet today?'

'Ah, already your head is in business. This is why you are so successful, *nipote mio*, but also why you need Poppy by your side. You risk becoming less human.'

'I'm human,' Sebastiano ground out. Right now he was having a very human reaction to the woman seated so serenely at his family's breakfast table.

'Speaking of plans for the day, Bastian,' Nicolette said, 'I've asked Poppy if she'd like to come sailing on *Destino*. I thought it would be nice to show her some of the Riviera since you're going to be in meetings all day. And she's never been on a boat before. It will be her first time.'

Somehow the words *first time* stirred something in his Italian blood and, remembering Poppy's words from the day before about how 'focused' he was, Sebastiano found himself announcing that it was a great idea but that he would take her himself.

Poppy immediately objected, saying that she understood he was here to work and not entertain her. She sounded sincere but Sebastiano heard a note of panic in her voice and guessed that her reticence had more to do with last night's kiss than any altruistic concerns for his business goals. Certainly she had barely looked at him since he'd arrived on the terrace, and he didn't like it.

'Va bene, va bene,' his grandfather chimed in. 'Why do not we all go? We don't need an office to talk business and the house is about to be overrun with preparations for the party tonight.'

Unable to fault his grandfather's logic, especially with his grandmother's murmured approval, Sebastiano nearly groaned out loud. First he'd made a suggestion he hadn't meant to make, and now he and Poppy would be under scrutiny the whole time. Not that they wouldn't have been anyway with Nicolette present, but his grandparents were far more astute than his bubbly cousin.

'Terrific,' he said, grabbing a pastry from the breadbasket. 'Let me take a shower.'

'Sebastiano?'

Poppy had made her excuses at the table and rushed after Sebastiano, catching him halfway up the stairs.

His gaze swept over her as he turned and waited for her to reach him, making her agonisingly aware of her body in a way only he managed to do.

'What is it, *bella*?'

Flustered by the time she reached him, Poppy took a deep breath to steady her heart rate. 'I just wanted to say that if you would prefer to stay here and work then please do. I have some studying to get done for an exam I have in a couple of weeks anyway.'

'It's too late now,' he said unhelpfully. 'But by all means, bring your study notes if you want. And a jacket. The sun is out, but it will be cold on the water.'

'I don't expect you to babysit me, Sebastiano.'

Liking the sound of his name on her proper English tongue a little too much, Sebastiano scowled. 'I'm not babysitting you. I'm taking your advice and showing my grandfather my reformed ways. I would have thought you would be commending me rather than reprimanding me.'

Poppy might have commended him if she wasn't feeling so out of sorts. Something had changed when he had kissed her last night. She hadn't wanted to admit it but now it was all she could think about and she didn't know how to stop it.

'Why don't we just go and enjoy ourselves?' he suggested. 'If nothing else it will be a good distraction from the realities of life.'

* * *

Poppy had no time to ponder that esoteric comment until later. It came back to her as she watched Sebastiano, his legs braced wide as he steered the sleekly hulled vessel through wind-ruffled waves. Poppy pulled her jacket more firmly around her and turned her face up to the sun, the yacht's billowing white sails catching the wind as they raced across the water. She had to admit the whole experience of skimming over the clear blue sea in a shiny yacht and taking in the romantic Italian coastline was nothing short of exhilarating: the smell of the sea and the call of seagulls flying over head, the feel of the salt water spray intermittently carried on the wind as the waves crashed against the side of the boat. It was almost as exhilarating as the thrill she got from watching the man at the helm.

Sebastiano had taken over from the captain after lunch and she could tell he loved being out on the water. It was the most relaxed she had seen him since they had arrived, and again she wondered at his cryptic comment about wanting to be distracted from the realities of life.

As far as Poppy could see Sebastiano had a pretty good one, born to a privileged family who loved him dearly, and having amassed enough money to last him several lifetimes without having to think about it. Looking at him now, he was like a modern-day pirate, commanding everything and everyone around him with the authority of a man born to power, his thick sweater moulding to his broad shoulders, his glossy black hair blowing in the wind. She couldn't imagine what was missing from his life. Other than his grandfather's endorsement for him to take over as CEO, but any fool could see that that was imminent. Especially if she played her part well.

'Poppy, can you take this to Bastian?'

She glanced behind her to see Evelina holding up two steaming mugs of coffee.

'Of course.'

Rising to her feet, she made her way towards the helm, her ponytail whipping around her in the breeze. Just before she got to him his eyes gleamed with interest. 'You planning to hand that to me, or throw it at me?'

'That depends on whether you plan to keep reminding me of my faux pas every time I bring you coffee,' she countered, warning herself to keep her emotional walls in place when he showed his more playful side.

'Since it's too cold to lose my shirt, I'll not mention it again,' he promised, a slight smile tugging at his lips as he took the mug from her. 'How are you enjoying your first boating experience?'

'It's fantastic. Thank you. You've given me so many firsts I can hardly keep track.' First ride on a plane—private or commercial—first trip to Italy, first truly passionate kiss. Blushing at the direction of her thoughts, and worried he could read exactly what she was thinking, she sipped her own coffee. 'How did your meeting with your grandfather go earlier?'

'So so.' He grimaced. 'The old goat is still stalling.'

'Why would he be stalling?' Poppy asked, instantly worried. 'Do you think he doesn't believe we're a couple?'

'No, it's not that. I think he doesn't want to give up control of CE. He's as stubborn as an ox and wants everything to go his way.'

Poppy couldn't help the small smile that touched her lips, and of course he noticed.

'I do not have to have everything my way,' he denied with an arrogant tilt to his head, his eyes narrowing menacingly.

Poppy laughed softly. 'If it helps, you're usually right. Or so everyone in your office thinks.'

His eyebrow rose with cynical amusement. 'Tell my grandfather that. He might listen if it comes from you.'

He gave a frustrated sigh. 'His problem is that he doesn't trust the latest innovations, and thinks I'm going to continue current trends and off-shore our workforce.'

'It is a valid concern in this shifting employment market,' Poppy said. 'So many companies are doing it and it means less jobs now and in the future. Labour forces around the world are going to suffer.'

'I know. But I have no intention of offloading our loyal employees like yesterday's garbage. There are other measures that can be taken to lower operational costs and I intend to implement those first.'

'Give your grandfather time. I'm sure it's not easy for him to think about retiring after so many years in charge. But I'm sure you'll do right by everyone.'

'You are?'

'Don't look so surprised,' she said. 'You've done right by me so far.' Which was a surprise in itself, given her earlier experiences of human nature. 'You're a good person. I wasn't so sure of it at first.'

'I would never have guessed,' he said dryly.

Poppy chuckled. 'It's not totally my fault. You weren't very approachable that first morning, and then you were extremely pushy.' She glanced at him over the top of her mug. 'I also thought you wanted to take over your family business to increase your net worth, but I was wrong to judge you when I didn't really know you.'

'Don't make me out to be more than I am, Poppy,' he said gruffly. 'I'm nobody's hero.'

Poppy tilted her head, smoothing down her ponytail as it caught in the wind again. 'Are you afraid I'll fall for you?' She smiled easily, but the pulse in her throat had picked up speed and she was very much afraid Sebastiano had noticed it. 'I promise you, I won't. I'm innately sensible, and besides…' She glanced out to sea. 'I'm not looking for love either.'

'Why not?' Sebastiano spun the wheel and deftly manoeuvred the yacht towards the family's private jetty.

Poppy shrugged. 'I have Simon to take care of and he's at that difficult teenager stage where he needs someone solid in his life to show him the way. I've seen what happens to kids without direction and I don't want that to happen to him. On top of that, I really don't have time. Between work, Simon and study, I'm done in most days.'

'A man could help ease your load.'

'He could also add to it.' She shuddered. 'I've worked out how to get by on my own and I like it.' She looked at him a little self-consciously. 'Boy, conversations with you get personal quickly.' She stepped away from him lightly. 'What time are we heading back to London tomorrow? I have to let Simon and Maryann know.'

As the yacht docked, two burly men moved forward to secure the ropes Sebastiano threw to them.

'I'll tell my grandparents we'll have to leave mid-morning, if that suits you.'

'Yes. Thanks.'

A small bubble inside her burst at his easy acceptance of the end to their weekend and she told herself not to be silly. Only naïve women fell for men like Sebastiano Castiglione and she'd let go of naïve a long time ago.

Coming above board, Giuseppe waited to help Nicolette and Evelina down the gangplank. Without asking, Sebastiano held out his hand to Poppy. Before letting her go to follow the others up the stone pathway, he turned her towards him.

Wondering if he was going to kiss her, she didn't realise she had held her breath until he started talking.

'I wanted to thank you for giving my grandparents a gift.'

'Oh.' She touched her hair self-consciously. 'That's okay. It was very small, and it is their anniversary.'

'It meant a lot.'

'Okay, well…' Too aware of her hand still caught in his, Poppy tried to tug it free.

'One more thing.' He held her firm. 'At the risk of putting you off-side again, I asked Giulietta to organise something for you to wear tonight. And, before you refuse and tell me you don't need anything, it didn't cost me a thing.'

Poppy could see that he was expecting her to argue, but truthfully she had already worn the only dress that might have been remotely appropriate to dinner last night. Refusing another of his offerings because of pride would just be petulant. 'Thank you,' she murmured, smiling widely at the bemused expression on his face.

He blinked down at her. 'Any time, intern.'

CHAPTER NINE

POPPY STARED AT her reflection in the mirror. She was wearing a flowing halter-neck silver gown with matching stilettos that made her feel like a movie star.

She had found the gown hanging in the closet when she'd returned upstairs and even if she hadn't already agreed there was not enough pride in the world to stop her from wearing it.

Taking a deep breath, she walked through to Sebastiano's private sitting room. 'Didn't cost a thing, hey?' she chided gently, trying to offset her nerves.

Sebastiano turned, his phone to his ear, and Poppy forgot to breathe. She had never seen a man wearing a tuxedo in real life before and she doubted she'd ever see one who looked this good ever again.

Good?

Try amazing. Sexy. Powerful. *Edible.* Once again a nagging longing rose up inside her that only seemed to stir to life when he was around. She swallowed heavily.

Mr Powerful, I'm-In-Control, Multi-Billionaire Castiglione, meet Miss Average, Not-So-In-Control, Poppy Connolly.

He gave her one of his slow grins. 'It was worth every penny. You look ravishing.'

'Oh!' She swiped moist hands down over her middle, her brow arching as she fought to contain the thrill his compliment had given her. 'You lied to me!'

'Yes,' he said, completely unapologetic. He advanced towards her and heat bloomed beneath the surface of her skin at the look of intent on his face. Surely he wasn't going to…going to…?

'Turn around.'

Turn around? Dumbly, she glanced down to see that he was holding the blue velvet box she had handed back to him on the plane. His lips twisted sardonically as she stood unmoving. Then he gave her a gesture to turn to face the mirror hanging over the mantle, and unbelievably she did, her hands going to the deep vee between her breasts as he placed the exquisite pearl and diamond necklace around her neck.

What would it be like to sleep with a man like him for one night? she thought in a moment of helpless longing.

Dangerous, her sensible side returned, giving her backbone a much-needed boost of common sense.

'Like it or not, you're going to wear this for me tonight. If we were in a normal relationship I would insist on it.'

Poppy watched as he fastened the clasp at her nape, a shiver chasing itself down her spine. If they were in a normal relationship she would want to wear it for him.

Ignoring that thought, she noted that despite her being in high heels he was still so much taller than she was, so much broader. She was unable to take her eyes from him; their gazes collided and held when he looked up. Green on blue. Blue on green.

Suddenly it was difficult to breathe and Poppy was gripped by a ferocious shock of sexual arousal so powerful she couldn't move. She didn't want to move. Instead she wanted to lean back into him and rub her check along his freshly shaven jaw. She wanted to turn her head, find his mouth and have him kiss her as he had done the night before.

A throbbing awareness rose up between them and Poppy was shaken to realise that his gaze was full of the same heat and fire she imagined was in hers. Everything inside her urged her to turn in his arms, place her hands around his neck and bury her fingers in his short, dark hair before pulling his mouth down to hers.

His words from the previous night came back to her once more.

'If I was completely ruthless, I'd already have you upstairs. Naked.'

The tenor of the air thickened between them as if he too was remembering the same thing. Poppy couldn't move to save herself and Sebastiano seemed equally as riveted as his searing gaze drifted down to where the pearl nestled between her breasts.

'Sebastiano…'

His nostrils flared at her soft tone and, just when she thought he might reach for her, was desperate for him to reach for her, he stepped back.

'We should go down before my grandparents send up a search party.'

'Of course.' He didn't want her. Not like that. *Fool!*

She took a moment to smooth her hair back from her face. She had coiled it into what she had hoped was a sophisticated style, but now she felt awkward. Gauche.

'Poppy—'

'Yes, yes.' She pinned a smile on her face and prevented any further comment by placing her hand in the crook of his arm, and propelling him from the room. She suspected he knew exactly what had gone through her mind and she didn't want him to make some lame overture to make her feel better.

When they stopped at the top of the staircase Poppy threw him an enquiring glance. Tension radiated from him like a testosterone-driven force; a dark expression turning his features hard.

The murmur of voices and the clinking of glassware reached them, drawing her attention. Poppy felt her heart seize as a group of beautifully dressed guests entered the foyer, a white-coated servant draping jackets across his arm that most likely cost more than her yearly rent.

'Why have we stopped?' she asked. 'Is everything okay?'

His tanned throat convulsed as he swallowed. 'Why wouldn't it be?'

'I don't know—but you're frowning. This is a really big deal, isn't it?'

'It is.'

'Is that what's bothering you? You don't like parties? Because if you don't I'd be happy to rent a movie on my laptop and eat popcorn.'

He shook his head, a reluctant smile starting at the edge of his mouth. 'And what movie would you choose?'

'I don't know.' She hunted around in her brain for one of her all-time favourites. '*His Girl Friday*?'

'Never heard of it.'

'I'm not surprised,' she said. 'They don't show it often in Business School for Beginners.'

His eyes narrowed on her face, a curious light in his eyes. 'What is your story, Poppy Connolly?'

'My story?' She almost laughed. 'I'm probably the most boring person you'll ever come across.'

'Actually, you're one of the most fascinating. Do you really not know that?'

'Now you're embarrassing me,' she said softly. He couldn't possibly mean that, not after the way he had rejected her upstairs.

'I do mean it.'

She gave a soft laugh. 'You read minds now?'

'Your face is very expressive. It's like you wear your heart on your sleeve.'

'It's my worst trait.' She sighed. 'Whereas your worst trait is that you aren't expressive enough.'

'Still, you manage to read me. How is that?'

'I'm just observant, I guess. It comes from years of not fitting in.' She smiled uneasily at having revealed something so personal about herself, forcing a lightness into her voice. 'Am I going to be confronted tonight by an old girlfriend who will try and scratch my eyes out? Is that what's bothering you?'

Sebastiano shook his head. 'No. You will eat delicate canapés, sip the finest champagne and have a wonderful time.'

But what about you? she wanted to ask. If she didn't know better, she would say he was dreading his grandparents' party. 'That's a relief.' She gave him another bright smile. 'But, just so you know, I get fidgety when I'm nervous so I'll apologise now if I embarrass you in some way.'

He glanced down at where her fingers were pleating the fabric of his jacket. 'I had noticed that, yes.'

'Oh, sorry,' she muttered. 'Maybe you should pinch me so I know this isn't real.'

His eyebrow quirked. 'Isn't it supposed to be for the opposite reason? So you know something is real.'

'No. This already feels too real for my liking. I need a hard reality check. Your family makes me feel like I fit in.'

'You do fit in.'

'Yeah, like a ballerina at a bullfight.'

Sebastiano threw his head back and laughed. 'Look at me, Poppy.' He sobered and reached out to tilt her chin up so that her eyes met his, a frisson of awareness darting between them. 'You can fit in anywhere.'

Her heart bumped inside her chest. 'That's not true.' She had tried many times before and never fit in. 'And you know it.'

'I know some people are callous snobs, but only you can let them reduce who you are.'

'So says the man who grew up with a silver spoon in his mouth.'

'But you are wearing the silver dress, *bella*.' His smile was disarming, his eyes steady on hers. 'You're smart and beautiful, Poppy. You probably didn't hear that enough growing up, but you can take my word for it. My HR department don't hire duds.'

She let out a shaky breath; she hadn't heard those words at all growing up. But Sebastiano made her feel both those things, and that made him even more dangerous than he'd been when they had been standing in front of the mirror. At least then she'd known her reaction to him was purely physical. This felt a whole lot deeper.

'You still have one wish left, you know. Have you decided what it is that you want?'

Poppy looked at him askance. 'You're asking me that now?'

'Why not?'

'Because…' She felt light-headed standing this close to him. 'Can I wish myself away from here right now?'

'I said it had to be within my power to deliver, *bella*.' His fingers stroked lightly across her jawline. 'That I cannot do without alarming everyone.'

'Then, no, I haven't.'

She shifted back a pace and his hand fell to his side. 'Is being here with me really that bad, Poppy?'

'No. Actually, it's not.' She made a face. 'Which is why I need pinching. I've never seen anything like this place and it feels like I've fallen into my very own fairy tale. And that only makes me feel worse, because it accentuates our differences.'

'I told you, whatever you want, I will get for you.'

'You don't get it, Sebastiano.' She shook her head. 'You can click your fingers and have anything you want. That's not real life for most people.'

His eyes cooled on hers. 'Actually, I learned a long time ago that you can't click your fingers and have whatever you want, which is why I work so hard. I make sure nothing will ever be taken away from me again.'

Aware that the conversation had deviated down a path they hadn't been down before, Poppy stared at him. She wanted to ask him what he was talking about but she was also aware that he had withdrawn from her and most likely wouldn't answer.

'Sebastiano, come sta? Tutto bene!' a disembodied male voice called from below.

Sebastiano turned to her. 'Ready?' he asked, his gaze hooded as he held his arm out for her once more. Nodding, Poppy descended the stairs beside him, aware of curious eyes turning to watch their progress.

A well-groomed Italian man with an air of confidence about him met them at the bottom of the stairs, a half-empty champagne flute in hand. His eyes did a slow tour of Poppy's figure. *'Chi e questa donna affascinante?'*

'Mine,' Sebastiano supplied smoothly. 'Poppy, this is a soon-to-be ex-friend of the family, Sergio Stavarone. Be careful; he is unattached and looking to receive a black eye.'

Sergio laughed and took her hand, kissing the back with a wicked glint in his eyes. 'Just say you don't want this ugly cretin, *bellisima*, and I am yours.'

Poppy grinned, she had no idea what he had said but his light-hearted banter seemed to ease Sebastiano's tension from moments ago. She caught the intense gleam in Sebastiano's gaze that said, *'Back off!'* to the debonair Italian and her stomach impersonated a tumble dryer.

'You're a really good actor,' she murmured as he led her to a part of the villa she hadn't been in before. 'I almost believed you myself back there.' Which would be to her detriment, she knew. 'Is this a ballroom?' Her astonished gaze swept the vast room lined with ornate mirrors and floor-to-ceiling windows facing the night-dark sea. Beautifully dressed men and women mingled while white-coated servants wove between them, offering drinks and finger food on silver trays.

'Yes, it is a ballroom.' Sebastiano grabbed two fluted glasses from a passing waiter, handing her one. 'And I wasn't acting. I didn't like the way he looked at you.'

'You're very possessive for a fake boyfriend,' she commented.

His eyes held hers. 'I'm very possessive full-stop.'

Poppy's heart did a little quickstep and she was very glad when a small group of well-turned-out Italians interrupted them. For some reason her defences regarding Sebastiano were lower tonight and, try as she might, she couldn't seem to find the wherewithal to resist his animal magnetism.

Knowing that could only lead to one outcome—a bad one—she decided to focus on the party and not the man beside her. It was a good idea, because she found that she actually enjoyed meeting and chatting with such a wide variety of people. Most of them were incredibly lovely, although one or two women shot daggers at her as they vied for Sebastiano's attention. Of course, he was a consummate fake boyfriend and played the part to perfection, always making sure she had a drink, including her in conversations and insisting that anyone who spoke to him did so in English. It was all a bit much, really.

Even so, there was often an undercurrent of something not quite right when some of the older Italians grabbed his attention.

After one particularly circumspect group departed, Poppy turned to him. 'Why does everyone treat you as if they haven't seen you in for ever?'

'Because they haven't.'

'Oh, well, that explains it,' she returned, deadpan. 'Seriously, though—that lovely couple before, for example, seemed awfully careful about what they said to you. It was almost as if they were walking on eggshells. The husband turned brick-red when he mentioned your parents and I thought his wife was going to stomp on his foot.'

'Don't you know, *bella*?' Sebastiano's teeth flashed white beneath the impressive chandeliers. 'I am the big, bad wolf. Or—what did you call me?—a shark.'

Poppy scoffed. 'You know I don't think that any more. I've seen your softer side and I'm not so easily fooled by your bad-boy exterior.'

'You are not only terrible for my ego, *bella*, but if I'm not careful my reputation as well.'

'Be serious,' she admonished. 'What am I missing?'

He raised his champagne flute to his lips. 'My mouth on yours.'

Poppy blinked, not sure she had heard him correctly. 'What did you just say?'

'I want to kiss you again, *bella mia*. Why do you look so shocked after the incredible kiss we shared yesterday?'

Poppy swallowed heavily. 'Because I am. That kiss was for show and—'

'Was the way your eyes ate me up back in my office that Sunday morning for show?'

Heat surged through her at the memory. 'My eyes did not eat you up.'

'I nearly kissed you then, you know,' he said almost conversationally. 'When your busy fingers were knotting my tie.'

'Sebastiano…'

'You know the only reason I told you to get me a shirt was to get your hands off me.'

'Well, I'm sorry if I over—'

'Because I was aroused.'

Poppy's breath caught in her lungs. His words were stripping away her more sensible side and rendering it obsolete.

He chuckled at her mute expression. 'You seem surprised.'

'I am. You date supermodels and beautiful actresses.'

'And now I date women who wear Mickey Mouse watches. I bet no one in my office put money on that.'

'No,' she agreed. 'But I knew I should have taken this off.' She fidgeted with the band. 'It's never looked so out of place before, but I forgot.'

Refusing to let her retreat behind her safe walls, Sebastiano curled his hand around her waist. 'Leave it on. It looks charming. Different. Original. You'll probably see a couture version selling on the Internet by morning.'

'I really don't think—'

'Poppy! Sebastiano! *Eccovi.* I have been looking for you everywhere.'

Poppy swung around at the sound of Giuseppe's voice, her eyes wide, her cheeks on fire. After listening to Sebastiano tell her how much he wanted her, all she could picture was her and Sebastiano's reflection in the mirror, his darker head bent to hers, his lips grazing her neck, his lean hands touching her. Stroking her.

'How are you enjoying the party?' his grandfather asked, clearly not picking up on the sexual tension that vibrated like a live wire between them.

'It's very good, Nonno,' Sebastiano answered for both of them, and Poppy was glad that he had, because she couldn't have strung a sensible sentence together if she'd tried.

Stunned by the strength of his need to enclose Poppy in his arms and lay claim to her, Sebastiano released her and shoved his hands deep into his pockets. He'd been trying to distract her from her perceptive questioning by telling her the effect she had on him but he'd only served to turn himself on. Big time.

Which wasn't like him. He never struggled to keep himself in check. He was always cool. Always in control. His grandfather would expect it. And yet here he was, about to ravish a woman he shouldn't even want. A woman, who despite her claims to the contrary, wanted him just as much but who would no doubt behave like every other woman he had bedded and want more from him in the end.

Even knowing that, he wanted her with a hunger that floored him. He wanted to claim her and soak up her softness. Soak up her goodness.

He took a deep breath. At some point over the last few days she had gone from not being his type to being the only woman he could think about. Even the beautiful Daria Perone, a woman he had wanted to bed for a long time but whose path he had never crossed at the right time, paled in comparison to the woman at his side. A fact she had reluctantly conceded earlier in the evening when he had introduced her to Poppy.

Poppy had known something was up by the way Daria's hungry eyes had lingered on him.

'I thought you said there would be no ex-girlfriend's here,' Poppy had said with her proud little nose in the air after Daria had sauntered off to find more easy prey.

Sebastiano had laughed. 'She's not an ex.'

'Oh.' Realisation had made her innocent blue eyes sparkle. 'Maybe she's heard you give really good kiss-off presents.'

She had fingered the pearl happily nestled between her round breasts, and he had wanted to pull her in close and never let her go.

Right now he'd like to end the evening early and take her to his bed. Stamp out the hollow feeling in his heart with her sweet body underneath his.

But his *nonno* had other ideas.

'Wait here,' his grandfather said, nodding to the musicians, who automatically stopped playing. 'I have an announcement that will make you happy, *nipote mio*.'

Sebastiano felt the blood move through his veins in a slow, dull thud when his grandfather took the microphone. Surely his grandfather wasn't going to make the announcement that he was going to take over CE here, tonight?

'Friends. Family. We are here tonight to celebrate *l'amore della mia vita*.' His grandfather gestured to Evelina who had come to stand beside him. He gave her a soft kiss and joined their hands together.

'What did he say?' Poppy whispered.

'The love of his life,' Sebastiano rasped.

He felt Poppy sigh beside him and his gut clenched. Yes, she would definitely want more from a man than he had it in him to give.

His grandfather waxed lyrical about his wife for a few more minutes to the avid enjoyment of the crowd. Then he held up his hand, his expression serious. 'And of course, most of you know that fifteen years ago on this night our family was dealt a cruel blow that we have struggled to overcome. It is fair to say that the intervening years have not been easy. But tonight…' His moist eyes scanned the crowd and locked with Sebastiano's. 'Tonight I want to create new, happier memories for all of us. So it is with great pleasure that I announce that my grandson, Sebastiano Castiglione, will be taking over as CEO of Castiglione Europa. Effective immediately.'

Sebastiano heard the applause and well wishes from the crowd but it sounded as if it came from far away. He had expected the announcement of his appointment to be more along the lines of a memo. A public statement written up by his PR people in a way that created little fanfare. The last thing he wanted was to be the centre of attention. Not tonight. Not when it should have been his father taking over this position instead of him.

Taking the dais to thunderous applause, he said a few words about his grandfather's non-existent retirement plans that lightened the air considerably, then he signalled to the musicians to start playing again.

Needing a drink, he raised his hand to those nearby in a gesture of thanks and made his way to the bar, the guests he passed giving him little more than a pat on the back and a, 'Well done, congratulations'.

'Scotch. Neat,' he grated at the hapless bartender who had a goofy grin on his face. The man's grin slipped a little as he quickly did what he was asked. In the blink of an eye, the drink was gone and Sebastiano slapped the now empty glass back down on the bar. 'Another.'

'Sebastiano…' Not realising that Poppy had followed him, he glanced at her. 'Sebastiano, your parents died today?'

'Please spare me the mini-violin, *bella*. I'm over it.'

She watched him, her blue eyes frankly appraising. 'Does anyone actually believe that when you say it?' she asked softly, sympathy leaching out of every one of her beautiful pores.

'Don't push, Poppy. Another,' he said to the hovering bartender.

Her mouth firmed into a stubborn line. 'Why are you drinking Scotch if you're so over it?'

'I like the taste.'

'Sebastiano…'

Deciding he needed air as well as Scotch, he pushed away from the bar. 'Excuse me, would you? There's someone I have to talk to.'

Moving past her, Sebastiano made his way out of the ballroom taking the stone steps down to the leafy garden. He had no idea where he was going, but being alone seemed like a good idea right now.

CHAPTER TEN

POPPY CAME AWAKE with a start and pushed herself into a sitting position. The sofa Sebastiano had slept on the night before was possibly the most uncomfortable piece of furniture she had ever fallen asleep on. Not that she had meant to fall asleep.

'Why aren't you in bed?'

She glanced across the room to find the cause of her disturbance silhouetted in the doorway. 'I was waiting for you.'

Sebastiano stepped into the room, closing the door behind him, enveloping them in semi-darkness, the floor lamp Poppy had put on the only light source in the room.

He strolled towards her with the loose-limbed grace of a professional marauder, his bow-tie swinging from his collar, his jacket tossed carelessly over his shoulder.

Dumping the jacket on a chair, he made his way to the drinks cabinet. 'Why?'

Poppy's heart thudded heavily inside her chest as he poured himself a drink. 'I wanted to make sure you were all right. It's what I would do if we were in a normal relationship.'

'Only we're not in a normal relationship,' he pointed out.

Poppy pushed her hair back from her face impatiently. 'Why do you get to pull that card out when it suits you but I can't?'

His lips twisted as if she amused him. 'Because I make the rules, intern, not you.' He tossed ice into the glass, not looking at her. 'You should go to bed.'

The fact that he'd called her 'intern' in his deep, sexy

voice set her insides ablaze. There was something so intimate and affectionate in the way he said it, although right now he probably hadn't meant it to sound either of those. 'And you should stop drinking,' she offered pleasantly.

'Where's the fun in that?'

Poppy stood up and smoothed her hand down her beautiful dress. 'Are you very drunk?'

His eyes skimmed her. 'Not nearly enough that I want to listen to your "good little girlfriend" act.'

Poppy pursed her lips. 'How about my bad one?'

His smile didn't quite meet his eyes. 'Now that one has potential.'

Poppy remembered everything he had said to her downstairs, every seductively appealing word he had uttered to prevent her from asking probing questions, and warned herself not to fall for his pretences again. The man was a ruthless shark, after all. 'Isn't your grandfather's announcement of you taking over CE supposed to have made you happy?'

Sebastiano smiled at her. 'You know, that's the strangest thing. It didn't.' He downed another finger of Scotch. 'Go figure.'

She crossed the floor and stood in front of him, her arms folded defensively across her chest.

'I was really angry with you for walking off and leaving me before but now...' She sighed. 'If I'd known about your parents I could have—'

'What?' His blank eyes met hers. 'Dressed me in flannel pyjamas and brewed me a pot of tea? Isn't that what you English do when you feel sorry for someone?'

Her mouth settled into a stubborn line. 'Maybe it would help if you talked about your feelings, Sebastiano, instead of pretending you don't have any.'

'You know, I spent most of last night wondering what you wear to bed and I couldn't decide if it would be silk.' He took a long slug of Scotch. 'Or cotton.'

'Don't,' Poppy said warningly. 'Don't pretend you want me to distract me. That trick might have worked once but only a fool would fall for it twice.'

'And you're no fool, are you, Poppy?'

'Sebastiano…'

'You're really very cute when you're riled. It turns me on immensely. In fact, everything about you turns me on, *bella*. Especially in that dress. *Por Dio*, but you look hot. Deliciously, sensually hot.'

Even though she knew he was toying with her, Poppy felt the warm flush of desire flow through her. Clearly her hormones did not require honesty as a prerequisite to arousal, and wishing it were otherwise wasn't going to change anything.

Especially since she suspected that Sebastiano's superficial guise was a way to keep the world at bay just as her sarcasm often achieved the same result. In that they were alike.

Disconcerted by that observation, she glanced up to find him watching her with a hunting stillness that caused her breath to back up in her lungs. The tension in his large frame was palpable and her pulse raced.

She shivered, doing her best to suppress the desperate ache that had bloomed deep inside her. Right now she could walk away from this fake arrangement unscathed. It was important that she remember that because, while her heart might think that throwing herself at Sebastiano was a great idea, her sensible side was of the opposite opinion.

Taking a deep breath, she zoned in on her sensible side. Anything was better than being at the mercy of her more dangerous, libidinous one that wanted nothing more than for her to throw herself at him.

'So is this what you normally do on the anniversary of your parents' deaths?' she queried lightly. 'Get drunk?'

Sebastiano held up his half-empty Scotch glass like a proud Boy Scout presenting a shiny new badge. Then he turned to refill it. 'I think your judgmental side is showing again, Miss Connolly.'

Ignoring his dig, Poppy moved closer. 'Wouldn't it be nicer to be with other people on a night like this? People who care about you? Like your family? A girlfriend?'

'Inviting a woman to my home for anything other than sex would undoubtedly give her the wrong message. I don't ever want someone to imagine that I might be her next meal ticket.'

Poppy rolled her eyes. 'I hate to point out the obvious, Sebastiano, but you've basically offered to be mine.'

'Ah, but not for life, *bella mia*.'

It was both a statement and a warning. A warning she'd do well to heed. She was merely a guest in this extraordinarily opulent land, not a resident. And that was a role she definitely knew how to play because no one had ever wanted her around for long.

Usually she would throw out a deflecting line about now to lighten the atmosphere, but she couldn't muster one up right now, because she knew this strong, capable man was hurting and all she wanted to do was ease his pain. 'I know what it's like to lose a parent, Sebastiano,' she said softly. 'I know how it hurts. How it makes you feel lost. Scared.'

Sebastiano poured himself another drink and settled back against the cabinet, watching the play of tender emotions cross Poppy's beautiful, unguarded face, pity being the prime emotion, and the last one he wanted to see.

He wasn't sure if she was aware of it but her tongue kept darting out to moisten her lips as if she was preparing for his kiss; his muscles automatically drew tight at the thought.

The best thing she could do for the both of them was to take herself off to bed and he knew exactly how to send her there. 'But do you know what it's like to *cause* their deaths?' he rasped, the words burning like vinegar in his throat.

Her stunned eyes met his and there was a touch of sadness in their depths. 'Sometimes I did wonder if my mother chose drugs over me because I wasn't nice enough,' she admitted softly. 'But, no, I don't in the way I suspect you're talking about. What happened?'

Unprepared for her to take his disclosure with such equanimity, Sebastiano answered before he thought better of it. 'I was a selfish little bastard who wanted to spend time with his new girlfriend rather than go on a holiday with my family, that's what happened.' He let out a harsh laugh. 'What I didn't realise at the time was that my new friends were more interested in my money and social connections, and when we were caught buying drugs my parents had to drive to Rome to collect me. They were upset, disappointed, but I was too self-righteous and embarrassed to apologise. Some time after that my father lost control of the car on the icy roads.' He swallowed heavily at the memory. 'I walked away unscathed. They didn't walk away at all.'

The blood pounded in his head and he hadn't realised she had moved so close to him until her scent drifted towards him. 'But you didn't walk away unscathed,' she murmured. 'You carry the pain here.' She laid her palm against his chest, directly over his heart. 'Don't you?'

Sebastiano swore softly, his emotions boiling over inside him. The deep core of ice he'd encased himself in for so long preventing him from whispering that she was right. He did carry the pain of that day in his heart and he never let himself forget what a little *bastardo* he had been.

He stepped back from her and came up against the drinks cabinet. 'I don't want your pity, Poppy.'

She stepped closer. So close he could see that betraying pulse beating like a trapped bird inside her throat. 'I wasn't offering it.'

His gaze lingered on her lips before rising to hers again,

and her breath gave that betraying little hitch that told him she was as aroused as he was right now.

Dio, how was that possible when he had just been talking about his parents.

His muscles drew tight with the need to touch her. His mind and body were at war about the right thing to do, and the searing-hot, blistering need to make her his.

His?

He shook his head to clear it. 'You should go to bed,' he advised silkily. The sooner she was there, the safer she would be from the darkness that wanted to engulf him.

Her nostrils flared as if she had just scented danger. But still she didn't move. 'I will if you stop drinking.'

If he stopped drinking he'd do more than wonder if she was wearing the thong he had bought to match the gown.

Turning his back to her, he poured another finger of Scotch and then swung back to lean against the cabinet, raising his glass in a self-mocking toast. Before it touched his lips, she reached out and took hold of it, staying it in mid-air.

Adrenalin fuelled by sexual arousal turned his voice rough. 'You need to go to bed, Poppy.'

When he didn't release the glass to her, she brought her other hand up and slowly peeled his fingers away one by one. Sebastiano's heart beat a primal rhythm in his blood, heat and need turning his muscles hard.

'Or what?' she asked, her voice low, the sexy cadence scoring his skin.

In one swift move Sebastiano straightened to his full height, turned her and backed her against the cabinet. 'Or I'll ruin you for any other man.'

Her breath hitched again, her gaze on his mouth. 'Maybe your grandfather is right, Sebastiano. Maybe it's time to create new memories tonight.' Her blue eyes looked as luminous as the pearl nestled between her pert breasts. 'Memories that conjure up pleasure rather than pain.'

'You want pleasure, *bella mia*, I've got pleasure.'

He jerked her against him, the impact of her soft body against his like drinking water after trawling through a hot desert for months on end. The press of her round breasts against his chest shut down his reasonable, cool brain and replaced it with a greedy hunger that pushed at the limits of his civility.

She stared up at him, her hands trembling as they slowly pulled the short lengths of his bowtie from around his neck. 'Sometimes you look at me as if you know how to give me more pleasure than I've ever experienced in my whole life,' she said on a breathless rush. 'I want that. I *need* that.'

A low growl rumbled out of his chest at her admission, and he scattered the pins in her hair when he fisted his hands in it, bringing her mouth to his. He kissed her the way he had wanted to kiss her all night. Hard and deep. '*Dio*, I want you,' he murmured. 'So much I ache.'

She moaned, her hands twisting around his neck, her hips lifting against his as if seeking something just out of reach.

Bending his knees a little, he pressed his erection between the juncture of her thighs, rewarded for his efforts when she opened her mouth wider, her tongue tangling with his.

Driven by a need he could neither explain nor resist, Sebastiano kissed his way down the tender skin of her neck. They were both unattached, consenting adults who wanted each other, and he was done fighting something that had started the minute he'd laid eyes on her.

She moaned softly, her hands moving over his chest, his sides, his back as she tried to shift even closer.

'Poppy.' Sebastiano swore under his breath as the need

to be inside her drove all else from his mind. 'I have to have you.'

'Yes, yes.' Her urgency drove his own and he released the snap holding her bodice in place, letting the twin sides fall so that only the iridescent pearl lay between her exposed breasts. Cupping her, he brushed the tips with his thumbs before leaning down to fasten his lips around one proud peak, laving it with his tongue.

She cried out and he hefted her higher, pressing her against the wall to hold her steady.

Some small semblance of sanity reached him and told him he couldn't take her here against a wall, and he clamped his mouth over hers as he carried her into the bedroom.

She lay dazed, spread out before him on the large bed, the silky fabric of her dress falling between her shapely thighs like a silver waterfall.

Breathing deeply, he yanked his shirt open, uncaring that buttons scattered over the carpet. Shucking out of it, his hands reached for his belt buckle and he stilled. His raging hard-on pressed against his zipper as he drank her in: her hair now tumbled from its sleek knot and spread around her; her naked breasts rosy and full; her slender arms raised in supplication above her head.

'You should come with a health warning,' he growled. 'One touch and you'll be changed for ever.'

Her eyes lifted to his, scorching a path up over his stomach and chest. 'That's you, not me.'

Her legs shifted together and he ran his hand along the outside of her thighs, gentling her. 'You're going to have to open these, *dolce mia.*' His eyes dropped to her legs. 'If you want me to take care of that ache.'

He came down beside her and she squirmed against him, her nails scoring his shoulders. Her movements were almost untutored; her soft pleas for more sounding as if she had never had a man touch her like this before.

Knowing that couldn't be the case in this day and age, Sebastiano reached for a condom and moved over her, his knee pressing high between her legs. 'You like that?' He nipped at the exposed skin above her hip, loving the way she moaned his name. 'When I press here.' He moved up to her breasts. 'When I suckle you there?'

'Yes. Please…' Her hands reached for him, smoothing over his shoulders, following the line of muscle either side of his spine.

Feeling as if he was about to possess something rare and unique, Sebastiano planted a soft, pre-emptive kiss beside her navel and dragged her gown down past her hips. It slithered to the floor but his eyes were riveted to the tiny white thong covering her femininity. His finger slid down the centre of the lace, his eyes trained on her face. She bit her lip to stop herself from crying out, her hips jerking upwards. He'd been right. She was all fire and wild passion, and now she was his. One-hundred-percent his.

'Sebastiano!' Her fingers dug into his scalp and she writhed against the moist kisses he planted along her collarbone, his fingers finding her slick and hot and ready. Her cry of pleasure as her body opened for his touch almost wrecked his self-control.

'Oh, yes, I know what you want.'

Nudging her legs apart, he ripped the thong from her body and rose above her. He settled between her thighs, latching on to a raspberry nipple as he pressed into the soft folds of her femininity, feeling her body give as it stretched to accommodate his.

Sweat broke out on his forehead as he eased inside her slick centre. She undulated against him, as if the pressure was too much, and he gave up trying to go slow and plunged deep, immediately stiffening as he felt her jerk beneath the power of his thrust.

Smoothing her hair back from her forehead, he took his

weight on his elbows, staring down at her. 'Poppy, *amore mia*, are you all right? Did I hurt you?'

She gazed up at him, a mixture of wonder and wariness in her gaze. 'I'm fine. It doesn't hurt...now.'

Sebastiano swore softly in Italian. 'Poppy was that...? Were you a virgin?'

She panted what sounded like a yes, her fingers digging into his lower back, her legs widening to take him deeper.

'Wait,' he ordered roughly. 'Let your body get used to mine.'

'Oh, that feels good again.'

Sebastiano growled under his breath. The cool part of his brain shrieked entrapment, but the primal, instinctive part overrode it, telling him to go deeper and harder in a mating ritual too powerful to ignore.

'Just relax, Poppy.' He groaned as she pressed upwards, his hands finding her hips to force her to go slow. 'Let me show you.'

She moaned softly as he pushed slowly into her, her arms clinging to him, her legs high around his waist to take him all in.

He whispered her name, petting her, watching her, learning what she liked. If sex had ever felt this good, he couldn't remember it. 'You're mine now, *bella*,' he growled. 'Mine.'

He brought her eyes to his, forging a deeper connection with her as he slowly started to move inside her, some primal part of him thrilling to the fact that he was her first.

'Sebastiano...' She hooked her ankles around his lean hips, her body straining for something no man had ever given her before.

'That's it, Poppy,' he murmured. 'Give yourself to me, let me pleasure you. I've got you, *dolce mia*, I've got you.'

'I can't... I don't think...' She panted his name and then he felt it, the moment her body tightened before flinging her into a mind-bending orgasm.

Sebastiano rode it out with her, holding her, soothing her, glorying in the wonderment shining out of her blue eyes.

The ripples of her body pushed at his self-control, making her soft and open for his possession. And Sebastiano did possess her, driven by the demons of his past and a woman who made him want more than any other... Then suddenly it was just her and him, and right before he found his own powerful release she wound her arms around his torso and held him tight with her whole body, sending him to a place he'd never been to before.

'Oh, my...' she murmured drowsily, her arms loosening their hold around his neck.

Sebastiano slipped from her body, his heart still pounding inside his chest.

She whimpered as he disposed of the condom, quickly returning to tuck her replete body against his side.

'That was your first time,' he said, trying to sort through the myriad emotions coursing through him. Disbelief. Pride. Wariness. *Contentment.*

His mind couldn't seem to decide how he was supposed to feel about taking Poppy's virginity but, damn it, he wished she had told him. 'You should have told me.'

'Mmm...' She snuggled closer against his side, one arm flung across his middle. 'I didn't think of it.'

'You didn't think of it?'

Now that he couldn't believe. How could a woman who was about to have sex for the first time not think of something so important?

'Well, I thought about it, but then...' She sighed with her whole body. 'Then I forgot until you pushed inside me.'

Just hearing those words on her lips made him hard again. He clenched his jaw. He didn't do virgins as a general rule—he'd never had a virgin before in his life—and the fact that Poppy had chosen him to be her first...

'Why me?' he asked softly, holding his breath as he waited for her answer.

When all that came was the soft, even sound of her breathing, he glanced down to find she had fallen asleep.

Fallen asleep?

That was usually his modus operandi, his body too sated to do anything but shut down. Only he wasn't sated right now, he was raring to go again, his brain trying to convince him that he could wake her up, roll her onto her back and slip inside her warm, welcoming body without any need for foreplay.

Emotions he couldn't—and didn't particularly want to—identify rolled through him. The night had been going well right up until his grandfather had made his speech and reminded him all over again how he had stuffed up in his youth.

Feeling the old sense of remorse rise up in him again, he turned his head into Poppy's hair and inhaled her unique female scent, smoothing his fingers down her spine.

She shifted against him, sighing deeply, and he immediately felt calmer, as if she were the port his icy heart was seeking like a battle-weary ship caught in a storm.

Shaking his head at his uncharacteristically whimsical thoughts, he knew that only one thing here was true. Poetic.

Sex had been very effective at keeping his demons at bay.

CHAPTER ELEVEN

A PERSON SHOULD feel good the day after they reached a much-longed-for milestone. Great, even.

Sebastiano felt like crap. The only milestone his brain could focus on was the one that had been reached in his bed last night, and that one wasn't even his.

He told himself that if Poppy wasn't troubled about losing her virginity then he shouldn't be either. Unfortunately logic was in short supply right now and he scowled darkly as he sipped his rapidly cooling coffee and stared out at the slate-grey sea, almost indistinguishable from the sky above.

As far as he could tell, Poppy hadn't stirred from his bed yet and he wasn't completely surprised. He'd woken her twice during the night to have her again and he'd had to force himself to leave her before doing so again this morning. Only the notion that he wanted her a little too much for comfort, and the knowledge that she must be sore, drove him from the tangled sheets and out onto the sofa made of bricks.

Remembering how those sheets had become so tangled, and her soft cries of pleasure as he'd shown her what her body was made for, had him hardening once more like one of Pavlov's dogs on speed. It would be pointless to deny that he wanted more than one night with her, but his guard was up, and putting some emotional distance between them seemed like the best move he could make.

He hadn't meant to complicate their arrangement with sex, but what was he to do when she'd bailed him up against the drinks cabinet and told him she wanted to experience real pleasure?

The woman never stopped surprising him. But the last thing he wanted was for her to read more into last night than what it was—phenomenally hot sex—and, having been a virgin, she undoubtedly would. So he'd tread carefully and let her down gently. Not that his kindness made him feel any less of a bastard. The fact was, he'd taken advantage of their situation and now he had to deal with the consequences. Which made what he had to tell her when she woke up all the more complicated.

Hearing a noise behind him, he turned like a man about to face a firing squad.

Maledizione. What was wrong with him? So he'd stuffed up—again. Time to take it like a man.

'Hi.'

Her soft, almost shy smile told a thousand stories and he knew none he'd want to hear. She wanted more. More than he could ever give. His gaze raked down over her thin cotton dressing gown. His heart lurched. She looked sleep-mussed and utterly beautiful. 'You're awake.'

Way to go, Castiglione; state the obvious, why don't you?

'Sort of.' She touched her hair self-consciously. 'I'm not a morning person.'

'That's good, because morning finished about a half an hour ago.'

'Really?' She glanced around searchingly, presumably for her watch or phone. 'My body clock is all out.'

He frowned. 'Because you're usually just finishing up a late shift?'

'Mmm... I suppose. Is that coffee hot?'

'Yes.' He poured her a cup and she moaned with pleasure at the first sip. 'Thanks.'

'You're welcome.'

They were acting like polite strangers and he found it

impossible to get a read on her. Normally a woman would be wrapping herself around him about now and telling him how wonderful he was.

'So.' She broke the growing silence between them. 'What happens now?'

'Usually…' Sebastiano began, wanting to shake up her insouciance when he had taken her damned virginity last night. 'I take the woman I'm with back to bed,' he continued softly. 'And repeat everything that happened the night before. Several times.' It was a lie. Usually he couldn't wait to go for a run and get to the office. Except this morning it wasn't true. This morning he'd happily drag her back through that door and repeat the night they'd just shared ad infinitum.

'Oh.' Her eyebrows rose. 'No wonder that woman was crying on the phone.'

It took him a minute to place her comment and when he did he shook his head. 'Why do you never say what I'm expecting you to say?'

Poppy sucked in a deep breath and let it out slowly.

It was no great feat to guess what Sebastiano was thinking. He'd given in to the emotion—and alcohol—last night and slept with her, and now he regretted it. No doubt he regretted telling her about his parents too, but at least she understood him a little better now. Understood that he carried guilt and pain around for his part in their deaths, but really, he'd only been a normal teenager rebelling against the bounds of his parents' restrictions. It was something she could easily imagine Simon doing. That it had ended in such tragedy was a tragedy in itself.

Given that last night had been the anniversary of their deaths, she was under no illusion that had another woman offered herself to him he would have chosen her to ease his burden instead. Poppy had just been in the right place at the right time—or not, depending on how you viewed it.

And she refused to view it as a bad thing. How could she, after the way he had made her feel? He was every woman's dream man. And not because of his money, as he thought, but because of his strength, his determination, even his arrogance. He was the kind of man a woman could rely on, if he ever chose to let one get close enough to fall in love with her.

A lump formed in her throat. For a while in his arms the night before her world had seemed perfect. He had been perfect. Caring. Considerate. Passionate. He had made her feel like the most beautiful woman in the world and she couldn't regret that. No doubt it was how he made every woman feel.

Okay, time for her to get back to the reality of her life. And the reality was that the only thing she could rely on with any degree of certainty was herself. Life was harsh and people could be brutal. Why open yourself up to that kind of pain unnecessarily, as her mother had done over and over?

And clearly Sebastiano's polite stranger routine was his way of trying to avoid a nasty scene between them now. But she had no intention of bawling him out, or blaming him for last night. After all, she had slept with him willingly, and she would put him out of his misery and show him that she was not going to be one of his women who clung and begged him to love them.

A tight, invisible band formed around her chest as if of their own accord her ribs had contracted to hold everything inside.

'So I think it's safe to say,' she began amicably, 'That last night was a mistake, don't you?'

'You're damned right it was a mistake.'

'Okay then…' She hadn't expected him to agree quite so vehemently but, whatever; *move on*.

He ran a hand through his already tousled hair. 'What I meant to say was that I don't bed virgins.'

'Okay—I'm not sure how to respond to that.' She gave a small laugh. 'Do you want an apology?'

'No I do not want a damned apology,' he grated. 'Damn it, Poppy, what kind of game are you playing? Why didn't you tell me?'

'Didn't we already cover this off last night?'

'Not to my satisfaction.'

Poppy expelled a pent-up breath. 'Look, Sebastiano, I'm not great at the whole morning-after thing so—'

'That would be because it's your first.'

'Right.' She cleared her throat. 'Another one. Okay—' she held her hand up as he glowered at her '—I don't know why this is such a big deal for you. It was my virginity to give away. And if you're worried that I'll expect more from you than one night, rest assured that I don't.'

'I could have hurt you.'

'I think we covered that off too…'

'And we'll cover it off again until I'm satisfied.' He growled. 'Are you sore?'

She was, but it was such a pleasurable ache it made her want to do everything they had done to cause it all over again. 'I'm fine, Sebastiano, but clearly you're not. And I think it's because you're afraid that I'm going to fall for you and start demanding rings and pre-nuptial agreements.' His jaw tightened. 'It's tempting,' she said with a slight laugh. 'But I promise you I won't. I know what this is, and if there's one thing I excel at its temporary relationships. Especially fake ones.' She'd meant that last to be humorous, but he wasn't laughing.

Thankfully her phone chimed a message and she dove on it like a seagull on a salted chip, a soft smile curling her lips when she read the name on the screen. 'It's Maryann,' she said, as if he would want to know. 'She and Simon are feasting on pancakes and ice-cream.'

Her eyes shone just thinking about them and she realised

how much she looked forward to seeing Simon and giving him a hug. 'What time should I tell them we'll be returning? You said yesterday it would be in the morning but I guess we've missed that time slot. Although I would like to take a shower if there's time.'

'There's time.'

He stared at her, brooding, and Poppy forced herself to smile. An hour to get ready, two to fly to London, another hour in traffic and maybe, just maybe, after that her shoulders would no longer be pinned up around her ears. 'Great.'

'Because we've hit a snag.'

Her eyes narrowed. 'A snag?'

'A problem,' he clarified. 'It seems my grandfather organised a business meeting in Venice later this week but it's been moved to tonight.'

'Okay.'

'Since I'm the new CEO, and the guy happens to be a friend of mine, I have to take the meeting.'

Poppy couldn't see any problem with that. 'Well that's great, isn't it? It's what you wanted. Control of your family's company.'

'Yes, but you have to come with me.'

'Me? I'm heading back to London.'

'You *were* heading to London, *now* you're heading to Venice. For a night.'

Poppy's lips went dry. 'But it's a Sunday.' Exactly a week since they'd met. 'I only know one person who works on a Sunday.'

He gave her a sardonic look and she crinkled her nose.

'I was only working that day because I had something to finish up. Usually I'm home studying, or sleeping.'

'Well, tonight you're dining at Harry's Bar. It's the only time Lukas has free, and I need to capitalise on the negotiations my grandfather started with his company six months ago.'

'You know I could just fly back to London on a commercial flight. I don't mind.'

'I do. And how will it look to my grandparents if you don't go with me? Especially since Lukas is bringing his wife.'

'Like I'm busy and have my own life.'

'We agreed on the weekend, *dolce mia*, and it's still the weekend.'

Poppy gave an exasperated sigh. 'You know, you're like one of those enormous earth-movers when you want something.'

'What can I say? It's my best trait.'

Poppy instantly thought about all the things he had done to her body last night. 'I wouldn't say that,' she murmured, excusing herself before he saw her face flame with embarrassment.

'Poppy?'

She turned back to look at him.

'If your reticence about Venice is because you think I'll expect a repeat performance after last night, you're wrong. I've already organised a suite with two rooms for tonight.'

Poppy let out a soft breath. Sadly, after his polite stranger routine this morning she hadn't thought that he would want anything from her, let alone a repeat performance.

'Does anyone ever say no to you?' she asked quietly.

'Only you, *bella*. Only you.'

But she didn't say no to him all the time, and she was very much afraid that if he touched her once more she wouldn't say no to him again.

'So, who is the guy again? Lukas Kursnet—Lukas Kornis—'

'Kuznetskov.' Sebastiano guided her out of the small launch and onto the red-carpeted jetty in front of the palatial Cipriani Hotel. Poppy was wide-eyed as she stared up at the blush-coloured Moorish building that rose out of the water like an elegant apparition.

They had arrived in Venice just over two hours ago, the city's unique beauty captivating and seducing her from the first glimpse of its elegant, centuries old architecture.

She smiled at the liveried hotel employee as she moved towards the main entrance. 'And his wife, Eleanore, you said? They're in shipping, right?'

'Lukas started in shipping and expanded into hotels. Eleanore runs her own consulting and design business.' Sebastiano's hand brushed her lower back as they passed through the incredible foyer towards the main restaurant. 'But relax, intern, I'm not going to grill you on this later.'

'That's a rel— Say, is that Julia Roberts?'

'Who?'

'The actress— Oh, never mind, I was probably wrong anyway.' She smoothed down the knee-length skirt of her silky dress and gazed around her in wonder. 'I'm just glad I lowered my pride and borrowed one of the dresses you bought at the start of the weekend. I thought the beautiful guests at your grandparents' party were intimidating but the women here could give a girl a complex for life.'

'You look stunning. You always look stunning.'

His low voice brought her eyes to his. He was wearing a suit with an open-neck shirt and he looked so handsome he made her heart ache. For all her good intentions on the flight to Venice—simply to enjoy a night in another exotic city and treat Sebastiano as if he were just any other man— she wasn't succeeding very well. 'Thanks. So do you.'

He stared down at her and Poppy willed her racing heart rate to settle. It would be mortifying if he realised that, far from thinking last night had been a mistake, she had in fact spent the day thinking about his impressive naked body. And no amount of internal pep talks about his 'love 'em and leave 'em' attitude towards women seemed to make a spit of difference to her treacherous hormones.

Suddenly he reached out to tug a strand of her hair away from where it had caught on her lip gloss and Poppy's breath backed up in her lungs. The way he was looking at her right now, she would swear he didn't think last night had been a mistake either.

'Castiglione.' A man cleared his throat behind them.

'Ah, Lukas… Eleanore.' Sebastiano turned to the couple as if the moment they had just shared had never happened. 'You look lovely as usual.' Sebastiano gave the requisite double kisses to the woman's cheeks. 'This is Poppy Connolly. Poppy, may I present Eleanore and Lukas Kuznetskov?'

'Harrington,' Eleanore corrected with a smile.

'Really?'

Clearly surprised Sebastiano glanced at Lukas who merely shook his head. 'Don't ask.'

Eleanore laughed delightedly at the men's wry grins and Poppy felt a bubble of happiness well up inside her as she watched the glamorous couple—Lukas with his dark-blond hair and striking blue eyes, and Eleanore with her cat-like elegance and wide smile. They looked relaxed and at ease with each other as if they had been together forever. Poppy knew MaryAnn would have taken one look at them and said, 'True love.'

'Poppy, it's lovely to meet you,' Eleanore said with genuine warmth. 'I'm so glad you could join us. Is this your first visit to Venice?'

'Yes, it is.'

'Mine too,' Eleanore said. 'I love it. You?'

'It's magical.'

'Exactly the word Eleanore used when we landed,' Lukas said, giving his wife an indulgent smile. 'Hello, Poppy, I'm the luggage handler.'

Poppy laughed, already liking this couple immensely.

'Oh, you're more than that,' Eleanore assured him. 'You organise incredible sleigh rides too.'

Lukas flushed at the in joke and Sebastiano gave a low laugh at the other man's discomfort. Groaning, Lukas shook his head. 'See what married life does to you, Castiglione? It breaks you.'

Eleanore elbowed her husband in the ribs. 'Stop complaining; you love it.'

Lukas's eyes gleamed, as if he wanted to show her just how much he loved it, and Poppy found herself entranced.

'I don't know about you lot,' Sebastiano interjected suavely, 'But the last meal I ate was pizza about—was it yesterday or the day before?' he asked Poppy.

Poppy shook her head. 'I swear men are born with hollow stomachs. My brother is exactly the same.'

'My sister Olivia eats like a horse,' Eleanore said. 'I was always so jealous growing up because she never put on a pound.'

'Table. Conversation,' Lukas instructed, guiding his wife with a hand at the small of her back. 'I think my last meal was yesterday as well.'

Eleanore, it turned out, was incredibly creative and had dabbled in art classes when she'd been younger, informing Lukas that they would be visiting the Gritti Palace some time the following day after Poppy had gushed about the Byzantine artwork in the foyer.

Poppy thought that Lukas would quite possibly fly to the moon and wrangle a star back for Eleanore if she was so inclined.

True love indeed, she mused, unconsciously taking in how relaxed the other couple was with each other—the covert touches, the possessive way Lukas leaned his arm along the back of Eleanore's chair and the soft glow in his eyes when he looked at her. Just being with them made her feel warm and included.

Included?

Yes, she felt included. Like she had with Sebastiano's family, as if she actually had a valuable contribution to make to the order of things.

A lump formed in her throat and she blinked back a shimmer of tears that was forming behind her eyes. If Sebastiano had asked her for her third wish right now, it would be to make this moment last for ever. Or maybe to make last night last for ever.

She was falling for him, she realised on a frantic rush of understanding, falling hard and fast, and she knew the landing would definitely not be soft this time.

Feeling unaccountably panicked, Poppy scraped back her chair and excused herself to go to the ladies' room. She had been the one to call last night a mistake, and he'd agreed, hadn't he?

'Hey, wait up.' Poppy nearly groaned to hear Sebastiano behind her. She stopped in the smoky corridor that led to the bathrooms but didn't look up at him. 'Are you okay?'

'Great,' she said, pinning a bright smile on her face.

'Really?' His intense gaze probed hers.

No! She was terrible. Panicked. Scared. 'Of course.'

'Poppy…'

'Sebastiano, don't.'

The last thing she wanted was for him to know how she felt and pity her. It would make her feel too pathetic for words.

His hands lifted to frame her face, bringing her eyes up to his. His nostrils flared as if he was drawing her scent into his body. She felt him shudder and then something came over his face. A softness. A sort of giving in. 'I want you.' The words sounded as though they'd been wrenched from a deep part of him and Poppy's traitorous heart started to sing. 'I know you said last night was a mistake but for me it was like nothing I've ever experienced before. You walk into a room, Poppy, and my body salivates to have you. You're like a drug. You're under my skin.'

Poppy stared up at him, incredulous, her mind barely able to register what she was hearing. 'I want you too,' she admitted huskily.

A woman glanced at them curiously as she made to move past and Sebastiano dragged Poppy closer against him. Then his mouth was on hers, open and demanding, and leaving her in no doubt as to how much he wanted her.

When they were jostled by a second person, Sebastiano raised his head with a groan. He looked at her. Took a deep breath. 'You need to fix your lipstick, *bella*,' he said gruffly. 'I'll meet you back at the table.'

'I like her.'

Sebastiano glanced at Lukas. The man's eyes were trained on Eleanore as she left the room to take a phone call. 'I hope so. You married her.'

'Interesting.' Lukas chuckled, giving him a look. 'Deflecting with humour. I had thought it was just casual between the two of you. Thanks for the clarification.'

Sebastiano narrowed his eyes. Frankly he was still reeling from what had just happened with Poppy in the corridor. He hadn't meant to say any of those things to her, they'd just spilled out and he certainly didn't need his old friend digging at him. 'Just because you're now married off, Kuznetskov, don't try and ruin it for the rest of us.'

'Safety in numbers and all that?' the Russian mused.

'Exactly. But there's nothing going on between Poppy and myself.' That was if you discounted last night and that savage kiss in the corridor just now. *Dio mio*, he could really pick his moments.

'Could have fooled me.'

'It's true,' he said, tossing an olive into his mouth. 'She was my intern and she helped me out of a tight spot.' Another olive. 'The important thing is that you'll be dealing with me from now on instead of my grandfather—and fair warning, but I'm about to fleece you so that we're the only contractor you use on your hotels in the foreseeable future.' He leaned back in his chair and raised his glass to his friend. 'What more could a man want?'

Lukas gave a helpless shrug. 'Poppy Connolly?'

Sebastiano scowled. 'Look, Kuznetskov, while I'm very pleased love has worked out for you not all of us want the same thing, or need it.' His scowl deepened as those words suddenly had a hollow ring to them. 'Personally, I'm not interested in capping my batting average just yet.' Or ever!

'Here, here,' Lukas drawled, raising his beer in a toast. 'So you won't mind if I get her number and text it to a few of my single friends?'

'Don't be an ass,' Sebastiano said. 'I doubt she'd have time to see any of your friends anyway.'

Not with the amount of nights she worked. Which bothered him immensely. He hated the idea that Poppy had to work nights to make ends meet. Damn it, that third wish of hers better be for ten million pounds or he was going to give her a piece of his mind.

'Castiglione?'

Unaware that he had started drumming his fingers on the table, Sebastiano frowned. 'Sorry, I missed that.'

Lukas smiled. 'I asked when you wanted to come to St Petersburg to go over the plans for the hotel restoration at Prospekt Avenue.'

'I'll touch base with the Head of Marketing as soon as she's back from New York and let you know.'

Sebastiano only faintly heard Lukas's reply, his eyes trained on Poppy as she wove her way towards them between the tables.

'By the way, I highly recommend it.'

Sebastiano stared blankly at the slow grin that spread across Lukas's face. 'Recommend what?'

'Married life.'

Mouthing a rude word, Sebastiano pulled Poppy's chair out for her as she sat down. Fortunately his friend didn't labour the point about marriage and the conversation resumed an easy flow.

The whole night had been easy, he realised. Poppy fitted in beautifully with the other couple. Not that Sebastiano had thought she wouldn't—but he'd just never done the double date thing before. Usually he met a woman, took her for a meal then back to either his place or hers where they had sex and went their separate ways, the pattern continuing until one or the other tired of it.

Sebastiano frowned. Running a global operation as successful as his meant a lot of contact hours, which didn't leave much down time.

Even nights out with male friends usually revolved around work. He rarely had time to indulge in boring chit-chat and yet that was exactly what tonight had morphed into. But it hadn't been boring. In fact, it had been relaxing and highly enjoyable.

His eyes ate up the woman at his side. It had been enjoyable because of Poppy Connolly. She was smart, caring, challenging, and the most sexually responsive woman he had ever known.

Which was when it hit him that his end goal had shifted without him even being aware of it. This was no longer about him trying to convince his grandfather that their relationship was real, it was about—it was about... He frowned. He had no idea what it was about; he just knew that he wanted her again.

He brooded over that, unable to take his eyes from Poppy's mouth as she devoured her ice-cream dessert, enjoyment evident every time she licked the spoon clean.

She chose that moment to look at him, her eyes darkening as she caught his gaze. 'Want some?'

She held the spoon out and his eyes never left hers as he dipped his head and sucked the ice-cream inside his mouth. Her eyes darkened even more, her long lashes lowering to mask the desire he'd already registered.

A strange sensation fluttered inside his chest.

He had always believed that true happiness was something he would never feel again but it welled up inside him, unexpected and full. A tentative, bubbling brook that scared him as much as it ensnared him.

'Okay, lovebirds,' Lukas drawled, breaking their connection and causing Poppy to blush. 'Time for us to hit the sack.'

'Lukas!' Eleanore whacked his shoulder with her clutch bag. 'Please excuse my husband, Poppy,' Eleanore implored with dignity. 'He's not usually so rude.'

'Not at all. It's been amazing meeting you both. I had a wonderful night.'

Sebastiano pushed his chair back. 'Time for us to go too, *bella*.'

CHAPTER TWELVE

SETTLING HIS HAND at Poppy's lower back, Sebastiano led her to the main foyer. 'Wait here while I order a water taxi.'

A thrill raced up Poppy's spine at the thought of returning to their hotel room. A thrill she needed to find some way to contain. Her intention to keep her heart safe from Sebastiano had gone up in smoke as soon as he had kissed her again. But it didn't change anything, did it? He only wanted her physically while she...she... *Was she really falling in love with him?*

No. She couldn't be. She was just doing the age-old thing of confusing lust with love even though she thought she knew better.

Confident that she could handle whatever this night brought without falling into her mother's trap of thinking that a man wanted more from her than he did, Poppy glanced around the opulent space, her eyes lingering on two fashionably dressed women with wistful smiles on their faces.

Wondering if they had recognised a celebrity of some sort, Poppy followed the line of their stares to find that it was Sebastiano who had captured their appreciative gazes.

No doubt they were noting the powerful width of his shoulders beneath his dinner jacket, the thick curl of his hair that would soon need a trim and those piercing green eyes he had just turned her way.

Poppy's breath stalled as his lips curved into a lazy smile, his gaze raking down over her in a slow burn.

Was there ever a man so gloriously male? So sensually

appealing? No doubt he'd had so many women give themselves to him, just as she had done, that he couldn't even remember their names.

She noticed one of the women eyeing her suspiciously, the other more openly hostile.

Don't worry, ladies, she wanted to say. *I know how just the look of him makes a woman's heart skip a beat but he'll be back on the market soon.*

And in real life they were exactly the type he would choose. Beautiful. Refined. Elegant.

A dismal feeling jolted inside her chest. By contrast, she was just an ordinary girl who had stumbled into an extraordinary situation.

Poppy watched him walk towards her, his stride powerfully male, sexual intent etched into every long, measured stride. For a moment she felt real fear invade her limbs. Everything inside her said that this couldn't end well. That it *wouldn't* end well.

'Ready, intern?'

He planted himself in front of her, shutting out the world behind him. She knew on some level that she was mad to put herself in the way of this freight train but she also knew that she would.

Not trusting that her voice wouldn't tremble when she spoke, she nodded, letting Sebastiano usher her outside to their waiting water taxi.

Excitement coursed through her and she turned her face up to the soft fall of snowflakes that fell softly like confetti from the sky. 'Oh,' she breathed. 'How magical.' Impulsively she curved her arm through Sebastiano's, snuggling close. 'Can we walk?'

'Walk?' Sebastiano looked at her as if she'd just asked him to swim.

'Yes.' She laughed at his pained expression. 'Please, Bastian. It's so beautiful with the snow falling all around us and I don't know if I'll ever make it back to Venice again.'

Sebastiano bit back a curse, sexual need pushing him to get her back to the hotel as quickly as possible. 'Of course.'

He fell into step beside her, an easy silence enfolding them as the enchantment of Venice wrapped them in its hazy black magic.

'Where are we?' she asked, looking around.

'Venezia,' he drawled.

'You do have a sense of humour.' She laughed, punching his shoulder lightly. Sebastiano smiled, enjoying the comfortable feeling between them.

'Are you warm enough?'

'Yes. And I meant *where* in Venice?' She pressed closer to his body and he tucked her against his shoulder. 'Where does this lane lead to?'

She pointed over a small wooden bridge and down a dimly lit alleyway. Sebastiano shrugged. 'Let's find out.'

They wandered aimlessly, traversing a series of narrow storybook canals and tiny lanes with elaborate shop fronts below lighted apartments, the smell of the sea heavy in the night air.

'Oh, that's a beautiful building.'

'The Peggy Guggenheim Museum,' Sebastiano said. 'It has a wonderful sculpture garden at the back.'

'The Nesher Garden,' Poppy provided. 'Eleanore said they have a new controversial artwork. It sounds interesting.'

'Want to take a look?'

'I'd love to, but it's closed.'

Sebastiano palmed his phone. 'Not to us.'

'What are you doing?' She pulled his arm downwards. 'You can't possibly think of trying to get it open.'

'Why not?'

'It's midnight and—' She shook her head. 'Could you?'

'Of course. CE did the restoration work on the building a few years back. On top of that, we are key patrons.'

Poppy shook her head. 'That's great, but put your phone away. We don't have to disturb the poor curator, or whoever would have to wake up to open the doors. We can see it tomorrow.'

Pocketing his phone, he turned to her, giving her a look she couldn't mistake. 'I might already have plans for tomorrow.'

'Such as?'

Her soft whisper was like the sirens' lure Odysseus would have warned his sailors to ignore. It heated his blood and called to that most primitive, that most male, part of him. The part that wanted to take her right here up against a stone bridge.

He sucked in a deep breath, misty air mixed with strains of Poppy. He slipped his arm around her waist and drew her closer. Her breath hitched and she whispered his name.

Another call. Another lure to his senses. He stared down at her beautiful upturned face, her flushed cheeks, her snow-damp hair.

His arms tightened around her, his nostrils flaring as he looked at her. 'Such as plans to inspect an important work of art of my own.'

'Really?' Another breathy whisper that hung on his senses. She arched towards him just a little, her breasts rising between them as if seeking the palms of his hands. 'What kind of art work?'

'Mmm…' Sebastiano leant close, inhaling her but not yet touching her; torturing them both. 'It's soft and curvy.' He demonstrated with the sweep of his hands. 'And it has these hidden valleys and wonderful peaks.'

Unable to help himself, he cupped one of those masterful peaks, moulding her in his hand, soaking in her soft moans of pleasure.

'It sounds—wonderful.' Her hands drifted over his arms and shoulders. Stroking. Petting. 'I wouldn't mind exploring myself.'

'Oh, yes, *dolce mia*.' He groaned. 'I have much that you can explore.'

And then he kissed her. Deeply. Drawing tiny cries of pleasure from her throat, murmuring to her in Italian, urging her to give him more. To give him everything. Again a pesky voice in his head said, *mine*, and his body tightened with need.

'Bastian, I want…' Poppy widened her legs and he slid his thigh between them. 'Oh yes, that. Right there.'

'Yes, Poppy,' he breathed against her mouth. 'Tell me what you want. What you need.'

Because he didn't know what he needed, apart from filling her body with his until he couldn't think. Until this intense hunger to make her his drove out this feeling that something was missing from his life.

Missing?

His life was full. Complete. There was nothing missing. And yet he couldn't deny the nagging sense that something definitely was.

Her?

The unbidden thought was almost enough to have him pulling back but then she moaned and twisted higher against him, her teeth grazing his jaw.

He should have shaved, he realised, so that he wouldn't mark her pale skin. And as soon as the thought entered his head it was all he wanted to do: mark her. Fill her. *Brand* her.

'Sebastiano, please…'

Uncaring as to where they were, Sebastiano firmed his hand over her bottom and urged their lower bodies together.

Minutes passed where all they did was kiss, tasting each other until he was so hard he was about to disgrace himself.

'Enough playing.' Sebastiano growled, having indulged her desire to walk long enough. 'We need to take this indoors before we get locked up.'

'I don't want to wait,' she moaned. 'I'm so desperate for you.'

'The feeling is mutual, *bella*, believe me.'

'*Buonasera, signor, signorina.* Gondola ride?'

Dazed with desire, Sebastiano turned to focus on the smiling gondolier in the stupid shirt and dark trousers. No, he did not want a damned gondola ride, he wanted a bed, wall, floor—any flat surface—but he knew, as soon as he heard Poppy's happy sigh, that he was thwarted again.

'When we finally get back to our hotel room,' he warned, 'You better be wet and ready for me because I won't be waiting.'

He turned to the gondolier and bared his teeth.

'Can you take us to the Gritti Palace?' he asked, hoping his voice revealed his desire for haste.

'*Si, si. Salire a bordo.* Come aboard.'

'Thank you.' Poppy's eyes shone in the hazy moonlight. 'This is so magical.' She turned in the curve of Sebastiano's arms. 'I love it.' She reached up and kissed him. It lacked the heat of her previous kisses but the sweetness of it lingered along with a sense of utter satisfaction. He slung his arm around her shoulders and pulled her in close.

'You want a song, *signor*? *Signorina?*'

'No.'

'Yes.'

Sebastiano sighed and Poppy laughed.

'Yes,' he amended gruffly.

The gondolier grinned, starting a low, melodic tune he became completely caught up in as the little boat rocked gently beneath tiny arched bridges and passed softly lit, enchanting buildings.

Poppy burrowed closer to him, her body replete as it

rested against his, as if they had already made love. But they hadn't and yet he felt just as contented as if they had. He felt...he felt... He frowned. What did he feel? A sense of rightness? A sense of—happiness? The realisation was like the unfurling of a corpse flower after a decade of dormancy. Something had been going on with him since he'd agreed to come to Italy, something he couldn't put a name to yet, but he would. He absolutely would.

'By the way.' Poppy turned her face up to his, a secret smile on her lips. 'I already am.'

Sebastiano's gaze lingered on her mouth. 'Already what?'

'Wet,' she whispered impishly.

'You are in so much trouble when we get back to our room, Miss Connolly,' he warned menacingly, turning her towards him and slipping his hand along her thigh.

'Stop that,' she admonished softly, checking to see if the gondolier had noticed his hand move beneath her skirt.

Of course, the man was too discreet for that.

'We are here, *signor.*'

Grazie a Dio!

'Bene,' Sebastiano said, deftly lifting Poppy out of the gondola, and paying the gondolier who knew what amount.

Poppy's face was flushed, her eyes fever-bright as they ran over his arms and chest, her gaze making him burn hotter than the sun.

Whisking her through the double doors the concierge held open, Sebastiano let her precede him into the narrow confines of the hotel lift. He followed her in, barely pausing to insert the keycard for their floor before pressing her flat against the back wall, angling her head to the side to kiss the breath from her body.

Her bottom pressed into his groin, her mouth opening wide beneath his, hungry and sweet. Sebastiano groaned. He wanted her. *Dio*, but he wanted her.

His hands slipped beneath the hem of her dress, raising it along the outside of her thighs as he stroked her stocking-clad legs.

'These have to go.' His fingers came into contact with sheer tights, the cloth tearing easily beneath his rough fingers. He groaned her name as he came into contact with warm baby-soft skin. He flattened her against the wall, pressing into her. 'You feel fantastic. So damned sexy.'

The lift juddered to a halt and Sebastiano shot his hand against the wall to steady them both, his breathing ragged. 'Room. Now.'

Once inside, he shucked out of his jacket and threw off his shirt.

'You are so magnificent,' she murmured huskily, stepping forward to comb her fingers through the smattering of hair on his chest. 'I wanted to run my hands over you that morning in your office.'

'Do it now,' he commanded, reaching around to slide the zipper of her dress down, going stock-still when she leant forward to press her lips against his pectoral muscles.

They clenched and he felt her smile against his skin. 'I like that you're so hard everywhere.'

Her lips drifted over his nipples and his breath rasped in his throat as she licked him. He forked his fingers in her hair, holding her lightly, letting her explore, but only just. Her lips drifted lower, tracking the trail of hair down the centre of his body, a trail that ended at his throbbing erection.

'Poppy...' He grabbed her arms and held her in front of him. 'I need you, *bella*. Desperately.'

With swift, unsteady movements he divested her of her dress and scooped her into his arms, his lips finding hers.

As soon as he reached the bed he dropped her onto it and came down over the top of her, clamping his mouth over one of her gorgeous little nipples and feasting on it.

She cried out, music to his ears, and he didn't hold back from delving his hand between her legs, moaning deep in his chest as he found her wet and swollen.

'Poppy, *amore mia*...' Senses overloaded, Sebastiano moved lower, peppering her silky abdomen with soft, open-mouthed kisses as he settled his shoulders between her thighs, urging them wider still.

'Sebastiano, I haven't—' Her hands lowered to hold him off and he kissed the backs of her hands.

'Now you want to be shy?'

'I'm not shy.' She moaned as he flicked her with his tongue. 'But this is so intimate.'

'More intimate than when I'm inside you?'

'Yes, if you must know.'

He laughed softly. 'You're so sexy, Poppy *mia*.' He gently shifted her hands and placed them on the bed beside her hips. 'When it gets too much for you, grab the sheets.'

His nose nuzzled her silky mound. 'You're beautiful, Poppy. Like the Venus de Milo come to life.' His mouth drifted lower. 'Perfect here...' He inhaled deeply. 'And here where you're soft and wet and waiting for me to fill you up.' He licked her, moaning his pleasure at her taste. 'Mine,' he said, the word rumbling from deep inside his chest. 'You're mine.'

CHAPTER THIRTEEN

HOURS LATER THE pale light of the winter sun washed over Poppy, disturbing her sleep. Again she woke alone, the sheets beside her cool to the touch. Feeling a pang of anxiety, she reminded herself that Sebastiano was an early riser and she pulled on the hotel robe and belted it lightly, her feet quiet as she crossed the carpeted floor.

She found him outside on the small stone terrace, the faint strains of the dawn sun shimmering off the silvery green canal. The sky beyond looked clear, but it was the man filling the small space that took all of her attention.

A cold breeze ruffled his thick, dark hair and she remembered tunnelling her fingers into the lushness of it the night before as he took her to the dizzying heights of absolute pleasure and far, far beyond. The connection she felt with him when his body joined with hers indescribable and totally scary. It was everything she had unknowingly craved and more.

Her heart sped up inside her chest.

He was so powerfully male, standing there with his arms on the balustrade, his muscular legs tanned and long beneath the white robe. He was a miracle of manhood in the prime of his life and he was all hers—or temporarily all hers. Temporarily and fakely all hers.

Fakely?

It wasn't even a word, but it described their situation perfectly. A situation that was fake but didn't quite feel fake. At least not for her.

Or at least not right now.

When she had agreed to this deal over a week ago she had imagined her biggest challenge would be to convince his family that they were a couple. In the end that had been the easy part. The hard part was keeping her hands of her boss-cum-fake-boyfriend and in that she had most definitely not succeeded.

But she wasn't going to dwell on that now. She knew what this was. She knew he was out of her league and that he had no long-term intentions towards her. Just as she had none towards him.

Sure, a cool voice in her head mocked, *if he wanted more, you'd jump at the chance.*

'*Buongiorno.*' His deep, sexy voice dragged her eyes up to his. 'How did you sleep?'

Knowing that she had been caught staring, she felt suddenly shy. 'Like a log.'

'Then I must not have been doing my job properly.' He held his hand out to her, beckoning her into his arms. 'It's a beautiful morning; come see.'

Pushing her wistful thoughts to the back of her mind, Poppy slipped into place, relaxing in his solid embrace, her back to his front. His arms tightened around her, his chin resting on the crown of her head. 'What did I tell you?'

Momentarily confused, Poppy realised he was talking about the view, and she forced herself to focus on the slumbering ancient city as the sun gilded the rooftops bronze and gold. 'It's exquisite. Maryann told me it was but I thought she was exaggerating.'

'Who is this Maryann to you?' he asked quietly.

'Maryann is a saviour to me. She lost her husband to cancer many years ago and when she found us we were like lost souls.' She smiled at the memory.

'Found *us*?'

'Simon and I.'

Sebastiano frowned. 'How old were you?'

Not wanting to ruin the moment by delving into the past, Poppy spoke quickly. 'I was seventeen. Simon was seven. Is that the island of Murano over there? I hear they have fantastic glassware for sale.'

Turning her in the circle of his arms, Sebastiano studied her face. 'Explain.'

Knowing she was thwarted, she pulled a face and let her mind drift back to that awful time, hoping he wouldn't look at her differently at the end of it. 'The day I met Maryann, I was at Paddington station trying to find a warm place for Simon to sleep since he was sick and—'

'Trying to find a warm place to sleep?' His voice deepened in alarm. 'Why didn't you go home? Or to a hospital, if your brother was ill?'

'I couldn't go to a hospital because I wasn't yet eighteen and I was afraid Social Services would separate us.' She bit her lip. 'And we didn't have a home.'

'Why not?'

She swallowed heavily. 'The last foster home we were placed in wasn't great and—I thought I could do better on my own.' She gave a self-mocking little laugh. 'Turns out I was pretty naïve on that score.'

'Go on.'

'Do I have to?'

He gave her a look that she knew from working for him scared CEOs and chairmen everywhere.

'Fine.' She rolled her eyes. 'I met a guy on the train to London and I was taken in by him. He was well-spoken and well-dressed and I somehow confided my situation to him. Looking back, I think I wanted to believe that there were good people in the world, so when he offered to help us out by lending us his spare room I jumped at the chance.'

A muscle ticked in Sebastiano's jaw. 'I'm not going to like where this story is headed, am I?'

Poppy pulled a face. 'Suffice to say he wanted payment

for the room, but not of a fiscal variety, and I told him I wasn't interested.'

'What did the lowlife do then?' His voice was so deep, Poppy blinked in surprise.

'He forced me to wake Simon and threw us out onto the street.' She didn't tell him she had been so foolish she had taken all her money out of her bank account so that Social Services couldn't trace her and he'd stolen the lot. That was too excruciatingly shameful.

Sebastiano swore viciously under his breath. '*Maledizione*, Poppy, you could have been hurt. Or killed.'

'It's just lucky Simon is deaf because he slept through the whole thing.'

'Your brother is deaf?' His eyebrows hit his hairline.

'Yes, but it doesn't define who he is. He's a perfectly normal teenage boy.'

'And you've taken care of him your whole life?'

'Since he was two. I used to throw a hissy fit whenever the social workers tried to separate us. It nearly didn't work on one occasion, but basically no one wanted a deaf toddler, and he would only be soothed when I was around.'

Sebastiano stared down at her, some of the steely rage that had come into his eyes easing. 'You're amazing, you know that?' He cupped her face in his hands. 'Strong. Sexy. Beautiful. Inside and out.'

'Don't,' she said, uncomfortable hearing his praise. She was nothing special and it was only a matter of time before he figured that out.

'You are,' he asserted softly. 'But I agree.' He sat down in the corner chair and tugged on the belt of her robe. 'We have done enough talking.' He kissed a trail down her midline and turned her to face the railing.

'What are you doing?' she asked breathlessly.

'I'm going to show you how you make me feel. Bend

forward, *bella*,' he crooned in her ear, placing her hands on the balustrading. 'And don't let go.'

Hours later Sebastiano jolted awake; the only sound in the room was Poppy's soft breathing as she lay beside him. Carefully, he turned his head to confirm that she was sleeping. She was, her soft curves pressed into his side, her kiss-swollen lips parted, her silky hair spread out on the pillow.

Their love-making this time had been different from the other times. Less intense, but somehow more powerful. If that was even possible.

He adjusted the bedcovers over her shoulder and she nestled deeper against him. He smiled and slid his hand over her thigh. Her skin felt like silk beneath his rougher fingertips. She sighed, a whisper of a sound that feathered across his chest. He contemplated waking her up, kissing her brow, her cheeks, the little dimple beside her mouth. She was so responsive to his touch he could already imagine her turning towards him, arching against him, giving him one of those tiny whimpers he loved so much.

Dio, this was supposed to have been just one more night. Not that either of them had stipulated as much—but, regardless, he had thought that was all it would be and now, if he was honest, he wanted more. The irony of which was not lost on him.

And somewhere in his psyche he must have known this would happen because on the flight to Venice he had decided to put as much distance between them as possible.

Si, Castiglione, you tried really hard.

Annoyed with himself, he gently extracted his arm from beneath Poppy's neck and headed for the shower.

Damn it, he *had* tried. Only she had worn him down.

By breathing?

He hit the shower mixer and hot water jetted out over his tense body.

The thing was that opening up about his parents the previous night had made him feel vulnerable. Somehow she milked information out of him like a zookeeper getting venom from a snake. If he wasn't careful he'd be depleted before he knew it.

And what about her story on the terrace? *Por Dio*, he was still reeling from that, and he wanted to hunt down the animal who had jumped her and beat him to a pulp. Her experiences in life were far worse than anything he had been forced to face yet she didn't seem to feel sorry for herself the way he sometimes did.

He shoved his head under a water jet.

What had started out one-hundred-percent fake had at some point during the weekend shifted to being only fifty-percent fake. And that fifty percent was all on her side. Because once he'd taken her into his bed it had become real for him, and now he didn't want it to end.

Not yet anyway.

And why should it? They weren't hurting anyone. They weren't breaking any laws. What they were doing was working this attraction out of their systems until it was no longer there.

A slow, satisfied smile broke across his face and he felt lighter as he towelled himself off. More in control. He padded out into the bedroom. Working this attraction out of their systems made complete sense.

'Rise and shine, sleepy head. The Guggenheim awaits.'

Poppy groaned and covered her head with a pillow. 'If you've seen one painting, you've seen them all.'

Sebastiano grinned. 'Sacrilegious, intern! Picasso is rolling over in his grave about now.'

'Picasso could be skywriting outside our window and I wouldn't care,' she grumbled.

Laughing softly, he lifted the pillow from her head and bent to kiss her.

Had he ever felt this happy?

Yes, he thought as a feather-stroke of unease raised the hair along his forearms. His grin faded. He'd felt this happy when he'd been a child. Blindingly, blissfully happy, and completely unaware of how easily all that could be lost with one bad decision.

By the time Sebastiano's jet touched down in Naples it was late and Poppy's joy at the day had morphed into something mellower. Giuseppe's smiling limo driver greeted them and put his foot down as he whisked them through the dusky evening towards Villa Castiglione.

A soft, dreamy smile curved her lips as her mind drifted over the afternoon they had shared in Venice: eating pizza beneath a shop awning to dodge the rain, checking out the Guggenheim and visiting the island of Murano where she had bought two small glass figurines, one for her brother and one for Maryann. Sebastiano had also bought her a tiny bluebird he'd said was the exact colour of her eyes when she was happy.

It had all been so perfect. So wonderfully normal she had quite forgotten that it wasn't. Had Sebastiano forgotten too? Did he feel any of the things she did?

She glanced at his carved profile. Being with him was like a dream, a dream she never wanted to wake up from. But the closer they got to the Villa, the closer they got to flying home to London, and the real world. The real world where yet again she would be required to be stoic and move on when things didn't work out as she hoped.

Memories of past homes she and Simon had stayed at crowded in on her. Not all of them had been bad. Some had seemed almost promising but in the end even those families hadn't wanted them. Not long term.

Feeling her stomach pitch Poppy pressed her hand to her abdomen. Sebastiano noticed.

'Everything okay?'

'Of course,' she murmured, staring at their hands as he linked their fingers together.

The fact was she would follow Sebastiano's lead on this. She would collect the things they had left at the villa the day before, say goodbye when he dropped her at her front door, maybe shake his hand, thank him for everything and— Oh God, the third wish...

She had nearly forgotten about the third wish.

Her throat tightened. She had already decided to let that go. How could she not when she loved him so much? Because, yes, she did love him, she acknowledged with a sigh. What was the point in denying it to herself any longer?

But she had a sneaking suspicion that Sebastiano wouldn't let her off the hook about that last wish so easily. He wasn't a man who left his debts unpaid, another thing that made him so lovable.

But what could she ask for when he was the only thing she wanted? The one thing she couldn't have because, even though he had said he wanted her, even though they had shared another night together, nothing had really changed between them. She was still Poppy Connolly, the daughter of a drug user, and he was still Sebastiano Castiglione, descendent of a royal household. Their getting together would be like Zeus pairing up with a Hyde Park squirrel!

'Look at the colour of the sea,' she said, wanting to distract herself. 'It's almost black in this light.'

'Yes.'

'And those houses.' She crinkled her nose. 'Maintenance must be really difficult, seeing as how they're built so close together. Do you think—? Hey!'

Suddenly she felt his hands on her waist. 'I want to see you in London.'

His roughly spoken words startled her and she must

have stared at him a full minute before responding, elation sending a wave of emotion through her whole body. 'Did I just hear you right?'

'*Si*. Our relationship might have started out fake, but it's not fake any more.' He flashed her a quick smile, his eyes searing her with a blaze of heat. 'Why end things prematurely when we don't have to?'

Reeling from his request, and his warm hands either side of her waist, a laugh welled up inside her. What had started out as fake for her had turned real in a very short space of time too.

Very real.

But continue to see him in London? A niggle in the back of her mind stopped her from jumping at the idea and throwing her hands around his neck. A niggle that warned her that if something was too good to be true then it usually was.

'But how do we make it work?' she asked, easing back from him. 'I have so little free time as it is. And...' She shrugged helplessly. 'Between our two schedules we'd never get to see each other.'

'I'll make it work.'

Poppy rolled her eyes at his confident tone. 'But how? Give me the logistics.'

'The logistics, Miss Connolly?' He smiled and kissed her. 'The logistics are that I'm going to get you a new place. Somewhere I'm a little less likely to lose a wheel whenever I visit.'

'A new place?'

'And you can quit your night job. I'll give you an allowance I think you'll find more than generous.'

'An allowance?'

He smiled indulgently. 'That's right. Your new role is to be exclusively mine.'

A lump formed in Poppy's throat. 'You're doing that

earth-moving thing again,' she said thickly, unable to take in everything he was saying.

'Not yet I'm not.' He nuzzled kisses along her neck. 'But give me time.'

She laughed. 'Sebastiano, be serious.'

'I've never been more serious.' His smile was panther-like. 'Say yes.'

The car pulled up smoothly outside the villa and Poppy stared at it absently. Her mind was foggy and, even though she knew she shouldn't, she said the only thing in her head to say. 'Yes, but—'

Before she could voice her objections about the apartment and the allowance Sebastiano kissed her soundly, rendering the thinking part of her brain obsolete.

Sebastiano poured more wine in Poppy's glass as she recounted their trip to Venice, to the delight of his transfixed grandparents. They couldn't get enough of Poppy. It was as if she had cast a spell over all of them. Even Lukas had been taken by her, and Eleanore had texted him earlier in the day asking for Poppy's number so they could catch up when she was next in London.

If he wasn't careful, Sebastiano thought bemusedly, she would become a permanent fixture in his life without him even noticing it.

A cool sense of disquiet brushed over his skin like a spider's web and he swept it aside.

Poppy already knew that he didn't do permanent and, after all, it wasn't his apartment he intended to set her up in.

He grinned as he recalled her shocked face when he had suggested it. All those claims about him not being her type—in the end she had jumped at the chance to sleep with him, as he had her, and she certainly hadn't put the brakes on things since then, despite her claim that sleeping with him had been a mistake. That had surprised him a little, but hell, who was he to complain?

He slowly twirled the wine in his glass and glanced across at her. She'd worn another one of the outfits he'd provided for her and he loved seeing her wearing his clothes. He loved seeing her smiling as she was now, her eyes sparkly like the bluebird he hadn't been able to resist getting her on Murano.

His grandmother was talking and he tuned back in before his *nonno* accused him of daydreaming.

'That would be lovely,' Poppy murmured carefully.

Sebastiano frowned, catching her guilty look. He raised an eyebrow. *What would be lovely?*

She dabbed her mouth with her napkin. 'I know Simon would love to meet you both too. And Maryann. And I can cook lunch if you like?'

She was going to cook lunch for his grandparents?

Sebastiano's eyebrow rose higher. What on earth was she talking about?

This wasn't supposed to be a long-term arrangement; he hoped she realised that. He was happy to set her up in an apartment, visit her whenever he wanted, but as to the rest—as to her playing domestic goddess for his family... And what about her family? He hadn't even thought about meeting them.

And how exactly was he going to call in on her with her brother hanging around? How would that look to a young teenager? 'Yes, hello, I've just come over to make love to your sister.'

If some guy had tried that with Nicolette, he'd have floored him.

Sweat broke out on his forehead, a sick feeling clawing at his stomach. And why *had* Poppy jumped at the chance to move into an apartment?

Little Miss I Like Paying My Own Bills hadn't so much

as batted an eyelash when he'd told her. It was almost as if she had been waiting for him to offer it.

He frowned. Had he been taken in by a slick operator? Had he, a man who'd had women try every trick in the book to turn his head, fallen for the oldest one of all? The one who played hard to get?

'Sebastiano, you've gone pale,' his grandmother said.

Sebastiano carefully put down his knife and fork. *'Si; scusa, Nonna.'* He pushed back from the table. 'Poppy and I have to leave.'

'Is something wrong?'

Poppy nearly rolled her eyes at her own stupid question. Was the sky blue? Was the Arctic cold? Yes, but not as cold as Sebastiano's expression as he stood before her with his hands on his hips.

'Why did my grandparents say they were coming to London?'

'I'm not sure.'

He folded his arms across his chest. 'Why did you offer to cook them lunch?'

'I didn't mean to do that.' She laughed nervously, not understanding where this was headed. 'I'm a terrible cook but when they said they were coming to visit it just popped out.'

His dark brows climbed his forehead. 'It just popped out?'

'Yes. Why are you looking at me like that?' She frowned. 'What would you have had me say? That I wouldn't have them over?'

'No, of course not.' He ran a hand through his hair. 'I just—I just wasn't expecting it.'

Poppy gnawed on the inside of her cheek. Why wasn't he taking her in his arms? Why wasn't he kissing her? 'And?'

He paced away from her and stared out of the window. 'And what?'

'And what else is wrong?' Suddenly her heart felt heavy instead of light. 'Are you regretting telling me that you want to continue our relationship? Is that why you've gone all broody?'

'I haven't gone all broody.'

'Yes you have. And you were very quiet at dinner and now you can barely look at me.'

'You're exaggerating,' he said with a small laugh. 'And what happened to "Bastian"?'

'Excuse me?'

'You called me Bastian in Venice.'

Well, she'd felt closer to him in Venice. The man in front of her now was the one who had greeted her yesterday morning after regretting the night before. The polite stranger. Poppy felt her stomach roil again. 'Did I?'

'Yes, you did. You were also very quick to jump at my offer to set you up in an apartment. Is that the place you were imagining cooking for my grandparents?'

'Yes,' she said evenly, suddenly understanding what was motivating Sebastiano's strange behaviour. 'I pictured a lovely galley kitchen with slate tiles and, eh, oak cabinets.' Poppy wracked her brain for what else an expensive kitchen would have as hurt and outrage roiled inside her stomach. She had thought—she had imagined—that he had fallen for her too. 'And a stainless steel splashback,' she finished with a belligerent flourish.

'Really?'

Sebastiano had come to a stop in front of her and Poppy wanted to hit him for not being able to see that she was hurting. That she wasn't the kind of person he was silently accusing her of being. Hit him and rail at him for hurting her so much. For making her believe in fairy tales again. 'Yes.' She tilted her chin up, unable to stop herself. 'And then I thought we'd retire to the living area and have wine on the marble terrace overlooking St Paul's Cathedral. You are intending to get me an apartment overlooking St Paul's Cathedral, aren't you?'

'Poppy?'

'Yes, *Bastian*?'

'I'm sorry.' He crossed the room and put his arms around her. 'I shouldn't have said what I did.'

Poppy carefully stepped out of his embrace. 'No, you shouldn't have.'

He frowned as she moved toward the bedroom. 'Where are you going?'

'To pack,' she said wearily. Anywhere really where he wouldn't see the tears glittering behind her eyes.

'You're angry.'

'Yes. But it's with myself, so don't worry about it. I'm the one who should have known better.'

'Poppy, listen.' He grabbed her again and swung her around to face him. 'You can hardly blame me for thinking what I just did. You said yourself that this is like a fairy tale. You wanted me to pinch you, remember?'

'I remember.' She gave him a smile but everything inside her had already closed down and moved on. Now all she had to do was fetch her bags. 'Excuse me.'

'Don't be unreasonable about this.'

Poppy threw her own clothes into her duffle bag, hurt now morphing into anger. *Don't be unreasonable?*

'I mean, you were the one who came into my office that Sunday morning in your sexy jeans and tight sweater and telling my grandfather you could handle me. Can you really blame me if I briefly wondered if you had been hoping something like this would happen?'

'Not at all,' she said blithely. 'In fact, you're right. I was hoping your grandfather would walk in and think we were a couple so we could pretend to be one, and eventually you would fall in love with me so we could live happily ever after in a penthouse in the sky. A great plan don't you think?'

A muscle ticked in his jaw. 'I'm sorry. I was wrong to say what I did.'

'Yes you were.' She stood before him, her duffle bag in her hand. 'But you thought it and the truth is…' Poppy swallowed heavily. 'The truth is you don't want more from me than a temporary affair anyway. So in the end it's irrelevant.'

He raked a hand through his hair. 'Are you saying you do?'

'No.' She stared at him. His words, his very aloofness, confirmed everything she already knew. He didn't want her. Not really. Not in the way she wanted him. 'But I will ask for my third wish.'

His gaze turned wary. 'What is it?'

'That we never see each other again.'

CHAPTER FOURTEEN

'You are heading back to London, I see?'

Sebastiano didn't look up as his grandfather entered the library, just continued to stare at the photo in his hand before he set it aside. 'Yes. It was a good idea to spend the week in the Rome office. I feel as if I've got a handle on everything that needs to be done now.' He set his laptop in his carry-on bag. He'd do more work on the plane, though God knew he was so tired he might just crash instead. And wouldn't that be a godsend? The blissful oblivion of sleep.

'And will you be seeing Poppy in London?'

'No.' He knew his grandfather had sensed something wrong between them when she had bid them a teary goodbye last Monday night, but they'd respected his unwillingness to talk about it, as they had done in the past.

'Why not?'

The frown on his grandfather's face told a thousand stories. The most blatant being that Sebastiano had disappointed him. Again.

'Because Poppy was never a long-term proposition,' he grated, knowing it was the truth. He was a loner. It was how he had conditioned himself since his parents' deaths. Poppy leaving when she did had been a good thing. Hurting her hadn't but—he didn't want to think about how that made him feel.

'Proposition?' His grandfather frowned. 'What kind of a word is this to use about a woman like Poppy?'

Sebastiano swore under his breath. 'Look I have an admission to make.' He held his grandfather's gaze. 'It doesn't make me feel particularly proud of myself, but it's done and I can't change it.' He grimaced. 'I lied to you about my relationship with Poppy to force you to retire and hand me CE. So, if you want to reverse your decision and pass the job onto someone else—the CFO?—I won't argue.'

'Stefan is not the right man for the job. And he is not family.'

'You're going to have to move with the times at some point, Nonno.' He ran a hand through his hair, his chest tight. 'I'll support whatever decision you want to make.'

'You are the only man for the job. You always were.'

Sebastiano grimaced. 'You mean my father was.'

'*Si*. But he is not here. And it is time you stopped living in the past which you cannot change.'

'I do not live in the past.'

'You do. But what is this lie you speak of? I did not see a lie between you and Poppy.'

'You thought we were a couple.' And they had been for a short while. 'We weren't.'

His grandfather frowned. 'When did I say you were a couple?'

'In my office. You said…' His eyes narrowed. What exactly had his grandfather said? 'You told me to bring her here for the party. To meet Nonna.'

'*Si*. Why would I not? She is a beautiful young woman. I saw something between you and I thought she was the one to bring you alive again. And I was right. She did. Now your stubborn pride is going to ruin everything.'

Sebastiano stared at the man who had taken over the job of raising him after his parents had died. Then he shook his head.

'*Dio*, you're right.'

'I usually am.' His grandfather laid his hand on his shoulder. 'How long are you going to keep punishing yourself for what happened fifteen years ago, *nipote mio*?' he asked quietly.

For ever.

The words jumped into his head, startling him. Was he really going to blame himself for ever?

And how could he have treated Poppy the way that he had? How could he have thought she was after him for his money? His status? She, the woman who had baulked at him buying her a small figurine, and who had refused to let him have the Guggenheim opened because she hadn't wanted to wake the curator. *Cristo.* Any other woman he had dated would have simpered about how important he was.

He stared down at the photo he'd unconsciously picked up again. He swallowed heavily. 'Here,' he said gruffly, handing to his grandfather the photo he'd found facedown in a drawer. 'This belongs on Nonna's photo wall, doesn't it?'

'Si,' his grandfather said thickly, his gaze riveted to the photo of Sebastiano and his parents taken the day before their fatal accident.

They looked at each other a long time, understanding flowing between them. The abominable weight Sebastiano had carried around for too long slowly easing.

'What about Poppy?' his grandfather prompted.

Sebastiano took a deep breath. With the clarity of how much he had held himself back came the realisation that it had been easier to let Poppy walk away than to face his own feelings. 'I stuffed up.'

Because without a doubt in his mind he loved her. Completely and totally.

'I told your grandmother that this time I was not going to respect your privacy and let you try and work this out for yourself. You are too thick headed.'

Sebastiano shook his head. 'I should be angry with you.'

'*Si.*' His grandfather waved him off, his eyes suspiciously moist. 'You can thank me later.'

'It sounds like a Cinderella story!' Maryann sighed.

Yes, it did, Poppy thought. Even up to her leaving the silvery gown and shoes behind as if they'd never existed. 'It's not a Cinderella story. Cinderella wasn't studying law, and she had magic mice to help her along.' And the Prince had searched the land for Cinderella afterwards, but already a week had gone by and she'd not heard a word from Sebastiano. She didn't even know what country he was in. 'And there are more important things to worry about. Like you. How are you? What did the doctor say today?'

'I'm fine. My tingling wasn't so bad yesterday and my hands aren't numb at all today. And I start the new drug trials next week, which should reverse that even more.'

'That's great.'

Every day since she had walked out on Sebastiano Poppy had expected someone to come knocking on her door and take back the trainers and the keys to Maryann's apartment. So far they hadn't. But deep down she knew they wouldn't. It was what she had asked for after all and Sebastiano was definitely a man of his word.

Poppy glanced around at the large bay windows that looked out over a small front garden and the wonderful green parkland opposite. Maryann's apartment was beyond the scope of Poppy's expectations and she didn't know how Sebastiano had managed to organise such a perfect place so quickly, but then maybe she did. When he wanted something, there wasn't much that stood in his way.

But she wasn't supposed to be thinking about him any more.

She glanced over at where Simon was absorbed in a video game. 'Are you sure you're okay having Simon stay over tonight?' She'd taken a double shift to make up for

Monday night and she didn't like Simon being alone for so long.

'Of course. He's an enormous help to me, Poppy.'

Poppy smiled at her beautiful brother. 'He's the best,' she agreed.

She heaved a heavy sigh. 'How do you do it?' she asked Maryann. 'How do you forge on when it all seems so hopeless?'

'I try and remember that there's always something to be grateful for, no matter how small.'

'God, you're wise,' Poppy choked out. 'I'm so lucky to have found you.'

She wrapped her arms around the woman who had literally saved her life.

'I think I'm the lucky one, Poppy. You brightened my life the day you came into it.'

Poppy scrubbed at her eyes. 'I was a mess.'

'You were.'

They laughed and held each other.

Later, on the Tube, Poppy looked around at the various commuters, most with their heads bent over their mobile phones. As heavy as she felt right now, she did have a lot to be grateful for. Simon. Maryann. The lovely cleaning crew she would be working with tonight. The fact that she would always have the memory of Italy and how she had once spilled coffee over one of the most powerful businessmen on the globe. How she had once slept in his arms for one glorious weekend. How she had loved him. How she would always love him...

Her breath caught and she stumbled to her feet as her train pulled into her stop. She kept her head down as she followed the mass of commuters to the nearest exit and didn't even feel the rain as it fell over her bent head.

Dodging the late-night traffic, she headed into the first

building they would be cleaning tonight, a large one off Charing Cross.

She had found comfort in working this week, getting herself into a rhythm that exhausted her to the point she couldn't think too much.

Two hours in, she dropped her rag into a bucket and stretched her back.

'Hey, popsicle. Want a coffee? Bernie's heading out to the shop across the street.'

Convenience store coffee? *Brilliant!* 'Love one,' she said. 'Thanks, Tom.' She had been spoiled by authentic Italian coffee but she was going to have to get over that. The quicker, the better.

Finishing up another office, Poppy was just doing an inventory to make sure she hadn't missed anything when she heard Bernie return. 'Just put it on the desk, Bernie. Thanks.'

'It's not Bernie.'

Startled by the sound of Sebastiano's deep voice, Poppy swung around, the long feather duster tucked under her arm sweeping out and catching him on the elbow. He made to dodge it, the to-go cup of coffee he was holding flying upwards, a spray of milky liquid fountaining out and landing all over his clean shirt.

A string of Italian curse words left his mouth. 'Are you kidding me?'

Poppy stared at him open-mouthed. 'Oh God, I'm so sorry.' Then her brain came online. 'Sebastiano! What are you doing here?'

'Looking for you.' He shook his head and pulled at his shirt. 'And getting covered in coffee. Again.'

Galvanised by his words Poppy grabbed a wad of tissues and thrust them at him. He took them and stared at her.

Please don't look at me like that, she thought, wrapping her arms around her waist. 'Why are you looking for me?'

He sat the half-empty cup on the desk and took a deep breath. 'I was looking for you because about five hours ago I realised I've been a monumental idiot and I wanted to tell you that I love you and ask you to marry me. I thought it would be better to do it face-to-face than over the phone.'

Poppy's jaw hit the floor. 'I'm sorry?'

'So am I, *bella*. I'm sorry I panicked and made you feel less than you are the other night. I'm sorry it's taken me a week to figure everything out and I'm sorry I associated love with pain for so long I actually believed I was better off without it.' He swallowed heavily. 'But I'm not. Better off, that is. You've shown me that.'

'I have?'

'Absolutely. You face everything that happens to you head-on and you only look for the best in others. I on the other hand look for the worst. Looked.' He smiled faintly. 'Past tense. But I love you, Poppy, with all my heart, and I know I promised to give you three wishes but that last one… If you want me to honour it of course I will, but you have to know it's not what I want.'

Poppy's heart climbed into her throat. She wanted so much to believe him but she knew she was difficult to love. Difficult to have around. 'Sebastiano—'

Sebastiano stepped closer, clasping her shaking hands in his. 'I know you're scared, *amore mia*. I am too, but I'm taking a leaf out of your book and going with what feels right.'

Poppy felt light-headed. 'You are?'

'I am.' He smiled softly. 'I've been walking around half-alive before you came into my life and I don't want to live like that anymore.'

He drew her forward slowly and Poppy went, still wondering if she wouldn't wake up and find this was all a lovely dream. 'I think I might need you to pinch me.'

'To prove this isn't real?'

'To prove that it is.' She gave him a tremulous smile. 'I can't believe this is happening.'

'That's because you've been let down by too many of the people closest to you,' he said gently. 'Including me.' He put his arms around her waist. 'I knew something was up when my grandfather handed me the CEO position and it didn't make me happy. That was one of the reasons I was drinking. Apart from it being the night my parents died, I couldn't face what it said about me. Not until you pushed me to feel again. I love you, Poppy, and if you'll let me I'll gladly spend the rest of my life proving it to you.'

Tears shone in Poppy's eyes.

Sebastiano went down on bended knee, pulling a ring box out of his pocket. 'Traditionally giving you things hasn't gone well for me. I'm hoping this time will be the exception.'

He opened the box and an enormous diamond winked back, dazzling her. 'Oh, my God. I will get mugged wearing that!'

'No, you won't, because I'll be there to protect you.' He took her hand in his. 'Poppy Connolly, will you marry me and let me love you and take care of you and Simon and Maryann for the rest of my life?'

'Blimey, Poppy, if you don't say yes, I will.'

Bernie's impromptu interruption from the doorway made Poppy laugh. She swiped at the tears leaking out of the corner of her eyes.

'Sorry, love, I didn't mean to interrupt,' Bernie said sheepishly. 'I was just checking on you. I'll tell Tom you're otherwise disposed.'

Poppy stared at Sebastiano, so happy she thought she might burst. 'I didn't exactly fight for what I felt the other night either. I think deep down I expected you to ditch me, and so when it seemed like you were I went into survival mode.'

'I don't blame you. Can you forgive me?'

'Of course I can forgive you,' she said softly. 'I love you.'

Sebastiano groaned and rose to his feet, pulling her into his arms and kissing her. 'Is that a yes to my proposal, then?'

She smiled up at him. 'Are you going to offer me another three wishes if I say no?'

A grin spread slowly across his face. 'No, you're going to give me three wishes this time.'

'Oh?'

'Yes. Wish number one is that you don't ever bring me coffee again.' He grimaced as he glanced at his chest and Poppy realised they were both now covered in coffee! 'You were actually bringing me coffee this time,' she pointed out, almost giddy with the happiness fit to burst from inside her chest.

'Two: you walk around naked in our house for the rest of your life.'

'That is so not going to happen.' She laughed. 'And three?'

'Three: you promise to love me for ever, even though I'm likely to stuff up from time to time.'

'Deal,' she said, wrapping her arms around his neck. 'Oh God, Bastian. I love you so much.'

'*Grazie a Dio,*' he said softly. 'Now, you need to text Simon and Maryann. They said if they hadn't heard from you within the hour they were sending out a search party. Maryann also said to say thank you for her new apartment.'

'You told her?'

'I didn't have to. You have a terrible poker face, *amore mia*.' He scooped her into his arms.

'I know. I really need to change that.'

'Don't change it. I don't want you to change a hair on your beautiful head. You're perfect, Poppy. My perfect Poppy.'

She clung to him, her arms tight around his neck. 'I feel like I'm in a scene from a movie.'

'You're not. This is one-hundred-percent real. And every year we're going to celebrate in Venice. Would you like that?'

'I don't care where I am as long as you're by my side.'

'For ever, intern. For ever.'

* * * * *

BLACKMAILED INTO
THE MARRIAGE BED

MELANIE MILBURNE

To Franca Poli,
thank you for being such a loyal fan.

This Italian hero is for you, even though
I know you already have one. Xxxx

CHAPTER ONE

AILSA DECIDED THERE was only one thing worse than having to see Vinn Gagliardi after almost two years of separation, and that was being made to wait to see him.

And wait.

And wait.

And wait.

Not a couple of minutes. Not ten or fifteen or even twenty, but a whole stomach-knotting, nerve-jangling hour that crawled by like a wet century.

Ailsa pretended to read every glossy magazine Vinn's young and impossibly glamorous receptionist had artfully fanned on the handcrafted coffee table in front of her. She drank the perfectly brewed coffee and then the sparkling lemon-infused mineral water. She ignored the bowl of breath mints and chewed her nails instead. Right down to her elbow, and if Vinn didn't open his office door soon her shoulder would be next.

Of course he was doing it deliberately. She could picture him sitting behind his acre of French polished desk, idly passing the time sketching new furniture designs, a lazy smile tilting his mouth as he enjoyed every excruciating minute of the torture she was enduring out here at the prospect of seeing him again.

Ailsa squeezed her eyes shut, trying to rid her mind of the image of his smiling mouth. *Oh, dear God, his mouth.* The things his mouth had made her feel. The places on her body his mouth had kissed and caressed and left tingling for hours after.

No. No. No. Must not think about his mouth. She repeated the mantra she had been saying for the last twenty-two months. She was over him. Over. Him. There was a thick black line through her relationship with Vinn Gagliardi, and she had been the one to put it there.

'Mr Gagliardi will see you now.' The receptionist's voice made Ailsa's eyes spring open and her heart stutter like a lawnmower running over rocks. She shouldn't be feeling so…so nervous. What did she have to be nervous about? She had a perfect right to demand an audience with him, especially when it involved her younger brother.

Although…maybe she shouldn't have flown to Milan without making an appointment first, but she'd been in Florence for an appointment with some new clients when she got the call from her brother Isaac, informing her Vinn was going to sponsor his professional sporting career. She wasn't going to leave the country without confronting Vinn about his motive in investing in her brother's dream of becoming a pro golfer. She'd made up her mind if Vinn wouldn't see her today then she would damn well camp in his office building until he did. She had her overnight bag with her from her short trip to Florence so at least she had a change of clothes if it came to that.

Ailsa rose from the butter-soft leather sofa, but she'd been sitting for so long her legs gave a credible impression of belonging to a newborn foal. A premature newborn foal. She smoothed her damp hands down the front of her skirt, hitched her tote bag more securely over her shoulder and wheeled her overnight bag with the other hand, approaching the still closed office door with resentment bubbling like a boiling pot in her belly. Why didn't Vinn come and greet her out here in Reception? Why make her walk all the way to his door and knock on it like she was some servile little nobody? Damn it. She'd been his wife. Slept in his bed. Shared everything with him.

Not quite everything…

Ailsa ignored the prod of her conscience. Who said husbands and wives had to share every single detail of their background? Especially with the sort of marriage she'd had with Vinn. It had been a lust match, not a love match. She'd married him knowing he didn't love her, but she'd convinced herself his desire for her more than made up for that. She'd convinced herself it would be enough. That *she* would be enough. But he'd wanted more than a trophy wife. Much more. More than she was prepared to give.

Ailsa was pretty sure Vinn hadn't told her everything about his background. He'd always been reluctant to talk about the time his father went to jail for fraud and how it impacted on his family's business. She'd soon got tired of pushing him to talk to her about it and let it slide, figuring she would hate it if he, or anyone for that matter, kept on at her to slide back the doors on her family's closet. She didn't have too many skeletons in there, just one big, stinking rotten carcass.

Ailsa stood in front of his office door and aligned her shoulders as if she were preparing for battle. No way was she going to knock on his door and wait for his permission to enter.

No flipping way.

She switched her tote bag to the other shoulder and, grasping her overnight bag with her other clammy hand, took a deep breath and turned the knob and stepped over the threshold to find him standing with his back to her at the window overlooking the bustling streets of Milan. If that wasn't insult enough, he was seemingly engrossed in a conversation on his phone. He barely gave her a glance over his shoulder, just cursorily waved his hand towards one of the chairs opposite his desk and turned back to the view and continued his conversation as if she were some anonymous blow-in whom he had graciously shoehorned into his incredibly busy day.

A sharp pain seized her in the chest, his casual dismissal piercing the protective *I'm over him* membrane around her heart like a carelessly flung dart. How could he ignore her after not seeing her for so long? Hadn't she meant anything to him?

Anything at all?

The conversation was in Italian and Ailsa tried not to listen because listening to Vinn speak in his mother tongue always did strange things to her. Even when he talked in English it did strange things to her. She suspected even if he talked gibberish her spine would still go all mushy and every inch of her skin would tighten and tingle.

While he was talking she took a moment to surreptitiously study him...or at least she hoped it was surreptitious. Every now and again he would move slightly so she could see a little bit more of his face. It was as if he was rationing her vision of him, which was annoying in itself. She wanted to look him in the eye, to see if he carried any scars from their doomed relationship.

He changed the phone to his other hand and turned to the computer on his desk, his brow frowning in concentration as he clicked on the mouse. Why wasn't he looking at her? Surely he could show a bit more interest? She wasn't vain but she knew she looked good. Damn it, she paid a lot of money to look this good. She'd bought a new designer outfit for her meeting with her clients and had her hair done and had spent extra time on her make-up. Looking good on the outside made up for feeling rubbish and worthless on the inside.

Vinn moved something on the computer screen and then continued with his conversation. Ailsa was starting to wonder if she should have worn something with a little more cleavage to show him what he'd been missing. He was still as jaw-droppingly gorgeous as the last time she'd seen him. And if she hadn't been grinding her teeth to powder her jaw would be embedded in the plush ankle-deep carpet right then and there. His jet-black hair was neither long nor short nor straight nor curly, but somewhere sexily in the middle, reminding her of all the times she had trailed her fingers through those thick glossy strands, or fisted her hands in them during earth-shattering, planet-dislodging sex. He was clean-shaven but the rich dark stubble surrounding his nose and mouth and along his chiselled jaw was a heady reminder of all the times he'd left stubble rash on her softer skin. It had been like a sexy brand on her face, on her breasts, between her thighs...

Ailsa suppressed a shudder and, ignoring the chair he'd offered, threw him a look that would have frozen lava. In mid-flow. 'I want a word with you. Now.' She leaned on the word 'now' like a schoolmistress dressing down a disrespectful pupil.

The corners of Vinn's mouth flickered as if he were trying to stop a smile...or one of his trademark lip curls. He ended his phone call after another few moments and placed the phone on his desk with unnerving precision. 'If you'd made an appointment like everyone else then I would have plenty of time to talk to you.'

'I'm not everyone else.' Ailsa flashed him another glare. 'I'm your wife.'

A dark light gleamed in his espresso-brown gaze like the flick of a dangerous match. 'Don't you mean soon-to-be ex-wife?'

Did that mean he was finally going to sign off on their divorce? Because they'd married in England they were subject to English divorce law, which stated a couple had to be legally separated for two years. It was strange to think if they had married in Italy they would have been granted a divorce by now because Italian divorce law only required one year of separation.

'This may surprise you, Vinn, but I'm not here about our imminent divorce.'

'Let me guess.' He glanced at the overnight bag by her side and his eyes glinted again. 'You want to come back to me.'

Ailsa curled her hand around the handle of her bag so tightly her bitten-down nail beds stung. 'No. I do not want to come back to you. I'm here about my brother. Isaac told me you're offering to sponsor him for the international golfing circuit next year.'

'That's correct.'

She disguised a swallow. 'But…but why?'

'Why?' One dark eyebrow rose as if he found her question ludicrous and her imbecilic to have asked it. 'He asked me, that's why.'

'He…*asked* you?' Ailsa's mouth dropped open so wide she could have parked one of her brother's golf buggies inside. 'He didn't tell me that…' She took a much-needed breath and, letting go of her bag, gripped the back of the chair opposite his desk instead and swallowed again. 'He said you told him you would sponsor him but there were conditions on the deal. Conditions that involved me.'

Vinn's expression changed from mocking to masked. 'Sit down and we'll discuss them.'

Ailsa sat, not because he told her but because her legs were threatening to go from under her like damp drinking straws. Why had Isaac led her to believe Vinn had approached him over sponsorship? Why had her brother been so…so *insensitive* to invite her soon-to-be ex-husband back into her orbit? Vinn's involvement with her brother's golfing career would mean she wouldn't be able to avoid him the way she'd been doing for the last two years.

She had to avoid him.

She had to.

She didn't trust herself around him. She turned into someone else when she was with him. Someone who had all the hopes and dreams of a normal person—someone who didn't have a horrible secret in her background. A secret not even her brother knew about.

Her *half*-brother.

Ailsa was fifteen years old when she stumbled upon the truth about her biological father. For all that time she'd believed, along with everyone else, that her stepfather Michael was her dad. For fifteen years that lie had kept her family knitted together...well, knitted together was maybe stretching it a bit, because there were a few dropped stitches here and there. Her parents, while individually decent and respectable people, hadn't been happy in their relationship, but she had always blamed them for not trying hard enough to get on.

She hadn't thought it was *her* fault.

That the lie about her was the thing that made their lives so wretchedly miserable. But after finding out the truth about her biological father and the circumstances surrounding her conception, she could understand why.

Ailsa straightened her skirt over her thighs and took a calming breath, but then her gaze spied a silver photograph frame on Vinn's desk and her heart stumbled like a foot missing a rung on a ladder. Why had he kept that? She had given him that frame after their wedding, with her favourite photo of them smiling at each other with the sun setting in the background. Giving him that photo had been her way of deluding herself she was in a real marriage and not one that was simply convenient for Vinn because he wanted a beautiful and accomplished wife to grace his home. She couldn't see the photo from her side of the desk. Perhaps he had someone else's image in there now. The thought of it churned her belly into a cauldron of caustic jealousy. She knew it was missish of her since she was the one to walk out on their marriage, but it hurt her pride to think he could so easily move on with his life.

And not just her pride was hurt…

Ailsa had always held a thread of hope that Vinn would fall in love with her. What bride didn't want her handsome husband to love her? She had fooled herself it would be enough to be his bride, to be in his bed. To be in his life.

But she had longed to be in his heart. To be the first person he thought of in the morning and the last he thought of at night. To be the person he valued over everyone else or anything else. But Vinn didn't value her. He didn't prioritise her. He didn't love her. Never had. Never would. He was incapable of it.

Vinn leaned back in his chair with one ankle crossed over his muscle-packed thigh, his dark unreadable gaze moving over her body like a minesweeper. 'You're looking good, *cara*.'

Ailsa stiffened. 'Don't call me that.'

His mouth curved upwards as if he found her anger amusing. 'Still the same old bad attitude Ailsa.'

'And why wouldn't I have a bad attitude where you're concerned?' Ailsa said. 'How do I know you didn't plant the idea of sponsorship in Isaac's mind? How often have you been in contact with him since we separated?'

'My relationship with your brother has nothing to do with my relationship with you,' Vinn said. 'That is entirely separate.'

'We don't have a relationship any more, Vinn.'

His eyes became obsidian-hard. 'And whose fault is that, hmm?'

Ailsa was trying to contain her temper but it was like trying to restrain a rabid Rottweiler on a Teacup Chihuahua's leash. 'We didn't have a relationship in the first place. You married me for all the wrong reasons. You wanted a trophy wife. Someone to do little nineteen-fifties wifey things for you while you got on with your business as if my career meant nothing to me.'

A tight line appeared around his mouth as if he too was having trouble reining in his temper. 'I trust your aforementioned career is keeping you warm at night? Or have you found yourself a lover to do that?'

She put up her chin. 'My private life is no longer any of your business.'

He made a sound that was suspiciously like a snort. 'Isaac tells me you haven't even been on a date.'

Ailsa was going to kill her younger brother. She would chain him to the sofa and force him to watch animated Disney classics instead of the sports channel. She would take away his golf clubs and flush all his golf balls down the toilet. She would force-feed him junk food instead of the healthy organic stuff his sports dietician recommended.

'Well—' she gave Vinn a deliberately provocative look '—none that he knows about, that is.'

A muscle in the lower quadrant of his jaw moved in and out like an erratic pulse. 'Any lovers you've collected will have to move aside for the next three months as I have other plans for you.'

Plans? What plans? Now it was Ailsa's pulse that was erratic. So erratic it would have made any decent cardiologist reach for defibrillator paddles.

'Excuse me?' She injected derision into every word. 'You don't get to make plans for me, Vinn. Not any more. I'm in the driver's seat of my life and you're not even in the pit lane.'

He made a steeple with his fingers and rested them against his mouth, watching her with an unwavering gaze that made the hairs on the back of her neck prickle at the roots. But then she noticed the gold band of his wedding ring on his left hand and something in her stomach tilted. Why would he still be wearing that?

'Isaac will never make the professional circuit without adequate sponsorship,' he said after a long moment. 'That nightclub incident he was involved in last year has scared off any potential sponsors. I'm his only chance. His last chance.'

Ailsa mentally gulped. That nightclub incident could well have ended not just her brother's career prospects but his or someone else's life as well. The group of friends he'd been hanging around with since school attracted trouble and invariably Isaac got caught in the middle. It wasn't that he was easily led, more that he was a little slow to see the potential for trouble until it was too late to do anything—his approaching Vinn for sponsorship being a case in point. But if he got on the professional circuit he would be away from those troublemaking friends.

'Why are you doing this? Why are you involving me? If you want to sponsor him then do it. Leave me out of it.'

Vinn slowly shook his head. 'Not how it works, *cara*. You're the reason I'm sponsoring him. The only reason.'

Ailsa blinked. Could she have got it wrong about Vinn? Had he married her because he *loved* her, not just because he fancied having a glamorous wife to hang off his arm? Was that why he was still wearing his wedding ring? Had he meant every one of those promises he'd made on their wedding day?

No. Of course he hadn't loved her.

He had never said those three little magical words. But then, nor had she. She had deliberately held back from saying them because she hadn't liked the feeling of being so out of balance in their relationship. The person who loved the most had the least power. She hadn't been prepared to give him even more power over her than he already had. His power over her body was enough. More than enough.

He'd reeled her in with his charm and planted her in his life as his wife, on the surface fine with her decision not to have kids, but then he'd changed his mind a few months into their marriage. Or maybe he hadn't changed his mind at all. He had gambled on his ability to change her mind.

Gambled and lost.

She glanced at the photo frame again. 'Is that what I think it is?'

Vinn turned the frame around so she could see the image of their wedding day. Ailsa hadn't looked at their wedding photos since their separation. She had put the specially monogrammed albums at the back of her wardrobe under some clothes she no longer wore. It had been too embarrassing to look at her smiling face in all of those pictures where she had foolishly agreed to be a trophy wife. She had agreed to become a possession, not a person who had longings and hopes and dreams of her own. Looking at those photos was like looking at all the mistakes she had made. How could she have been so stupid to think an arrangement like that would ever work? That marrying anyone—especially someone like Vinn—would make her feel normal in a way she hadn't felt since she was fifteen? Their marriage hadn't even lasted a year. Eleven months and thirteen days, to be precise.

Vinn had mentioned the B word. A baby—a family to continue the Gagliardi dynasty. She would have ended up a breeding machine, her career left to wither, while his business boomed.

Her interior decorating business was her baby. She had given birth to it, nurtured it and made numerous sacrifices for it. Having a real baby was out of the question. There were too many unknowns about her background.

How could she give birth to a child, not knowing what sort of bad blood flowed in its veins?

Ailsa swallowed against the barbed ball of bitterness in her throat and cast her gaze back to Vinn's onyx one. 'Why do you keep it on your desk?'

He turned the frame back so it was facing him, his expression now as inscrutable as his computer screen in sleep mode. 'One of the best bits of business advice I've ever received is never forget the mistakes of the past. Use them as learning platforms and move on.'

It wasn't the first time Ailsa had thought of herself as a mistake. Ever since she'd found out the circumstances surrounding her conception she had trouble thinking about herself as anything else. Most babies were conceived out of love but she had been conceived by brute force. 'What do your new lovers think when they see that photo on your desk?'

'It hasn't been a problem so far.'

Ailsa wasn't sure if he'd answered the question or not. Was he saying he'd had numerous lovers or that none of them had been inside his office? Or had he taken his new lovers elsewhere, not wanting to remind himself of all the times he had made love to her on that desk? Did he wear his wedding ring when he made love to other women? Or did he take it off when it suited him? She glanced at his face to see if there was any hint of the turmoil she was feeling, but his features were as indifferent as if she were a stranger who had walked in off the street.

'So...the conditions you're proposing...' she began.

'My grandfather is facing a do-or-die liver transplant,' Vinn said. 'The surgeon isn't giving any guarantee he will make it through the operation, but without it he will die within a matter of weeks.'

'I'm sorry to hear he's so unwell,' Ailsa said. 'But I hardly see how this has anything to do with—'

'If he dies, and there's a very big chance he will, then I want him to die at peace.'

Ailsa knew how much respect Vinn had for his grandfather Domenico Gagliardi and how the old man had helped him during the time when Vinn's father was in jail. She had genuinely liked Dom and, although she'd always found him a bit austere and even aloof on occasion, she could well imagine for Vinn the prospect of losing his grandfather was immensely painful. She wouldn't be human if she didn't feel for him during such a sad and difficult time, but she still couldn't see how it had anything to do with her.

'I know how much you care for your grandfather, Vinn. I wish there was something I could do to—'

'There *is* something you can do,' Vinn said. 'I want us to be reconciled until he is safely through the surgery.'

Ailsa looked at him as if he'd told her to jump out of the window, her heart thumping so heavily she could hear it like an echo in her ears. 'What?'

'You heard me.' The set to his mouth was grimly determined, as if he had made up his mind how things would be and nothing and no one was going to talk him out of it. Not even her.

She licked her parchment-dry lips. He wanted her back? Vinn wanted her to come back to him? As his wife? She opened and closed her mouth, trying to locate her voice. 'Are you mad?'

'Not mad. Determined to get my grandfather through this without adding to the stress he's already going through,' Vinn said. 'He's a family man with strong values. I want those values respected and honoured by resuming our marriage until he is well and truly out of danger. I will allow nothing and no one to compromise his recovery.'

Ailsa got to her feet so abruptly the chair almost toppled over. 'I've never heard anything so outrageous. You can't expect me to come back to you as if the last two years didn't happen. I won't do it. You can't make me.'

He remained seated with his unwavering gaze locked on hers. Something about his stillness made the floor of her belly flutter like a deck of rapidly shuffled cards.

'Isaac is talented but that talent will be wasted without my help and you know it,' he said. 'I will provide him with not one, not two, but three years of full sponsorship if you'll agree to come back to me for three months.'

Ailsa wanted to refuse. She needed to refuse. But if she refused her younger brother might never reach his potential. It was within her power to give Isaac this opportunity of a lifetime. But how could she go back to Vinn? Even for three minutes, let alone three months? She clutched the strap of her bag like it was a lifeline and blindly reached for her overnight bag, her hand curling around the handle for support.

'Aren't you forgetting something? I have a career in London. I can't just pack up everything and relocate here.'

'You could open a temporary branch of your business here in Milan,' he said. 'You could even set up a franchise arrangement. You already have some wealthy Italian clients, *sì*?'

Ailsa frowned so hard she could almost hear her eyebrows saying *ouch* at the collision. How had he heard about her Italian clients? Had Isaac told him? But she rarely mentioned anything much to her brother about her work. Isaac talked about his stuff not hers: his golfing dreams, his exercise regime, his frustration that their parents didn't understand how important his sport was to him and that, since their divorce, they weren't wealthy enough to help him get where he needed to be, etc. Ailsa hadn't told Isaac this last trip to Florence was to meet with a professional couple who had employed her to decorate their centuries-old villa. They had come to her studio in London and liked her work and engaged her services on the spot.

'How do you *know* that?'

Vinn's mouth curved in a mocking smile. 'I'm Italian. I have Italian friends and associates across the country.'

Suspicion crawled across Ailsa's scalp like a stick insect on stilts. 'So... Do I have *you* to thank for the di Capellis' villa in Florence? And the Ferrantes' in Rome?'

'Why shouldn't I recommend you? Your work is superb.'

Ailsa narrowed her gaze. 'Presumably, you mean as an interior decorator, not as a wife.'

'Maybe you'll be better at it the second time around.'

'There isn't going to be a second time around,' Ailsa said. 'You tricked me into marrying you the first time. Do you really think I'm so stupid I'd fall for it again?'

He leaned back in his leather chair with indolent grace, reminding her of a lion pausing before he pounced on his prey. 'I didn't say it would be a real marriage this time around.'

Ailsa wasn't sure whether to be relieved or insulted. Could he have made it any more obvious he didn't find her attractive any more? Sex was the only thing they were good at in the past. Better than good…brilliant. The chemistry they'd shared had been nothing short of electrifying. From their first kiss her body had sparked with incendiary sexual heat. She had never orgasmed with anyone but him. She hadn't even enjoyed sex before him. And, even more telling, she hadn't had sex *since* him. So why wouldn't he want to cash in on the amazing chemistry they'd shared?

'Not real…as in—?'

'We won't be sleeping together.'

'We…we won't?' She was annoyed her voice sounded so tentative and uncertain. So…crushed.

'We'll be together in public for the sake of appearances. But we'll have separate rooms in private.'

Ailsa couldn't understand why she was feeling so hurt. She didn't want to sleep with him. Well, maybe her traitorous body did, but her mind was dead set against it. Her body would have to get a grip and behave itself because there was no way she was going to dive back into bed with Vinn… She had a sneaking suspicion she might not want to get out of it.

'Look, this is a pointless discussion because I'm not coming back to you in public or private or even in this century. Understood?'

He held her gaze with such quiet, steely intensity a shiver shimmied down her spine like rolling ice cubes. 'Once the three months is up I will grant you a divorce without contest.'

Ailsa swallowed again. This was what she'd wanted—an uncomplicated straightforward divorce. He would give it to her if she agreed to a three month charade. 'But if we're seen to be living together it will cancel out the last two years of separation according to English divorce law.'

'It will delay the divorce for another couple of years, but that would only be a problem if you're intending to marry someone else.' He waited a beat before adding, 'Are you?'

Ailsa forced herself to hold his gaze. 'That depends.'

'On?'

'On whether I find a man who'll treat me as an equal instead of a brood mare.'

He rose from his chair with an expelled breath as if his patience had come to the end of its leash. 'For God's sake, Ailsa. I raised the topic back then as a discussion, not as an imperative. I felt it was something we should at least talk about.'

'But you knew my opinion on having children when you asked me to marry you,' Ailsa said. 'You gave me the impression you were fine with not having a family. I wouldn't have married you if I'd thought you were going to hanker after a bunch of kids before the ink was barely dry on our marriage certificate.'

His expression was storm cloud broody and lightning flashed in his eyes. 'You have no idea of the word compromise, do you?'

Ailsa gave a mocking laugh. 'That's rich, coming from you. I didn't hear any talk of you offering to stay home and bring up the babies while I worked. You assumed I would gladly kick off my shoes and pad barefoot around your kitchen with my belly protruding, didn't you?'

His expression locked down into his trademark intractable manner. 'I've never understood why someone from such a normal and loving family would be so against having one of her own.'

Normal? There was nothing normal about her background. On the surface, yes, her family life looked normal and loving. Even since their divorce both her mother and stepfather had tried hard to keep things reasonably civil, but it was all smoke and mirrors and closed cupboards because the truth was too awful, too shameful and too horrifying to name.

On one level Ailsa understood her mother and step-father's decision to keep the information about her mother's rape by a friend of a friend—who'd turned out to be a complete stranger gate-crashing a party—a secret from her. Her mother had been traumatised enough by the event, so traumatised she hadn't reported it to the police, nor had she told her boyfriend—Ailsa's stepfather—until it was too late to do anything about the pregnancy that had resulted. Her stepfather had always been against having a DNA test but her mother had insisted on it, saying she needed to know. When Ailsa was fifteen she had come home earlier than normal from school to overhear her mother and stepfather arguing in their bedroom. She'd overheard many arguments between her parents before but this one had been different. Overhearing the awful truth about her origin meant that her life and all her dreams and hopes for her own family had died in that stomach-curdling moment.

Ailsa met Vinn's flinty gaze. 'In spite of my refusal to play this game of charades with you, I hope you will still sponsor Isaac. He looks up to you and would be devastated if you—'

'That's not how I do business.'

She raised her chin a little higher. 'And I don't respond to blackmail.'

His gaze warred with hers for endless seconds, like so many of their battles in the past. It was strange, but this was one of the things she'd missed most about him. He was never one to shy away from an argument and nor was she. She had always secretly enjoyed their verbal skirmishes because most, if not all, of their arguments had ended in bed-wrecking make-up sex. She wondered if he was thinking about that now—how passionate and explosive their sex life had been. Did he miss it as much as she did? Did he ever reach for her in the middle of the night and feel a hollow ache deep inside to find the other side of the bed empty?

No, because his bed was probably never empty.

Ailsa was determined not to be the first to look away even though, as every heart-chugging second passed, she could feel her courage failing. His dark brown eyes had a hard glaze of bitterness and two taut lines of grimness bracketed his mouth, as if, these days, he only rarely smiled.

The sound of his phone ringing on the desk broke the deadlock and Vinn turned to pick it up. 'Nonno?' The conversation was brief and in Italian but Ailsa didn't need to be fluent to pick up the gist of it. She could see the host of emotions flickering across Vinn's face and the way the tanned column of his throat moved up and down. He put down the phone and looked at her blankly for a moment as if he'd forgotten she was even there.

'Is everything all right?' Ailsa took a step towards him before she checked herself. 'Is your grandfather—?'

'A donor has become available.' His voice sounded strangely hollow, as if it was coming through a vacuum. 'I thought there would be more time to prepare. A week or two or something but... The surgery will be carried out within a matter of hours.' He reached for his car keys on the desk and scooped up his jacket where it was hanging over the back of his office chair, his manner uncharacteristically flustered, distracted. In his haste to find his keys several papers slipped off the desk to the floor and he didn't even stop to retrieve them. 'I'm sorry to cut this meeting short but I'm going to see him now before—' another convulsive swallow '—it's too late.'

Ailsa had never seen Vinn so out of sorts. Nothing ever seemed to faze him. Even when she'd told him she was leaving two years ago, he'd been as emotionless as a robot. It intrigued her to see him feeling something. Was there actually a heart beating inside that impossibly broad chest? She bent down to pick up the scattered papers and, tidying them into a neat pile, silently handed them to him. He took them from her and tossed them on the desk, where a couple of pages fluttered back to the floor.

'I can't let him down,' he said in a low mumble, as if talking to himself. 'Not now. Not like this.'

'Would you like me to go with you?' The offer was out before Ailsa could stop it. 'My flight doesn't leave for a few hours so...'

His expression snapped out of its distracted mode and got straight back to cold, hard business. 'If you come with me, you come as my wife. Deal or no deal.'

Ailsa was torn between wanting to tell him where to put his deal and wanting to see more of this vulnerable side of him. She could agree to the charade verbally but he could hardly hold her to anything without having her sign something.

'I'll go with you to the hospital because I've always liked your grandfather. That's if you think he'd like to see me?'

'He would like to see you,' Vinn said and searched through the papers on his desk for something, muttering a curse word in the process.

'Is this what you're looking for?' Ailsa handed him the pages that had fallen the second time.

He took them from her and, reaching for a pen, slid them in front of her on the desk. 'Sign here.'

She ignored the pen and met his steely gaze. 'Do we have to do it now? Your grandfather is—'

'Sign it.'

Ailsa could feel her will preparing for battle. Her spine stiffened to concrete, her jaw set to stone and her gaze sent a round of fire at his. 'I'm not signing it unless you give me time to read it.'

'Damn it, Ailsa, there isn't time,' Vinn said, slamming his hand down on the desk. 'I need to see my grandfather. Trust me, okay? Just for once in your life trust me. I can't let Nonno down. I can't fail him. He's depending on me to get him through this. Along with Isaac's sponsorship, I'll pay you a lump sum of ten million.'

Ailsa's eyebrows shot up so high she thought they might hit the light fitting above her head. 'Ten...*million*?'

The line of his mouth was white-tight. 'If you don't sign in the next five seconds the deal is off. Permanently.'

Ailsa took the pen from him, his fingers brushing hers in the exchange, sending a riot of fiery sensations from her fingertips to her feminine core. The pen was still warm from where he'd been holding it. She remembered all too well his warmth. The way it lit the wick of her desire like a match on dry tinder. She could feel the smouldering of his touch moving through her body, awakening sensual memories.

Memories she had tried so hard to suppress.

She took a shaky breath and ran her gaze over the document. It was reasonably straightforward: three years of sponsorship for Isaac and giving her a lump sum of ten million on signing. While it annoyed her he'd used money as a lure, she realised it was the primary language he spoke. Money was his mother tongue, not Italian. Well, she could learn to speak Money too. Ten million was a lot of money. She was successful in her business but with ten million in her bank account she could expand her studio to Europe.

But then she realised how trapped she would be once she signed that agreement. She would have to spend three months with Vinn. She needed time to think about this. She had rushed into marriage with him in the past. How foolish would it be to rush into this without proper and careful consideration? She left the document unsigned and pushed it and the pen back to him. 'I need a couple of days to think about this. It's a lot of money and... I need more time.'

He showed no emotion on his face, which surprised her given how insistent he had been moments earlier. But maybe behind that masked expression he was already planning another tactic to force her to comply with his will. 'We will discuss this further after we've been to the hospital.' He put the paper under a paperweight and, picking up her overnight bag, ushered her out of his office.

He spoke a few quick words to his receptionist Claudia, explaining what was happening, and Claudia expressed her concern and assured him she would take care of everything back here at the office. Ailsa felt a twinge of jealousy at the way the young woman seemed to be such an integral part of the business. She wondered what had happened to the receptionist who had worked for him during their marriage. Vinn liked surrounding himself with beautiful women and they didn't come more beautiful than Claudia, who looked as if she'd just stepped out of a photo shoot.

Ailsa waited until they were in Vinn's car and on

their way to the hospital before she brought up the subject. 'What happened to your other receptionist, Rosa?'

'I fired her.'

She rounded her eyes in surprise. She'd thought his relationship with the middle-aged Rosa had been excellent. She'd often heard him describe Rosa as the backbone of the business and how he would be lost without her. Why on earth would he have fired her? 'Really? Why?'

He worked his way through the gears with an almost savage intensity. 'She overstepped the mark. I fired her. End of story.'

'Overstepped it in what way?'

He sent her a speaking glance. 'Could we leave this until another time?'

Ailsa bit her lip. 'I'm sorry… I know you're feeling stressed and this must be so upsetting for you with your grandfather so desperately ill…'

There was a long silence.

'He's all I have,' Vinn said in the same hollow-sounding voice he'd used back in his office. 'I'm not ready to lose him.'

She wanted to reach for his hand or to put her hand on his thigh the way she used to do, but instead she kept to her side of the car. He probably wouldn't welcome her comfort or he might push her away, which would be even worse. 'You still have your dad, don't you?' she said.

'No.' He made another gear change. 'He died. Car crash. He was driving under the influence and killed himself and his new girlfriend and seriously injured a couple and their two children travelling in the other car.'

'I'm so sorry…' Ailsa said. 'I didn't know that.'

It pained her to think Vinn had gone through such a tragic loss since she'd left and she'd known nothing about it. She hadn't even sent a card or flowers. Had he kept his dad's death out of the press? Not that she went looking for news about Vinn and his family…well, not unless she'd had one too many glasses of wine late at night when she was feeling particularly lonely and miserable.

He shrugged off her sympathy. 'He was on a fast track to disaster from the moment my mother died when I was a child. Without her steadying influence he was a train wreck waiting to happen.'

Ailsa had rarely heard Vinn mention his mother's death. It was something he never spoke of, even in passing. But she knew his relationship with his father had never truly recovered after his father was charged with fraud when Vinn was barely out of his teens. The shame on the family's name and the reputation of the bespoke furniture business had been hard to come back from, but coming back from it had been Vinn's blood, sweat and tears mission and he had done it, building the company into a global success.

'I guess not everyone gets to have a father-of-the-year dad,' she said, sighing as he turned into the entrance of the hospital. 'Both of us lucked out on that one.'

Vinn had pulled into a parking spot and glanced at her again with a frown. 'What do you mean? You've got a great dad. Michael's one of the most decent, hard-working men I've ever met.'

Ailsa wanted to kick herself. She even lifted one

foot to do it, welcoming the stab of pain from her high heel because she was a fool to let her guard slip. A damn fool.

'Yes…yes, I know. He's wonderful…even since the divorce he still makes an effort to—'

'Then why say something like that? He'll always be your dad even though he's divorced from your mother.'

'Forget I said it. I… I wasn't thinking.' Ailsa hated that she sounded so flustered and hoped he'd put it down to the emotion of seeing his grandfather under such tense and potentially tragic circumstances. She had a feeling if he hadn't been in such a rush to see his grandfather before the surgery he might well have pushed her to explain herself a little more. It was a reprieve, but how long before he came back to it with his dog-with-a-bone determination?

It was a timely reminder she would have to be careful around Vinn. He knew her in a way few people did. Her knew her body like a maestro did an instrument. He knew her moods, her likes and dislikes, her tendency to use her sharp tongue as a weapon when she got cornered.

He didn't know her shameful secret, but how soon before he made it his business to find out?

CHAPTER TWO

VINN DIDN'T KNOW what was worse—seeing Ailsa again without a little more notice or walking into the hospital to see his grandfather, possibly for the last time. But, in a way, he'd been expecting to lose his grandfather... eventually. But two years ago when Ailsa called time on their marriage it had not only blindsided him but hit him in the chest like a freight train. Sure, they argued a bit now and again. What newly married couple didn't?

But he'd never thought she'd leave him.

They hadn't even made it to the first anniversary. For some reason that annoyed him more than anything else. He had given her everything money could buy. He had showered her with gifts and jewellery. Surrounded her with luxury and comfort, as was fitting for the wife of a successful man. He might not have loved her the way most wives expected to be loved, but she hadn't married him for love either. Lust was what brought them together and he'd been perfectly fine with that and so had she, or so he'd thought. She had never said the words and he hadn't fished for them. He'd just assumed she would be happy with the arrangement because most women wanted security over everything else and the one thing he was good at was providing financial security. Financial security was what you could bank on—*pardon the pun*—because emotions were fickle. People were fickle.

But Ailsa had been unwilling to even discuss the subject of having a child. He knew her career was important to her, as was his to him, but surely she could have been mature enough to sit down and discuss it like an adult? He'd told her he wasn't all that interested in having a family when they'd first got together because back then he wasn't. But after a few months of marriage, his grandfather had his first health scare with his liver and had spoken to Vinn privately about his desire for a grandchild to hold in his arms before he died. He had made it sound like Vinn would be letting down the family name by not providing an heir. That it would be a failure on Vinn's part not to secure the family business for future generations.

Letting the family down.

Failure.

With his father already the Gagliardi family's big failure, those words haunted Vinn. They stalked him in quiet moments. It reminded him of how close to losing everything he had been when his father had jeopardised everything with his fraudulent behaviour. Vinn couldn't allow himself to fail at anything. Being an only child had never really bothered him before then, but with his father acting like a born-again teenager at that time and his grandfather rapidly ageing, it had made Vinn think more and more about the future. Who would he leave his vast wealth to? What was the point of working so hard if you had no one to pass on your legacy to when you left this mortal coil?

But no, practically as soon as he'd brought up the topic, Ailsa had stormed out of his life like a petulant child, refusing to communicate with him except through their respective lawyers. She had dropped another failure on him—their marriage. He would give her the divorce when it suited him and not a moment before. He had far more pressing priorities and top of that list was getting his grandfather through this surgery.

Vinn was banking on Ailsa's love for her younger brother Isaac to get her to agree to his plan for the next three months. But her turning up unannounced at his office was a reminder of how careful he had to be around her.

Careful. Guarded. Controlled.

He'd assumed she would call and make an appointment, but the one thing he knew he should never do with Ailsa was assume anything. She had an unnerving ability to catch him off guard. Like when she'd point blank refused to sign his agreement even though he'd dangled ten million pounds in front of her. He hadn't expected her to ask for time to think about it. He'd expected her to sign it then and there. But with the pressure of getting to the hospital in time to see his grandfather before the surgery, Vinn had allowed her to get away without signing. He had never allowed anyone to do that to him before. Push him around. Manipulate him. He had always put measures in place to avoid being exploited or fooled or thwarted.

All through his life he had aced everything he had ever set out to do, but his marriage to Ailsa was a failure. A big fat failure. How he hated that word—*failure*. Hated. Hated. Hated it. It made him feel out of control, incompetent.

But it wasn't just him who had been affected by Ailsa walking out on him. The breakup of their marriage had shattered his grandfather and it was no surprise the old man's health had gone into a steep decline shortly after Ailsa had left. The death of Vinn's father so soon after her leaving certainly hadn't helped. But in some ways his grandfather had coped better with Vinn's father's death than the breakup of Vinn's marriage. His marriage to Ailsa had been the hope his grandfather had clung to for the future—a future ripe with promise of a new generation, new beginnings and new success. But that hope had been snatched away when Ailsa left.

But just lately, as the two-year mark of the separation crept closer, he'd noticed his grandfather becoming more and more stressed and his health suffering as a result. His grandfather had always been a devoted family man and had stayed faithful and true to Vinn's grandmother, Maria, until her death five years ago. If Vinn could do this one thing—make his grandfather believe he and Ailsa were back together—then at least the old man's recovery wouldn't be compromised by the stress and worry about their imminent divorce.

Besides, this time around, Vinn would be the one in control of their relationship and he would stay in control. He wouldn't allow Ailsa to throw him over again. He had put a time limit on their 'reunion' and he'd mentioned the no-sex rule just to be on the safe side. When he'd seen her walk into his office unannounced, his loins had pulsed with a drumbeat of primal lust so powerful it nearly knocked him off his feet. And if he hadn't been talking to one of his senior staff on the phone about a tricky problem in one of his workshops, he might well have taken Ailsa into his arms then and there and challenged her to deny the spark that arced between them. The spark that had always arced between them from the first time they'd met at a furniture exhibition in Paris. He was attracted to her natural beauty—her long silky curtain of ash-blonde hair and creamy complexion and coltish model-like figure, and the way her bewitching grey-blue eyes seemed to change with her mood.

The other thing he'd liked about her back then was she hadn't been easy to pick up. With his sort of wealth and profile it had been a new experience meeting a woman who didn't dive head first into bed with him. She had taken playing hard to get to a whole new level. The thrill of the chase had been the biggest turn-on of his adult life. He had seen it as a challenge to get her to finally capitulate and, if he were honest, he would have to admit it was one of the reasons he'd married her instead of offering her an affair like anyone else. Maybe even the major reason. Because nothing shouted *I won* more than getting that wedding ring on her finger.

But that iron-strong determination of hers that had so attracted him in the first place was the same thing that had ultimately destroyed their marriage. She refused to back down over a position she adopted. It was her way or the highway and to hell with you if you didn't agree.

But Vinn was equally determined, and this next three months would prove it.

Ailsa followed Vinn into the private room where Domenico was being monitored prior to the transplant. Strict sterilisation procedures were being conducted and, according to the nurse, they would be a hundred times more stringent once the surgery was over.

The old man was lying in a bed with medical apparatus tethering him seemingly from every limb. He opened his eyes when Vinn approached the bed and gave a weak smile. 'You made it in time.'

Vinn gently took his grandfather's hand in his and Ailsa was touched to see the warmth and tenderness in Vinn's gaze. Had he ever looked at her like that? As if *she* mattered more than anything at that moment? She felt guilty for thinking such thoughts at such a time with his grandfather so desperately ill, but how could she not wish Vinn had felt something more than just earthy lust for her?

'I made it,' Vinn said. 'And I brought someone with me to see you.'

Domenico looked to where Ailsa was standing and his weary bloodshot eyes lit up like stadium lights. 'Ailsa? Is it really you?'

She stepped forward and put her hand on the old man's forearm, so close to where Vinn's hand was resting she felt a little electric tingle shoot up her arm. 'Hello, Dom.'

Dom's eyes began to water and he blinked a few times as if trying to control his emotions. 'My dear girl… You have no idea how much it thrills me to see you back with Vinn. I've prayed for this day. Prayed and prayed and prayed.'

Back with Vinn.

Those three words sent a wave of heat through her body and two hot pools of it firing in her cheeks. Had Vinn already told his grandfather they were back together? Had he been so arrogantly confident she would sign the agreement? She was glad now she hadn't signed it. Fervently glad. He had given her ten million very good reasons to sign it, but still, it rankled that he thought he could so easily buy her acquiescence by waving indecent amounts of money in front of her.

'But I'm not really—' Ailsa stopped mid-sentence. How could she tell Dom the opposite of what he clearly wanted to hear? She might not have signed Vinn's agreement, but his poor old grandfather was being wheeled into surgery within a matter of minutes for an operation, which he might not survive. What harm would it do to allow Dom this one moment?

She wasn't back with Vinn as in Back With Vinn. She was playing a game of charades to keep an old man happy. Standing here by this old man's bedside with the prospect of his life with a clock ticking on it made her want to do everything in her power to make Dom feel settled and peaceful before his life-saving or, God forbid, life-ending surgery.

'I'm here,' she said and moved her hand so it was on top of Vinn's on Dom's hand. 'We're both here. Together.'

Tears dripped down from Dom's eyes and Ailsa leaned over to pluck a tissue from the box beside the bed and gently mopped them away, her eyes feeling suspiciously moist and her chest so tight it felt like she was having her own medical crisis.

'If I don't make it through this operation then at least I have the assurance you two have patched things up,' Dom said, his voice choked with emotion. 'You're meant to be together. I knew that the first time Vinn introduced me to you. You're a strong woman, Ailsa. And my grandson is a strong man and needs someone with enough backbone to handle him.'

Ailsa was going to handle Vinn all right. She was going to grab him by the front of the shirt and tell him what she thought of him manipulating her into this crazy charade by default. Even though she hadn't committed herself on paper, he must have known she wouldn't be able to help herself once she saw his desperately ill grandfather. No wonder he hadn't made a fuss back in his office when she'd refused to sign the wretched agreement. He had simply bided his time so he could play on her emotions because he knew it was her weak spot. Just like he was using her love and affection for her brother as a bargaining tool, forcing her to bend to his will.

'Time to go to Theatre,' a hospital orderly announced from the door.

Vinn leaned down to kiss his grandfather on both cheeks European style, his voice husky and deep. 'Good luck, Nonno. We'll be waiting for you once you come out of Recovery.'

If you come out of Recovery...

Ailsa could hear the unspoken words like a haunting echo inside her head. Vinn had lost his mother when he was a small child barely old enough to remember her. He had lost his grandmother—who had effectively raised him—five years ago, and lost his father during the last two years. Now he was facing the prospect of losing his grandfather. The grandfather who, in many ways, had been more of a father to him than his own father.

She hadn't expected to feel anything other than hate towards Vinn because of the way he had married her because he wanted a wife and she had somehow measured up to his standards. Little did he know how far below those standards she actually fell. But now she felt an enormous wave of sympathy for what he must be going through. She wasn't supposed to feel anything where Vinn was concerned. She was in the process of divorcing him.

But who wouldn't feel sorry for someone saying goodbye to a grandfather who had been there for them all of their life? Dom and his wife Maria had stepped in when Vinn's mother died when he was so young and again when his father had caused so much financial and emotional mayhem. Dom had been there for Vinn in every way possible and now he was facing the very real prospect of losing him. Not that she had found out any of that information about his grandparents' role in his life from Vinn. She had found out most of it from his previous secretary Rosa, who had filled her in on some of the Gagliardi family dynamics.

Ailsa leaned down to kiss Dom's cheeks and wish him well and, when she straightened, Vinn's arm encircled her waist and drew her close to his body. In spite of the layers of her clothes, his touch set off fireworks through her flesh. He was so much taller than she was and even in her high heels she barely came up to his shoulder. She had never been more aware of her femininity than when standing next to him. It was as if his body had secret radar that was finely tuned to hers, signalling to it, making it ping back responses she had little or no control over. She could feel them now. *Ping. Ping. Ping. Tingle. Tingle. Tingle.* The warm press of his hand on her left hip was sending a message straight to her core, like a network of fiery hot wires fizzing and whizzing. Her breasts began to stir, as if remembering the slightly calloused glide of his hands caressing them, his thumbs rolling over her nipples…

Ailsa gave herself a mental slap and eased out of Vinn's hold once Dom had been wheeled away, accompanied by the nurse and three other clinicians. She waited until they were alone before she turned to face Vinn with a skewering glare. 'Did you tell him we were back together before you'd even spoken to me?'

His expression showed faint signs of irritation. 'No. But he must've put two and two together when he saw you come in with me.' He rubbed a hand over his face, the sound of his stubble catching against his skin making something in her belly turn over. 'Thanks, by the way. You've made a frail old man very happy.'

Ailsa shifted her lips from side to side—a habit she'd had since childhood. She did it when she was stressed and she did it when she was thinking. 'But what about when he wakes up? He'll know there's something not right between us. He might be desperately sick but he's not a fool.'

His dark-as-pitch eyes moved between each of hers in a back and forth motion, as if looking for a gap in her firewall. 'You'll have to work a little harder on convincing him you're in love with me.'

Ailsa gave him an arch look. 'Maybe you could show me how to do it by example.'

His hooded gaze went to her mouth and something dropped off a shelf in her stomach. That was the look that had started their crazy lust-driven relationship. The I-want-to-have-jungle-sex-with-you look. The look that melted her self-control like a scorching flame on sorbet. But then, as if he remembered they were still in a hospital room and likely to be interrupted, he brought his gaze back to hers. 'I'm sure you'll do a great job once you see ten million pounds in your bank account.' He took out his phone and started pressing the keys, adding, 'I'll transfer a quarter of the funds now and the rest on signing.'

Ailsa bristled again at the suggestion she could be bought. 'I don't care if you put twenty million in my account, it won't change the fact that I hate you. And I told you, I'm not signing it until I've had time to think about it.'

He looked up from his phone with an unreadable look. 'Hate me all you like in private, *cara*, but in public—signed agreement or not—you will act like a blissfully happy bride or answer for the consequences.'

She ground her teeth together. 'Don't go all macho man on me, Vinn. It won't work.'

One side of his mouth lifted in an indolent smile

as if he was enjoying her strong will colliding with his. He stepped closer and lifted her chin with the tip of his finger. She knew she should have jerked away from him but for some reason her body was locked in a mesmerised stasis. His eyes were so dark she couldn't make out his pupils and they pulsed with little flashes of heat that could have been anger or red-hot desire or a combination of the two.

'You really are spoiling for a fight, aren't you, *tesoro mio*? But you know where our fights end up, hmm? In bed with you raking your fingernails down my back as I make you come again and again and again.'

Ailsa could feel her cheeks blushing like an industrial furnace. How dare he remind her of how wanton she had been in his arms? He made her turn into an animal in his bed. A wild animal with needs and desires and hungers that had never been awakened, much less satisfied, by anyone but him.

The need to get away from him so she could think straight was suddenly paramount. She didn't care what agreement he wanted her to sign or for how much, but right then and there she had to put some space between them.

'Dream on, Vinn. I need the bathroom. Will you excuse me for a minute?'

'There's a bathroom in here.' He pointed to the signed door in his grandfather's room. 'I'll wait for you.'

Ailsa gave him a tight smile that didn't show her teeth. 'Strange as this may seem given our previous relationship, but I would actually like a little privacy. I'll use the bathroom down the hall.' She moved past him and mentally steeled herself for him trying to stop her but she managed to escape without him touching her. She glanced back from the doorway but he had already taken out his phone and was tapping again at the screen.

Ailsa walked straight past the bathroom down the corridor and stepped into the first available lift. She would have taken the stairs but she was in too much of a hurry. She had left her overnight bag in Vinn's car but at least she had her passport in her tote bag. But then she began to weigh her options. If she flew back to London he would immediately withdraw his offer of Isaac's sponsorship. She had no reason to think he didn't mean every single word. She had run up against his steely will too many times to count. The only time she had won an argument with him was when she'd walked out on their marriage.

But in a way she hadn't really won.

She had left him almost two years ago but a secret part of her had hoped he would come after her. While on one level she accepted he didn't love her in the traditional sense, on another level she had been so desperate for a sign—any sign—he cared something for her that her walk out had been far more impulsive and dramatic than she'd intended. In hindsight, she realised she had been hormonal and moody and feeling neglected because he'd been working extra long hours. She'd felt like a toy that had been put to one side that no longer held its earlier appeal. When he'd mentioned having kids it had triggered all her fears about their relationship. It had triggered all her fears about herself. What sort of mother would she be? How could she risk having a child when she didn't know whose DNA she carried?

But Vinn hadn't come after her. He hadn't even called her. It seemed to prove how little he cared about her that he would let her call time on their marriage and not even put up a fight to beg her to stay.

But then, men like Vinn Gagliardi didn't beg. They commanded and people obeyed.

The lift doors opened and Ailsa looked towards the hospital entrance. Could she walk out those doors and hope some decent part of Vinn would make him go ahead with Isaac's sponsorship? But then she noticed a gathering of people outside and her heart began to skip in her chest. Paparazzi. Were they here for a visiting celebrity? It only took her a moment to realise *she* was the celebrity. Why hadn't she realised Vinn would contact the press about their 'reconciliation'? He was always a step or two ahead of her. It was as if he could read her mind as well as her body. She hadn't signed his stupid agreement so he had a Plan B and C and God knew how many others up his designer sleeve.

One of the paparazzo looked Ailsa's way and said something to his colleagues and then they came rushing through the front doors of the hospital.

Ailsa turned and stabbed at the lift button but when she looked up at the numbers she could see it was still on the fourth floor. She went to the next lift and, just as she pressed the button, the doors opened and she came face to face with Vinn.

He took her hand and looped her arm through his. His expression was hard to read but the tensile strength in his grip was not. She would have to think twice before trying to outwit him. 'Our first press conference is about to begin,' he said. 'Nice that you could join me for it.'

Ailsa had no choice but to paint a plastic smile on her face as he swung her to face the press. The back and forth conversation was mostly in Italian so she could only pick up a few words here and there, but it was clear the press were delighted to hear the runaway wife of high profile billionaire furniture designer Vinn Gagliardi was back.

'Let's have a kiss for the cameras,' one of the journalists said in English.

Ailsa's heart began to race at the thought of Vinn's mouth coming down on hers, but he held up his hand like a stop sign. 'Please respect our privacy. This is a difficult day for both of us with my grandfather undergoing life-saving surgery. *Grazie.*'

The press gang parted like the Red Sea as Vinn led her towards the front doors of the hospital. She understood the gravity of the situation, with his grandfather hovering between life and death upstairs in Theatre, but why hadn't Vinn taken this opportunity to kiss her? Had she misinterpreted the way he'd looked at her mouth earlier? Was he really serious about the no-sex rule? Did it mean he already had someone in his life who serviced those needs for him? A sudden pain gripped her at the thought of him with someone else. For the last twenty-two months she had forced herself not to think about it. He was a man with a healthy sexual appetite. Not just healthy—voracious. He was thirty-five years old—in the prime of his life.

Vinn led her to where he'd parked his car and silently handed her into it. Ailsa knew he was angry. She could feel it simmering in the air like humidity before a storm. He got in behind the driver's wheel and gave her a look that would have blistered paint. 'You might not have signed the agreement yet, but you told my grandfather you're back with me. If you try to run away again I will not only withdraw my offer of sponsorship from Isaac, but I will make sure no one else ever offers to sponsor him. He won't be able to walk onto any golf course in Europe as a spectator, much less play in a tournament. Have I made myself clear?'

Ailsa would have loved to throw his agreement and his ten million back in his face. She would have loved to tear up the money note by note and stuff the pieces down the front of his shirt. But she loved her brother more than she hated Vinn. Much more. Which was kind of scary because she needed to vehemently hate him in order to keep herself safe. But could she ever be safe from Vinn? She raised her chin a fraction, unwilling to let go of her pride. 'You might think you can cleverly blackmail me back into your life for three months but I will always hate you. Ten million, twenty million— even fifty million—won't ever change that.'

'If I thought you were worth fifty million I would pay it.'

His words were as cruel and stinging as a slap and shocked and pained her into silence.

She watched out of the corner of her eye as his hands opened and closed on the steering wheel, his knuckles straining white against the stretched tendons. The air inside the cocoon of the car felt thick, dense, as if all the oxygen atoms had been sucked out.

Ailsa felt dangerously close to tears, which annoyed her because she wasn't a crier. She was a fighter not a crier. She gave as good as she got and never showed her vulnerability. She didn't like showing her neediness. She fought against her emotional weakness. She'd taught herself from a young age when her mother would turn away from her outstretched arms as if she couldn't bear to be touched, let alone hugged, by her own child.

Ailsa turned her head to stare blindly out of the window, vaguely registering people coming and going from the hospital. People going through the various cycles of life: birth, death, illness and recovery, sadness and happiness and hope and loss and everything in between.

Vinn released a heavy sigh and turned to face her. 'I'm sorry. That was…unkind of me.'

'Unkind?' Ailsa wasn't ready to forgive him. Her hurt was festering, pulsating and throbbing like a re-opened wound. Old hurts and new hurts were twisting around each other like rough ropes tied too tightly against wounded flesh. 'But true in my case. I'm not worth anything to you. In fact, I'm surprised you offered ten million.'

He reached across the space between them and put a gentle hand to the nape of her neck where it seemed every nerve in her body had gathered to welcome his touch. 'I would pay any amount of money to get my grandfather safely through this surgery.' His mouth twisted in a rueful movement that wasn't quite a smile. 'I'm not ready to let him go.'

You were ready to let me go. The words hovered on the tip of her tongue but she didn't say them out loud. 'You really love him, don't you?'

His hand moved closer to the base of her scalp, his fingers moving through her hair sending shivers down her spine. 'He's family. The only family I have left.'

'Don't you have cousins and uncles and aunts and—?'

He made a dismissive sound. 'They ran for cover when my father's shady dealings became public knowledge. I have no time for fair weather family or friends.'

Ailsa hadn't realised until then how isolated he was. She knew there were numerous Gagliardi relatives because she had met a lot of them at their wedding. Some had refused the invitation because of his father's reputation but Vinn had shrugged it off as if it hadn't bothered him one way or the other. But where were they today, the day his grandfather faced the biggest battle of his life? Had anyone reached out to support Vinn? To offer comfort at such a difficult time? Who were his closest friends these days? She had met a few of his business associates in the past but none of them appeared to be close to him or he to them. He had a tendency to hold people at a distance.

And who knew that better than her?

Even though she had shared his body and his home for nearly a year he was as much of an enigma to her as ever.

Ailsa looked into his gaze and felt her resolve melting like an ice cube in a hot tub. She didn't have too many pressing engagements back in London. She had planned to have a week or two out of the studio to work on some designs for some clients at home. What would it matter if she rescheduled her flight for a day or two? Just until Dom got out of surgery or Recovery. Her assistant, Brooke, could handle anything urgent.

'How soon will you know if your grandfather is going to be out of immediate danger? I could stay in a hotel for a day or two...until I've made up my mind about the agreement.' Would he allow her that much leeway? A day or two wasn't much of a reprieve but she needed to keep as much distance from him as she could—while she still could.

His hand moved further along her scalp, the glide of his fingers sending her senses spinning and her willpower wilting like a daffodil in the desert. 'Is it me you don't trust or is it yourself?' His voice was rich dark honey and gravel swirled together.

Ailsa could feel his body just inches away from hers, his tall frame like a powerful magnet, pulling her body, drawing it inexorably towards his. Her lips were suddenly so dry they felt like cardboard but she daren't moisten them because she knew Vinn would read that as a signal that she wanted him to kiss her.

Damn it. She *did* want him to kiss her. Wanted. Wanted. Wanted. But no way was she going to let him know that. She would get her willpower back into line. Right here. Right now. She glanced at his mouth. *Where the hell was her flipping willpower?* Why did he have to have such a beautiful mouth? Sculptured and firm and yet the lower lip had a sensual fullness to it that her mouth, and other parts of her body, remembered with a frisson of excitement.

Ailsa raised her chin and locked her gaze with his. 'You think I still want you?' She affected a little laugh. 'That ego of yours really is something, isn't it? I feel nothing for you. A big fat nothing.'

His eyes darkened and a knowing smile lifted one corner of his mouth and his fingers shifted back to her nape to toy with the underside of her hair. A sensation shimmied down her spine like a warm flow of melted caramel, gathering in a hot whirlpool between her thighs. His gaze went to her mouth and back to her eyes and back again as if he were in the process of deciding whether to kiss her or not. Every nerve in her lips prepared itself—leaping and dancing and clapping their hands in anticipation. Every cell of her body vibrated with a hum of primal longing as needs she had ignored, suppressed or denied for the last two years came to throbbing life.

But then he suddenly moved away from her and a mask came down over his features like a curtain lowering on a stage. 'Someone's waiting for this car space. We'd better get moving.'

Ailsa had completely forgotten they were still in the hospital car park. But that was typical of being in Vinn's company. She forgot stuff, like how he had only married her so he could tick the job of 'finding a wife' off his to-do list. She was a fool to think he still wanted *her*. Maybe he did physically, but that was a male thing. Men could separate the physical from the emotional far more easily than most women.

Vinn had never been emotionally connected with her. And she had been a fool to accept his proposal on those terms. He'd offered her marriage but she had a feeling that was only because she had been the first woman to resist him. He'd seen her as a challenge, a conquest, and putting a ring on her finger and having a big flashy society wedding had publicly broadcast his success in claiming her as his prize. Even if he hadn't loved her at the start of their marriage, she had been happy with his desire for her. It had been enough because no one had ever made her feel that way before.

Wanted.

Needed.

As if she was irreplaceable.

But if she had been so irreplaceable, surely he would have fought a little harder to keep her? She'd been let go without a whisper of protest. Sure, he'd been a little difficult over the divorce proceedings, but that was because of the wording of the pre-nuptial agreement. The fact that he'd insisted on a pre-nup was another stark reminder of the sort of marriage they had. She had ignored it at the time, telling herself that of course a man with that sort of hard-earned wealth would want to make sure it was well protected. She had dutifully signed the document, pretending she was happy to do so while a tiny alarm bell tinkled in the back of her mind. She'd slammed the door on it, but now the door was swinging wide open and the alarm bell was clanging with a warning.

Be careful.

CHAPTER THREE

VINN DROVE OUT of the hospital car park with his gut clenched around brutal balls of barbed wire. He would have stayed on the ward until his grandfather was out of surgery but he knew it would be many hours, and then even more, before Nonno was out of Recovery.

If he ever got out of Recovery.

He hated hospitals. Hospitals were places people you cared about went in and never came out. He had been young when his mother had come into hospital for routine surgery—four years old—but he'd been old enough to realise something was horribly wrong when the doctor came out to speak to his father. The look on his father's face was something he would never forget. But his father had lied to him, pretended everything was fine and that *Mamma* was coming home when she got better. It was the first of many lies his father had told him over the next few days, until his grandparents had stepped in and insisted he be told the truth.

Where would Vinn be without his grandfather? Nonno had been there for him through thick and thin and each and every one of his father's sins. He had stalwartly stood by Vinn, refusing to allow the shame of his father's behaviour to leave a stain on him.

And then when his father died, two days after Ailsa left, and the distraught family of those poor innocent victims had been baying for blood, Nonno had been steady and supportive, even though his grief at losing his only son must have been devastating. Vinn had mechanically organised his father's funeral and gave a short but respectful eulogy, but he'd done all of it like an automaton. He couldn't remember feeling anything during that time. He'd been blank. Like his motherboard had frozen. People had come up to him at the funeral expressing their condolences and casting their questioning gazes around for Ailsa. He'd made up some excuse for her absence, fully believing at that time she would be back.

But, in a way, his father's death had been a good distraction from Ailsa walking out on him. It meant weeks, almost a month, had passed before he had to face the fact she wasn't coming back. He had assumed she would call him in a couple of days or text him, telling him she didn't mean it, that she was sorry and could they make up. She had often blown off steam like that and, once she got over her little temper tantrum, everything would return to normal.

But it hadn't returned to normal because she hadn't returned.

There had been no phone calls.

No text messages.

Vinn hadn't called her to inform her about his father's death. But then, why would he? She hadn't met his father and even Vinn rarely had much contact with him during their brief marriage. He'd assumed she'd find out from the press coverage, because there had been plenty of that at the time. Although the London tabloids didn't always carry what the Italian ones carried, which was a good thing as far as Vinn was concerned. The less the rest of the world knew about his father's shady dealings and the misery he'd inflicted on others the better.

But none of that mattered now because Ailsa was back and Vinn was going to make sure that when she left the second time around it would be on his terms not hers. He would get her to sign the agreement if it was the last thing he did.

Ailsa was expecting Vinn to take her to a hotel, but when he took the road that led to his villa in the up-market district of Magenta she sent him a questioning look, her insides fluttering and flopping with panic… or maybe it wasn't panic. Maybe it was a feeling of excitement, but she refused to acknowledge it. She had no right getting excited around Vinn. That part of their relationship was over. Dead and buried over. 'I said I'll stay in a hotel, not with you.'

'Don't be ridiculous. What will the press make of that if they see you staying at a hotel now our reconciliation has been announced?' he said. 'It might get back to Nonno. You'll stay with me. It's the most sensible thing to do.'

Sensible? Nothing about being in the same country— the same geological era—with Vinn was sensible—never mind being alone with him in his villa. Not that they would be truly alone since he had a housekeeper and two gardeners. Ailsa had grown up with comfortable wealth—not rich, not poor but somewhere in between. But nothing had prepared her for the wealth Vinn had accumulated.

One of the things she'd enjoyed most about their brief months of marriage was how he'd let her decorate his villa. It had been her project—one of the biggest she'd done—and she'd relished the opportunity to bring the grand old beauty into full glory. Of course, she'd had to deal with the interference of Vinn's grumpy old housekeeper Carlotta, who'd always seemed to take issue with Ailsa over each and every change she'd wanted to bring about. But in the end Ailsa had ignored the old woman's comments and asides and got on with the job. It was her proudest achievement and, while she'd since removed the photos from her website, barely a day went past when she didn't think of the love and hard work she had poured into that beautiful old building.

Had Vinn changed it? Had he stripped every room of her influence? Purged the villa of her? Taken away every trace of her presence in his life? The thought of him undoing all of her work squeezed at her chest like a giant claw.

But then she remembered the one room that had triggered the final breakdown of their relationship.

The room that Vinn thought would make a great nursery. At first she'd thought he was joking, but day after day he kept bringing up the subject to the point where she would childishly plug her ears and walk away. She had planned to decorate the room as a guest-room with en suite bathroom and a lovely reading area near the windows overlooking the garden below. In the end she had left the room untouched.

She had closed the door on it and on their marriage.

'Same old Vinn,' Ailsa said, shooting him a murderous glare. 'Ordering me about as if I'm a child. But aren't you forgetting something? I haven't signed up for this. I'm only here for a day or two, max.'

He released a slow breath as if trying to remain patient. 'Can we just get through the next twenty-four hours without the verbal fisticuffs? I'm not in the mood for it.'

Ailsa remained silent until he pulled up outside the villa. Her chest was tight and her breathing shallow when he helped her out of the car and led her towards the front door. So many memories assailed her. He'd carried her over the threshold the day they returned from their honeymoon. Memories of making love in each room of the house in those first blissfully happy months. Kissing in doorways. Touching, wanting. This house was where they had their first argument…and their last.

Vinn opened the front door and silently gestured for her to enter. Ailsa stepped past him, breathing in the scent of him—the lemon and lime top notes of his aftershave with the base notes of something woodsy, reminding her of a deep, dark secluded forest.

She stepped into the hallway and it was like stepping back in time. Nothing had changed. The colours she had chosen, the furniture and fittings and little touches she had placed about were still there. Was every room still the same?

Ailsa swung her gaze back to his. 'I thought you would've gutted the place after I left. You know, got rid of my handiwork.'

He shrugged. 'Couldn't be bothered, to be frank.'

'Are all the rooms still the same?'

'Why wouldn't they be?' His expression was hard to read. 'I spent a fortune having it redecorated. I wasn't going to let the walk-out of my wife make me waste even more of my money.'

Ailsa could feel herself bristling like a cornered cat. 'I thought it was *our* money. We were married, for God's sake. Anyway, I spent a lot of my own money on this house because, unlike you, I don't have a problem with sharing.'

His eyes became hard, as if they had been coated with an impermeable sheen. 'I wasn't the one who forgot we were married, Ailsa. That was you.'

She blew out a whooshing breath, anger flooding her like a tide. 'Why is everything always *my* fault? What about your role in this? You shifted the goalposts, just like you did today. You overrode my opinions as if I hadn't spoken. You tried to force me to sign that stupid agreement and then you brought me here even though I expressly told you I wanted to go to a hotel. You don't listen, Vinn. You never have. You just do what you damn well want and to hell with anyone else's wishes. That's not how a marriage is supposed to work.'

His features had a boxed-up look about them, as if he was retreating inside himself. Or maybe it was more a case of him locking her out. 'I told you my reasons for bringing you here.'

'Yes, but we didn't discuss it first,' Ailsa said. 'You just got behind the wheel of your car and drove here, not once asking if it was okay with me.'

He rolled his eyes in a God-give-me-patience manner. 'Okay. We'll discuss it now.' He folded his arms and planted his feet as if he was settling in for a century or two. 'Talk to me. Tell me why you want to stay in a hotel.'

Because I don't trust myself around you. Because you're still the sexiest man I've ever met and I can barely keep my hands off you. Ailsa kept her expression masked. 'I prefer my own space. I've got used to it after the last twenty-two months.'

His gaze studied hers as if he was seeing through the lie like a detective saw through a false alibi. Then his gaze went to her mouth and something molten-hot spilled in her belly. 'Really.' He didn't say it as a question but in a tone that was faintly mocking.

Ailsa fussed with a loose strand of her hair, securing it back behind her ear for something to do with her hands in case they took it upon themselves to reach for him. A possibility that terrified her as much as it tempted her. Why was she so...so *weak* around him? It was like her body had no connection with her mind. It was running on autopilot and no amount of self-discipline or self-control had any impact.

'Yes. Really,' she said. 'I haven't missed you at all. Not a bit. In fact, on the contrary, I—hey, what are you doing?'

Vinn suddenly placed his hands on her hips, drawing her close enough for their lower bodies to touch pelvis-to-pelvis, heat-to-heat. Male to female. His eyes locked on hers, the slow burn of his gaze unravelling something tightly knotted in her body. 'You've always been a terrible liar.' One of his hands came up to cradle her face, his thumb moving over her cheek in a lazy caress that sent a frisson of electric awareness through her body. If her self-control had been in serious trouble before, now it was on life support. Nothing could have made her move away even though his hold was light.

No one had held her for the last twenty-two months. No one.

Her skin craved human touch. She ached to be crushed to his body, to feel his warm male skin pressed to hers—to feel his mouth come crashing down to hers with its hot erotic promise. She fought the desire to close her eyes and lean into the hard heat of his tempting body. Need pulsed and pounded in each and every cell of her body, making her aware of every inch of her flesh. Flesh he had touched and teased and tantalised with such thrilling expertise in the past.

'I'm n-not lying.' Ailsa was ashamed her voice betrayed her with its wobble and whisper-softness.

Vinn's half smile switched off the ventilator on her self-control. His fingers splayed through her hair and his mouth came down to within a breath of hers, the sexy mingle of their breaths a heart-stopping reminder of other intimacies they'd shared. Intimacies she craved like an addict did a drug they had long been denied. Vinn was exactly like a drug—potent and powerful and with the unnerving ability to totally consume her.

Ailsa knew she should push him away. Knew it in her mind but her body was offline—it wasn't even in the same Wi-Fi zone. She even got as far as placing her hands on his chest but, instead of pushing, they fisted the front of his shirt until the buttons strained against their buttonholes.

'You think I still *want* you?' she said in a tone that was meant to be scornful but somehow sounded exactly like the cover-up it was.

His gaze flicked to her mouth and back again to her eyes, the pad of his thumb moving against her lower lip in a soft-as-a-puff-of-air motion. 'You want me. I want you. Some things never change.'

Ailsa frowned. 'But you told me before you didn't want to sleep with me. You said our reconciliation would be a hands-off arrangement—or words to that effect.'

He gave a lip shrug as if the prospect of sleeping with her was not much of an issue. Not for him maybe, but for her it was The Issue. 'Why not make the most of what's still between us?'

'There's nothing still between us.' Ailsa tried to pull away but his hold subtly tightened…and a part of her—a part she didn't want to believe existed any more—clapped its hands in glee and cried, *He still wants you!*

Vinn's thumb gently pressed down on the middle of her lower lip—the most sensitive spot where thousands of nerves were already firing off in anticipation for the pressure of his mouth. 'Are you sure about that, *cara*?'

Ailsa knew she had to resist him. She had to stop him kissing her. If he kissed her she was not going to be able to control herself. When had she ever been able to control herself when his mouth connected with hers? But with the tantalising presence of his thumb on her lips, she suddenly found herself parting them and tasting his salty skin with the tip of her tongue as if the connection between her rational brain and her body had been sabotaged. A bomb of lust exploded in his bottomless black gaze. The same explosion went off in her own body, sending flaming-hot darts of longing to sizzle in her core.

One corner of his mouth came up in a sexy slant. 'You really shouldn't have done that.' His deep voice was a silky caress in places that hadn't been caressed in so long Ailsa had almost forgotten what it was to be a woman. Almost.

She knew it was a mistake to moisten her mouth, but there was nothing she could do to stop her tongue sweeping over her lower lip where his thumb had rested. She kept her gaze locked on his. Not that she could have looked away if she'd tried. 'Why not?'

'Because now I have to do this.' And his mouth came down and covered hers.

His mouth was deceptively soft against hers, luring her into a sensual whirlpool in which she knew she could so easily drown. But the feel of his lips moving against hers with such exquisitely gentle pressure left her defenceless, disarmed and desperate for more. She made a sound against his lips—a whimpering, mewling, approving sound that betrayed her as shockingly as if she had shouted, *I want you*.

His tongue glided through her softly parted lips and rediscovered every corner of her mouth in deliciously arousing detail. The taste of him, the feel of him, the sheer maleness of him excited her senses into a madcap frenzy like someone poking at a hive of bees. Sensations buzzed through her flesh, hot prickles of want and cascading shivers of delight, and sweet little stabs of memory as his lips and tongue danced with hers like two ideally suited dancing partners coming together after a long absence.

Ailsa welcomed each stroke and glide of his tongue, relishing the way his breathing quickened and his hold tightened. At least she wasn't the only one who was affected. But it still worried her that one kiss could do this to her—turn her into a breathless, limbless wanton with zero willpower. She linked her arms around his neck and leaned into him, her breasts tingling at the contact with warm, hard male muscles.

Vinn slid his hands down to her hips, holding her against the potent ridge of his erection, his mouth making teasing little nips and nudges against hers.

'Want to do it here or shall we go upstairs?'

His blunt statement was a shot of adrenalin to her comatose willpower. Ailsa unwound her arms from around his neck and stepped back, throwing him a look that would have curdled milk. Long-life milk.

'Do you really think I would subject myself to more of your…your disgusting pawing?'

He made a soft sound of amusement and his eyes

gleamed. 'You started it, *tesoro*. You know how hot I get for you when you use your tongue on me.'

Ailsa remembered all too well. Over the last two years she'd vainly tried to forget the things she had done with him. Wickedly sexy things she had not done with anyone else, or ever wanted to. It made her hate him all the more for being so damn...*special*.

She straightened her shoulders and looked down her nose at him like a haughty Victorian schoolmistress. 'I merely opened my mouth and your thumb was in the way.'

He gave a deep chuckle that made the floor of her belly shiver like an unset jelly. 'You're unbelievable.'

She forced herself to hold his gaze. 'Right back at you, buddy.'

He closed the distance between them and traced a slow pathway from the front of her left ear and along the line of her jaw, sending every nerve under her skin into raptures. His expression went from amused to serious. 'Thank you.'

It was such an unexpected thing for him to say it shocked her into silence for a moment. She looked at him in confusion. 'For?'

His fingertip traced a lazy circle on her cheek, his eyes holding hers captive. 'For making me forget about Nonno for a while.'

Ailsa was a little shocked that she too had forgotten Dom. But hadn't it always been this way between her and Vinn? It was as if no one else existed when they were in each other's arms. 'Is it too early to call the hospital to see how he is?'

'Way too early.' His hand fell away from her face and went to scrape back his hair from his forehead instead. 'It will be hours and hours before we find out anything…' a worried frown flickered across his forehead '…unless, of course, something goes wrong.'

Ailsa put her hand on his forearm. 'Try not to think like that, Vinn. Your grandfather might be frail but they wouldn't have offered the surgery if they didn't think he had a fair chance.'

'He has no chance without it,' he said, releasing a sigh. 'No chance at all.'

She squeezed her fingers around the muscles of his forearm. 'Is there anything I can do?'

His eyes met hers. 'You're doing it by agreeing to come back to me.'

Ailsa dropped her hand from his arm as if it had been scorched. 'I'll stay one night or two maximum. That's all. Just till he gets out of surgery.' *Or doesn't.* She didn't need to say the words out loud because she knew they were both thinking about the very real possibility that Dom wouldn't make it through the surgery. She crossed her arms over her body and glared at Vinn. 'You can't make me stay any longer than that. I haven't signed the agreement and I have commitments back home and—'

'Cancel them.'

'Oh, like you did during our marriage whenever I needed you?' Ailsa injected a stinging dose of sarcasm in her tone.

A brooding frown formed on his forehead. 'I run a large business that involves a lot of responsibility. I can't just take a day off to keep my bored wife amused. I have people relying on me for their incomes.'

'And why was I bored? Because you insisted I move to Milan and forget about my job back in London. I wasn't used to having so much spare time on my hands.'

'But you told me you were unhappy in that job,' Vinn said. 'You were working for someone else who was exploiting you.'

'Yeah, funny that,' Ailsa said with a pert tilt of her brow. 'I seem to attract those sort of people, don't I?'

His mouth flattened to a line of white. 'I did not exploit you. I told you what I was prepared to give you and—'

'And then you went and changed the rules,' Ailsa said. 'You thought you'd get me to pop out a baby or two while you go on with your terribly important career that can't be interrupted under any circumstances.'

'You are the most maddening young woman I've ever met,' Vinn said with a thread of anger running through his voice. 'It's impossible to discuss anything with you without it turning into World War Three. I've made it clear how this is going to work. I need you here for this week at the very least. I realise you have responsibilities back in London so I'll allow you to travel back and forth as needs be—'

'You'll *allow* me?' Ailsa could feel her eyes popping in outrage and her pulse thundering.

'I'm prepared to be reasonable.'

She laughed a mirthless laugh. 'Somehow you and the word *reasonable* don't fit too well together. I'll travel to London whenever I want or need to. I will not be ordered about by you, nor can you kidnap me.'

'Don't tempt me.'

Ditto. He was temptation personified. Putting her anger aside, Ailsa didn't know how she was going to keep her distance, and was privately impressed with herself for how she'd got this far without throwing herself upon him and begging him to make love to her. She blew out a breath and picked up her bag from where she'd left it on the floor.

'I need a cup of tea or something. Do you mind if I make myself one?' It seemed strange to be asking permission to do something in the home she used to call her own, but with the surly presence of his housekeeper Carlotta, no doubt still guarding her territory like a junkyard dog, Ailsa was reluctant to breeze in there as she had in the past. She didn't have the same rights and privileges now…but then, maybe she never had, which was something his housekeeper had made clear whenever she'd had an opportunity. Ailsa had tried to strike up a friendship with his housekeeper because she had felt a little daunted by being so far away from everything familiar. She had secretly hoped Carlotta would be a sort of stand-in mother figure for her since her own mother had never been the nurturing type. But Carlotta hadn't been interested in connecting with Ailsa on any level. The older woman had been cold and dismissive towards any attempts on Ailsa's part to offer to help around the villa. Ailsa had felt unwelcome, a hindrance, an inconvenience. A burden to be borne.

Just like she'd felt back at home with her mother.

Vinn waved a hand in the direction of the kitchen. 'Make yourself at home—you know where everything is. I'm going out for a while. I don't know when I'll be back. But call or text me if you want me.'

That was the whole trouble—Ailsa did want him. She wanted him so badly it was a persistent ache in her flesh. When would she stop wanting him? Would that day ever come? Or had he left his mark on her like a brand? Making her his for ever by the simple fact of making her desire only him and him alone?

'What about Carlotta? Is she going to frogmarch me out of the house as soon as she sees me or have you given her the heads-up?'

His mouth tightened as if he were recalling all the arguments they'd had over his housekeeper's attitude towards her. An attitude he had never witnessed and therefore didn't believe existed. 'She's having the week off.'

'A week off? Wow, wonders will never cease.' Ailsa didn't bother pulling back on the sarcasm. 'I didn't think Carlotta had a life outside this house. She never even had a day off when I was here. Not once.'

He let out a breath that sounded faintly exasperated. 'I hope you're not going to make things difficult for her while you're here.'

'Difficult for *her*?' Ailsa laughed even though she felt like crying at the injustice. 'What about her making things difficult for me? I tried to get close to her and she shut me down like I was a stray dog who'd turned up at the back door looking for scraps.'

'Look, she's an old woman and I don't want—'

'She should've retired by now,' Ailsa said. 'She doesn't even clean the house properly. I was always going around after her, redoing stuff she'd missed, which I'm sure was another reason why she hated me so much. Why do you still employ her when she's obviously past it?'

He let out an impatient-sounding breath. 'She did not hate you.'

'Not while you were around, no,' Ailsa said. 'She saved it for when you weren't there to witness it. How old is she anyway?'

'Seventy-three.'

Ailsa widened her eyes. 'Seventy-three? That's surely a bit old to be still in full-time employment, isn't it?'

'She's been working for my family for a long time.' He paused for a beat and then continued. 'Since before my mother died. They were…close, or as close as a housekeeper and an employer could be.'

Ailsa tried to read his expression but it was like trying to read invisible ink. 'So you keep her on because of her link to your mother?' He had so rarely mentioned his mother in the past. She had tried to draw him out about what he could remember about his mother but she had got the impression he'd been too young when his mother died to remember much at all.

A shadow passed over his gaze but then his mouth became tightly compressed as if he regretted his uncharacteristic disclosure. 'Please—make yourself at home. I'll let you know if there is any news on Nonno.' And with that he turned and left her in the hallway with just the echo of his footsteps for company.

Ailsa made her way to the kitchen, but instead of making herself a cup of tea, she stood and looked out of the windows to the courtyard and garden beyond. The two-lane lap pool sparkled in the warm spring sunshine and, even without opening the French doors, she could almost smell the purple wisteria hanging in a scented arras.

How many other women had Vinn made love to in that pool? How many other women had he made love to under the dappled shade of those trees? Her stomach clenched into a fist of anguish.

How many women had he made love to in the bed he had once shared with her?

She turned away from the window and sighed. Why was she even thinking about things like that? She had been the one to leave their marriage. If Vinn had taken up with other women since, surely that was his prerogative? They had been separated almost two years. Longer than they'd been together. Two years was a long time to be celibate for a man who had been having sex since his teens. *Damn it.* It was a long time for her and she'd only been having sex—the sort of sex that was worth mentioning, that was—while she had been married to Vinn.

Ailsa left the kitchen and made her way upstairs to the master bedroom she had once shared with him. Even as she walked towards it, she knew she was inflicting unbearable torture on herself but she felt compelled to revisit that room, to see if anything had been changed. There were numerous other rooms she could have visited first, but no, her legs were carrying her, step by step, to that room.

She pushed open the door and for a moment just stood there, breathing in the faint scent of Vinn's aftershave that was still lingering in the air. The king-size bed was neatly made and she wondered again who was the last woman to sleep in it with him.

Ailsa swallowed a tight lump as she walked towards the walk-in wardrobe, drawn there like a hapless moth to a deadly flame. *This is going to hurt.* But, even as she mentally said the words, she pulled back the sliding doors…

CHAPTER FOUR

A$_{ILSA}$ $_{STOOD}$ $_{AS}$ still as one of the marble statues in the garden below and stared at the rows and rows of her clothes. At first she thought they might have been someone else's but she recognised the fabrics, the styles, the colours. Things Vinn had bought her, expensive things—things she could never have afforded herself.

She'd stormed out in such a hurry that she hadn't bothered packing, mostly because a secret stubborn part of her had always hoped to come back when Vinn pleaded and begged her to, which of course he hadn't done. She hadn't asked him to return anything to her London address because, once it was clear he wasn't going to fight for her, she'd wanted to put her life with him in Milan behind her. She had wanted no reminders, no triggers for memories that could make her regret her impulsive decision to call time on their marriage.

For she could see now, with the benefit of hindsight, how impulsive it had been. How…how immature to storm out like a tantrum-throwing child instead of trying to work at better communication. Why hadn't she tried harder to understand where Vinn was coming from? If he'd wanted to talk about the possibility of having children then surely she should have been mature enough to have the discussion even if her opinion remained the same. It was becoming apparent to her that his inability to see the flaws in his housekeeper was deeply rooted in his attachment to Carlotta that stretched back to his early childhood. A childhood he had told Ailsa virtually nothing about.

Why hadn't he told her about Carlotta's connection with his mother before?

And why hadn't she made it her business to find out more about his childhood?

Because she hadn't wanted him digging about in her own.

Ailsa trailed her fingers through the silky fabrics on the velvet hangers, releasing a tidal wave of memories as the clothes moved past her fingers. Why hadn't he got rid of them? Why not toss them out in the rubbish or donate them to charity?

Why keep them here, so close to his clothes?

Ailsa slid the doors closed and let out a serrated sigh. How well did she know Vinn? She knew the way he took his coffee and that he absolutely hated tea. She knew what books he liked to read and what movies he liked to watch. She knew he had a ticklish spot at the backs of his knees and that he always slept on the right side of the bed—no exceptions.

But how well did she *know* him?

Was his keeping her clothes a sentimental thing or a tactical thing? What if he wanted her to believe he hadn't given up hope on her returning? What if this very minute she was being masterfully manipulated?

Anger prickled her skin like a rash. Vinn was ruthless—she had always known that about him. He detested failure. He saw it as a weakness, even as a character flaw. He wanted her back for three months to prove what, exactly? That she couldn't resist him?

Ailsa smiled a secret smile.

She would *show* him how well she could resist him.

Vinn paced his Milan office floor like a tiger on a treadmill. He wondered now if he should have stayed back at the villa in case Ailsa did another runner on him. She still hadn't signed the agreement. He might be considered a little ruthless at times but he could hardly force her to sign it. He could offer her more money but he had a feeling it wasn't about the money. It was about her wanting to stand up to him. She could stand up to him all she liked but he didn't want anything to compromise his grandfather's recovery.

He had to have her here with him, otherwise people would suspect it was all a ruse. He wanted his grandfather to believe he and Ailsa were back together. He'd seen the joy on Nonno's face when she'd walked into his hospital room. Vinn hadn't seen his grandfather so animated, so overjoyed since the day Vinn had presented Ailsa to him as his fiancée. His grandfather had always approved of Vinn's choice of bride, which had not surprised him because Ailsa was everything a man could want in a bride: beautiful and smart, accomplished and quick-witted—the downside of that being, of course, she was a little sharp-tongued. His grandfather liked strong women and no one could describe Ailsa as anything but strong.

But Vinn hadn't chosen Ailsa as his bride to gain his grandfather's approval. He had chosen her because he couldn't imagine a time when he wouldn't feel attracted to her. He had never felt such powerful chemistry for a woman before. The sexual energy she triggered in him was shockingly primitive. No one had ever pushed his self-control to the edge the way she did. He wanted her with a fierce, burning ache that pulsed in his loins even now. He had tried for almost two years to rid his brain of the images of her going down on him, the way her lips and tongue could undo him until he was weak-kneed and shuddering. He knew she still wanted him as much as he wanted her. He could feel it in the air when they were in the same room together. It changed the atmosphere. Charged the atmosphere until the air all but crackled with tension.

Vinn couldn't settle to work—not with his grandfather still on the operating table and his almost-ex-wife no doubt searching through the bedroom they'd shared during their marriage. He'd heard Ailsa's footsteps going up the stairs on his way out of the villa and knew it wouldn't take her long to see he had left her things in the wardrobe. It seemed a foolish oversight now that she was back. What would she make of it? Why hadn't he tossed the lot out? Or shipped it to her? *Damn it.* He could have got Carlotta to do it.

But no, he had left things as a reminder of what happened when he let his guard down. What they'd had together was not something he'd had with anyone else and he'd expected it to continue. He'd had great sex before, yes. He'd even enjoyed some great relationships, and had even thought one or two might go the distance, but it wasn't until he'd met Ailsa that he'd realised what he'd been missing. She was feisty and opinionated and while it annoyed him at times, it also thrilled him. Because of his wealth and influence, he was used to people dancing around him—people-pleasers and sycophants all wanting to get on his good side.

But Ailsa wasn't afraid to stand up to him. She seemed to relish the opportunity to not just lock horns with him but to rip his horns off and stomp on them and smile sweetly while she was doing it. He'd always liked that about her. Her drive and determination rivalled his and it secretly impressed him as few others impressed him.

But she had left him and it still rankled. It rankled like the very devil. He couldn't countenance failure. Failure was for people who didn't try hard enough, who didn't work hard enough, who didn't *want* hard enough.

He hated surprises. He was a planner, an organiser, a goal-setter. Things didn't just happen—he *made* them happen. Success didn't come about by pure chance. Opportunity knocked on the door of preparation, and that was why, when Ailsa's younger brother had asked him for sponsorship, Vinn realised he had a chance to turn things around so he was back on the winner's podium.

Blackmail wasn't a word he was comfortable using but he would use it if he had to. He wanted Ailsa back for three months. Back in his house. Back in his life.

And, even more importantly, back in his bed.

He wouldn't have made an issue out of it if he hadn't seen the raw desire on her face, felt it in her body, felt it in her mouth as it was fused to his. She might baulk at signing the agreement but he had other ways to get her to change her mind. Much more satisfying ways.

He smiled and silently congratulated himself. *You've got this nailed.*

Ailsa waited for Vinn to come back that evening but he simply sent a text to say he had an urgent matter to see to and not to wait up. She hadn't realised how much she had been looking forward to another showdown with him until the opportunity for it was taken away. Wasn't he concerned she might leave and fly back to London? She hadn't signed his agreement. Yet. She couldn't get that ten million out of her mind.

She had never been the sort of person motivated by money. She enjoyed the good living she earned and was grateful she hadn't grown up in abject poverty. But the thought of all that money and the good she could do with it was tempting. Not just to build and expand her business but to help others. There must be other children born of rape out in the community. Perhaps she could set up a counselling service or a safe place where they could talk about their issues. She could even offer to pay for her mother to have counselling, something her mother had always shied away from. But if the prohibitive cost of long-term therapy were taken away, perhaps it would help her mother finally heal?

But signing the agreement would mean she would

be back in Vinn's life for three months. He thought he had her cornered. Wasn't that why he'd left her here unaccompanied tonight? He was confident she wouldn't leave. And if it hadn't been for his grandfather still undergoing surgery, she would have left.

Ailsa barely slept that night, not just because she was in one of the spare rooms instead of the bed she used to share with Vinn, but also because she was listening for his return. Every time there was a sound in the house she sprang upright, but each time it was just the villa creaking or a noise outside on the street. She kept glancing at her watch, her anger at him escalating as each hour passed. One o'clock. Two o'clock. Three. Four. Five. Why would he be at work at this hour? Or wasn't he at work? Was he with someone? Someone he had on standby to assuage his needs?

Needs Ailsa used to satisfy.

Her anger turned to hurt. Deep scoring hurt like someone had taken a blistering-hot blade to her belly. She curled up in a ball and rocked against the pain. Why had she allowed herself to get into this situation? Exposing herself to Vinn's power to hurt her like no one else had hurt her?

Somehow she must have slept but when she finally woke up around nine the next morning there was still no sign of Vinn. He texted her at about ten to let her know he was at the hospital with his grandfather. Had he been there all night? She wanted to believe he had been sitting by his grandfather's bed but would that be allowed? Wouldn't it be more likely he'd gone to spend the night with someone? Someone female?

It was later that following night when Ailsa realised she wasn't alone in the villa. She'd been listening out for the return of Vinn's car or the sound of the front door opening and closing, annoyed with herself for being on such tenterhooks. She had lost so much sleep over him and tied herself into such big choking emotional knots, she felt rattled to the core of her being. She was supposed to be over him. He wasn't supposed to have this sort of power over her now.

But when she heard sounds coming from within his study she realised he must have come back without telling her. It infuriated her that he was treating her as if she were a houseguest he had no desire to interact with unless it was absolutely necessary.

Ailsa didn't knock on Vinn's study door but barged right in and stalked over to his desk, where he was sitting. 'How long have you been back? I've been waiting for you since yesterday. Did you not think it would be polite to tell me you'd come back? I thought we had a burglar.'

He leaned back in his chair with a squeaking protest of expensive leather, his expression as inscrutable as a MI5 spy's. 'And what were you going to do if there had been a burglar in my office just now?'

Ailsa hated how he always criticised her impetuosity. So she was a little impulsive? He'd liked that about her in the bedroom. He'd been delighted and dazzled by it. *Stop thinking about you and him in bed.* She decided it was time for a change of subject. 'Why are my clothes still in your wardrobe?'

'I've been waiting for you to come back and collect them.'

She sucked in a breath, trying to contain her temper but it was like trying to stop a pot from boiling over while someone else was deliberately turning up the heat underneath. 'How long were you prepared to keep them?'

He picked up a gold ballpoint pen off his desk and clicked it on and off in a carefully measured sequence of clicks. On. Off. On. Off. 'As long as it took.'

Ailsa refused to back down from the challenge in his dark-as-night gaze. 'I might never have come back.'

Something glinted in the back of his eyes and his pen clicked again, acting as a punctuation mark. 'But you did.'

Ailsa ground her teeth so hard she was sure she would be on liquids for the rest of her life. 'You had no right to keep my things.'

'You didn't ask for them back.'

'That's beside the point.'

His gaze was unwavering on hers. 'Why didn't you?'

'I think you know why.'

'I don't.' Another click-click of the pen. 'Enlighten me.'

Ailsa compressed her lips. 'You bought me all that stuff. They were clothes to fit the role of trophy wife.'

'Are you saying you didn't like them?'

She had liked them too damn much. 'I'm not saying you haven't got good taste, I'm just saying you wanted me to act a role I was no longer prepared to play.'

He dropped the pen and pushed back his chair and

stood, coming around to sit on the corner of his desk right near where she was standing. She was conscious of his long strong legs within touching distance of hers and the way his eyes were almost level with hers because he was seated. She considered moving but didn't want to betray how vulnerable she felt around him. She put her game face on and stared back into his quietly assessing gaze.

'When did you change your mind?'

Ailsa tried to keep her expression under tight control but she could feel her left eyelid flickering. 'About what?'

'About not wanting to be a trophy wife, as you call it.'

She tucked a strand of hair back behind her ear for something to do with her hands. How could she tell him she had never been happy in the first place? That their marriage was not the fairy tale she had longed for since she was a little girl. That she had only accepted his offer of marriage because it made her feel marginally normal. The white dress and veil, the congregation-packed church, the vows, the hymns, the traditions that made her—for a short time at least—forget she was the daughter of a faceless monster. That for the first time in her life she had felt wanted and needed by someone. Someone who could have had anyone but had somehow chosen her. 'We should never have got married. We should have had a fling and left it at that. At least then we could have parted as friends.'

His eyes held hers for a long heart-chugging beat before his gaze went to her mouth. Then he lifted his hand and drew a line from the top of her cheekbone to the centre of her chin, not touching her mouth but close enough for the sensitive nerves in her lips to get all excited in case he did. 'You don't think we could one day be friends, *cara?*'

Ailsa pressed her lips together to stop them from tingling. Her heart was thudding like a couch potato at a fun run and her resolve was nowhere to be seen. 'We've never been friends, Vinn. We were just two people who had sex and got married in a hurry and had more sex.'

His mouth shifted in a rueful manner and he slowly underscored her lower lip with his fingertip, just brushing along her vermillion border, creating a storm of longing in her flesh. His hand fell away from her face and his gaze met hers. 'Perhaps you're right.' He released a short sigh. 'But it was great sex, *sì?*'

Ailsa wished they weren't talking about sex. Talking about sex with Vinn was almost as good as doing it with him. Almost. The way he looked at her with those dark, sexily hooded eyes, the way his body was so close but not close enough, the way his hands kept touching her as if he couldn't help himself. Talking about sex—about *their* lovemaking—made her want him so badly it was like an unbearable itch taking over her entire body. 'Yes, but that doesn't mean I want it now. Or ever. From you, I mean. We're practically divorced and—'

His hands captured both of hers and drew her so close to him she was standing between his muscular thighs. Everything that was female in her started cheering like cheerleaders at a grand final. Her hands were flat against his chest, her breasts pushed so tightly against him she could feel the ridges of his muscles against her nipples. 'You do want it. You want me. That's why you haven't had anyone since me.'

Ailsa made a vain effort to pull away. Well, maybe it was more of a token effort if she were to be perfectly honest. She didn't want to pull away. She wanted to smack her lips on his and rip off all his clothes and get down to business to assuage this treacherous need spiralling through her body. But some small vestige of her pride refused to allow her to capitulate so easily. 'I'm sure you've had dozens since me. How soon did you replace me? A week? Two? Or are we talking days or maybe even hours?'

His hands released her and he set her from him and stood from where he had perched on the corner of the desk. He went back around the other side of the desk as if he were putting a barricade between them. His expression was just as barricaded. 'Until our divorce is finalised, I consider myself still legally married.'

Ailsa looked at him in shock. 'What are you saying? That you haven't had anyone since me? No one at all? But I saw pictures of you in the press with...' She stopped before she betrayed her almost obsessional perusal of the press for any mention of him. She had even gone as far as buying Italian gossip magazines. Ridiculous. And expensive and practically useless since she couldn't read Italian.

'I have a social life, but I've refrained from getting involved with anyone until our divorce is done and dusted. I didn't think it would be fair to bring a new partner into such a complicated situation. Why are you looking so shocked?'

Ailsa tried to rearrange her features into blank impassivity. Tried but failed. 'I just thought you'd…you know…move on quickly.'

He straightened some papers on his desk that, as far as Ailsa could tell, didn't need straightening. His eyes met hers across the desk—dark and glinting and dangerously sexy. 'You mean for a man with my appetite for sex?'

The less she thought about his appetite for sex, the better. It was *her* appetite for sex that was the problem right now. She couldn't get it out of her mind. She couldn't get the ache out of her body. 'I never took you to be a man who'd be celibate for two days let alone almost two years.'

He gave a shrug. 'I've eased the tension in other ways. If nothing else, it's been good for business. All that redirected drive has paid off big time.'

Ailsa couldn't get her head around the fact he hadn't replaced her. Not with anyone. She'd spent the last two years torturing herself with images of him making love with other women, doing all the things he had done with her, saying all the things he had said to her, and yet…he hadn't.

He'd been celibate the whole time.

But why? What did it mean? He had more opportunity than most men to attract another lover. Many other lovers. And since they were officially separated and in the process of divorcing, then why wouldn't he have replaced her with someone else? Few people these days waited until the ink was dry on the divorce papers.

She had been celibate because having sex with someone else had never even crossed her mind. She'd looked at men in passing but mentally compared them to Vinn and found them lacking. No one came even close. No one stirred her senses the way he did. No one made her feel more like a woman than he did.

Ailsa slowly brought her gaze back to his, but somehow the knowledge that he had been celibate for so long only intensified the sexual energy that pulsated between them. She'd been aware of it before. Well aware. But now it was crackling in the air like static electricity. She ran her tongue over her suddenly dry lips, her chest fluttering as if there were a hummingbird trapped in one of her heart valves. Two hummingbirds. Possibly three. 'So…that explains why our kiss in the hallway got a little…heated…'

Vinn came back around from behind his desk and, standing right in front of her, slowly tucked a loose strand of her hair back behind her ear, just as she had done moments earlier. But her fingers brushing against her skin hadn't set her nerves abuzz like his did. Ailsa could feel her body drawn towards him as if he were an industrial-strength magnet and she was a tiny iron filing. 'Three months, *cara*. That's all I want. After that you can have your divorce.'

Ailsa watched his mouth as he spoke, her mind and her body seesawing over whether to accept his terms. If she didn't and left right now she would be divorced from him within weeks and free to move on with her life, leaving him free to move on with his. Isaac would miss out on his chance at a golfing career, but she could only hope that he would find another career. He was young, and who didn't change career a couple of times these days anyway?

But if she accepted the three months arrangement she would be back in Vinn's life.

And even more tempting…back in his bed.

Could she do it? Could she risk three months with him just to get him out of her system once and for all? It wasn't as if she was committing to for ever. He didn't want for ever…or so he said.

Just three months.

She could have all the sex she wanted with him. She could indulge in a red-hot affair that had a time limit on it so she didn't have to feel trapped or worried he would suddenly start talking about making babies. It was risky. It was dangerous. But it was so tempting— especially since she'd found out he hadn't replaced her.

What did that mean?

Ailsa slowly brought her gaze back up to his. 'Why are you doing this?'

He slid a hand under the back of her hair, his fingers splaying through the strands, making her shiver in sensory delight. 'I told you—I want my grandfather to have a stress-free recovery.'

She swallowed back a whimper of pleasure as his fingers started a gentle massage at the nape of her tense-as-a-knotted-rope neck. 'This isn't just about your grandfather. It's about us. About this…this chemistry we have.'

He brought his mouth down to the side of hers, nudging against her lips without taking it further. 'So you feel it too, hmm?'

Ailsa couldn't deny it. Her body was betraying her second by second. She angled her head to give him greater access to her neck, where he was now leaving a blazing trail of fire as his lips moved over her skin, the slight graze of his stubble stirring her senses into a frenzy. Desire slithered in quicksilver streaks to all her secret places. 'I want it to go away.' Her voice was too soft and whispery but she couldn't seem to help it. 'It *has* to go away.'

His mouth came back to just above hers, his breath mingling with hers and making every reason to resist him slink away in defeat. 'Maybe three months together will burn it out of our systems.' He nudged her lips— an invitation to nudge him back.

Ailsa shuddered and slid her arms around his waist and placed her mouth on his, giving herself up to the flame of lust that threatened to consume them both. The heat of his mouth engulfed her, sending her senses spinning out of control. His tongue found hers in an erotic collision that made her inner core instantly contract with need. His lips moved on hers with an almost desperate hunger, as if he had been waiting for years for the chance to feed off her lips. She kissed him back with the same greedy fervour, her tongue darting and dancing with his, her body on fire, her blood racing, her heart giving a good impression of trying to pump its way out of her chest.

Vinn brought one of his hands to the front of her silky blouse, where her breasts were already aching for his touch. He skated his hands over her shape without undoing the buttons and her flesh leapt and peaked at the promise of more of his touch. He tugged her blouse out of her skirt with an almost ruthless disregard for the price she'd paid for it. He slid his hands up her ribcage to just below her breasts, the slightly calloused pads of his fingers sending her into a paroxysm of pleasure.

His mouth continued its magic on hers, drawing from it a response that was just as feverish as his. Their tongues duelled and tangoed in a sexy combat that triggered a tug and release sensation between her thighs. He reached behind her back and deftly unclipped her bra, freeing her breasts to the caress of his hands. Delight rippled through her as he took possession of each breast in his hands, his thumb pads rolling over the budded nipples until she was breathless with need. He brought his mouth down to one breast, licking and stroking her areola with his tongue, sending her senses into raptures before he did the same to the other breast. His stubbly jaw abraded her tender flesh but she welcomed the rough caress, relishing the marks he would no doubt leave on her skin because it would prove that they were really doing this and it wasn't just her imagination playing tricks on her.

'I want you.' His admission was delivered with gruff urgency that made her blood pound all the harder.

Ailsa was beyond speech and began to work at his clothes, not caring that buttons were being popped. She had to get her hands on his body. She had to get her mouth on his hot skin. She had to get her desperate, unbearable desire for him sated.

A phone began to ring but she ignored it, too intent on freeing Vinn's belt from his trousers. But then his hand came down and stalled her, and he reached past her to pick up his phone off his desk. 'Vinn Gagliardi.'

Even the way he said his own name made Ailsa want to swoon, especially with his desire-roughened voice making it sound all the more sexy. He continued the conversation in Italian and she gestured to him to see if it was news from the hospital but he simply shook his head and mouthed the word 'work' and turned slightly away to complete the call.

It made her feel shut out. Put aside. Put on pause, just like all the times in the past when his work took priority. Just like last night. Just like it would always be because she wasn't anything to him other than someone to have sex with when he wanted.

Ailsa did up her bra and tucked her blouse back into her skirt and finger-combed her hair into some semblance of order. She would have excused a call from the hospital, but a work-related call was a stinging reminder of where she stood on his list of priorities. She was a plaything, something he picked up and put down when it suited him. Hadn't it always been that way? She had fooled herself he would one day see her as more than a trophy wife. But he could have married anyone. She was nothing special and never had been.

Ailsa mouthed at him she would be waiting for him upstairs, feeling a glimmer of triumph when she saw the anticipatory gleam in his gaze. But she wasn't going to be upstairs waiting for him like the old days. She was going to leave while she still had the willpower and the sense to do so.

CHAPTER FIVE

AILSA SLIPPED OUT of the villa and once she'd walked a short distance she hailed a cab. 'The airport, thank you,' she said to the driver. She sat back against the seat and rummaged in her tote bag for her phone and her passport. She planned to book a flight on her phone on the way to the airport but when she looked at her screen she saw it was almost out of battery. Why hadn't she thought to charge it? Never mind. At least if she turned it off Vinn wouldn't be able to call her. She knew she should really be calling Isaac to explain and/or apologise about the bitter disappointment he was in for, but she couldn't face it just yet. She had to get a flight booked, which she would have to do once she got to the airport.

She dug deeper in her bag for her passport but she couldn't find it. She upended the bag and its contents spilled out onto the back seat of the taxi. She wanted to scream. She wanted to scream and pummel the seat until the stuffing came out. How could Vinn do this to her? It was virtually kidnap. He'd taken her passport. He'd actually taken it out of her bag without her permission. She had always known him to be ruthless but this was getting ridiculous. Why was he so determined to make her stay with him? Was it just about his grandfather? Or was this about revenge?

'Is everything all right?' the driver asked.

Ailsa pasted a frozen smile on her face. 'Erm, I've changed my mind. I think I'll go to a hotel in the city instead.' She rattled off the first name she could think of, where she and Vinn had once had a drink after seeing a show. She would have no choice but to go back to his villa to demand he give back her passport but she wasn't going back until the morning. She wanted him to spend a sleepless night—like she had last night— worrying about where the hell she was.

It would serve him damn well right.

Vinn had only just got his work colleague off the phone when his phone rang again. His heart jumped when he saw it was the hospital calling. He'd spent the night before at the hospital, sitting in the waiting room, wanting to be on site when his grandfather came out of Theatre. But there had been a complication with the surgery and the operation had gone on well into the night. He had finally left the hospital after speaking to the surgeon, once his grandfather was transferred to Recovery, but he knew it was still way too early to be confident his grandfather was out of danger.

He mentally prepared himself for the worst this phone call might bring. His skin prickled from the top of his scalp to the soles of his feet, dread chugging through his veins at the anticipation of bad news. 'Vinn Gagliardi.'

'Signore Gagliardi, your grandfather is doing as well as can be expected and is now out of Recovery and in ICU. It's still early days but he's stable at the moment. We'll call you as soon as there is any change.'

'*Grazie.*' For a moment it was the only word Vinn could get past the sudden constriction in his throat. Emotions he hadn't visited since he was four years old were banked up there until he could scarcely draw a breath. 'Can I see him?'

'Best to leave it until tomorrow or even the day after,' the doctor said. 'He looks worse than he is and he won't know if you're there or not. We're keeping him on a ventilator for a couple of days to get him through the worst of it.'

Vinn put the phone down once the doctor had rung off. Things had changed a lot from thirty years ago, when relatives were often shielded from the truth out of a misguided sense of compassion. He wanted to know all there was to know about his grandfather's condition. He didn't want to be left in the dark like he had been as a child, expecting his mother to come home, excited at the thought of seeing her again, only to find out she was lying dead and cold in the morgue. Nothing could have prepared him for the shock and heartache, but he still believed if he'd been told earlier he would have handled it better. He hadn't even been given the chance to say goodbye to his mother. He hadn't been allowed to even see her. For years, too many torturous years, he had fooled himself into believing she wasn't actually dead. That she had simply gone away and would one day walk back in the door and reach for him with one of her enveloping perfume-scented hugs.

But of course she hadn't come back. His childish mind had struggled to cope with the enormous loss the only way it could by conjuring up an explanation that was far more palatable than a young mother in her prime going into hospital for routine surgery only to die five days later from complications.

Vinn gave himself a mental shake. He hated thinking about his childhood. The loneliness of it. The sheer agony of it. The sickening realisation that at four years old he was without a reliable parent. His father had never been an involved father so Vinn couldn't excuse him on the basis of his grief. His father had grieved, certainly. But, within a month of the funeral, he had a new mistress, one of many who came and went over the years. Vinn had learned not to show his disapproval or his own ongoing grief for his mother. He'd buried it deep inside, locked it away with all his feelings and vulnerabilities because it was the only way he could cope. His grandfather and grandmother had understood, however. They'd never pressed him to talk about it but he knew they were conscious of his deep inner sadness and made every attempt to make up for his father's shortcomings by always being there as a solid, secure and steady influence in his life.

Vinn was suddenly conscious of the quietness of his villa. Had Ailsa given up on him joining her? He hadn't intended being away as long as he had the night before but he hadn't been able to tear himself away from the hospital until he'd spoken to the surgeon in person. Was she still angry with him for leaving her so long? Wasn't her anger another sign she wanted him as much as he wanted her? He had been longer on the phone than he'd expected. Some smoking-hot sex with her was just what he needed to make himself forget the tragedy of the past. He smiled to himself, picturing her waiting for him, naked in the bed they had once shared. His body thickened at the thought of her silken golden limbs wrapping around him.

He took the stairs two at a time, anticipation making his heart race. But when he opened the master bedroom door, the bed and the room were empty. He swung to the en suite bathroom but it too was empty. He went through each of the spare rooms on that floor, wondering if she had chosen to wait for him in another room.

He went to the spare bedroom furthest from his that she'd apparently slept in the night before and that was when he saw her passport lying almost out of sight next to the bed. Had she dropped it and inadvertently kicked it further out of sight? He picked it up and flicked through the pages. She had been to Italy four times since their separation, but then he already knew that because he had sent her clients to make sure she came back. He'd liked the thought of her returning to the scene of the crime, so to speak. To remind her of everything she had thrown away by walking out on him.

Vinn slipped the passport into his pocket and took out his phone to call her. If she were still in the villa at least he would hear it ringing. He didn't hear it and within seconds it went through to the message service.

Before he could think what to do next a text message came through, but it wasn't from Ailsa. It was from an acquaintance of his who owned a luxury hotel in the centre of Milan, informing him that Ailsa had just checked in for the night. Nico Di Sante had heard the news of their reconciliation in the press the day before and wondered if anything was amiss. Vinn quickly replied, telling him everything was fine and that he would be joining Ailsa shortly, but to keep it a secret as he wanted to surprise her because she thought he was still caught up with work.

Vinn wanted to do more than surprise her. He was going to put the wedding and engagement rings she'd left behind two years ago back on her finger and that was where they would stay until he gave her permission to remove them. She knew the terms. If she didn't sign the agreement her brother's golfing career would be over before it began. He wouldn't sabotage her brother's career as he'd threatened. The boy deserved a chance even if Vinn wouldn't end up being the one to give it to him. Isaac was typical of other lads his age, dreaming of the big time without putting in the hard yards. He liked the boy and thought he had genuine potential but there was no way Vinn was going to get screwed around by Ailsa. Not again. Had he misjudged her love for her brother? Did she hate him more than she loved Isaac?

He didn't care if she hated him or not. A bit of hate never got in the way of good sex. As far as he was concerned, the more hate the better.

And right now he was damn near boiling with it.

* * *

Ailsa lay back in the luxury hotel bath that was as big as a swimming pool and sipped the complimentary champagne that had been delivered to the door a short time ago. It was a frightfully expensive show of defiance. She had never paid so much for a night's accommodation before but she figured it was worth it for one night of freedom before Vinn made her toe the line. Because, of course, she would have to do as he commanded.

Commanded, not asked. *Argh*.

She had thought about it long and hard. She couldn't let Isaac's chance slip away from him. After all, she knew what it felt like to give up on a dream. It hurt. The hurt and disappointment never went away. It sat like a weight in her chest, dragging her spirits down like a battleship's anchor.

You can't have what you want. You can never have what you want.

The words tortured her every time she heard them inside her head. Ailsa topped up her champagne glass. So what if she was getting tipsy and maudlin? So what if she felt sad and lonely and worthless? She was considering whether to have a good old self-pitying cry when the door of the bathroom suddenly opened and Vinn stood framed in the doorway. She gasped and drew her knees up to her chest, her heart knocking against her chest wall like a pendulum in an earthquake. 'How did you find me?'

His gaze raked her partially naked breasts—partially because of the amount of bubble bath she had poured into the water. 'Don't push me too far, *cara*. You know how it will end.'

Ailsa put up her chin and sent him a look as icy as the North Sea in winter. 'You stole my passport.'

'I did not steal your passport.' He took something out of his top pocket and handed it to her. 'I found it on the floor next to the bed in the spare bedroom.'

Ailsa took the passport with a bubble-coated hand and put it to one side on a marble shelf next to the bath. 'I don't believe you.'

He shrugged as if that didn't concern him. 'It's the truth whether you believe it or not.'

Ailsa wasn't sure what to think. She wouldn't put it past him to have taken her passport, but she also knew her tendency to lose things. She was clumsy and careless under stress and being anywhere near Vinn created more stress than she could handle.

He pulled out a folded document from his back pocket and, using one of the glossy magazines she'd brought into the bathroom as a firm backing, he unfolded it before handing her a pen. 'Sign it.'

Ailsa wished she had the courage to push the wretched document into the bathwater. She wanted to make it dissolve until it was nothing but flotsam floating around her. She wanted to take his stupid gold pen and stab him in the eyes with it. But instead she took the pen and, giving him a beady look, signed her name with an exaggerated flourish. 'Happy now?'

He folded the document and put it to one side and then put his hand back in his trouser pocket and took out the ring box she'd left behind two years ago. 'I want you to wear these until the three months is over.' There was something about his voice that warned her she would be wise to put the rings back on her finger without an argument, even though it went against her nature to be told what to do.

She took the rings from the box and slipped them on her finger, shooting him another glare. She didn't want to let him know how much she'd missed wearing those rings. The engagement ring was the most beautiful she had ever seen. He'd had it designed specially for her and, while he had never told her how much it cost, she had a feeling it was more than what most people earned in a lifetime. But it wasn't the ring's value she loved. She would have been happy with a cheap ring if he had given it to her with his love. He started to undo his shirt buttons and she reared back in horror. 'What are you doing?'

'We were interrupted an hour or so ago.' His shirt dropped to the floor and his hands went to the waistband of his trousers. 'I was telling you how much I wanted you, remember?'

Ailsa wished she hadn't drunk so much champagne. Her willpower was never a match for Vinn's charm but with alcohol on board it was as good as useless. 'You were telling me how much you wanted me, yes. But, you might recall, I didn't say it back to you.'

Something tightened in his jaw and a guarded sheen hardened his gaze. 'You didn't have to say it. You were ripping my clothes off, and if it hadn't been for that phone call you'd be onto your second or third orgasm by now.'

Argh! How dare he remind her how many times he could make her come? She affected a scornful laugh.

'You think? I would have had to fake it because I do not want you, Vinn. Do you hear me? I. Do. Not. Want. You.'

He stripped off the rest of his clothes and stepped into the bath, sending a miniature tsunami over her body. 'How many times do you reckon you'll have to say it so you actually believe it, hmm?' There was a dangerously silky edge to his tone and he moved up close, capturing her chin between his finger and thumb.

Ailsa tried to brush off his hold like she was swatting an annoying insect. 'Stop touching me.'

His other hand slipped back under the curtain of her hair and he nudged his nose against hers in a playful bump that made her self-control fall over like a house of cards in a hurricane. 'You want me so bad you're shaking with it.'

'I'm shaking with anger and if you don't get your hands off me this instant I'll show you just how angry,' Ailsa said through gritted teeth.

He gave a deep chuckle and slowly but surely coiled a strand of her damp hair around one of his fingers, inexorably tethering her to him. 'I've missed your temper, *cara*. No one does angry quite as sexily as you. It turns me on.'

His pelvis was close enough for her to feel it—the swollen ridge of his arousal calling out to her feminine core like a primal drumbeat, sending an echo through her blood and through her body. 'No one makes me as angry as you do,' Ailsa said. 'I hate you for it. I hate you period.'

'You don't hate me, *cara*.' He slowly unwound her hair from around his finger. 'If you hated me you wouldn't have come home with me from the hospital yesterday.'

Ailsa wrenched out of his hold with a strength she hadn't known she possessed, sending a wave of bathwater over the edge of the tub. 'I didn't have a flipping choice. You brought me there instead of to a hotel as I requested. It was basically abduction, that's what it was. Then you stole my passport and—'

'You know what your trouble is, *cara*? You don't trust yourself around me. That's why you have to paint me as the bad guy because you can't bear the thought that you're the one with the issue.'

How typical of him to make it seem as if *she* was the problem. It was her self-control that was the problem but that was beside the point. 'You think I can't resist you? Think again. I can and I will.' Dangerous words since his hairy legs were currently nudging hers under the soapy water and everything that was female in her was getting hot and bothered.

His smile was confident. I'll-have-you-eating-those-words-in-no-time confident. 'Come here.'

Ailsa sent him a look that would have withered a cactus. 'Dream on, buddy. The days when you could crook your little finger and I would come running are well and truly over.'

He laughed and moved closer, trailing a fingertip down between her soap-covered breasts. 'Then maybe I'll have to come to you, hmm?'

She suppressed a whimper of pleasure as his finger found her nipple beneath the bubbles. *Why wasn't she moving away?* The slow glide of his finger undid every vertebra on her spine. Only he knew how to dismantle her defences. She could feel her body moistening in preparation, the signal of high arousal. The ache intensified, the need dragging at her, clawing at her, making her desperate in a way that threatened her pride as it had never been threatened before. She tried to think of a way out of the tight corner Vinn had backed her into. How could she satisfy him—*bad choice of word*—without compromising herself? Was there a way she could get Isaac that sponsorship without committing to three months of living with Vinn? 'What if we negotiated the time frame a little?' she said. 'What if I stayed for a week instead of—?'

'One month.'

She gave herself a mental high five. The old Vinn would never negotiate over anything. There was hope after all. 'I was thinking in days rather than—'

He shook his head and sent his finger down her breastbone. 'No deal. One month or nothing. I realise three months is a little long to be away from your business but a month is hardly more than a holiday. And, from what I've heard from Isaac, you haven't had one of those in a while.'

Like you can talk, Mr Workaholic. Ailsa chewed the side of her mouth. One month was better than three and she could catch up on all her Italian clients, giving them the attention they deserved instead of fitting them around her other work. Besides, Vinn's villa was huge. Surely she could keep her distance from him in a house that size? It was a win-win. Well, sort of... 'What have you told Isaac about this...arrangement?'

'I told him the sponsorship would ultimately be up to you.'

Ailsa frowned. 'You told him you were effectively blackmailing me back into your bed?'

'No. I simply told him it was your decision whether I went ahead with the sponsorship.'

'So he'll blame *me* if it doesn't go ahead?'

He gave her an on-off smile that didn't involve his teeth. 'It would be a pity to disappoint him, *sì*?'

Ailsa couldn't refuse. She had no room to refuse. If she refused, her relationship with her brother would end up like her relationship with her mother and stepfather. Damaged. Maybe even destroyed. Isaac would blame her for ever for not being able to follow his dream. It would be *her* fault. Vinn had cleverly orchestrated it so she had no choice but to agree. 'Okay. It's a deal.' She lifted her chin to a combative height. 'But I'm absolutely not sleeping with you.'

His eyes strayed to her mouth as if he couldn't stop himself. 'Who said anything about sleeping?' And then his mouth came crashing down on hers.

It was a kiss she had no way of resisting. No amount of self-control, no amount of anger, no amount of anything was going to be a match for the desire she felt for him. As soon as his lips met hers she was swept up in a maelstrom of lust that threatened to boil the water they were in.

Vinn's hands went to her breasts in a possessive movement that thrilled her as much as it annoyed her. How dare he think she was his for the asking? Not that he'd asked. He'd assumed and he'd assumed right, which was even more annoying. Why did she have no will-power when it came to this man? Why him? What was it about him that made her so weak and needy?

His mouth left hers to suckle on her breasts in a way that lifted every hair on her scalp and sent shivers skating down her spine. No one knew her breasts like he did. No one handled them with such exquisite care and attention. He cradled them as if they were precious and tender, his touch evoking a fevered response from her that had her gasping and mewling like a wanton. His tongue circled her right nipple, rolling and grazing and teasing until she was mindless and limbless. Then he used his teeth in a gentle bite that made an arrow of lust shoot straight to her core. A possessive, you-are-mine-and-only-mine-bite that made her throw herself on his body, desperate for the release only he could give.

His fingers found her folds and within seconds she was flying, careening like an out of control vehicle, her gasps and cries so loud she was almost ashamed of them. She bit down on his shoulder to block the trai-torous sound, vaguely satisfied when he grunted and winced. She wanted him to feel pain. Why should it be just her who suffered for this crazy out of control need?

But within moments that was exactly what he seemed to want, for as soon as her stormy, tumultuous orgasm was over he withdrew and sat back against the edge of the bathtub, his arms draped either side, with a cat-standing-beside-an-empty-canary's-cage smile. 'Good?'

Ailsa glanced at the soapy water surrounding his groin that barely concealed his erection. 'Aren't you going to—?'

'Not right now.' He vaulted out of the bathtub in one effortless movement and reached for one of the fluffy white towels and began roughly drying himself.

Ailsa silently seethed at the way he was demonstrating his superior self-control. He'd made her come but he wasn't going to indulge his own pleasure just to show how he could resist her. *Damn it.* She would show him how hard it was to resist her. She got out of the bath and began drying herself with one of the towels, not roughly as he had done but with slow sensual strokes. She put one foot on the edge of the bath and leaned over to dry between her toes, feeling his eyes devour her derrière. She changed feet and swung her wet hair behind one shoulder and leaned forward again. He was the only man she had ever felt completely comfortable with being naked. She had the same hang-ups most women did about their bodies, but Vinn had always made her feel like a goddess.

She put her foot back down to the floor and turned to face him. 'Would you pass me that body moisturiser over there?'

He picked up a bottle of luxurious honeysuckle-scented creamy lotion. 'This one?'

Ailsa took it from him with a coy smile. 'Want me to rub your back for you?'

His eyes darkened with simmering lust. 'You're playing a dangerous game, *cara*.'

Ailsa squirted some lotion into one of her hands and then put the bottle aside to emulsify the lotion between her hands before smoothing some over her breasts. 'It's really important to moisturise after a hot bath. It keeps your skin supple and smooth.'

His eyes watched every movement of her hands moving over her breasts, the tension in the air at snapping point. When she reached for the bottle of lotion again his hand was already on it. He held her gaze while he poured some out into the middle of his palm. 'Turn around.'

Ailsa turned and shivered when his hand began a slow, sensual stroking motion from the tops of her shoulders to the base of her spine and then even further into the cleavage of her buttocks. Her body clenched tight with need, the sexy glide of his hands in the intimate spaces of her flesh making her forget everything but the desire that throbbed with every single beat of her pulse. He moved his hands to the front of her body, stroking over her breasts and down over her stomach before going lower. She could feel the brush of his body from behind, the hard ridge of his erection against her bottom making her need for him escalating to the point of pain.

He turned her in his arms and looked at her through sexily hooded eyes. 'You know I want you.'

Ailsa moved closer so the jut of his erection was pushed against her belly. 'Make love to me, Vinn.'

He framed her face in his hands, his eyes holding hers. 'That wasn't what you were saying a few minutes ago.'

'I'm saying it now.'

His eyes dipped to her mouth, lingering there for a pulsing moment. Then his mouth came down and covered hers in a searing kiss that inflamed her need like petrol on a fire. He held her body closer, the glide of naked flesh against naked flesh stirring her senses into rapture. Ailsa linked her arms around his neck, stepping on tiptoe so she could feel the proud bulge of his arousal close to where she throbbed the most.

Vinn deepened the kiss, tangling his tongue with hers, making her whimper at the back of her throat. With his mouth still clamped to hers, they moved almost blindly to the bedroom where he laid her down on the bed and came down over her, propping his weight on his forearms with his legs in a sexy tangle with hers.

He lifted his mouth off hers, looking at her with a direct and probing gaze. 'Are you sure about this?'

Ailsa had never felt surer of anything. She would think about the implications of making love with Vinn again later. For now all she could think of was how wonderful it felt to be pinned to the bed with his weight, with his engorged length thick and heavy between her thighs. She traced a fingertip over his bottom lip, her stomach tilting when she encountered his prickly stubble just below. 'I want you. I don't want to want you, but I can't seem to help it.'

He pressed a brief hard kiss to her mouth. 'I feel the same.'

Ailsa moved beneath him, opening her legs to accommodate him, breathing in a quick sharp breath when he entered her swiftly and smoothly. Her body gripped him, welcoming him back with a tight clench of greedy muscles. He began a torturously slow rhythm but she egged him on by clutching him by the buttocks and bringing him closer with each slick thrust. She could feel the pressure building, the tension in her core so intense but unable to finally let go without that extra bit of friction. He slipped a hand between their bodies, finding the swollen heart of her and caressing it with just the right amount of pressure to send her flying over the edge.

The orgasm smashed into her, rolling her over and over and over, sending waves and currents and eddies of pleasure through her body. It was almost too much and she tried to shrink back from it but Vinn wouldn't allow her to do so and kept on caressing her until she was in the middle of another orgasm, even more powerful than the first. She gasped and cried out as the storm broke over her, tossing her every which way like a shaken rag doll. She gained enough consciousness to feel Vinn pump his way through his own powerful orgasm, his guttural groan thrilling her because it made her feel wanted and needed and desired. She knew she could have been anybody, but he hadn't chosen anybody.

He had chosen her.

He hadn't made love with anyone since she'd left. It didn't mean he loved her. It meant he wanted to draw a line under their relationship once it was finally over, but she didn't want to think about that now. She closed her eyes and sighed as his arms gathered her close, just like the old days when she'd fooled herself this was a normal relationship with no secrets and hidden agendas.

Vinn stroked a hand down her thigh. 'I would have used a condom but since neither of us has been with anyone else I thought it'd be okay. I assume you've still got your contraceptive implant?'

Ailsa's stomach pitched. Her implant had been up for

renewal a couple of months ago but she'd put off making an appointment with her doctor. Why had she left it so late to get it changed? She knew exactly why—because she hadn't had sex with anyone.

Because she hadn't been able to even *think* about having sex with anyone other than Vinn.

Would the device still be working? She hoped and prayed…and yet a tiny part of her couldn't help thinking about a baby that looked exactly like Vinn. *No. No. No.* She mustn't think about it. *Must not. Must not. Must not think about it.* Allowing those thoughts into her head made it harder to ignore them the next time.

And there would be a next time.

There had been a lot of them lately. Thoughts. Treacherous thoughts of holding a baby in her arms. She was nearly thirty years old. Her mother had given birth to her at eighteen and to Isaac at twenty-eight. But how could Ailsa think of being a mother to a child?

She pushed those thoughts away and gave Vinn a you-know-me-so-well smile. 'Yep. I sure do.'

He traced a slow circle around her belly button. 'You're the only person I've ever made love to without a condom.'

'Because we were married, right?'

'Not just that…' His eyes went to her mouth for a moment before coming back to her gaze. 'I never felt any other relationship had the potential to work as ours did.'

Ailsa lowered her gaze to concentrate on the dark stubble on his chin. 'It would only have worked if I'd caved in to every one of your commands. I wasn't prepared to do that. I'm still not.'

He brushed the hair back from her forehead with a wistful look on his face. 'Maybe you're right. We should have had a fling and left it at that.'

Ailsa tiptoed her fingertip down from his sternum to his belly button. 'Changed your mind about that back rub?'

His eyes glinted. 'You've talked me into it.' And then his mouth came down and covered hers.

CHAPTER SIX

WHEN AILSA WOKE the next morning back at the villa there was no sign of Vinn. Well, apart from the indentation of his head on the pillow beside her and the little twinges in her intimate muscles, that was. He had taken her back to the villa late last night rather than spending the whole night at the hotel, and made love to her all over again. It made her wonder how she had gone so long without him making love to her. It made her wonder how she would cope once their 'reconciliation' was over.

She had a refreshing shower and, wrapping herself in a fluffy white bath towel, looked balefully at her creased clothes from the day before. There was any number of outfits in the walk-in wardrobe but somehow stepping back into the role of trophy wife—temporary as it was—was a little off-putting. Was she losing herself all over again? Capitulating to Vinn's demands as if she had no will and mind of her own?

But this was about his grandfather more than about her and Vinn. Dom was the one they were doing this for. She was still trying to make up her mind what to do about her clothes when her phone rang from her handbag on the end of the bed. She took it out and saw it was a call from her brother. 'Hi Isaac.'

'Vinn told me you're okay with him sponsoring me,' Isaac said with such excitement in his voice it soothed some of her residual anger at Vinn. Some. Not all. 'I don't know how to thank you. I thought you'd be all dog-in-the-manger about it but he said you were amazing about it. Really amazing.'

'What else did he say about me?'

There was a little silence.

'He said you two were working on a reconciliation. Is it true? Are you back together?'

Ailsa hated lying to her brother but couldn't see any way out of it. If Isaac knew what was really going on he might refuse Vinn's sponsorship. She couldn't allow Isaac's one chance to hit the big time to be overshadowed by how Vinn had orchestrated things. 'It's true but it's only a trial reconciliation. Things might not work out so don't get your hopes up.'

'I'm happy for you, Ailsa. Really happy because you haven't been happy since you left him.'

'You don't have to worry about me, kiddo,' Ailsa said. 'I'm a big girl who can take care of herself.'

'What actually broke you guys up? You've always changed the subject when anyone mentions—'

'I'd rather not talk about it if you don't mind—'

'He didn't cheat on you, did he? I know he was a bit of a playboy before he met you but he wouldn't have married you if he didn't want to settle down.'

Ailsa let out a short sigh. 'No. He didn't cheat on me. We just…disagreed on stuff.'

'Like having kids?'

She was a little shocked at the direct way her brother was speaking. She had never overtly discussed her decision not to have children with him or with her mother and stepfather. It was something she didn't like discussing because it reminded her of why she'd made the decision in the first place. They knew her career was her top priority and she allowed them to think that was her main reason. Her only reason. 'Why would you say that?'

'I just wondered if you've been put off the idea of having kids because of Mum and Dad breaking up.'

Alisa knew the divorce had hit Isaac harder than it had her. She had moved out of home soon after but he had still been at school and had to move between two households for access visits. Their parents had done their best to keep things civil, but Ailsa knew there were times when things had been a little messy emotionally. 'Lots of people come from broken homes these days,' she said, skirting around the issue. 'It's the new normal.'

'So you do want kids?'

'For God's sake, Isaac.' Ailsa laughed but, to her chagrin, it sounded a little fake. 'I'm only twenty-nine. There's still plenty of time yet to decide if I want to go down that track.'

'Remember when you gave away all your childhood toys a few years back? All your dolls and stuff? I wondered why you would do that if you planned to have kids of your own some day.'

'I was doing a clean-up,' Ailsa said. 'All that stuff was taking up too much space at Mum's place after the divorce.'

'That wasn't the only thing,' Isaac said. 'You used to go all goochy-goochy-goo and embarrassing when you saw someone with a pram. Now you look the other way.'

No wonder her brother was an ace golfer. He had eyesight like an eagle's. 'Not every woman is cut out to be a mother. I have my career in any case and—'

'But you'd be a great mum, Ails.' He used his pet name for her, the name he had called her when he'd been too young to pronounce her name properly—except back then he'd had an adorable lisp. 'Sometimes I think you've been better at it than Mum. She's never been all that maternal, especially with you.'

'It's not going to happen,' Ailsa said. 'And certainly not with Vinn.'

'Oh… I didn't realise there were problems. But you can have IVF. It's not like Vinn couldn't afford it.'

'I do not need IVF.' And she could almost guarantee nor did Vinn. 'It's a choice I've made and I would appreciate it if everyone would damn well accept it.'

'Sorry. I didn't mean to upset you. I just wanted to call and say thanks for agreeing to the sponsorship. You have no idea what this means to me. I wouldn't be able to get anywhere near the pro circuit without Vinn's help. Three years all expenses paid. It's a dream offer.'

Ailsa wished she hadn't sounded so…so defensive. 'I'm sorry for biting your head off. I'm just feeling a little emotional right now. Vinn's grandfather is still in ICU and it's—'

'Yeah, he told me about that. It's kind of cool you're there with him, supporting him through such a tough time.'

I'm not here by choice. The words were on the tip of her tongue but she didn't say them out loud. Besides, she had made a choice. She had chosen to accept Vinn's deal and now she had to lie on the bed she had made.

Her only consolation was Vinn had joined her in it.

Vinn had left Ailsa to sleep in because he didn't trust himself not to reach for her again. And again and again and again. The need she awakened in him was ferocious. Ferocious and greedy and out of control, and the one thing he needed right now was to be in control. They could have a one-month fling. It would serve two purposes: get his grandfather through the danger period and draw a final line under Vinn's relationship with Ailsa.

He'd phoned the hospital first thing and the ICU specialist had informed him his grandfather was still stable. It was good news but he didn't feel he could relax until his grandfather was off the ventilator and conscious again and truly out of danger.

Vinn knew Ailsa had only slept with him to prove a point—to prove he couldn't resist her. Which was pretty much true. He couldn't. But in time he would be able to. He would make sure of it. He would have to because their relationship had a time limit on it and he was adamant about enforcing it. He would have liked three months with her because three months would have given his grandfather ample time to recuperate. But he'd agreed to the compromise because three months was a long time for her to be away from her business. In the two years since she'd left him she had built up a successful interior decorating business that had enormous potential for expansion. It was a little unsettling to think she had only achieved that success once she'd left him. He hadn't intended to hold her back career-wise but she had seemed unhappy and unfulfilled in her previous job and he'd thought she would jump at the chance of being his wife, with all the benefits the position entailed.

Their affair had been so intense and passionate and he hadn't wanted to lose her...or at least not like that. He'd thought an offer of marriage would demonstrate his commitment even if he hadn't been in love with her. He had never been in love with anyone. He wasn't sure he had the falling in love gene. Maybe he was more like his father than he realised.

Although, unlike his father, he devoted himself to his work, to the business he had saved and rebuilt out of the ashes his father had left. He was proud of what he had achieved. It had taken guts and sacrifice and discipline to bring it back from the brink but he had done it. He'd owed it to his grandfather to restore the family business built over generations, to undo the damage his father had inflicted. He had built up the Gagliardi name to be something to be proud of again, instead of something of which to be ashamed.

But making love with Ailsa again reminded him of all the reasons why he'd wanted her in the first place. Would a month be enough to get her out of his system?

Or would it only feed the fire still smouldering deep inside him that he had relentlessly, ruthlessly tried to smother with work?

Ailsa came downstairs but was a little miffed to find Vinn had left the villa without speaking to her first. There was a note left on the kitchen bench informing her he had gone to visit his grandfather. Surely he could have walked upstairs to deliver the message in person? Why hadn't he? And why hadn't he taken her with him to the hospital? Wouldn't his grandfather be expecting her to be by Vinn's side? But then she recalled Vinn telling her his grandfather was being kept on a ventilator for a few days until he recovered from the surgery. It appeased her slightly, but still it was a chilling reminder of the charade they were playing. He would only want her 'on task' when his grandfather was awake and conscious.

And, of course, when Vinn had her in his bed. She was annoyed with herself for making love with him so soon. *Damn it.* Why hadn't she kept her distance? It was as if he had the upper hand again. He knew how much she wanted him. He wanted her too, which was some minor consolation, but she would be a fool to think he would always want her. Once their divorce was final he would move on. He would not spend weeks, months, almost two years remembering and missing and aching for every touch, every kiss, every passionate encounter. He wouldn't be curled up lonely in bed, wishing she were back in his arms. He would find someone else to have his babies for him and would not give her another thought, while she would be left with her memories of him and her regrets over what she wanted but couldn't have.

Ailsa had finished making some calls to her assistant Brooke in her studio back in London when she heard the front door of the villa open. But the footsteps sounded nothing like Vinn's firm purposeful stride. She poked her head around the sitting room door to see the elderly housekeeper Carlotta shuffling in carrying some shopping.

'So you're back.' The old woman's tone could hardly be described as welcoming but Ailsa refused to be intimidated.

'Can I help you with those bags?'

Carlotta grudgingly allowed Ailsa to take the bags and carry them to the kitchen. Ailsa placed them on the bench and began unpacking them. 'Why are you here today? Vinn told me you had this week off.'

'How long are you staying?' The housekeeper's gaze was as sharp as her voice.

Ailsa shifted her lips from side to side, wondering if she should try a different tack with Vinn's housekeeper. In the past she had been quick to bite out of hurt, but she wondered now if that had been the wrong approach. 'I'm only staying a month. I presume Vinn told you his plan to keep me here until Dom is out of danger?'

Carlotta made a sound like a snort and glanced at the rings on Ailsa's hand. 'Long enough for you to get your hands on more expensive jewellery, no doubt. I'm surprised you didn't pawn those when you had the chance.'

Ailsa reined in her temper with an effort. 'I didn't

take them with me. I left them in Vinn's bedside drawer. I left everything he gave me behind—but surely you know that?'

Carlotta's expression flickered with puzzlement for a moment but then her features came back to her default position of haughty disapproval. 'Why are you back now if not for money? How much is he paying you?'

Ailsa could feel her cheeks giving her away. 'It's not about the money… It's about Dom's health and my brother's—'

'It was always about the money,' Carlotta said. 'You didn't love him. You've never loved Vinn. You just wanted to be married to a rich and powerful man to bolster your self-esteem.'

Ailsa bit the inside of her mouth to stop herself flinging back a retort. But, in a way, Carlotta had hit the nail on the head with startling accuracy. She had married Vinn for the wrong reasons. She had so wanted to be normal and acceptable, and what better way to prove it than to marry a man everyone looked up to and admired for his drive and focus and wealth? It had certainly helped that she'd found him irresistibly attractive. But she had grown to love him over the short time they were married, which was why she'd been so terrified when he'd brought up the topic of having a family.

How could *she* give him what he most wanted?

'If you cared about him you would have come back when his father died,' Carlotta said.

'I didn't know his father had died until he told me about it the day before yesterday.' Had it only been two days? It shamed Ailsa to think Vinn had managed to lure her back into his bed in little more than forty-eight hours. Had she so little willpower? So little self-respect?

Carlotta gave her a disbelieving look and then made a business of unloading the shopping out of the bags. 'He wasn't close to his father but it brought back a lot of memories for him about when his mother died. And where was his wife when all this was going on? Living it up in London with not even the decency to call him or send a card and flowers.'

Ailsa decided to ignore the dig at her supposed lack of decency in order to pursue the subject of Vinn's mother's death and the impact it had on him. She'd tried to get him to talk about it but he'd always resisted. Should she try again? 'I didn't realise you were close to Vinn's mother. What was she like?'

Carlotta's expression lost some of its tightness. 'She was a wonderful person. Warm and friendly and loving and she loved Vinn so much. Motherhood suited her. Vinn was what she lived for. She should never have married Vinn's father but he was a charming suitor and she was shy and got swept off her feet before she realised what he was truly like.' She gave a heartfelt sigh and folded one of the shopping bags into a neat square. 'Vinn took her death hard, but then what four-year-old wouldn't? He used to be such a happy outgoing child but after his mother was taken from him he changed. Became more serious and hardly ever smiled. It was like he grew up overnight.'

'Her death must have hit you hard too,' Ailsa said.

Carlotta gave a sad twist of her mouth. 'I worked for her as a housekeeper but we became friends. When

Vinn moved in with his grandparents I came too. I've worked on and off for the Gagliardi family for most of my life. In some ways they *are* my family.'

'I can see now why you only wanted the best for Vinn,' Ailsa said, toying with an imaginary crumb on the kitchen bench. 'No wonder you didn't accept me.'

The elderly housekeeper looked at her for a long moment. 'I would have accepted you if I'd thought you loved him.'

'We didn't have that type of relationship,' Ailsa said. 'I know it's hard for you to understand but he didn't love me either so—'

'So you didn't have the courage to love him regardless.' The barb of disapproval was back in the old woman's tone.

Was loving Vinn a courageous or a crazy thing to do? Lusting after him was madness enough. Loving him would be emotional suicide because even if by some remote chance he grew to love her, what would he think of her once he found out she was the child of a ghastly criminal?

After spending the rest of the day reflecting on her conversation with Carlotta, Ailsa decided more could be served by drawing Vinn out about his childhood. She needed to try harder to understand him, to get to know the man he was behind the successful businessman. But she couldn't do that if she was constantly falling into bed with him. Making love with him within forty-eight hours of seeing him after a twenty-two month separation was a pathetic indictment on her part. How had she succumbed so quickly? So readily? Why couldn't she have gone ahead with the charade without sleeping with him, as he'd first proposed?

Like that was ever going to work.

She had to get a grip on her self-control. Sex with Vinn was delightfully distracting but she needed to get to know him better. What motivated him to work so hard? What had made him marry a woman he didn't love when he could have had anyone? What was it about her that made him make such a commitment without love as the motivation?

She knew the more she slept with him the harder it would be to leave when the month was up. She had to keep reminding herself she was in the process of divorcing him. This was not a fairy tale where the handsome prince came riding back into town to claim his princess bride. This was a fake reconciliation in order to reduce the stress on an elderly man during a medical crisis.

Ailsa moved some of her clothes out of the walk-in wardrobe and into the bedroom she'd used the first night, further down the corridor from Vinn's. She was resetting her boundaries, making sure he got the message she wasn't the pushover he thought she was. Did he really think ten million pounds would buy her back into his bed? She'd scratched the itch and now the itch would have to go away. Or if it didn't she would damn well ignore it because it was time she made it absolutely clear to him that he didn't have the same hold over her as he had in the past. If they were going to sleep together then they would have to talk as well. Use not just their bodies but also their minds. To connect in the way they should have done in the first place.

Ailsa came out of the en suite bathroom of the spare bedroom to find Vinn waiting for her.

'Why have you moved your things in here?' He waved a hand towards the pile of clothes on the bed she hadn't yet put away.

She tightened the towel she was wearing around her body. 'Because I think it's best if we keep things on a platonic basis for now.'

'Platonic?' The mockery in his tone was as jarring as the raking look he gave her towel-clad body. 'A bit late for that, don't you think?'

'I shouldn't have slept with you. You caught me in a weak moment. It won't be repeated. We need to talk to each other instead of having sex. Really talk.'

He came to stand in front of her. 'Such a stubborn little thing.' He stroked the upper curves of her breasts showing above the towel. 'You want me and yet you deny yourself because you think it will give me an edge.'

Ailsa wasn't too happy about being so transparent. 'The trouble with you, Vinn, is you're not used to someone saying no to you.'

He smiled a lazy smile and sent his finger on another slow journey, this time to her cleavage, dipping his finger into the space between her breasts. 'You say no with your words but your body says an emphatic yes.'

Ailsa trembled under his touch, the leisurely movement of his finger against the sensitive flesh of her breasts making her nipples tighten and ripples of pleasure flow through the rest of her body. Before she'd met Vinn, her breasts were just breasts. Things that had sprouted on her chest when she was thirteen. Things she put in her bra and checked once a month for lumps. But since his hands and mouth had explored and tasted and tantalised them, she couldn't even look at her breasts without thinking about his dark head bent over them and his wickedly clever lips and tongue and teeth, and the sensual havoc they could do to her.

She glanced at his tanned finger against the creamy whiteness of her cleavage, her breath stalling in her throat and rampant need spiralling through her body. How could her body betray her like this? How could it be so needy and hungry and greedy for his touch? He slid his finger deeper into the valley of her cleavage. Well, *valley* was probably a bit of an exaggeration. But, even though her breasts were on the small side, that had never seemed to matter to Vinn. He made her feel as if she could have been a lingerie model. 'Vinn... I...'

'Don't talk, *cara*.' He brought his mouth to the edge of hers, playing with her lips with his in a teasing come-and-play-with-me nudge. 'Just feel.'

Ailsa was pretty much incapable of speech. Saying no or pretending she didn't want him seemed point-less when her body was on fire and red-hot need was clawing at her insides with rapacious hunger. Had she ever been able to say no to Vinn? 'I'm going to hate myself for this tomorrow,' she said and bumped her lips against his.

'It's just sex.' He gave her lips another nudge and

then followed it up with a bone-melting sweep of his tongue.

Ailsa glanced up into his eyes. 'Is it just sex?'

'What else could it be?' His mouth did another teasing movement against hers, making any thought of resisting him move even further out of her reach.

She braced herself against the surge of lust roaring through her body by placing one of her hands flat against his chest, the other somehow holding her towel in place. 'But why now? It seems so…so out of the blue. We've had zero contact other than through our lawyers for almost two years.'

His stubble grazed her cheek as he shifted position to go back to just below her ear. 'Because I've missed you.'

Ailsa shivered when his tongue found the shell of her ear. *He'd missed her?* Her old friend sarcasm came on duty before any romantic notions could take a foothold. She eased back a little to look at him eye to eye. 'But you knew where I was. There was nothing to stop you coming to see me in London. You didn't even call me or send a text. The only communication I got was through your lawyer a month later, once I'd instigated the divorce.'

His expression became rueful and his hands fell away from her body. He put some distance between them and then he rubbed one of his hands over the back of his neck as if trying to release a knot of tension. 'I had planned to come and see you but then I got caught up with—'

'Work has always been your first priority, hasn't it? And yet you won't allow it to be mine.'

His hand dropped back by his side and his mouth took on a grim line. 'My father died two days after you left.'

Ailsa was shocked into silence. She'd been under the impression Vinn's father had died a few months ago, not within two days of her leaving. She tried to think back to her conversation with Carlotta. Had the housekeeper said when Vinn's father had died? Was that why Carlotta was so convinced Ailsa didn't care about him? Had he been going to contact her and then got caught up in the tragedy of burying his father? When she hadn't heard from him after a week she'd instigated the divorce proceedings with her lawyer, figuring Vinn had had plenty of time to say what needed to be said. She'd taken his silence as his answer and yet now she realised there had been a good reason for that silence.

Remorse, regret, shame at her impetuosity rained down on her like stinging hail. Why hadn't she waited a few more days? Why hadn't *she* contacted him? Pride. Stubborn mulish pride had kept her in London with her phone mostly turned off because she'd wanted him to sweat it out. To miss her. To feel threatened he might lose her.

But *she* had lost him…

Vinn released a rough-edged breath. 'I probably should've contacted you to at least tell you he'd passed away but it was such a hideous time, with that poor family he'd nearly wiped out and his grieving girlfriend's family… I don't know…' He sighed again. 'I just had to get through each day. There wasn't time to think about my own stuff with the police and coroner's investigation and the distraught relatives threatening legal action, not to mention the constant press attention. And then, when I got your lawyer's letter informing me you were demanding a divorce, I figured it was too late to change your mind.'

It hadn't been too late. Ailsa swallowed the words behind a wall of regret. If only she had waited a few more days. A week or two...even a month. Why had she been so insistent on drawing that line in the sand so firmly it cut her off from him completely? But what was the point in admitting how immature and foolish she'd been? Their relationship was beyond salvage because they wanted different things out of life.

'I had no idea your father died so soon after I left... I'm so sorry. It must have been an awful time for you and Dom. I didn't see anything in the press back in London, otherwise I would have—'

'What? Sent flowers?' A note of sarcasm entered his voice. 'Just think—you could've sent two for the price of one. A wreath for my father and another one for the death of our marriage.'

For once, Ailsa refrained from flinging back an equally sarcastic response. She realised, shamefully for the first time, that he used sarcasm as she did. As a shield to keep people from discovering the truth about his emotional state. He might not have been close to his father, but a parent's death was still a huge event in one's life. Sometimes the death of a difficult parent was even trickier to deal with because of the ambiguity of feelings, and the nagging regret that those issues couldn't be resolved once death had placed its final stamp on things.

'I'm really sorry you had such a horrible time dealing with your dad's death and all the other stuff so soon after we…split up. But maybe if you'd contacted me straight away to tell me about your father's accident—'

'You would have come crawling back?' The dark light in his eyes warned her she was flirting with danger. 'You are assuming, of course, that I would've taken you back.'

Ailsa straightened her spine and forced herself to hold his gaze. 'I wouldn't have come back unless you apologised first for being such an arrogant chauvinist.'

'I see no need to apologise for wanting what most people want, and if you're honest with yourself you want it too. You're allowing your parents' divorce to dictate your life. That's crazy. And childish.'

'It's not about my parents' divorce,' Ailsa said. 'Why is it so hard for you to understand I don't want children? When a man says he doesn't want kids no one says anything. But when a woman does, everyone takes it upon themselves to talk her out of her decision as if she's being impossibly selfish.'

'Okay, so if it's not about your parents' divorce then what is it about?' His gaze was so direct she felt like a bug on a corkboard.

'I just told you.'

'You told me you didn't want children, but is it just about the interruption to your career?'

Ailsa shifted her gaze and made a business of securing the towel around her body. 'I'm not maternal. I never have been. My career is the most important thing to me.'

'Isaac once told me you were more of a mother to him than your mother was,' Vinn said. 'He said in many ways you still are.'

Ailsa wondered exactly how chummy her brother and Vinn were these days. But then she realised Isaac had always idolised Vinn from the moment she'd introduced them to each other. Vinn talked to her brother man to man, not man to child or even man to teenager. But how much of their childhood had Isaac shared with him?

'I'm ten years older than Isaac. I was just being a big sister. Mum did her best, but she found being a mother hard, with me especially, but with Isaac too.'

His frown brought his eyebrows together. 'Why you especially?'

Ailsa wished she'd kept her mouth shut but for some strange reason it was becoming more and more tempting to tell him about her background. When she'd first met him she hadn't wanted him to see her as anything other than a normal young woman. As the normal young woman she had been until the age of fifteen when she'd stumbled across the ugly truth. She didn't want to be a freak. She didn't want to be the outcome of a hideous crime. She wanted to be normal. 'I was a difficult, fractious baby who refused to take the breast and slept fitfully. She had trouble bonding with me. And she was young—only eighteen when she had me so it was hard for her.'

'But she still loved you and wanted you.'

She met his frowning gaze. Could she risk telling him the whole truth or would it be safer to give him a cut-down version of it? She was tired of holding this dark secret inside.

Tired and lonely and utterly isolated.

No one but her mother and stepfather knew about the circumstances of her birth but they didn't like talking about it any more than she did. The lie was the elephant in the room quietly rotting in the corner. Wasn't it time to tell Vinn? He'd been her husband, her lover, and in some ways the first person who'd made her feel normal and acceptable. Then there would be one other person she could talk to about the shame that clung to her like grime. It wouldn't change the circumstances of her conception but it would mean she didn't have to keep it a secret from him any longer. It was too late to repair their marriage, mostly because they shouldn't have married in the first place, but surely she owed him the truth before the divorce was made final? 'She didn't want me, Vinn. That was the problem. She never wanted me.'

'Why do you say that? Surely she didn't say that to you?'

Ailsa gave him a tortured smile. 'Some things you don't have to say out loud, especially to kids. I was a mistake. I should never have been born.'

Vinn's expression was full of concern and he came up close to rest his hands on the top of her bare shoulders, his long tanned fingers warm and gentle on her flesh. 'But what about your dad, Michael? Does he make you feel the same as your mother?'

Ailsa knew she had come to a crossroads in her relationship with Vinn. If she took the truth turn, things would never be the same. If she took the white lie turn, things would be the same but different. It was strange because she was dressed in nothing but a fluffy white bath towel and it felt as if the towel symbolised the white lie she was hiding behind. Once she stripped it away she would be naked.

Emotionally naked.

Vinn's hands gave her shoulders an encouraging squeeze. 'Talk to me, *cara*.' His voice was deep and gravelly, making her insides melt.

Ironic he should say that when she'd been the one to insist he talk to her. 'Vinn…' Ailsa sighed and placed her hands on his chest and suppressed a shiver as she felt his warm hard muscles flex beneath her palms, as if her touch shook him to the core as his did to her. 'The thing is… Michael isn't really my father. He's my stepfather.' She took a deep breath and went on. 'I have never met my real father and nor would I ever want to.'

'Why's that?' There was a note of unease in Vinn's tone and a gentling in the way his hands held her.

Ailsa swallowed tightly. 'My mother was raped at a party. She didn't tell anyone about the assault as she blamed herself for getting tipsy. By the time she realised she was pregnant it was too late to do anything about it. She eventually told my stepfather, who was her boyfriend at the time, and he insisted on marrying her and bringing me up as his own.'

Vinn's face was riven with shock but overlying that was concern—rich, dark concern that pulsed in his gaze as it held hers. 'Oh, *cara*… That's so… I don't know what to say. When did you find out? Was it recently? Did they tell you or—?'

'I found out when I was fifteen. They were never going to tell me. They'd made a pact about it.'

A heavy frown carved deep into his forehead. 'You've known since you were *fifteen*?'

Ailsa tried not to be daunted by the slightly accusatory tone of his voice. 'I overheard them arguing about it one day when I came home earlier than expected. My stepfather thought I should be told but Mum didn't. I confronted them about it and my mother reluctantly told me about the assault.'

'But Ailsa, why didn't you tell me?' His voice was hoarse and his hands fell away from her as if he couldn't bear to touch her. 'Why keep something like that from me? Your own husband, for God's sake.'

Ailsa tried to read his expression. Was it anger or disgust that made his eyes so dark and glittery? 'So this is suddenly all about you now, is it?' she said. 'I didn't tell you because I didn't want you to look at me like you're looking at me now. As something disgusting and freakish and ghastly.'

'I am not looking at you like—'

'Do you know what it's like to find out you're the child of rape?' Ailsa said, not giving him time to answer. 'It's disgusting and freakish and ghastly. Every time I look in the mirror I'm reminded of it. I look nothing like my mother, and of course I don't look like my stepfather. The face my mother sees when she sees me is the face of her rapist. A man who has never been charged and is probably out there with a wife and kids of his own by now. How could my mother ever love me? I'm the embodiment of her worst nightmare. She thought she was doing the right thing in keeping me. Michael thought he was doing the right thing by marrying her and bringing me up as his own. But they wouldn't have got married if it hadn't been for me. Their relationship was doomed from the start and it was my fault. No surprise they got a divorce a few months after I found out. I've ruined so many lives.'

'*Cara*...' Vinn took a step towards her, his features still contorted with concern. 'You've done no such thing. You're the innocent victim here. Your mother too, and Michael. What happened was shocking. Even more shocking that justice hasn't been served.'

Ailsa turned away, frightened she might break down in front of him. Over the years she had taught herself not to cry. She vented her distress in other ways—tantrums, anger, sarcasm and put-downs.

She felt him come up behind her, his tall frame like a strong fortress. His hands went to her waist this time, resting there with such exquisite gentleness a ropey knot formed in her throat and she had to swallow furiously a couple of times to clear it.

Vinn rested his chin on the top of her head and cradled her against his body in a supportive embrace that stirred her body into feverish awareness. 'Thank you for telling me. It must have been difficult for you to keep that to yourself all this time.'

Ailsa slowly turned in his arms and somehow her arms were around his waist as if programmed to do so. The way their bodies fitted together felt so natural, so right, like two pieces of a complicated puzzle slotting together. She looked up into his gaze and was surprised to see tenderness. 'You have to promise me something, Vinn. Please don't tell Isaac.'

His frown was back. 'He doesn't know?'

'No, and I don't want him to, nor do my mother or stepfather want him to find out.'

'Is that wise? I mean…keeping this a secret hasn't helped you or your mother or stepfather. In fact, it's made things so much worse.'

Ailsa dropped her arms from around his waist and stepped away. 'Don't make me regret telling you, Vinn. I absolutely insist Isaac doesn't find out. I couldn't bear it if he no longer saw me as his sister. I just couldn't bear it.'

There was a beat or two of silence.

'All right.' His tone was both resigned and reluctant. 'If that's what you insist. But will you tell your mother and Michael I now know?'

Ailsa hadn't thought that far ahead. She chewed at her lower lip, wondering if she'd done the right thing in telling Vinn after all. 'I don't see either of them much these days.' She chanced a glance at him and saw he was frowning again. 'They weren't too happy with me when I announced I was divorcing you. They thought I should've tried harder.'

'I'm the one who should have tried harder, *cara*.' His voice was weighted with regret and his expression rueful.

Ailsa was still thinking of something to say in response when his phone rang from where he'd left it on the bedside table. Vinn moved across to pick it up and, after a brief conversation, the lines of worry etched into his face began to ease. 'Thank you for letting me know. *Ciao*.'

'Was that the hospital?'

Vinn nodded and let out a breath that sounded as if he'd been holding it for years. 'They've removed him from the ventilator. He's conscious and stable for the moment.'

Ailsa let out her own breath she hadn't realised she'd been holding. 'I'm so glad. Do you want to go and see him or is it too early?'

'I'll go in now but you stay here. It's just close relatives allowed at the moment.'

She tried not to feel shut out but how could she not? She wasn't close family any more. Strictly speaking, she was no longer Vinn's wife. She was nothing to him now. Sure, he might desire her but how long would that last? He'd set a time limit on their 'reconciliation'. She was little more than a mistress to him now. Someone to have sex with but not to build a future and a life together.

CHAPTER SEVEN

VINN DROVE LIKE a robot to the hospital to see his grand-father but it was Ailsa on his mind, not the frail old man. How could she have kept the secret of her background from him? Had he known her at all back then? Why had she felt she couldn't tell him something so important about her childhood? It explained so much about her reluctance to discuss having a family. He could only imagine what it must feel like, not knowing who her father was. He knew his all too well and, while deeply ashamed of the things his father had done and having been hurtfully and repeatedly let down by him, Vinn had still loved him.

While on one level he could understand Ailsa keep-ing her dark secret from him, another part was angry she hadn't trusted him with it earlier. There was a war going on inside him—a war between anger and compas-sion. One part of him recognised the trauma it must have been for Ailsa to find out her father was a criminal—a beast who'd taken advantage of her mother in the most despicable way. And yet another part of him felt angry Ailsa hadn't opened up to him. It was ironic but they had shared so much sexually, been adventurous and open about what they liked and didn't like. How could she have shared her body so openly and yet not her heart?

Not that he had any right to sit in judgement. He knew there were things he hadn't shared either. Things that had shaped him, moulded him, changed him. Like losing his mother so unexpectedly and the grief and bone-deep sadness that followed—sadness that still clung to him, haunting him with a lingering feeling of isolation and loneliness. He had learned from an early age to be self-sufficient.

To rely on no one but himself.

Even though his grandparents had been as support-ive as they could, Vinn had still kept a part of himself contained, held back in case they too were snatched away from him.

Finding out about Ailsa's past now, when they were so close to divorcing, deepened his regret. Made it harder to grapple with because he had always blamed her for the breakup. He had given her everything money could buy, spoilt her as most women loved to be spoilt, but she had given nothing of herself but access to her body.

He felt shut out.

Locked out.

Lied to.

He'd made it his business to know every inch of her body. He had prided himself on their sex life—the frequency of it, the power and potency of it. The mon-umental satisfaction of it. But she had kept the most important information about herself from him.

It reminded him of how his father had kept the truth about his mother's death from him. But in the end it had only made things worse. He hadn't been adequately prepared for the blunt shock of the truth. He'd always wondered if his father had gently led him through that time with honesty instead of cowardly lies and cover-ups, he might have coped better with the loss of his mother.

Now he was left floundering again. Shocked. Stunned. Angry that Ailsa hadn't trusted him enough with the truth, as painful and heartbreaking as it was. If he had known earlier he might have been able to rescue their relationship, to tread more carefully over the issue of having a family. But he hadn't had all the information back then because she had wanted his body but not his trust.

Was it too late to come back from this? What did she want from him now?

A divorce. That was what she wanted. She was only with him now under sufferance in order to secure her brother's sponsorship.

He wanted her. That hadn't changed one iota. The desire he felt for her was as strong and powerful as ever—maybe even more so. She'd said she wanted to keep things platonic but he knew she still wanted him as much as he wanted her. He didn't want her to come back at him when the month was up and accuse him of coercing her into having sex with him. He wanted her to come to him because she owned and accepted her need of him. That she was fully engaged in their 'affair' because it was what *she* wanted.

His conscience gave him a prod about the use of the

word *affair*. An affair was temporary, but that was all he was prepared to offer now. Letting anyone, particularly Ailsa, have that much power over him was anathema to him. He was back to being an affair man again. Short-term and satisfying, that was how he'd liked his relationships in the past and he would learn to like them that way again. His relationships would run to his timetable and be conducted on his terms.

And his relationship with Ailsa would be no different.

Ailsa tried to settle with a book until Vinn came back from the hospital, but her mind was whirling and her body still restless, aching for the weight of his arms. She was annoyed with herself for not being able to switch off her desire for him. She felt guilty her restlessness came not from her worry over Dom's condition but for the aching need Vinn had awakened in her body. Every time he touched her it ramped up her desire another notch.

It was strange to admit it, but she knew if they hadn't got talking about his father's death so soon after her leaving him, and her confession about the secret she had been keeping all these years, they would have made love again by now. She had been so close to capitulating. She had resigned herself to another quick scratch of the itch. The itch he alone generated in her flesh.

But then he'd told her about his father's accident. They had actually talked. Not just talked but *communicated*. He had allowed her to see the difficult situation he'd been in back then. The situation she had placed him in with her childish storming off. For almost two years she had seethed with anger at the way he had simply let her walk out of his life. Her anger had sustained her; it had motivated her to get her own business up and running. She had directed all those negative emotions into creating beauty and elegance in her clients' homes. Priding herself on how successful she had become in such a short time, not realising her most valuable clients had come her way via Vinn.

And now she had told him what she had told no one about her background. She had shared with him her pain and shame and he hadn't been revolted by her but rather by the situation. By the crime that was committed and the fact no justice was ever served.

You should have told him two years ago.

Ailsa closed her ears to the nudge of her conscience. She hadn't been ready two years ago. And anyway, they hadn't had that sort of relationship. They had communicated with their bodies but not their hearts and minds. She had allowed herself to be rushed into marriage because their lust for each other had been overwhelming. Vinn's passion for her had taken her by surprise, as had hers for him.

It had been like an explosion the first time they'd made love. Nothing in her experience could have prepared her for it. In the past, sex was something a partner did to her and, while she had sometimes enjoyed the physical closeness, until she'd made love with Vinn, full satisfying pleasure had mostly escaped her. But Vinn's expertise in bed had put an end to her orgasm drought. She'd become aware of her body's potential for pleasure and felt proud of the pleasure she brought to him. She liked to think he hadn't felt such intense pleasure with anyone else, but she knew it was fanciful thinking on her part. As soon as they were officially divorced he would be off with another partner.

It still surprised her he hadn't already done so.

Was it more fanciful thinking to hope he cared for her? That he had in fact loved her and loved her still and wanted her back in his life? If so, why was he insisting it be a temporary affair? She'd convinced him to cut it down to one month instead of three. Surely if he wanted her back permanently he would have said so? He had enough bargaining power with Isaac's sponsorship. He knew she would do just about anything for her younger brother.

But what if this was a plan for revenge? What if Vinn wanted her back long enough to make her fall in love with him all over again? What if his plan was to hurt her pride, the way his pride was hurt when she'd walked out of their marriage? He might feel sorry for the circumstances of her background but she knew him well enough to know that wouldn't be enough to distract him from a goal. If he wanted revenge then what better tool than to have her fall for him, *properly* fall for him?

Not just in lust but in life-changing, long-lasting love.

Vinn sat by his grandfather's bedside in ICU for a couple of hours but, apart from a brief flicker of Nonno's eyelids and a weak grasp of his hand when he'd first arrived, the old man had been sleeping ever since. The transplant team were cautiously optimistic about his grandfather's condition but Vinn couldn't quite quell a lingering sense of impending doom. The hospital sounds scraped at his nerves, bringing back memories he thought he had locked away. Even the squeak of a nurse's shoes along the corridor was enough to get his heart racing and his skin to break out in beads of sweat.

It wasn't that he didn't expect to lose his grandfather at some point. It was normal to outlive both your parents and grandparents, but still... Nonno was the only relative—the only person—Vinn trusted.

The only person he loved.

The only person he *allowed* himself to love.

What about Ailsa?

Vinn frowned at the thought of how he was fooling his grandfather about his relationship with Ailsa. Nonno had always liked her. He admired her spirit and feistiness and the way she stood up to Vinn. The only reason Vinn had orchestrated this charade was because of his grandfather's affection for Ailsa.

It had nothing to do with him—with *his* feelings for her, which right at this point in time were a little confusing, to say the least. For the last twenty-two months he'd been simmering and brooding with anger about the way she'd ended their relationship. He had concentrated on those negative feelings to the point of ignoring the presence of others. Other feelings he had ruthlessly suppressed because allowing himself to love someone exposed him to the potential for hurt.

For loss.

He was fine with the one-month plan. He had cut it down from three because he was not an unreasonable man. He was a business owner himself so he knew the difficulties of running a business at arm's length. One month with Ailsa gave him enough time to get his grandfather out of danger and stable and well enough to cope with the truth about the state of their marriage.

Vinn didn't like thinking beyond the month ahead. But he did know one thing—he would be the one to call time because no way was he going to let Ailsa walk out on him again.

Ailsa was half asleep when she heard Vinn come back from the hospital just after midnight. Keen to find out how his grandfather was doing, she put aside her determination to keep her distance from Vinn and found him standing by the window in his study downstairs. He hadn't even bothered to turn on the lights and was silhouetted by the moonlight.

'Vinn?'

He turned from the window, his features cast in shadow giving him an intimidating air. 'Go back to bed.'

Ailsa stepped further into the room, the floorboards creaking eerily as she moved closer to his tall imposing figure. 'How is your grandfather? Were you able to speak to him?'

'Not really.' He pushed a hand back over his forehead, making his hair even more tousled as if it hadn't been the first time that night he'd done so. 'He was conscious for a bit but heavily dosed up with painkillers so went straight back to sleep.'

She moved closer so she could touch him on the arm. 'Are you okay?'

He gave her a vestige of a smile and a crooked one at that. 'It's tough…seeing him like that. So…so helpless, hovering between life and death.'

'Are the doctors happy with his progress so far?'

Vinn took her hand off his arm and, turning it over, began absently stroking the middle of her palm with his thumb. 'Yes, so far, but who can predict how these things will go? There are risks with any surgery and this is one hell of an operation, especially for a man that age.'

Ailsa began her own absent stroking of his hand, well, maybe it wasn't so absent for she couldn't resist the feel of his skin under her touch—the warmth of it, the way his fingers were so long and tanned compared to hers. 'Carlotta told me a little bit about your mother. How lovely she was and how much she loved you.'

He frowned. 'When did you see her? I thought she was having the week off.'

'She came earlier today when you were out,' Ailsa said. 'She brought in some shopping but she didn't stay long. I got the feeling she wanted to see if I was really back or not.'

'Did you argue with her?'

She tried not to be annoyed by the way he so readily took his housekeeper's side. 'No, not really.'

One of his eyebrows lifted. 'What's that supposed to mean?'

Ailsa blew out a small breath and pulled her hand out of his hold. 'Look, I understand your connection with her and I also understand hers to you. She genuinely cares about you and wants you to be happy. I guess she realises, and did right from the start, that you would not be happy with me in the long-term.'

'Why would she think that?'

'Because… I don't love you.' Ailsa's mouth said the words but her heart wasn't in agreement. Why had it taken her so long to realise the depth of her feelings for him?

Something flickered across his features. 'Did you tell her that?'

'I didn't have to,' Ailsa said. 'She figured it out for herself. She thinks I married you to bolster my self-esteem.'

He took her left hand and ran the pad of his thumb over the setting of diamonds of her engagement ring. 'And is that why you married me, *cara*?' His voice was low and deep and with just the right amount of huski-ness to make her spine loosen.

Ailsa looked into his dark-as-pitch gaze and won-dered that he couldn't see it for himself. That along with her need to boost her self-esteem there had been another reason she had married him. A reason she had denied and disguised because if she admitted, even to herself, that she loved him it would make her decision to remain childless all the more heartbreaking. 'This is why I married you.' She stepped up on tiptoe and pressed her lips to his.

His hands settled on her hips, drawing her closer as he took control of the kiss. His tongue came in search of hers, making her whimper as his body stirred and thickened against hers. His stubble grazed her face as he changed position but she didn't care. She was hungry for his touch. She was aching in every cell of her body for his possession. No one kissed her the way he did. No one made her senses sing the way he did. No one could trigger this torrent of lust the way he did. Her hands went to the buttons of his shirt, tearing at them with careless disregard for their welfare. She wanted him with a fierce need that clawed at her insides. And if the surging potency of him pressing against her was any indication, he wanted her just as badly. Just as ferociously.

Ailsa was only wearing a silky wrap and a slip of a nightgown and soon it was on the floor in a silken puddle at her feet. His ruined shirt joined it and then his trousers and underwear and socks and shoes. Then she was on the floor on her back without any real memory of how she got there as she was so intent on devouring his mouth and clutching at his hard male flesh.

'We should slow down or things will get out of—'

'Don't you dare slow down.' Ailsa dug her hands into the taut muscles of his buttocks and held him to her pulsing need. 'I want you. *Now*.'

He smiled against her mouth and drove into her with a gasp-inducing thrust that made every intimate muscle in her body weep with relief. He set a fast pace but she was with him all the way, panting and clawing and whimpering as the sensations built like a tornado approaching. She could feel the carpet burning the back of her shoulders but she was beyond caring. The need for release was so overwhelming she thought she might die if it didn't come soon.

And then she was there when he added that extra

friction with his fingers against her swollen clitoris. She came with a cry that sounded so primal and wild she could hardly believe it came from her throat. Her body bucked and thrashed beneath his with the force of her orgasm, waves and waves rolling through her. His release came on the tail-end of hers, the sheer power of it reverberating through her flesh, his deep agonised groan as primal-sounding as hers.

Ailsa lay panting on the floor under the press of his now relaxed body, her hands moving up and down his back and shoulders in the quiet of the afterglow. The moonlight shone in from the window, casting their entwined bodies in a ghostly light. It could well have been two years ago after one of their passionate lovemaking sessions…but this time somehow it felt different. She couldn't explain it… Perhaps it was because he knew about her background and the sheer relief of not having to hide that from him any more made her feel freer, less weighted. Less abnormal.

Vinn propped himself up on his arms and looked into her eyes. 'I didn't rush you too much?'

Ailsa gave him a lopsided smile and brushed some tousled strands of his hair back off his face. 'I'm fine apart from some mild carpet burn and stubble rash.'

Concern shadowed his gaze and he moved his weight off her and gently turned her so her back was facing him. He brought his mouth down to both of her shoulder blades in turn, pressing soft soothing kisses to the skin. She couldn't remember a time when he had been so tender, as if she were something precious and fragile and he couldn't bear to hurt her even if inadvertently.

He turned her back over so she was face up and then he softly ran a fingertip over the circle of skin on her chin. 'I keep forgetting how sensitive you are.'

'My skin might be but I'm certainly not.' It was a lie and she was sure he knew it.

His finger circled her still tingling mouth, his gaze thoughtful as it held hers. 'I'm not so sure you're as tough as you make everyone think.'

Ailsa worried he might see more than she wanted him to see, like how she was falling back in love with him. But maybe a part of her had always been in love with him. Now that part was growing, expanding, swelling inside her until there was no room for the hate she had claimed to feel for him.

She averted her gaze from his and focused her attention instead on the dip at the base of his neck between his clavicles, tracing her finger down from there to his sternum. 'Are we going to lie here on the floor all night or go up to bed?'

Vinn tipped up her chin so her gaze had to meet his. 'Which bed are you thinking of occupying? Mine or the spare bedroom?'

Ailsa gave him a rueful twist of her mouth. 'Do I have a choice?'

'That depends.' He brushed her lips with his, once, twice, three times.

She ran her tongue over her tingling lips and tasted his salt. 'On what?'

He wound a strand of her hair around one of his fingertips, his eyes still holding hers with quiet intensity. 'On whether we're talking about my willpower or yours?'

Ailsa sent her fingertip down his abdomen to the hardened length of him, circling him with her fingers, moving the pad of her thumb over the moist tip where his body was signalling its readiness to mate. 'How's yours doing so far?'

His dark eyes glinted. 'It's toast,' he said and his mouth came down on hers.

CHAPTER EIGHT

THE FOLLOWING EVENING on their way back from visiting his grandfather at the hospital, Vinn suggested a night out. 'Just like old times.'

Ailsa wasn't so sure she wanted to go back to the 'old times'. It had been fun going out for dinner at amazing restaurants were they were waited on like royalty and to nightclubs or exclusive bars, but when had they talked to each other on those occasions? She wanted to know more about his mother's death and how it had impacted on him. And even though it intensified her guilt over leaving him the way she had, she wanted to know more about his father's accident and how he'd juggled everything in the aftermath.

She waited until they were seated in one of the restaurants where they'd dined in the past, with drinks in front of them and their meals ordered, before she brought up the subject. 'Vinn... I've been wondering how you managed everything when your father died. Your work, your grandfather's grief. The other accident victims.'

His expression flickered like he was masking deep physical pain. He seemed to waver for a moment, as if he was torn between wanting to change the subject and offloading some of the burden he'd gone through. 'It was difficult…' He paused for a beat. 'Different from when my mother died. I felt guilty about that, actually. That I wasn't grieving for my father the way I had for my mother. I don't miss him even now and yet not a day goes past without me thinking of her.'

Ailsa reached across the table and laid her hand on the top of his, her voice choking up as if it were her own mother she had lost. 'Oh, Vinn. You must have loved her so much and you were so terribly young.'

He turned over her hand and covered it with his. 'Even though I was young, I remember everything about her. Her smile, her hugs, the way she lit up a room when she walked into it.' His fingers began playing with hers. 'When my father injured those other innocent people I couldn't get them out of my mind. The kids, I mean, not just the parents, although that was bad enough. I couldn't bear the thought of those little kids growing up without their mother.'

Ailsa realised yet again how stupid and immature she had been to leave the way she had. Why hadn't she been there for him? Helping him, supporting him through such a harrowing time? 'I can't imagine how dreadful it must have been for you and for them. But they survived, yes?'

'Yes.' His hand briefly squeezed hers. 'I sent them presents at Christmas. I wasn't sure if they'd accept them, given it was my father who nearly destroyed their family, but they seem to like me contacting them. I think it helps them put it behind them. Or at least I hope so.'

'I'm sure it helps enormously,' Ailsa said. 'It shows what a generous and caring person you are.'

He gave a stiff on-off smile and withdrew his hand. 'But it still doesn't change the fact my father almost killed them. But he did kill his girlfriend and no amount of Christmas presents or financial compensation will ever make up for that.'

Ailsa's heart squeezed at the way he carried such a burden of guilt and shame about his father even now. 'You weren't driving that car, Vinn. That was your father. You've done everything you can to help those poor people. So many people in your situation wouldn't have done half of what you've done for them.'

Their meals arrived and the conversation switched to less emotionally charged topics. But after their main meal and dessert was cleared, Vinn reached for her hand and began a gentle stroking of her fingers. 'Have you ever tried to talk to your mother about what happened to her? How it affected her and, consequently, her parenting of you?'

Ailsa began to chew at her lower lip. 'She doesn't like talking about it. Michael wanted her to get counselling but she always refused.' She looked at Vinn's tanned fingers entwined with hers. 'I never understood it as a little kid, but whenever I needed a hug from my mother she would pull away from me. It was as if she couldn't bear to touch me. It hurt so much I taught myself not to need hugs.'

His fingers gave hers a brief squeeze. 'Can you see

it wasn't about you? That it was the trauma she associated with you that was the issue? That you're not personally to blame?'

Ailsa met his gaze. 'I do on an intellectual level but on an emotional level I still feel like that little kid needing a hug from her mum and being pushed away.'

Vinn cradled her hand so tenderly she felt like he was reaching back in time to her as that needy little child, offering her comfort and security. 'Do you think if you talked to your mother about your own issues with having a family it might help you and even her?'

Ailsa gave a non-committal shrug without speaking. What was the point of talking to her mother? It wouldn't change the fact she was the offspring of a criminal. No one could change that. She had to learn to live with it.

Vinn's fingers gently tapped her on the back of the hand as if to bring her out of her private reverie. 'Time to go home, or do you want coffee?'

Ailsa didn't want the evening to end. She had never felt so close to someone as she did right then. Not just a physical closeness, but an emotional closeness where walls had been lowered and screens and masks laid aside. Would this newfound intimacy between them last? What would happen when their month was up? What then? She gave him a tentative smile. 'No coffee for me.'

What I want is you.

Later, when they got home, Vinn reached for her without saying a word. His mouth came down on hers and his arms gathered her close. Their lovemaking was slow but intense, as if he was discovering her body's secrets all over again. There was an element of poignancy to his caresses and touches. They made her feel as if she was so much more than a woman he had wanted to marry because she ticked all the boxes. He made her feel as if she was the only woman he wanted to make love to. He might not love her the way she had grown to love him, but it was enough for her now to be held close enough for their hearts to beat against each other. Close enough for her to feel as if the last two painful years hadn't happened.

Close enough for her to feel as if she had finally come home.

Two weeks later, when Ailsa woke, she was starting to wonder how she would ever return to London and her former life of work, work and more work. Her days had formed a pattern of her sleeping in while Vinn rose early to see to his business commitments, then he would come back for her mid-morning so they could visit his grandfather together.

Dom was now fully awake and out of ICU and in a private room and, while he was still frail, at least he no longer had a jaundiced look about him. She was glad for him and for Vinn, for she could see the bond between them was strong and she couldn't help envying it. She had never felt close to her mother or stepfather and since both sets of grandparents had always lived abroad and two were now deceased, they hadn't been as involved with her and Isaac as much as other grandparents might have been. She was close to Isaac in that she loved him and would do anything for him but he didn't know her as well as he might think. And she didn't want him to. She couldn't bear him finding out she was only his half-sister.

Another thing that had happened over the last few days was an unspoken truce between her and Carlotta. The elderly housekeeper came in the morning soon after Vinn left for his office and only stayed long enough to tidy whatever needed tidying. She didn't cook the evening meal as she used to before as Ailsa had insisted she and Vinn would eat out most evenings and any evening they didn't she would cook. If Carlotta was annoyed to find her services were not required in the same capacity as before, she certainly didn't show it. If anything, Ailsa thought Carlotta was privately pleased she had stepped up to the wifely role she had been resisting two years ago with such vehemence.

She lay back against the pillows on Vinn's bed and sighed. It was increasingly hard to find the strong-willed career girl who had fallen in lust with Vinn. In her place was a mellow version, a woman who was content to listen instead of spout an opinion, a woman who was dangerously close to wanting much more than she could ever have. She tried to console herself that once this month was up she would have ten million reasons to be content and happy with her lot in life. She was so much better off than most people. She had no right to be hankering after the fairy tale when she was not the daughter of royalty but the daughter of darkness.

Ailsa threw the covers off the bed and got to her feet but the room started to spin and she had to sit down again before she fell down. Her stomach had a queasy feeling, a low-grade nausea that was annoying rather than debilitating. She waited for a moment or two before rising tentatively to her feet. *So far so good*. The room had stopped spinning but her stomach was still unsettled. She showered and dressed, deciding she'd better pull herself together before Vinn got back from the office, not wanting to add to his worries about his grandfather.

Carlotta was in the kitchen when Ailsa came down-stairs and narrowed her bird-like gaze when Ailsa came in. 'Are you unwell? You look pale.'

Ailsa put a hand on her stomach. 'It must be some-thing I ate last night when we went out for dinner. Too much rich food.'

Carlotta's expression was difficult to read, which was unusual because usually she had no qualms about showing what she felt, be it disapproval, censure or a grudging acceptance. 'Sit down, Signora Gagliardi,' she said, pulling out a chair. 'I will make you a cup of tea and some dry toast.'

Ailsa sat down but her mind kept tiptoeing around the reason why Carlotta would offer to make her tea and dry toast. There was no way she could be preg-nant. She still had a contraceptive implant in her arm. Yes, it was a little overdue for a change but she hadn't had a normal period since she'd had it implanted so it must still be working. A flutter of panic beat inside her belly and she put a hand over her abdomen in an effort to quell it. It had to be still working.

It *had* to.

Carlotta turned from switching on the kettle and Ailsa wasn't quite quick enough to remove her hand in time to escape the quick flick of the housekeeper's gaze. 'Will you tell him?'

Ailsa swallowed. 'Tell him what?'

'That you're having his *bambino*.'

She choked out a laugh. 'I'm not having his—'

'So it's not his child?'

Ailsa was struck dumb by the housekeeper's insinuation. She suddenly felt close to tears. This couldn't be happening. Not now. Not ever. She couldn't have Vinn's baby. She couldn't allow herself to dream of holding his child in her arms, of being with him permanently. He didn't want her for ever anyway. This was just for now, until his grandfather was well enough to handle the truth.

This was not part of the plan.

Carlotta came over with a steaming cup of tea and set in on the table in front of Ailsa. 'Drink it. The toast will be ready in a minute. Nibble on it slowly until your stomach settles.'

Ailsa wasn't sure if it was the nurturing the housekeeper was dishing out or the stress she was feeling about the possibility of being pregnant that made her emotions suddenly spill over. One sob rose in her throat and another closely followed it, then another and another until she sat with her head in her hands and with her shoulders shaking. 'This can't be happening... I can't do this... I can't have a baby. I just can't.'

Carlotta stroked the top of Ailsa's head with a touch so gentle it made her cry all the more. 'You are lucky to be with child. I would have given anything to have a *bambino* of my own but it wasn't to be. My husband left me because of it.'

Ailsa dragged her face out of her hands to look at the housekeeper's wistful expression. 'I'm sorry you weren't able to have children. I really am. But I've never wanted to have them. My career is too important to me.'

Carlotta brushed the hair back off Ailsa's face like she was a child, her gaze soft and full of wisdom. 'Have you really always not wanted to have children?'

Ailsa gave a shaky sigh and dropped her head back into her hands. 'Not always…but it's complicated and I don't want to talk about it.'

'He'll make a good father,' Carlotta said, still stroking the back of Ailsa's head. 'He won't be reckless and irresponsible like his father. He'll support you and the child—'

'But will he love me?' Ailsa looked up at her again.

Carlotta's expression became sombre. 'He might not say it the way other men would but he cares about you. Why else would he have asked you to come back to him?'

Ailsa got to her feet, holding onto the edge of the table in case she felt another wave of faintness. 'Please, I beg you. Don't tell him about this. I need to make sure first.'

'You're not going to get rid of—?'

'No,' Ailsa said, realising with a jolt it was true. 'No, I can't do that. It might be right for some people and I would never judge them for it, but it's not right for me.'

'But he has the right to know as soon as—'

'I'll cross that bridge if and when I come to it,' Ailsa said. 'This could be a false alarm. I don't want to get his hopes up. It would cause more hurt in the long run.'

Carlotta didn't look too convinced but she agreed to keep silent on the subject. 'Is there anything I can do for you, Signora Gagliardi?'

Ailsa attempted a smile but couldn't quite pull it off. 'Yes, call me Ailsa.'

Carlotta smiled back. 'Ailsa.'

Ailsa went back upstairs but, instead of going back to the master bedroom, she went to the one room she hadn't visited since she'd been back. The door was closed and she hadn't once been tempted to open it but now she held her breath and turned the doorknob and stepped inside. It was exactly the same as the last time she'd walked out of it with her ears stubbornly plugged against Vinn's suggestion they talk about having a family. It was the only room in the villa that was unfinished…incomplete, like an interrupted conversation. She looked at the room with new eyes, not seeing its potential as a reading room but as Vinn had seen it—as a nursery. A nursery for the child she might be carrying.

His child.

She looked at the empty space and in her mind's eye saw a white cradle with a pastel-coloured animal mobile dangling overhead. She saw soft toys—teddy bears and kittens and puppies and cute long-eared rabbits sitting on the shelf above the fireplace, next to a row of picture books and childhood classics. She saw neatly folded baby clothes—most of them handmade—in the chest of drawers.

And in the window…a rocking chair perfect for feeding or settling a baby…

Ailsa drew in a breath that pulled on something deep in her chest and turned and left the room, quietly closing the door behind her.

Vinn was late getting back to the villa to collect Ailsa to visit his grandfather. Work had been piling up while he'd been spending so much time with her and there were a few pressing meetings and some urgent paperwork he'd needed to see to. He was used to spending most of his time at work. Even during their marriage he had prioritised work over his time at home. He was always conscious of how close to losing everything he had been when his father had been convicted of fraud. It was a driving force inside him he had little or no control over. Working hard was in his blood as it was in his grandfather's and his great-grandfather's before him.

When he finally got back to the villa it was closer to lunch than he'd realised. He found Ailsa sitting outside in the garden with a magazine lying across her lap but she was staring into space rather than reading it. She gave a little start of surprise when she heard his footsteps on the flagstones and sprang out of the garden seat but then seemed to stumble and almost fell.

He rushed to stabilise her with a hand on her arm. '*Cara*, what's wrong?'

She squinted against the strong sunlight and leaned on him for support. 'It's hotter out here than I realised...'

It didn't feel hot to Vinn but then he was used to Milan in spring, which on balance was generally much warmer than what she'd be used to in London. 'Sit down for a bit here in the shade.' He guided her back to the garden seat and crouched down in front of her with his hands resting on her knees. 'Feeling better now?'

She gave him a funny little smile and her gaze kept skipping away from his. 'Yep, much better now.'

She certainly didn't look it. She had a waxen look to her features and there were tiny beads of perspiration around her temples. Vinn placed a hand on her forehead to check if she had a temperature but, while she was clammy to touch, she wasn't burning with a fever that he could tell. 'Maybe you shouldn't come with me to visit Nonno today. You must have a virus or something.'

'Okay…'

He stood and held out his hand to help her to her feet. 'Come on, *tesoro*. Let's get you inside and resting. I'll call the doctor to come round and—'

'No!' There was a shrill note of panic in her tone. 'I… I don't need to see a doctor. It's just a bug or…or something…' She bit down on her lip and for a moment he thought she was going to cry.

He put his hands on the tops of her shoulders. 'Are you sure you're okay, *cara*?'

'I just need to lie down for a while…'

Vinn helped her upstairs and got her settled in bed with a long cool drink beside her. 'I won't be long. I'll just check in on Nonno and come back to see how you're feeling.'

'Okay…'

Ailsa waited until she heard the sound of Vinn's car leaving the driveway before she threw off the light bed-covers he had drawn over her moments ago. Sick or not, she had to get her hands on a pregnancy test. Two or more tests. Possibly more. She felt a little guilty ducking out of the villa while he thought she was safely tucked up in bed but what else could she do?

She had to know, one way or the other.

The streets were crowded enough for her to blend in without being recognised…or so she hoped. She'd tied her hair back and pulled on a baseball cap and dressed in tracksuit pants and a T-shirt, making her look as if she was just out for a walk or a trip to the gym. She went into the first pharmacy she came to and bought two test kits, figuring if she bought too many from the one place it might draw too much attention to herself. She was about to walk into another pharmacy when she bumped into a man who was coming out. She mumbled an apology and went to sidestep him but he called her by name.

'Ailsa? I thought it was you hiding under that disguise.'

Ailsa looked up to see one of Vinn's acquaintances, Nico Di Sante, the owner of the hotel she had checked into on her first night in Milan two weeks ago. What quirk of fate had led her to that hotel and now to the very same pharmacy he was using? 'Oh…hi…'

His gaze narrowed. 'Are you okay?'

Ailsa tried to relax her tight features. 'Sure. I'm just trying to get some errands done without being recognised. You know what the paps are like.'

'Sure do.'

She shifted her weight from foot to foot, not wanting to extend their conversation past the greeting stage, but neither did she want to appear rude or draw unnecessary attention to herself. 'Well…it was nice seeing you again.'

'You too, Ailsa,' Nico said. 'Hey, I'm really glad you guys are back together. Vinn's really missed you.' He gave a short laugh. 'Not that he would ever admit it to anyone. He's too proud for that. Stubborn too.'

Ailsa managed a small smile. 'I missed him too.'

'Tell him to bring you in for cocktails in my new bar.' Nico smiled. 'On the house, of course.'

Ailsa stretched her mouth into an answering smile. 'Will do.'

But she had a horrible feeling it might be several months before she would be drinking alcohol again. Was this how her mother had felt, finding out she was pregnant? Feeling dread and shock and anguish instead of joy and excitement? She couldn't help feeling a wave of sadness for her mother. For how isolated and desperate she must have felt, unable to tell anyone what had happened to her and then the double blow of finding out she was pregnant. Her mother had said it had been too late to have a termination but why hadn't she put her up for adoption instead?

Maybe Vinn was right—she should try and talk to her mother. Even if she shut down the conversation, at least Ailsa would have tried instead of letting things go on the way they were for God knew how many more years.

She took out her phone on the walk back to Vinn's villa. She had never felt the need to talk to her mother as she did then and a wave of relief flooded her when she finally picked up on the seventh ring. 'Mum?'

'Ailsa…' Her mother sounded a little distracted and

Ailsa wondered if she had someone with her. A new man in her life perhaps?

'Is this a bad time to call?'

'No, of course not.'

'Mum…can I ask you something?'

'What's wrong? You sound upset. Is everything working out between you and—?'

Ailsa took a steadying breath. 'Why didn't you have me adopted? Did you ever think of—?'

'I did think of it…in the early days, but as the pregnancy went on I felt I couldn't do it.'

'So you…you *wanted* me?'

'I would be lying if I said I was completely happy about being pregnant,' her mother said. 'I wasn't the earth mother type. I wanted children but I probably wouldn't have been miserable without them either. But about six months into the pregnancy I knew I would never be able to let you go to someone else. But why are you asking me this now?'

'Mum, I think I'm pregnant,' Ailsa said. 'I don't know what to do.'

'Have you done a test?'

'Not yet. I just bought one. I just wanted to talk to someone…you, actually.'

'Oh, Ailsa…' Her mother gave a sigh. 'I'm probably not the best person to talk to. I felt so ambivalent about being pregnant with you and I know it's probably affected our relationship but—'

'I know and that's completely understandable,' Ailsa said. 'It must have been awful, so terrifying to know you had to carry a child you didn't want to term.'

'It wasn't just because of the…because of what happened,' her mother said. 'I was the same when I fell pregnant with Isaac. I'm not the nurturing type. I feel ashamed of it but I can't change it. It's hardwired into my personality. But it doesn't mean I don't love you and Isaac. I don't regret going ahead with the pregnancy. It was hard and I was in denial for a long time about how it affected me, but I'm glad I had you. I guess I'm not that good at showing it. But maybe you can help me work on that… I mean, if you'd like to?'

'I would love to,' Ailsa said, suddenly overcome with emotion. 'I'll do the test and let you know the results, okay?'

She ended the call with a bubble of hope expanding in her chest. Hope for a better relationship with her mother, hope for a future with Vinn.

Hope for a child.

Vinn's trip to the hospital to visit his grandfather was cut short because Nonno's specialists were doing a ward round. His grandfather had developed a slight temperature overnight and since Ailsa had some sort of virus, in spite of the thoroughness of the hygiene procedure on entering the ward, he thought it would be best to come back the following day when his grandfather was feeling better. His grandfather seemed more concerned about Ailsa than his own health when Vinn told him.

'Send her my love and tell her I hope she feels better soon,' Nonno said.

'Will do. Take care of yourself. I'll be in tomorrow and Ailsa will too if she's feeling well enough.'

Vinn decided to swing by a local florist on his way home and pick up some flowers for Ailsa. She'd looked so peaky and unwell and he thought a bunch of spring flowers would lift her spirits.

Two weeks had passed and he was becoming more and more conscious of the clock ticking on their relationship. It was way too early to know if his grandfather was out of danger—there were always things that could go wrong and he was still being closely monitored. Vinn wished now he'd insisted on the three months as he'd first proposed. That would have given him ample time to get his grandfather out of hospital and set up in the independent living apartment he'd bought for him so there would be twenty-four-hour medical care on hand.

Could he ask Ailsa to reconsider? They could come to some arrangement if she needed to go back to London for work. He could even go with her as he'd long thought about setting up a UK branch of his furniture business.

His mind started to run with the possibility of postponing the divorce, even taking it off the table altogether. They were a functional couple now. They communicated better than they ever had before and their sex life was as good, if not better, than when they were first married. And now that Ailsa had told him about her background, he realised how wrong it would have been to bring children into their marriage back then. But could he settle for a life without children? Could he take the risk that she might never change her mind?

His grandfather was in the winter of his life and his greatest wish was for a great-grandchild to hold before he died. But it was Vinn's wish too. He wanted to hold his own child in his arms, to share the bond of a child with Ailsa because he couldn't imagine wanting a child with anyone else.

But she doesn't love you.

Vinn shoved the thought aside. What did romantic love have to do with it? That sort of love was fleeting anyway. It often didn't last beyond the honeymoon phase of a relationship. Caring for someone, providing for them, sharing your life with them and creating and raising a family with them required commitment and steadfastness and maturity.

Two years ago, he hadn't understood Ailsa's reluctance to commit to having a family. But he did now and he couldn't see any reason why they couldn't work through it and, even if they didn't end up having kids, at least they would have made that decision together. Their relationship had undergone a change, a remodelling that made him look forward to coming home to her. He might not love her in the Hollywood movie sense but he damn well cared about her and wanted her in his life.

Not just for a month. Not just for three months.

For ever.

CHAPTER NINE

AILSA WAS IN one of the guest bathrooms upstairs when she heard Vinn's footsteps on the stairs. Her heart began to race. She hadn't had time to do the test; she had barely had time to read the instructions. What was he doing home so soon? Normally he stayed a couple of hours at the hospital with his grandfather. She quickly bundled the test back into the paper bag and shoved it into the cupboard under the marble basin.

'Ailsa?' Vinn's knuckles rapped on the bathroom door. 'Are you okay?'

She took a calming breath. 'Yes…j-just finishing up in here.' She flushed the toilet and then turned on the taps in the guise of washing her hands. Her hand crept to her abdomen… She had always been so adamant about not wanting children but she had never been pregnant before, or even suspected she was pregnant.

What if Vinn's DNA was this very minute getting it on with hers? What if a tiny being was being fashioned inside her womb, a tiny embryo that would one day lift up its little chubby arms and call her Mummy?

Ailsa bit her lip so hard she thought she'd break the

skin. It wasn't supposed to happen like this. She'd been fine with her decision not to have kids when she wasn't pregnant. Falling pregnant changed everything.

It changed *her*.

'Ailsa. Open the door.'

Her heart leapt to her throat and pushed out the sob she'd been holding there. 'Go away. I'll be out in a minute.'

'No. I will not go away.' Vinn's voice had a steely edge to it that made her heart thump all the harder.

Ailsa blew out a breath, put on her game face and opened the door. 'What does a girl have to do around here to get a little privacy?'

His concerned gaze ran over her. 'Why have you locked yourself in here? Have you been sick?'

Ailsa found it hard to hold his gaze. How could she tell him before she knew for sure? Or should she tell him? It was a set of scales tipping back and forth inside her head—*Tell him. Don't tell him. Tell him. Don't tell him.* She let go of a breath she hadn't realised she'd been holding. 'I… I went to the pharmacy.'

'I have painkillers here if only you'd asked me to—'

'Not for painkillers.' She took another breath and let it out in a rush. 'For a pregnancy test.'

Shock rippled over his features, but then his eyes lit up and a broad smile broke over his face. 'You're pregnant? Really? But, *tesoro*, that's wonderful. I was on my way home to ask you to call off the divorce so we can start again.'

He wanted to start again? Oh, the irony of his timing. Had he made that decision before or just now when he thought there was a chance she could be pregnant? How could she trust his offer was centred on his feelings for her, not his family-making plans? How could she accept knowing the one thing he wanted was a child, not the mother who came with it—her?

'I haven't done the test yet,' Ailsa said. 'I was about to when you started hammering on the door.'

He took her by the upper arms in a gentle hold, his face still wreathed in a smile. 'Sorry about that, *cara*. I was worried about you. Let's do the test now, shall we? It'll be fun doing it together—finding out at the same moment.'

Ailsa chewed at her lip. 'Don't get too excited, Vinn.'

His fingers tightened on her arms. 'You're not thinking about terminating?'

She pulled out of his hold and rubbed at her arms as if his touch had hurt her. 'Don't be ridiculous. Of course I'm not going to terminate.'

He reached for her again and his hands began a slow stroke of her arms. 'Let's do the test so we know one way or the other.'

Ailsa sighed and, pulling away, walked back to the bathroom where she'd stashed the test kits. He waited outside while she collected the sample of urine and then she opened the door again so he could join her as the test was processed.

'Is that two lines?' Vinn said, standing so close to her she could feel him all but shaking with excitement.

'No, it's too early.' Ailsa could feel her stomach doing cartwheels, her emotions in such turmoil she could barely breathe. It was as if she were holding her destiny in her hands. Two lines would mean she was to become a mother. Two lines that would change her life for ever.

There weren't two lines.

The wand stayed negative.

Ailsa could feel Vinn's disappointment by the way his breath left his body. She could feel her own disappointment coursing through her, making it hard for her to process her emotions. She should be feeling relieved, not disappointed. This was good news...wasn't it?

No. Because the one thing she wanted was a baby. But not with a man who didn't love her, who only wanted her now because she was the one who got away.

She didn't just want a baby. She wanted Vinn to love her the way she loved him. The way she had always loved him. How could she settle for a rerun of their marriage when nothing had changed? Sure, he knew about her past and she knew a bit more about his, but it hadn't made him fall in love with her. He hadn't said anything about loving her.

'Don't worry, *cara*,' Vinn said, winding an arm around her waist. 'We'll keep trying for a baby. It'll happen sooner or later.'

Ailsa moved out of his hold. 'Vinn, stop. Stop planning my future for me without asking me what *I* want.'

His expression flickered and then reset itself to frowning. 'What are you saying? You wanted that baby. I know you did. I could see it in your eyes, damn it, I could feel it in your body. You're as disappointed as me. I know you are.'

She saw no reason to deny it, not even to herself.

The time for denial was over. She had to be clear about what she wanted and not settle for anything less. 'You're right. I do want a baby. But I want to have a baby with a man who loves me more than anything else. You're not that man. You've told me yourself you can never be that man.'

'But we'll be great parents, *cara*,' Vinn said. 'We're great together. So what if neither of us is in love with each other? We want each other, we respect each other. Surely that is something to build on?'

Ailsa let out a frustrated sigh. 'I can't be with a man who refuses to love me. Who fights against it as if it's some sort of deadly virus. I want to be loved for me, Vinn. For *me* with all my faults and foibles.'

'I care about you, Ailsa. You surely don't doubt that?'

'You can't say the words, can you? What is so terrifying about admitting you feel more for me than just caring about my welfare?'

'But I do care about you. I always have—'

She let out a laugh that was borderline hysterical. 'You "care" about me.' She put her fingers up in air quotes. 'What does "care" really mean? I'll tell you what it means. It means you don't love me. It means you won't love me. You're not capable or not willing to love me.'

'But you don't love me either so what's the problem?'

Ailsa shook her head at him, exasperated by his inability to see what was staring him in the face. But she wasn't going to say it. She wasn't going to tell him she loved him only for him to throw that love back in her face. To have him cheapen her love by offering a relationship that was loveless. 'I'm going back to London,

Vinn. Today. I'm sorry if it upsets your grandfather but I'm sure he'll understand I can't do this. I can't be in a marriage like this. I deserve more and so do you.'

Vinn's expression went through various makeovers. First it looked blank, then angry, then shocked and then back to angry again. 'So. You're leaving.' His tone was clipped as if he was making an enormous effort to control himself. 'You do happen to realise what will happen to your brother's sponsorship if you walk out that door?'

'Yes, but I'm hoping you won't punish Isaac because you and I can't be together,' Ailsa said. 'And as to the money you gave me…of course I'll give it back.'

'Keep it.' His lips were so tight it was as if he was spitting out lemon pips instead of words. 'You've earned it.'

'There's no need to be insulting,' Ailsa said, stung by his cruel words. 'But this is exactly why I'm calling it off now before we end up doing even worse to each other. I don't want our divorce to be long and drawn-out and uncivilised. We can be better than that.'

His look was so cutting Ailsa was surprised she didn't end up in little slices on the floor. 'Civilised you say? Then you married the wrong man.'

And, without another word, he turned and left her with just her regrets and heartbreak for company.

Vinn was so furious he wanted to punch a hole in the nearest wall. She was leaving. Again. She had called time on their relationship in the same half hour when he'd seen a glimpse of the future they could have had together.

A future with children.

A family.

The family he wanted more than he wanted success.

But no. She was leaving because she had never intended to come back. He had *made* her come back. Lured her and blackmailed her, hoping it would change her mind, hoping it would make her see how good they were together.

So she wanted to be civilised about their divorce, did she? He wasn't feeling too civilised right now. He felt every emotion he had locked down deep inside was about to explode out of him. Was it his fault he couldn't say the words she wanted to hear? Was it his fault he had taught himself not to feel love in case it was taken away? How could he switch the ability to love back on? The loss of his mother so young had permanently changed him. It had flicked a switch inside him and he could no longer find the control board to switch it back on again. Loving and losing were so inextricably linked inside his head that he couldn't untangle them, no matter how hard he tried.

He had been so looking forward to seeing his grandfather with the news of Ailsa's pregnancy. He had pictured it in his mind, imagining how delighted Nonno would be to hear the news of the baby. But there wasn't going to be a baby. There wasn't even going to be a marriage any more.

He had failed.

He had failed to win her back and he had failed his grandfather.

He would have to give Ailsa the divorce. He had no

choice, the law saw to that. The only consolation was she would have to wait another two years.

He hoped they would be as miserable for her as the last two had been for him.

Ailsa got off the plane in London with a raging temperature and a splitting headache. The bug that had been masquerading as a baby hit her during the flight and she'd curled up in her seat under a blanket and wondered if she had ever felt this miserable.

No. Never. Not even when she'd left Vinn the first time. This was much harder, much more painful because, along with losing Vinn, she'd lost the future she'd longed for. Why couldn't he love her? Was she so awful, so *abnormal* that he couldn't bring himself to love her?

Even as she'd boarded the plane in Milan she'd hoped he would come after her and tell her he'd made a mistake. But he hadn't. She'd stared at the entrance of the boarding gate as she had stared at the wand of that test kit. Wanting something to happen didn't make it happen. It either happened or it didn't.

Vinn didn't love her and she had best get over her disappointment. She'd done it before and she would do it again.

Even if it damn well killed her.

CHAPTER TEN

VINN WAS DREADING telling his grandfather that Ailsa had left him. He even considered not telling him, but that would be doing what his father had done, pretending everything was fine when it wasn't. Pathetic. But in a strange way now he could understand why his father had kept the news of his mother's condition under wraps. It was too painful to face. His father had tried to spare him from pain in the only way he knew how. By pretending. By lying. By hiding the truth until it could be hidden no longer.

But Vinn had to face Ailsa's leaving him just as he'd had to face his mother's death. It was just as permanent for there was nothing he could do to bring her back. Ailsa didn't love him. And all this time he had fooled himself she was the one with more invested in their relationship.

When Vinn went to the hospital the day after Ailsa had left for London, his grandfather still had a temperature and a change of antibiotic had been arranged. He couldn't help feeling concerned at the frailty of his grandfather's appearance. Would the news he was about to break make things worse? How would he be able to live with himself if he sent Nonno over the edge? But how could he live with himself if he kept up the charade?

'Ailsa not coming in today?' Nonno said, glancing past Vinn's shoulders. 'Is she still feeling a little under the weather?'

Vinn pulled the visitor's chair closer to the bed and sat down and slowly released a breath. 'I don't know how to tell you this, Nonno, but she's gone back to London.'

'For work?'

How easy would it be to lie? All he had to say was yes and give his grandfather another day or two of peace before the ugly truth had to be faced. 'Not just for work,' Vinn said. 'The thing is…we weren't really back together.'

His grandfather put his gnarled hand on Vinn's forearm. 'You think I didn't know that?'

Vinn stared at his grandfather. 'You…*knew*?'

Nonno gave a single nod. 'I appreciate what you tried to do. I know you had my best interests at heart. But you have to want her back for you, not me. Because you can't live without her. Because no one else will fill the space she left.'

Vinn's throat was suddenly so constricted it felt as if he'd swallowed one of the pillows off his grandfather's bed. Two pillows. Plus the mattress. Ailsa had left a space so big and achingly empty his chest felt like it was being carved out with a rusty spoon. The inextricable knot was finally loosened inside him. He hadn't been able to say the words but the feelings were there and could no longer be denied or ignored or masqueraded as anything else. His biggest fear hadn't been falling in love. His biggest fear was losing the only person he had loved with all his heart and soul and body. He had to have the courage to own those feelings. To embrace them and express them. 'I love her, Nonno. But I think I've ruined everything. Again.'

'Have you told her you love her?'

Vinn couldn't meet his grandfather's gaze and looked down at the wedding ring on his left hand instead. Why hadn't he taken it off by now? *Because you love her and can't bear the thought of never seeing her again.* He loved her. He loved her so damn much he hadn't been able to move on with his life. He hadn't taken off his wedding ring because taking it off would mean finally letting go of the hope. The hope that their marriage still had a chance. That was why he'd sent those Italian clients to her studio. He'd been unwilling to finally sever the connection. He'd clung to whatever thread he could to keep her in his life.

He brought his gaze back to his grandfather's. 'What if I've poisoned that love? What if it's too late?'

'You won't find out by sitting here talking to me,' Nonno said. 'The person you need to talk to is Ailsa.'

Vinn sprang to his feet. 'You're right. But I hate leaving you while you're still in ICU. That infection is worrying your specialists. What if you—?' He couldn't finish the sentence for the lump of emotion in his throat.

Nonno waved his hand towards the door. 'Go. I'll

be all right. I'm not ready to leave this world yet.' His eyes twinkled. 'I have one more thing to tick off on my bucket list.'

Ailsa got over her virus but her spirits were still so low she could barely drag herself through the day. Forty-eight hours had passed since she'd left Italy and she hadn't heard anything from Vinn. Not that she'd expected him to contact her. Their relationship was over and the sooner she moved on with her life the better. But, even so, every time the studio door opened, her heart would give an extra beat in the hope Vinn might walk through the door.

She'd sent a text to her mother to let her know there wasn't going to be a baby, and told both her mother and stepfather she had left Vinn because she didn't want them reading about it first in the press. Her mother had replied, saying she would come and see her as soon as she could.

It was lunchtime when the bell at the top of the door tinkled again and Ailsa looked up to see her mother and stepfather come in. Normally when her mother said she would drop by it could mean days and days before it actually happened. Was this a sign things were improving in her relationship with her mother? 'Mum? Dad? Why are you both here?'

Her mother spoke first. 'We were worried about you. And sad about your news about Vinn and you calling it quits. Are you okay? Is there anything we can do?'

Ailsa shook her head and sighed. 'No, there's nothing anyone can do.'

Her mother looked anxious and kept darting glances at Ailsa's stepfather. 'We feel so bad about everything. Me particularly. I know I haven't been the best mother to you. I tried but I was so messed-up after... Well, I should have got some help instead of bottling it up. But that's going to change now so—'

'Mum, it's fine, really. You don't have to apologise.'

'But I want to be closer to you,' her mother said. 'Since your father and I divorced... Sorry, I can't help calling Michael your father even though—'

'It's fine, Mum. Michael *is* my father.' Ailsa turned to face him. 'You're the only father I've ever known and ever wanted.'

Michael blinked back tears and reached for Ailsa's mother's hand. 'Thank you, sweetheart. What your mother is trying to say is we're working at some stuff. We're both having counselling.'

Ailsa looked at her parents' joined hands and the light shining in her mother's usually haunted and shadowed eyes. 'What's going on?'

Her mother gave a sheepish smile. 'I feel bad saying this when you're going through a relationship breakup, but your dad and I have realised we're not happy without each other.'

'But you weren't happy together.'

'That was because we weren't being honest with each other,' Michael said. 'We're learning how to do that now. I don't want to lose your mother. I don't want to lose the family we made together.'

Ailsa couldn't believe her ears. 'So you're getting remarried?'

'Maybe,' her mother said. 'We're not making any promises. But for now we're enjoying putting the past aside and moving forward.'

Ailsa hugged both her parents in turn. 'I'm happy for you.'

She just wished she could put the past aside and move forward too.

Ailsa was about to close the studio for the day when she saw Vinn walking towards the front door. Her breath stalled in her throat and her hand on the key in the door fell away and went to her chest, where her heart was threatening to leap out of her chest. He'd left his grandfather back in Milan to come and see her? What did it mean? 'Vinn?'

'Can we talk?' Vinn said.

Ailsa stepped back to let him enter and closed the door behind him. 'Why are you here? Is your grand-father okay? Oh, God…don't tell me something's hap-pened.'

He smiled and reached for her hands, holding them within the cradle of his. 'Something has happened, *cara*. I've finally come to my senses and realised I love you. Can you forgive me for not telling you sooner?'

Ailsa did a rapid blink. 'You love me?'

He gave her hands a gentle squeeze, his dark eyes shining. 'So so much. I can't believe it's taken me this long to admit it. I was too frightened, too cowardly to admit I needed you, that I loved you so much I couldn't bear to take off my wedding ring because it was all I had left of you. That's why I fired Rosa. She told me I was a fool to let the wife I was madly in love with go without a fight. I fired her rather than face up to the truth. And I let you go—twice. Please say you'll forgive me and come back to me.'

Ailsa was crying and laughing at the same time and threw herself against him, winding her arms around his neck. 'I love you too.'

'You do? You really do? Even after all the stupid mistakes I've made?'

She smiled. 'Of course I do. You don't have to say the words to show it, you know.'

He grinned back. 'True, but given how stubborn and blockheaded I am, I think it'd be wise if you did tell me now and again. At least once or twice a day.'

'I love you.' She pressed a kiss to his mouth. 'I love, love, love you.'

'That's a start.' He pressed a kiss to her lips. 'Stay married to me, *cara?* Please? We don't have to live all the time in Milan. I've been thinking about launching a showroom over here. Maybe you could send some clients my way.'

Ailsa grimaced in shame. 'I feel so bad I deliberately directed clients away from your beautiful designs out of spite. And all the while you were sending me clients. You're a much better person than I am.'

He stroked her face with a tender hand. 'You are a wonderful person, *cara.* Don't ever think you're not.'

Ailsa smiled again. 'I've come to some realisations of my own in the last little while. I am much more than my DNA. I might not know who my father is but I know who *I* am and that's all that matters.'

Vinn hugged her close. 'And I love who you are and can't wait to spend the rest of my life proving it to you.'

'I thought you only wanted me because you thought I was pregnant. I wouldn't have left the way I did if I'd known you loved me.'

He gave her a rueful smile. 'I'd actually bought you flowers on my way home that day. I planned to ask you to stay with me. I guess it was a roundabout way of expressing the feelings I hadn't yet admitted to myself.'

Ailsa stroked his jaw. 'We've been such fools wasting so much time. We've been making war instead of making love.'

His dark eyes shone with deep emotion. 'I want you in my life no matter what. Having children is not as important to me as you are. I love you and you'll be more than enough for me.'

Ailsa looked at him through a blurry sheen of tears. 'Oh, Vinn, I do want a baby. I didn't realise how much until I stood with you in that bathroom with that test wand in my hand.'

'You do? Really?' His hands gripped her so tightly it was almost painful. 'But I don't want you just saying that to appease me.'

'I want to make a family with you, darling,' Ailsa said and gave him a twinkling smile. 'How soon can we get started?'

He gave her an answering smile and brought his mouth down to hers. 'Now.'

EPILOGUE

Three months later...

IT WAS THE most unusual way to find out if a pregnancy test was positive or not but Ailsa didn't care. Unusual because instead of just her and Vinn peering at the test wand in the bathroom with expectant breaths held, Vinn's grandfather and Carlotta and Rosa were waiting in the sitting room downstairs for the results. Rosa had come back to work for Vinn and was such an enormous asset to the company that Vinn had been able to step back a little and spend more time with Ailsa and his grandfather.

Ailsa started to well up when she saw the positive lines appear and Vinn's arm around her waist tightened. 'That looks like a positive to me,' he said, grinning at her. 'What do you think?'

She turned in his embrace and linked her arms around his neck, smiling up at him with such joy filling her heart she thought it would burst. 'I think you are going to be the best father in the world. I love you. Do you have any idea how much?'

He pressed a gentle kiss to her mouth. 'I love you too, more than I can ever say, although it has to be said I'm pretty damn good at saying it now, don't you agree?'

'You are.' She kissed his mouth back. 'And I never get tired of hearing you say it.'

Vinn brushed back an imaginary hair from her face, his expression so tender and loving it made her chest expand as if her heart was searching for more room. 'I'm dying to spread the good news to Nonno and Carlotta and Rosa but there's something I have to do first.'

'What's that?'

'This,' he said, and covered her mouth with his.

* * * * *

AN INNOCENT TO TAME THE ITALIAN

TARA PAMMI

For Jen – for talking me up when I'm down, for untangling complicated plots only we could come up with, and for always being there to discuss how much we can push these cranky, arrogant Modern heroes. This book wouldn't have been possible without you.

CHAPTER ONE

"DID YOU FIGURE out why the security breaches keep happening? And how?"

Massimo Brunetti looked up from the three monitors on his desk in the lab that was the hub of his cyber security business. It was a high-security center with thumbprint access only.

A measure he'd taken at the age of sixteen when his father, Silvio, had still been living with them, a matter of self-preservation for Massimo to keep him out. Now, this was his tech center where his servers were stored and where he designed software worth billions.

Only his older half brother, Leonardo, who was currently scrutinizing everything, and their grandmother Greta's stepdaughter, Alessandra, had access. On the condition that they disturb him only at the threat of the building burning down or an equivalent emergency.

Greta wasn't allowed. Her emergency the last time had been an epic tantrum on his thirtieth birthday three months ago. The cause was that Leo and he were going to die childless, leaving the dynastic legacy of the Brunettis to perish with them.

She should know Massimo didn't give a damn about family legacies, especially theirs.

"We have a meeting scheduled for an update in a half hour, Leo," he said, without raising his head. "You know I do not like it when you barge in here."

"You've been locked up in here for the better part of a week." Leo's mouth pinched. "I can't hide it from the board any longer, Massimo. If it gets to the press that BCS had clients' financials open for any little Dark Net hacker to find... *Merda!*"

It would be a disaster of epic proportions.

"It's bad enough we lost that ten-billion-dollar contract," Leo finished.

Massimo rubbed his eyes with the heels of his hands, hoping to alleviate the pulsing prick of pain in his forehead. He *had been* cooped up in here for too long. "It's not my fault if people remember the trail of destruction Silvio left in his wake."

It had taken Leo and him close to fifteen years to restore their family company—a multi-billion-dollar finance giant, Brunetti Finances, Inc.—to its original glory. In fact, it was still a work in progress.

For Greta, it was the family legacy, the name Brunetti synonymous with its prestige. Even now, she could call out half the skyscrapers littered through Milan that had housed the main offices of Brunetti Finances through its two-hundred-year history.

For Leo and him, however, it was the satisfaction of building it up again, bigger and better, a force to be reckoned with, after their father had almost brought it to its knees.

But...for the last six months, more than one contract had fallen through at the last minute. In the first one, they had found that an accountant had leaked their bid details. In the second one, the subcontractor they'd hired had been bought off. Leaving an unholy mess on Leo's hands.

On top of that, there was this security breach Massimo had discovered a week ago in his own brainchild company, Brunetti Cyber Securities.

Someone was clearly targeting their business. The security breach was far too much a direct attack to ignore. If Silvio wasn't being monitored 24/7 at a clinic with no resources at hand and no communications beyond Leo, they would know the culprit was him. Their father, once they had grown taller, bigger and stronger than him, despised being powerless.

"Are you sure Silvio's the only enemy we have?" Leo asked, cocking an eyebrow at his brother. "What about your recent fling? She's certainly making a lot of noise."

"Gisela and I are done. Four months ago now." Massimo let his displeasure show on his face. Leo had no business delving into his personal matters.

"Sì, you and I know that. Does the daughter of the most powerful banking tycoon in Italy know that? *Maledizione*, Massimo, the woman calls *me* now."

The pain behind his eye intensified. If everything hadn't been going so wrong, Massimo would have laughed at his brother's expression.

Leo didn't even give out his number to his own mistress. Who was, very conveniently, a supermodel who had a shot at the end of the world, with an expiry date of two more months, if Massimo's calculations were right. The last one had been a CEO who met his brother once every two weeks for six months. Before that, had been a photojournalist studying migration patterns of an exotic bird species in Antarctica who went into hibernation for about ten months out of a year.

Leo seemed to have the algorithm for the best kind of mistress all figured out—distance, just as ruthless as him and ambitious. All his relationships ended on amicable footings, too.

It wasn't that Massimo wanted a cold and clinical relationship like that. He just didn't have the time or the energy for a deeper one. And he wouldn't for the next twenty years at least. He doubted he knew what deep, meaningful relationships looked like, anyway. His mother and Silvio—it had been a war. Fought by her, for his sake.

"You need to do whatever is needed to make her understand," Leo added. "Do not antagonize her father in the process."

Massimo hated when Leonardo was right. "I'll take care of it."

It had been a stupid move tangling with the selfish, spoiled socialite Gisela Fiore. But after the months he'd spent designing his latest product—an e-commerce tool and its subsequent release hitting ten billion in revenue—he'd needed to play. Hard.

Which Gisela excelled at, according to her reputation. The *only* thing she excelled at. A torrid two-week affair had ensued. At the end of which, Massimo had been itching to get back to work. As was *his* reputation.

Except Gisela was still sending him alarmingly disturbing texts full of threats followed by sobbing messages. When she wasn't camping outside the Brunetti brothers' office building.

"Do you want to hear about the hacker or not?" he challenged Leo.

"Please."

"I found the trail last night. I also figured out how he gained access through the multiple firewalls I built. Both times."

"Two times?" Leo asked with cutting focus to the gist of the vast problem on their hands.

"Sì."

"Cristo, you're a freaking genius, Massimo. How is that even possible?"

It wasn't arrogance that made Massimo nod. Comput-

ers were his thing. The one thing he was the master of.
"The hacker is obviously extremely talented. A true genius, no doubt."

Leo's curse exploded in the basement. A few minutes
later, his brother was all business again. "But you have the
proof tying it to this person, right?"

"*Sì*. I used the bots to piggyback onto the malware he—"

"Normal people words, Massimo, *per favore*," his
brother said with a smile, for the millionth time in their
lives. "Words a small brain like mine can understand."

As always, a spurt of warmth jolted through his veins at
Leo's joke. His brother was no fool. But when Massimo had
been at his lowest, Leo, with his words, full of concern and
praise, had urged him toward realizing his full potential.
"I have proof. I have even triangulated the hacker's physical location. New York."

"That's fantastic. I can arrange for a meeting with the
commissioner in a half hour. He'll get the cybercrime divi-
sion involved. We'll have the hacker behind bars by tonight
and the identity of whoever orchestrated this—"

"*No.* I don't want the *polizia* involved. Not yet."

"What? Why the hell not?"

"I've already figured out a cyber club where this hacker
plays. I've established contact."

"Contact with the hacker? Why?"

Massimo shrugged. He couldn't exactly put it into
words—curiosity, thrill, even a certain amount of cama-
raderie. The hacker intrigued him. "I want to get to know
him. Learn how he operates."

"*Dios mio*, Massimo, he breached our security. Twice."

"*Essattemente!* He could do it again and again. You have
to admit that there's something…fishy about the whole
thing. None of the clients' financials were leaked. I have

bots working everywhere they could be sold, like black markets, on the Dark Net. They haven't surfaced anywhere.

"It's as if the hacker is taunting me, playing with me. He's hard to pin down."

"What are you suggesting?"

"Let me develop a relationship with him. Let me get into his head. When I know how he works, how he's doing it, I'll spring the trap."

"I want your word that he won't hit our servers again."

"You losing faith in me, Leo?" he taunted, that resentment in him finding voice. Reminding him that Massimo wasn't still the always sick runt their father went off on whenever he was on one of his frequent alcoholic tirades. That he wasn't the younger brother running to his older brother's arms to hide from his father. That he was the computer genius who'd designed products that generated billions in revenue.

Leo paused at the high-tech sliding doors, frowning.

"Give me a week and I'll give you the hacker, his life story and the proof of his illegal activities, all tied up with a bow like a Christmas present."

"A week. At the most," Leo pushed back. "I want him behind bars."

One week later

Massimo stood outside the cyber club exit—a metal door of undistinguishable color at the rear of a dilapidated building in one of the run-down neighborhoods of Brooklyn. A far cry from his penthouse that overlooked Central Park that he'd left behind an hour ago.

March snow carpeted the parking grounds in the dark alley, thankfully suppressing the odors emanating from the vast trash containers that stood two feet from him.

The hacker, he'd found, was very much a creature of habit. Unlike Massimo, and much against the popular culture's rendition of a chaotic, free-spirited genius. Two evenings a week, the hacker came to this club, at exactly eight minutes past nine p.m. and stayed for exactly forty-three minutes. Before going completely off-line.

Like a junkie allowing himself a very strictly mandated and measured fix.

Massimo hadn't found him anywhere else.

Which meant all Massimo had had were two sessions of forty-three minutes to get to know how the guy operated. And he had. Hackers were a mysterious and antisocial bunch, and yet boastful, too, especially someone at the level at which this particular one operated. All he'd needed to do was compliment him on his modification of a security challenge posed by the master of the club. He hadn't quite owned up to the breach but the connection had been made.

His heart fluttering against his rib cage like a caged bird, Massimo tucked his hands into the pockets of his trench coat. Adrenaline hadn't hit him this hard since the release of his latest software product. No, that wasn't true. The last time he'd been this excited had been when he'd shored up the tunnel this very same hacker had created into BCS.

The metallic whine of the heavy door made his spine lock. Buffeted by the collar of his coat against the harsh wind, Massimo watched a slight figure swathed in black from head to toe, a dark contrast against the snow clinging to every crevice and roof of the building, walk down the steps.

The howl of the frigid wind pushed the hood away from the figure's face, revealing a delicate jawline with a wide, plump mouth. A too-sharp nose and a high forehead. Broad but sharp cheekbones. A pointed chin. Slender shoulders held an almost boyish figure with long legs swathed in black denim and knee-high boots.

Jet-black hair, wild and curly, the only thing that betrayed the fact that she was a woman. No, the soft fragility, the sharply delicate bones, couldn't be mistaken for a man.

A painfully young, delicately beautiful woman.

It couldn't be her... This fragile young woman couldn't be the hacker that had taken down his firewall, could she? Couldn't be the diabolically intelligent computer genius that Massimo had been chatting up for the last week. The hacker that Leonardo wanted behind bars *pronto*. The one who'd kept him up for a fortnight now, given him sleepless nights...

Not a single one of his girlfriends had ever done it.

He laughed, a harsh bark that sounded loud in the silence.

Like a deer caught in the headlights, the hacker's feet frozen in the snow, her face turned toward him.

Brown eyes with long lashes alighted on his face and paused. He saw her swallow, felt that gaze dip to his mouth and trail back up to meet his eyes. A soft sound, almost like a kitten's sigh, filled the silence around them. Followed by the soft treads of her boots as she returned to the car.

No, he wasn't wrong.

He'd even had a quick chat with the hacker from his car before he'd stepped out. He...or *she* had been inside that building. On an impulse, Massimo grabbed his tablet from the car and sent a quick message through the chat boards.

It wasn't a sure thing since the hacker never used the chat boards outside of the cyber club. And yet, Massimo had teased him today with a glimpse of the new security software he was building for Gisela's father's company. He knew the hacker had been intrigued, had even stayed beyond the forty-three minutes he usually allowed himself.

Vitruvian Man: I can show you the double encryption layer for the new design.

His heart raced. *Dios mio*, he felt like a teenage boy waiting for his first kiss.

The woman paused, pulled her phone out from the coat jacket. Massimo realized what it meant to wait with bated breath.

His tablet sent out a soft chirp that sounded like a fire alarm in the dark silence.

Her reply shone up at him.

Gollum: Not tonight, thank you. My time's up. Maybe next time.

The message flashed on his screen and a smile curved his mouth, a flare of excitement running through his veins.

So polite, he'd thought during his chats with her. A certain softness buried even in the software jargon in contrast to the ruthlessness with which she'd attacked his firewalls.

It was her.

She was the hacker he'd been chasing, the hacker who it seemed was truly Massimo's match.

In the few seconds it took him to accept this new discovery, and course-correct his strategy for her, she'd reached her car.

His long legs ate up the distance. The tightening of her shoulders made him stay a few steps from her. He didn't want to scare her. Not yet.

"Why Gollum?" he said, keeping his tone soft, even as

anger and excitement roped through him. "Why not Aragorn, or Gandalf the Wizard?"

She turned. Her eyes ate him up, her breath coming in short, shallow spurts that had nothing to do with the cold. "I don't know what you're talking about."

When she made to pull the driver's door to her beaten down Beetle, he crowded her. Still not touching.

The subtle scent of lavender filled his breath, a jarring thread of softness that made him breathe hard. He lifted his phone, the screen showing the chat boards. "I know who you are. I have proof of what you did to Brunetti Cyber Securities. Every last bit."

The smile faded from his face just as the innocence dropped from hers.

The pointed chin lifted up, the expression in her eyes clear and sharp. "What do you want?"

He let the full power of his fury settle into his words. "Your purse, please."

She looked at the sea of white snow around them.

"There's nowhere to run. Nowhere to hide. I recommend doing as I ask."

Slowly, she pulled a wallet out of her back pocket and handed it over.

"Natalie Crosetto," he said loudly. The name reverberated in the silence, and he breathed a sigh. "You've led me on a merry chase all over the internet, Ms. Crosetto, and now, I will run this game. We will go back to my hotel and you'll explain to me why you've been attacking my systems."

"No!" She took a deep breath. "You're a stranger. You can't expect me to let you just…kidnap me!"

"What do you suggest, then?"

"My home. Please. Tomorrow morning."

"I didn't take a trip over the Atlantic to let you escape

me once I found you. We'll go to your home if that offers you a modicum of security. You're free to keep your cell phone and dial the police if you feel a threat to your person at any point, even.

"But you'll answer each and every one of my questions and you will do so tonight."

That stubborn chin raised even as her mouth quivered. Scared, and yet she challenged him. "Or else what?"

"Or else you'll be behind bars tonight. I will even let you call the cops yourself. And you'll stay there for the next decade, if I have anything to say about it."

CHAPTER TWO

NATALIE CROSETTO STARED at the man lounging on her couch—a soft but old piece she'd picked up at thrift store last month—as if he were a king sitting on his golden throne, surveying a subject brought up for judgment.

Her.

Sweat gathered on her upper lip and the nape of her neck. The tremors that had taken over her body wouldn't abate.

Jail. He could send her to jail...which meant any chance of her getting custody of Frankie would go up in flames. Christ, why the hell had she let Vincenzo talk her into this? What would happen to her brother if she ended up in jail? No, God, no...

"Head down between your knees. And deep breaths, Ms. Crosetto." He stood to give her room to sit.

She automatically followed the commanding voice and bent her torso down. The blackness taking over her vision faded, breath rushing into her lungs with the force of a storm. In, out. In, out.

Panic receded, bringing rational thought in its wake.

She couldn't count on Vincenzo coming to her rescue. Not when she didn't know how to contact him beyond a number she could text. Not when she didn't know what the stranger would do with that information.

She had no one to count on but herself. As always.

Still keeping her head down, she went over the jumble of thoughts in her head, unraveling each one.

She'd covered her tracks very well, the first time. This man…he'd have never tracked her by that. But then, she'd tunneled through the firewalls a second time. Albeit with utter reluctance at Vincenzo's behest. That had been her mistake.

Still, the man on the other end had to be a genius to have tracked her. With unlimited resources. And not just online but all the way here. To show up right outside the cyber club, to taunt her with that text, to trap her so neatly…

She looked up and panic threatened to overwhelm her again.

A stranger in her apartment.

Her sanctuary. Her only safe place from the cruel world outside. She had never even invited Vincenzo here.

God, what a mess.

She pushed a hand through her hair and tugged at it. Her scalp tingled, the pain dispersing the remnants of panic. She'd survived worse situations. She'd find a way out of this, too.

First, she needed to protect herself from him. Needed to get him out of her home.

From the trench coat he'd discarded to the crisp black suit, the cuff links at his wrists, which she'd guess to be platinum, all the way to the handmade black leather shoes he was tapping on her cheap linoleum floor—he was expensively dressed. She might not know all of Vincenzo's background but he had expensive tastes.

This man was no different.

Even his jet-black haircut, carefully piled artistically at the top of his head, looked expensive, catering to the high cheekbones and forehead, sharpening those features even more. He was no mere IT officer or a hound sent to track her down.

Even if she could get away from him, he or his higher-ups would come after her. Again. Neither could she be a fugitive for the rest of her life. And yet…the need to take control of the situation was overwhelming.

Keeping her eyes on his lean frame lounging against the opposite wall, Nat pushed herself to her feet. Shuffling her feet, she slowly reached for the baseball bat she kept next to the bookshelf. One of the numerous things she'd been collecting to make the tiny apartment a home for Frankie.

The wood felt solid in her hand as she lifted it.

"Drop it, Ms. Crosetto," he said in a mildly bored tone.

She couldn't. Not for the life of her.

For a man who topped a couple of inches over six feet, he moved with a grace and economy she couldn't believe. In two seconds, his lean frame was crowding her. A gasp fell from her mouth when his fingers wrapped around her wrist, forcing her to drop the bat. The *thunk* of it hitting the floor reverberated in the small space. With a firm grip, he pushed her arm behind her until her upper body arched toward him. Her skin tingled where he held her tightly, but not hurting her.

Head falling back against the wall of his chest, she looked up at him.

And the impact of the man beneath the expensive clothes hit her hard. Hit her in places she didn't want to think about in front of him.

Intelligence and something else glimmered in his gaze. Dark shadows hung under his penetrating gray eyes. His sharp nose had a small dent right in the middle. His mouth…wide, the bow of the upper lip carved, it was so… sexy.

Awareness rushed in through her blood, settling into a warm throb in her lower belly. A shocking heaviness in her breasts.

Her breaths became shallow. He stood so close that she

could see the slight flare of his pupils, the harsh breath he pulled in before his fingers tightened on her wrist.

She wouldn't be surprised to discover he was one of those male models that seemed to have been born with the perfect bone structure. To whom everything in life came easy. Women at their feet and millions in their bank account.

"Do not dig yourself a deeper hole, Ms. Crosetto."

The arrogance in his tone banished the airy lethargy in her limbs. "You're in my home. You cornered me and intruded into my apartment. You—"

He released her instantly. Stepped back, and Nat felt air rushing back into her lungs. "I mean you no harm. Not physically at least. Also, may I remind you that you invited me into your home. And I—" he cast a dismissive look around her living room, that upper lip turned up into a sneer "—expected to find you in something better than this hovel. Didn't you get paid enough for the hacking job to upgrade from…this?"

She rubbed the sensitive skin at her wrist, more to rid herself of the warmth he left behind than because of any hurt. And to stop herself from smacking the distaste off his curling mouth. "I've no idea what you're talking about."

He sat back onto the couch, leaning his arms onto his long legs, every movement utterly masculine. And yet graceful. "How much did you get paid for taking down the firewalls at BCS?"

"You're mistaking me for someone else. I'm nothing but a low-level clerk at a cheap easy-loan company in Brooklyn."

He rubbed a long finger over his left temple. "No more lies, *per favore*." His accent sent shivers down her spine that had nothing to do with fear.

When he looked up at her, impatience swirled in his

gaze. "Let's cut through the innocent act. Now that I have your actual identity, it will take me no time at all to find your financials, every personal record, from your date of birth to how often you visit your ATM."

In a bare, few words that sent all her assumptions of him grounding into dust, he rattled off, step by step, the date and time to the exact second when she had bypassed his security measures and brought down the firewalls at BCS. And not as if he had learned it by rote.

"So, you're not just a pretty, rich boy?"

He stilled, except for raising a brow on that gorgeous face. She could swear his eyes twinkled but then she didn't trust herself right now. "A pretty, rich boy, huh? Remind me to tell my older brother that, *si*? He'll find it amusing."

Nat could only stare.

"I don't think you comprehend the trouble you're in."

"I'm terrified at the trouble I'm in. You've no idea what…" She took a deep breath and pushed her shaking hands behind her. "But attacking even when you're cornered is sometimes the only defense you've left in life."

Something like interest dawned in his eyes before he went on to outline how he'd tracked her signature to the cyber club, made contact with her. How he'd triangulated her physical location. How when he'd given her a small opening in the guise of his latest tech, she'd all but opened herself to him.

Her foul curse rang like a gunshot.

"It was clever. No, not clever. It was sheer genius. But you made a mistake. You—"

"I came back a second time without masking my trail," she finished, a knot of tension in her throat. He had her. Nicely trapped. Without doubt.

"Yes, that. But you also shouldn't have returned to the scene of your crime—that cyber club. Why did you?"

She shrugged, refusing to give any more information. Like how every inch of her had been fascinated by his diabolical talent after he'd patched the tunnel she'd created. How she didn't even really have the kind of technology on hand to pull off something like this, how even membership to the cyber club had been gained for her by Vincenzo.

"Why are you talking to me instead of turning me in, then?" she challenged boldly, even as fear coated her skin with cold sweat.

If only she could somehow contact Vincenzo...

"How and why."

"What do you mean?" she said sharply, feeling as if she was a prisoner whose execution had been stayed.

He looked at his fingers and then up. Uncrossed his legs and then crossed them again. Pulling the material of his tailored trousers upward. She'd never realized how distracting a man's powerful thighs could be. "I want to know how you did it. My firewalls, every bit of technology I design, is cutting edge, the best in the world. What you did should have been...impossible."

"You're dangling jail time over my neck as a sword because your ego got dented?" The words pushed out of her. "You and I both know I didn't touch a single client's financials. I...didn't *steal* anything. I'm not a thief. In any sense of the word."

"Which brings me to the second question. Why attack the security, bring down the firewalls...something that would have taken you days, if not to steal millions worth of financial info—"

"Five hours," she chimed in, and could have kicked herself. Damn it, where the hell was her sense of self-preservation? What was it about this man that pushed all the wrong buttons in her?

A stillness came over him. He rotated his neck on his

shoulders with that casual masculine elegance. But this time, Natalie saw through it. He was shocked. It was clear in the pinched look around his mouth when he cleared his throat and said, "You did it in five hours?"

"Yes."

If she could trust her judgment right then, Nat would have called the expression in his eyes excited. No...fascinated. He sounded fascinated and thrilled, his body containing a violent energy. More than angry that someone had attacked his design.

This was personal to him, too, this security breach she'd caused. She had to use that to her benefit, to persuade him to be lenient with her.

But she didn't trust herself right then, didn't know if she could pull it off. Not when he distracted the wits out of her. Jesus, the man held her future in his palm.

"How long did it take you the second time?"

"Fourteen hours. I... You made it much more complicated and I was under...duress."

Another smile, this one flashing his perfect white teeth, the warmth of it reaching his eyes. Nat blinked at the sheer beauty of the man. Dark skin at his throat contrasted against his white shirt. "Nice to know I'm not the only who gives in to their ego. I had you penned right."

"You don't know anything about me," she whispered, a sane defense for once.

"I knew enough to put a tracker on the malware you introduced when you came back the second time. I have bots scouring through every black market, in case you stole the financials. I'll find out if you're part of a hacking syndicate. Any money you took for the job, I'll find the financial trail."

"There won't be any." Thank God she'd refused Vincenzo's financial offer. Thank God she'd retained some of her moral sensibilities. Her life had been too much of a bitch for her to afford them. But she'd refused. Because she hadn't wanted to benefit from illegal activity. "You'll see that I have two thousand and twenty-two dollars in my checking account and credit cards with over nine thousand dollars in debt. I live in this hovel, as you call it. I don't own a car. And most weeks, I live on ramen. I didn't make any money on this. It wasn't a job. I'm not… My services aren't for sale."

"So why do it? If it had been just the one time, I'd have assumed you had chickened out at the sheer scope of what you'd done and its consequences. But to come back…" He raised a hand when she opened her mouth. "Think carefully before you decide on an answer, Ms. Crosetto. And stick to the truth, if you can, *si*?

"I'm on a deadline to submit the security designs for a major project and I'm grouchy when I'm pulled away from my lab. Forget the fact that my older brother is breathing down my neck for not just having thrown you in jail when I first found you. One wrong word and I'll take his advice."

Sweat rolled down between her shoulder blades. A torrent of lies came and fell away from Nat's mouth. "I…" She swiped her tongue over her lips. Truth, as much as she could afford, was her only option. "I had no intention of stealing anything. I…have been stupid but I'm not greedy. I'm not a thief…by profession," she added at the last second.

His arrogant gaze bore through her. "I'm waiting, Ms. Crosetto."

"I did it on a challenge." It was the last answer he'd been expecting from his shocked expression. "I… Someone in the club issued a challenge."

"Who?" he demanded instantly, clearly not buying it.

"I don't know. All I gathered is that BCS's security was unbeatable. That your security guy's a genius. That he… no one could ever bring down his firewalls. I…

"I was foolish enough and egotistic enough to want to beat it. Not to prove anything to anyone. Just for myself."

"And the second time?"

"Hubris." This time, she was relieved to speak the truth. "You closed the tunnel minutes after I created it. It shouldn't have been possible. What you did the second time to put them up—to try to bring it down—it was a high." She'd constantly moaned about how wrong it was with Vincenzo, but it hadn't stopped her. He'd known how much she'd wanted to do it.

How exhilarating she found it to pit her mind against the security expert at BCS.

"Once I started, I… I lost the little sense I seem to have been born with. I… I swear, I'll never do it again. I… I've never done this before. Please, you've got to believe me."

"It's not that simple, Ms. Crosetto."

"Why not? You said—"

"I don't trust that brain of yours. I can't just…let you walk free."

She reached for the wall behind her, her knees giving out. Fear felt like shards of glass in her throat. "You'll send me to jail?"

He looked at her with a thoughtful expression, as if she were a bug under a microscope he was wondering whether to crush or not. He studied the beads of sweat over her upper lip. The shivers spewing over her entire body. "*No.* But I'm not letting you go, either."

"What does that mean?"

"You'll accompany me to Milan."

She shook her head, trying to swim through the emotions barreling through her. Fear and hope knotted painfully in her stomach. "I can't leave the country. I have… responsibilities."

"You should have thought of them before you decided

o embrace the criminal life. Until I get to the bottom of his, until I decide what to do with you, you'll be my... guest. If you give me your passport, I'll arrange for travel mmediately. I can't let you out of my sight and I do not ike the idea of—"

"That's kidnapping!" Nat broke through his casual plan-ning. "You're kidnapping me."

He didn't even blink. "The alternative is jail, Ms. Cro-setto. There's too much at stake to magnanimously forgive you." He turned to his tablet, as if the topic was done. "Pack our things. We leave as soon as possible."

"I can't just... I have to tell someone that I'm leaving he country."

"A boyfriend? Perhaps the man who put you up to this?"

"No one did," she repeated, biting away Vincenzo's name at the last second.

This man was dangerous, in more than one way.

More than panic shimmied through her veins as his gaze ouched her face. "My job, my... I don't even know who you re. What if you were a serial killer? A human trafficker? A harvester of organs who's salivating at the thought of getting his hands on my body?"

His hands on her body... What was wrong with her?

This time, there was no doubting the twinkle in his eyes. Or the languid heat flaring beneath.

Nat stepped back at the mere thought of what that meant. The last thing she needed was an...attraction between them. She knew squat about men. And less than squat about ambi-ious, ruthless, gorgeous men like her accuser. "Criminals, Ms. Crosetto, dead or alive, however diabolically clever—" his gaze raked her from top to toe and dismissed her in the ame breath "—are not my type." He couldn't sound more pper class, refined and sophisticated, if he tried.

Everything she wasn't.

"But since I do not want a hysterical female on my hands on a long transatlantic flight, I'll tell you." He looked around her tiny living room, frowned and then settled those broad shoulders onto the wall behind him. The action pushed his hips and thighs away from the wall, highlighting the lean masculinity of the man. Every gesture, every movement of his, called all her senses to attention.

"I'm Massimo Brunetti, the cyber security genius you took on with such ease. And since I won't let you near an electronic device in the near future, I'll also give you the Google version, *sì*?

"I founded Brunetti Cyber Securities a decade ago when I was nineteen. I'm also the CTO for Brunetti Finances, an international finance giant. My brother, Leonardo, is the CEO. That's the one who wants you behind bars *pronto*.

"Our family, if you hadn't realized already, is old power and wealth, the kind of European dynasty others try to emulate unsuccessfully," he added, with nothing of the pride that was in his tone when he spoke of his security company. "So, yes, far more than your average pretty, rich boy who likes to have his way. Proceed with caution, *sì*?

"Also, I'll allow you one single call and you'll make it in front of me."

CHAPTER THREE

ACK OF SLEEP made Nat grit her eyes as dawn painted the New York sky beautiful shades of pink and orange. Unlike the light pollution that dimmed its shine in the city, the sky here in the country that she'd been driven into at three a.m. in a tinted limo, her sad little bag in hand, was gorgeous. The private airstrip was a hubbub of activity.

Massimo Brunetti...that name and all the power, wealth and reach that came with it had kept Natalie up all night.

She had Googled him the moment Vincenzo had mentioned BCS to her. Him and his CEO brother, Leonardo Brunetti. If Massimo was the brains behind Brunetti Finances, Leonardo was the heart. Cut in the same cloth as Massimo, ruthless when wielding his power, but much more socially active among the glitterati of Milan. The face of their business, the man who flashed his teeth at his enemies, brought in investors, managed the funds, while Massimo built brilliant software that brought in billions of revenue.

"Powerful men make powerful friends or enemies," Vincenzo had said, when she'd asked if he knew them. "A small favor," he'd called it. *Easy for her incisive mind.*

"Can you bring down BCS's security, Natalie?"

When she had argued that she couldn't risk anything criminal, she could never go down that path again, he had clasped her hand.

"I'd let nothing happen to you, *cara mia*. Find a flaw, bring it down. Nothing more. I'll not ask you to retrieve

anything you discover, if you do crack it. Nothing to steal.
Just find a weakness in the system."

"Then why?"—the only question she'd even thought
to ask.

"Let's just say I have my eyes on the man who built it. I
need to know if he's as good as they say. Not a single hacker
I've hired so far has been able to get through."

And that had been his lure and she'd more than happily
taken the bait.

She could've refused. He hadn't insisted on it. He hadn't
called it as a return on all the favors he'd done for her and
Frankie. He hadn't once, in the ten years since they'd met,
mentioned how he'd saved her from a bullying foster parent
or from a wretched future in the juvie system. He hadn't
mentioned not turning in Nat herself when he'd caught her
stealing his wallet the first time they had met.

And yet, she'd done it.

Now she wondered at the questions she should've asked
then.

What did Vincenzo have against Massimo?
Why this particular man?
Why his company?
*Why had Vincenzo targeted the brainchild of tech ge-
nius Massimo Brunetti?*

Instead, she'd thrown caution to the wind, given in to
her one weakness and risked everything.

She hadn't even been able to reach Frankie during the
one call Massimo had allowed her. While he'd watched her
like a hawk circling a carcass, Natalie had left a message
that she was going out of the country for a friend's sudden
wedding, freeloading on the chance. That she would be out
of coverage for a while but would call when she could. Her
brother knew what a cheapskate she was.

"You're quite the storyteller, Ms. Crosetto," Massimo

had said in his delicious Italian accent, all sleep mussed before he'd rushed her out of her apartment in the middle of the night, to collect their documents.

Nat pressed her fingers around the coffee cup in her hand—no rest-stop diesel-like coffee for Mr. Pretty Rich Boy. The dark roast felt like heaven on her tongue, anchoring her.

Her spine straightened against the limo as she heard Massimo step out on the other side. His security detail—one broad six-and-half-footer—and his two assistants: a thin man in his twenties with thick glasses and messed-up curly hair. What she'd expected the computer genius to look like—not the sleek, lean, sex-on-legs stud that was Massimo, shame on her prejudice... And the second one—a woman with a dark complexion, in her forties—followed him while he spoke into his cell phone.

Coffee forgotten, Nat watched him with wide eyes as he walked back and forth in front of her speaking in rapid Italian that she couldn't understand a word of. After every other sentence, he paused, looked at her, and then started again.

Suit jacket gone, three buttons of the white dress shirt undone, that stylishly cut hair all rumpled up from his stint on her couch, he should've looked disheveled. At least a little tired. After all, he'd traveled across the Atlantic the previous day.

Instead, the stubble that coated his jaw and his upper lip, the V of his shirt glinting olive against the white of it, the snug fit of his trousers against lean hips—he was an erotic fantasy given form. The assault on her senses that had begun when she'd found him on her couch, trousers pulled up tight against powerful thighs, shirt equally snug against his shoulders, long lashes fanning against his sharp cheekbones... Her heart hadn't still recovered from it.

And then while she'd stared at him like an enthralled

idiot, he'd opened those gray eyes. For just a second, there had been something in his eyes. Something that made liquid desire float through her veins. Before he sat up with his ubiquitous cell phone attached to his ear.

"The jet is ready. Let's go."

That was all he'd said to her, before bundling her into the limo. Coffee had been acquired on the way.

When she'd refused, he'd frowned. "Drink up, Ms. Crosetto. I need you awake and alert."

She'd tensed so hard her shoulders hurt. "Why?"

"Don't worry. I'm not going to ask you to breach the security of another company."

She'd immediately relaxed and then cursed herself when a shrewd light dawned in his eyes. Afraid he'd see even more, more than what she'd already betrayed, she'd looked away.

"I want to know exactly how you were able to create that tunnel through the firewall. Both the first and the second time. Each and every step. I want to also know of any other ways you can breach BCS's security. All the truth, Ms. Crosetto. Not just the convenient parts.

"If I even get a sniff of duplicity from you, you'll wish I had sent you to prison in your own country."

Even the wonderful aroma of coffee had felt like poison then.

The threat still ringing in her ears, she swallowed when he beckoned her from the foot of the air stairs. The arrogance of the man scraped her raw. She'd survived the cruelty and negligence of a foster care system that was supposed to protect her, the heartbreak of knowing that she wasn't good enough, just yet, to be her younger brother's family.

No way was she going to let Massimo Brunetti control her with the threat of incarceration. No man was going to make her live in fear every day, not after everything she'd been through. Not this easily.

And just like that, an idea began to percolate in her mind. Her shoulders straight, she tilted her chin and walked toward him with confidence.

The narrowing of his eyes made her smile.

Yep, she'd do what he asked of her, but she'd do it on her terms.

"Call the cops if you'd like. But I'm not getting on that plane. Not until you hear me out."

Massimo disconnected his call with Leo, Natalie's husky voice filled with determination sliding over his skin like a sensuous whisper. That same voice whispering at his ear, after a night spent in bed together, limbs heavy around each other, those dark brown eyes languid with sated desire… His imagination fired up the picture faster than he could breathe.

Dios mio, of all the women to spur this insta-lust in him…she was the worst choice.

He wanted to blame the last six months of his self-imposed celibacy for it. But then, after the fiasco with Gisela, he'd been a little bit disgusted with himself. He should've known better than to play with a spoiled princess.

He'd been more than a little tired of playing the same old game of chasing a woman just for sex. He had nothing more to give right now. Not at this point in his life.

And now Leonardo had informed him that Greta had been pulled into the whole mess with Gisela. His *nonni* had decided that Gisela would make a suitable bride for the scion of the Brunetti dynasty, that she was rich enough, sophisticated enough and blue-blooded enough to spawn the next generation of Brunettis.

Which was happening…*never*. But it did mean handling

Gisela and, now, his *nonni* without giving offense to the former and hurting the second.

Of all the messes…

"Mr. Brunetti? Did you hear me? I'm not—"

He turned slowly, bracing himself. Still, the up-tilted chin and the wide brown eyes packed a punch.

This morning, she'd dressed in a light green-and-black sweater dress that hugged her slender frame, pointing out curves he'd missed last night. The loose neckline kept sliding off her shoulder showing glimpses of silky skin that beckoned his touch.

The dress ended beneath her buttocks—he'd seen enough when she'd walked ahead of him toward the limo, the knee-high leather boots displaying long legs that went on for miles. The mass of her black curls was pulled away into a tight knot at the top of her head, but in no way contained. Thick stray curls kept framing her face and she blew at them. A nervous tell that had made him smile in the limo. High forehead and a sharp nose only emphasized her gaunt face.

He frowned at the increasing appeal she held for him.

She wasn't the lush, curvaceous beauty he usually went after. Neither was she, he was sure, the experienced type he preferred, the way she'd jumped every time he came near. Women who owned their sexual desires usually meant uncomplicated but pleasurable affairs.

Delicate collarbones jutting out, the only lush thing about her was that mouth. Collagen had nothing on those luscious lips.

She had that million-dollar look that runway models seemed to have. A fragility that, despite her very clever mind, roused a protectiveness in his chest. The last thing she deserved, given the daggers she shot at him. He'd expected her to try to change his mind this morning, *sì*, but not with that brash confidence she exuded just then.

"Come, Ms. Crosetto." He gestured her back toward the limo, taking her wrist in his hand. She was truly delicate in his fingers, and they tightened instinctively. He guided her into the waiting limo and shut the door behind him. Even with the luxurious space, their knees bumped before she tucked them away.

Good, at least one of them needed to be wary of this attraction between them. "You seem to think you have a choice in this situation. My patience runs thin especially as my *nonni* is cooking up a scheme I abhor on the other side of the ocean."

"Your *nonni*?"

"My grandmother."

"I'll make this quick." She swallowed and looked up. "I'm calling your bluff."

He smiled. "You don't have any cards."

She leaned back against the seat, and crossed her legs. Her dress pulled up toward her thighs and he peeked at long, taut muscles. Shamelessly. "I'll not surrender my freedom to a stranger, a stranger moreover with the power and reach that you have, not only in your country but here, to arrange my visa at such short notice, without some security in place. God knows what you'll do to me when—" whatever she saw in his eyes, color darkened her cheeks and she cleared her throat "—what you'll decide for my fate. Even in the worst situations, one always has a choice."

She roused his curiosity so easily and held it. Turned his expectations upside down. So frequently. Unlike any woman he'd ever known. "Why do you think I'll accept any condition of yours?"

"Because you and I are alike. Hungry for new challenges. So full of arrogant belief that we're the best there

is. I knew what I was risking when I attacked your security the second time. I knew…and I still couldn't stop. And
you…you want to know how I did it. More than you want
me in jail. You want to know what other weaknesses there
could be in your design. You hate knowing someone better than you exists."

"You're not better than me." He hated that he sounded
like a juvenile teenager trying to get one over the smart
girl.

She smiled and grooves dug into her cheeks. Her front
two teeth were overlapped, a small imperfection that only
made her face more distinct, more memorable. More lovely
even. Challenge and knowledge simmered in that smile,
tugging at his awareness. "Sending me to jail right now
doesn't serve your purpose. I'd rot there for who knows
how long while what I was capable of doing eats away at
you. So I'll let you kidnap me, yes, but at a price."

Laughter punched out of his mouth. *Cristo*, she had guts.
And smarts. And a tart mouth he desperately wanted to
taste right then. Humor and arousal were an unusual combination but had a languorous effect on his limbs. He ran
a hand over his bristly jaw, trying to find the rationality,
the reason, beneath both.

If he had any sense, he'd dump her at the nearest police
station and wash his hands off.

It was what Leonardo was expecting. What the sane
part of him said to do.

But he hadn't arrived at his place in this world without
taking risks. By denying his instincts. Forget also the fact
that if she went to jail, all her secrets went with her.

He didn't believe for a second that she'd only done it
for the challenge. Either it was an impersonal job she took
on for money, or someone she knew was deliberately targeting them.

Leonardo and he had worked too hard, for too long, to let some unknown enemy destroy everything they'd built. For now, he'd play along. Plus he'd be no kind of businessman if he didn't use her talents to his benefit. At least in the short term. He'd just have to convince Leo of her usefulness to them.

"Bene," he said.

In the intimacy of the leather interior, her soft gasp pinged on his nerves. Her eyes wide, she stared at him, swallowed, looked away and then back at him again. Her knuckles white against the dark leather.

Cristo, the woman blushed even when she was cornered.

He couldn't help liking the little criminal. He knew what it was to be the weaker one against a stronger, terrifying opponent, to have no way out, the powerlessness that came with it. "State your condition."

"You'll pay me for any services I render, like an outside consultant."

He raised a brow. "You're not bargaining for me to destroy the proof of your crime?"

She shook her head. And he had a feeling it was to hide her expression. "You won't give that up. This way, if I end up in jail, I'll make money to show for it. During the stint, I'll work on proving to you that I have no agenda of my own."

"Making money for hacking my system and then more for fixing it? I was right about you."

"If you were the computer whiz kid the world calls you, you'd have my financials in hand by now."

"Believe me, I was tempted to find the salacious details of your criminal life last night. But my brother reminded me of the importance of doing this through official channels.

"So I ordered a background check on you. Your whole life will be in my hands in a matter of hours," he added, making sure she understood the consequences. "Just because I accept your condition doesn't mean I trust you. Or intend to let you get away with it forever."

Devoid of color, her skin looked alarmingly pale against the black leather. "Is a background check necessary? All you need is to confirm that I'm dirt poor."

He shrugged.

What else was she hiding? And how was he going to explain her presence near him, 24/7, to his family, to the world? The last time he'd been in an actual relationship had been…never. He worked hard, partied hard. For more than a decade, he'd worked sixteen-hour days, buried in his lab. Coming up only for refueling.

Brunetti Cyber Securities came first. Always would.

First because he'd needed to prove to his father that he wasn't the runt he'd been called all his childhood. And prove himself to Leo even, because he'd been the golden son, the adored Brunetti heir at first. Because Leonardo had been everything Massimo hadn't been able to be.

Later, when Leo had realized the extent of their father's bullying of Massimo, he'd hated Leo's pity, his concern for him. Resented him for thinking Massimo needed handouts, that Massimo was weak. But then success itself had become the motivator; the challenge of building better and better cyber systems had become its own drug.

The more he had, the more he'd wanted. The more he wanted his father and his family and his brother to be beholden to his company for fueling much needed funds into Brunetti Finances.

Suddenly, the answer came to him. Two problems and one solution. A tangible use of the attraction between them. An explanation for her presence with him, night and day.

He'd get her to trust him with the complete truth, then

he might even take her to bed. Scratch the itch out of his system. Her innocent act would have to drop when he had the background check in his hands.

He pulled up his phone and texted his assistant waiting outside to ready a contract with all the required confidentiality clauses. Another text to notify Leo about the slight modification to his plans. "You'll have the contract by the time we land. Under one—"

"I won't leave without it."

He shook his head. "Not even I can come up with a contract like that immediately. Not without having that background check in hand first."

"How do I know I can trust you?"

"You don't." He shrugged. The hiss of her breath, the filthy curse reverberating in the confined space, made his mouth twitch.

He was enjoying this—this pitting his will against hers, this anticipation in his gut as he waited to see what she'd do next. More than he enjoyed anything with a woman in a long time. Even more than sex. He frowned at the runaway thought. "I have a countercondition of my own."

"You're already blackmailing me, kidnapping me, threatening me with incarceration. What else is there?"

"You'll be my partner for the duration. I'll compensate you for that, too."

"Partner? What kind of a partner?" Color left her cheeks, her eyes searching his. "For the last time, Mr. Brunetti, I'm not for sale. I'm not what you think—"

"Calm down, Natalie," he interrupted her, trying her name on his tongue and liking it. Her eyes sought his in the relative dark, awareness shining through them. She hadn't missed the intimacy of it, either. "It's just another part of our deal, *si*?"

"Explain. Now, please."

"I have to explain your presence at my side, 24/7. I need a romantic partner for the foreseeable future. This way—"

"You've lost your mind. I'm not staying in Italy any longer than I have to. And I refuse to be your... Why the hell would a man like you need a pretend girlfriend?"

"A man like me?"

He grinned. She glared. "You're supersmart, obviously given you're one of the tech billionaires under thirty in the world. You're—" she licked her lips then and he waited with arrested breath "—a walking, talking stud muffin. Not counting all that dynasty crap you threw at me. Why—?"

"What does a woman do with a stud muffin?"

She rolled her eyes and he laughed. "Why do you need a pretend girlfriend?"

"I was thinking a pretend fiancée actually." Her eyes bugged and he grinned, explaining, "An ex-girlfriend that I can't shake off and my *nonni* have joined forces. Believe me, it's enough to scare a grown man."

"So you don't want to hurt their feelings?"

This time, when he laughed, it felt as if his chest would burst open. The minx was such a contrasting mix of street savvy and naïveté, of smarts and innocence. She'd make a hell of a distraction from the lethargy that had filled him of late when it came to women.

"Feelings, of any of the parties involved, are the least of my concern. Greta, my *nonni*, is extremely stubborn, and has antiquated views about the whole dynasty and its continuation and legacy and all that rot. For some unfathomable reason, apparently, she's decided that Gisela Fiore, who comes with a fortune of her own, would be a sweet, biddable wife for me. Gisela is a mistake I shouldn't have indulged in, and has been...problematic since I ended our purely physical relationship almost six months ago."

For all her sass, color skimmed up Natalie's cheeks. "Problematic how?"

"She knows my relationship patterns. She knew it was only an affair. When I retreated to my lab—refueled and ready—"

"What do you mean…refueled?"

"After every big project release, I need to fill the well, so to speak."

"And you do this…*refueling* by sleeping with a woman you don't care about?"

Her distaste made him frown. "I care about the woman's pleasure. And mine. But, *sì*. Gisela knew that. Knew my pattern. I made it clear. After it was over, she started texting me a hundred times a day. She'd cry, make a scene at the few social events I attended. She flew to San Francisco and accosted me at a cyber security conference.

"Showed up outside our estate in Lake Como. Cornered my brother, Leo, at one of the events where her father was present, too."

"And her father is someone whose feelings you do give a damn about?" she said tartly.

Massimo scowled. "Giuseppe Fiore is one of the most powerful banking tycoons in Milan, in all of Italy. BCS is in the running for a hundred-billion-euro security contract with his banks that spans a decade. Leo thinks it's going to make dealing with him awkward because of Gisela.

"Why should a fling she came into with her eyes open cause problems for me now?"

"Because people are not algorithms that give you the same, expected results every time?"

"Once Giuseppe sees me with you, he'll understand that Gisela and I are long over. And this is the best way for me to keep an eye on you."

"If this tycoon's so rich and powerful, and his daughter's

good enough to be your...*whatever*, why not just marry her? Or are you holding out for love?"

He stared at her, wondering if she was joking again. Steady brown eyes held his. "Tut, tut, Natalie...you disappoint me. The last thing I need in my life is a wife who wants love and all the rainbows it brings with it. I have nothing to give a wife at present. Or in the foreseeable future.

"Just do your part, *sì*? The compensation I provide should be big enough for you to get over your distaste for me," he mocked.

Her nostrils flared. "And if I say no? If I tell your ex and your grandmother that it's all a big pretense?"

"You won't do that."

"I just—"

"Be smart about this, Natalie." All humor fled his tone. "If I find you've told me the truth about your financials, about this not being a job, then what do you have to lose? For once in your life, maybe you could use your interesting capabilities to make a living. Spend a few months in the lap of luxury in Milan. Pretend to be the fiancée of the most—"

"Arrogant, high-handed man on the planet?"

"So?"

"Fine. I agree to your conditions."

"Bene."

He stepped out of the limo and helped her do the same, keeping his fingers around her wrist. He liked having the feel of her in his hands, this mystery hacker who'd haunted his days and nights for weeks.

"All that's left now is to swap our life histories and practice the intimacy we have to pretend in front of my family and the whole world."

A pithy curse fell from her mouth and Massimo looked down at her.

She was truly the most interesting woman he'd ever met. He wouldn't hesitate to send her to jail if he found her loyalties lay with their enemy, but he would regret it all the same.

And he didn't understand even that negligible emotion dogging his rationality, his judgment.

It had never done so before.

CHAPTER FOUR

AFTER A TRANSATLANTIC flight to Milan with a creative genius who peppered her with a million incisive questions meant to unsettle her lies. Throwing in a magnificent view of white-tipped Alps, which she'd probably never see again in her life—except maybe on the return flight on her way to jail in New York. Then a quick helicopter ride up to the shores of Lake Como—because, of course, the once-in-a-lifetime scenic drive from Milan to the lake would take forever and time was a precious commodity to a tech billionaire. Finally arriving at a destination where she was nothing but a prisoner, Natalie foolishly assumed she would become oblivious to her surroundings—not the man, of course—or at least be too exhausted mentally and physically to take much more in.

She was wrong.

The chopper landed on the side of a hill, in a sea of lush, perfectly manicured gardens with azaleas and gigantic rhododendrons and a long avenue of tall plane trees that created a walkway to the lakefront. A small boat floated at the end of the steps. Beyond, the calm waters of Lake Como glittered like a dark blanket creating a stunning sight littered with boats of various sizes floating lazily to the gorgeously lit-up houses and villages scattered about.

As Natalie followed Massimo, who seemed to have forgotten about her existence, amid carefully sculpted flower beds, she spotted a hidden cave enclosed by more azaleas and even an artificial Japanese-style pond.

"Your family owns this villa?" she said, her breath catching in her throat.

Massimo stopped, took a look around absentmindedly and then turned to her. "*Sì*. One of the Brunettis, a count or a duke, maybe, I think in the nineteenth century, took possession of a Benedictine monastery in these grounds and converted it into a sumptuous noble residence. It's been in the family's possession ever since. Greta will cram a history lesson down your throat if she catches you staring at it like that."

Even his mockery couldn't fracture the awe in her chest. Fountains with water glittering out like liquid gold because of strategically placed lights, a gazebo with creepers enveloping it, two statues of majestic lions at the sides of the carriage entrance… How could he sound so dismissive and unaffected by his family's legacy? "I've never seen such beautiful gardens."

"You'd love it in spring when they're a riot of color. They're Leonardo's pride. He personally tends to them along with a team of gardeners. He can make the most reluctant plant blossom. He…loves the land and the villa and the…legacy of it all."

She was out of breath as they walked up the small, steep path while he simply marched on. "You don't?" she asked, something in his tone snagging her attention.

"I like being the one who saved it, the one who held it for the Brunettis so that they could show it off for another century," he added mysteriously.

She frowned, wondering at the contradictions of the man.

Finally, they came around the bend to a square plot that

housed the villa itself. A grand entrance portico with wide stairs that sloped toward the lake straddled the villa, which would offer three-sixty-degree views of the lake and the mountains from the grand terrace even now overflowing with guests.

The white stucco facade gleamed under the light thrown from the lake. Nat sucked in a breath as the sounds of music and people chatting in Italian flowed over her skin. A line of luxury cars stood like gatekeepers, tasked with keeping riffraff, like her, out.

She shivered even though the wind coming off the lake was more balmy than cold. Cicadas whispered all around them, the scents from the orangery they'd walked by thick and pungent in the air.

It was a world away from Brooklyn and her cheap studio apartment, a world away from everything she'd ever known.

Through the high arched front entrance, she could see suave men dressed in black suits and refined women dressed in cocktail finery with diamonds glittering at their throats and wrists. Uniformed waiters passing around champagne flutes so fine that Nat wondered if they'd break at the slightest pressure.

She rubbed her sweating palms on her hips, which only brought her attention to her own outfit. A thread of shame filled her chest and she chased it away with much needed anger. God, she'd worked hard for every small thing she owned. To make an honest living for herself and for Frankie.

She felt the heat of Massimo's body next to her, before she heard the curse from his mouth. Frowning, she craned her neck to see him. Flashes of light revealed the tension in his brow, that perfectly carved jaw so tight that it almost seemed fragile. If she didn't know better, she'd have thought he was no more inclined to go in than she was.

The suavely sophisticated man who'd taunted her was

nowhere to be seen. In his place was a stranger with tension thrumming tightly through his lean frame.

"Massimo?" she whispered, unable to stem the concern she heard in her voice. "Is something wrong?"

"My father is here," he answered softly, before he blew out another soft curse and shook his head. "He is a bully of the worst kind."

"Must run in the family, then," she quipped.

"No." His soft denial was emphatic enough that her head jerked to him. Glittering gray eyes held hers. "I'm nothing like my father." He rubbed his jaw, a tell she was beginning to recognize he did when stressed. "*Dios mio*, I forgot it's his birthday week. That means Greta checks him out of the rehabilitation clinic and parades him in front of our family and friends in an annual tradition. That means—" his gaze swung to the luxury vehicles "—everyone is here."

"Your father lives at a clinic?" She'd gotten the sense from him that family was important to him. Yet, he stared at his family's villa like it was a nest of vipers.

"He's a recovering alcoholic. The recovery, if we can call it that, has been in progress for a decade now. Leonardo put him there years ago. My brother...he's the best at eliminating anything that could damage our name, our business. Our legacy."

The bitterness in his words was unmistakable. "What do you mean your grandmother parades him?"

"You didn't get the sordid Brunetti history online before you attacked BCS?"

The man changed skins as easily as a chameleon—one minute a charming rogue, the next a cunning businessman determined to make her spill her secrets against her own best interests. "I told you, I knew nothing about who and what you are."

Hesitation flickered in his eyes, before he cast another

glance toward the villa. "If you're to be exposed to them... My father, for most of my childhood, went on alcohol-fueled rampages. He embezzled funds from the company account for his personal use. Affairs with numerous women—both willing and unwilling—lavish parties at the villa... Think of it as a decades-long, out-of-control party that Greta turned away from.

"By the time his misuse of company funds and resources came to Leonardo's notice, Brunetti Finances, which had once been the leading finance giant in all of Italy, had been on the verge of bankruptcy. A dynasty reduced to nothing but a deck of cards standing on quicksand.

"Leo had to use every inch of his business acumen to stop it from crumbling around our ears. He slogged night and day to get us out from under debt, took control of the board. I designed an e-commerce tool at the same time. He brought in millions in investors, persuaded me to build and release it myself instead of selling the design like I had planned to. I created Brunetti Cyber Securities under the family company's umbrella and launched the tool. With the revenue from it, we stopped Brunetti Finances from going under.

"Silvio, kicking and screaming, was checked into rehab. My father's still a powerful man—so many of the investors Leo brought in are of his generation. So...lest the world think we're any less than the grand dynasty we're supposed to be, lest they wonder we're not all one big happy family, we parade him annually and pretend to be his adoring sons."

Natalie refused to let the stringent quality of his words, something that almost sounded like pain, touch her.

Massimo Brunetti had blackmailed her. He was a ruthless bastard who thought women were for refueling his... He was the scion of a powerful if *dysfunctional* dynasty;

he wouldn't have even noticed her if she'd fallen at his feet. There was no need to see him as anything but a two-dimensional enemy.

No need to feel this…answering emotion in her chest, this urge to touch him and smooth out his brow.

Nope, nope, nope. So not going there.

She tugged his wrist. "We don't have to go in, then. It's not as if you can't go against their wishes, is it? I mean, you're a grown man. You run your own company. Who cares if—"

His laughter cut through her persuasive tirade, sending shock waves through her body. The warm, masculine sounds reached through her skin, into her chest, enveloping her. Burrowing inside of her.

She turned to look at him and it got worse. Much worse.

Moonlight bathed his perfect bone structure, caressing the high planes of his forehead and cheekbones, lavishing that lush mouth with tender care. His nostrils flared, grooves digging around his mouth.

She tried to ignore the attention his laughter had drawn toward them. A shiver went through her as she felt more than one set of eyes watching her, watching them from the lounge and from the terrace above. "What?" she said, channeling sarcasm.

The flash of his white smile in the darkness sent awareness through her. It wasn't fair that one man could be that gorgeous.

"You sounded as though you were championing me. Is it possible I'm growing on you, *cara mia?*"

The endearment threw her even more off balance. "As much as a malware bot could grow on an encrypted system," she threw at him. "Seriously, Massimo, can we leave?" she implored.

This time, his smile reached his gray eyes, deepening

them into molten pools of warmth. "It would only be post-poning the drama. With Greta, it's better to get it done as soon as possible. All you have to do is bat your eyelashes, pretend to adore me and thank the guests when they tell you what a lucky woman you are."

"At what time during our short and forced acquaintance did I give the impression that I'm of the kind to bat my eye-lashes and adore a man for simply existing?"

He reached for her, his large hands encompassing her in warmth. "What worries you so much, anyway?"

"I'm not worried. I…"

His gaze held hers, searching, studying. "Natalie…"

"No one's going to believe you, Massimo."

"Believe what?"

"That I'm your fiancée. That you could fall for me. I don't—" she moved her arm to encompass the sheer elegance of everything surrounding them "—belong in this world."

His gaze raked over her, from her wavy, curly hair—even more uncontrollable after the flight—to her off-shoulder sweater, which instead of looking stylish, to her just felt tacky in this environment, to the scuff marks on her secondhand leather boots. "*No*, you don't."

No way was she going to let him see the ridiculous dismay settling like a boulder in her throat. What the hell was wrong with her? "We finally agree on something."

"They'll believe exactly because of that," he said cryptically. "It's too late, anyway. Even she's here."

"She who?"

He turned completely toward her and ate up the little distance separating them. When he raised his hand to her face, every inch of her froze. Her mouth felt dry, her pulse racing through her.

"She who I need to send a message to in the most diplomatic way possible." Gray gaze holding hers, he paused an inch away from her face. "I'm going to touch you, *cara mia*—*sì*?"

"Not *sì*, Massimo," she said, panic brewing in her belly, and his mouth twitched. "Why do you want to touch me?"

"For the audience," he said, his eyes saying something else completely. "I'm going to touch you and kiss you, and maybe… All you have to do is close your eyes and think of your future, unmarred by visits to jail cells."

"You're a rogue and twisted to get your kicks from a woman you're blackmailing."

Instead of anger, his eyes glittered with warmth and desire. "Shall I tell you the bare truth, then, *bella mia*? The one small nugget that distracts me when I should be focused on a hundred other priorities?"

It took everything she had to not give in to the urge to lean into him. Already, the scent of him—cologne, sweat and the cigar she'd seen him smoking this morning—entrenched deep under her skin. "What?"

"It's for the audience, *sì*. But also, for me. For us. I should very much like to learn what you taste like, Natalie, and every time you lick your lower lip, which you do, any time I set my eyes on that mouth, it's like you're inviting me to do the same. Every time you devour me with those big eyes, my nose, my mouth, my hair…you're—"

Warmth unlike she'd ever experienced uncurled low in her belly, spreading its wicked fingers to each limb until she was made of honey. He'd barely even touched her and she was branded by the honesty in his words. Desire pervaded his every word, his accent deepening with each breath. "I'm not, I mean… I wasn't…"

Something almost like possessiveness flitted in his eyes. Because, really, what did she know of men. Especially of men like Massimo Brunetti. "One kiss, Natalie. Be honest. Tell me you haven't wondered, too. Tell me you haven't been thinking of the heat between us and I'll make do with a kiss on the cheek."

She simply nodded, no words coming to her aid. A light-headedness traversed through her entire body, stealing her good sense.

If he'd coerced her, if he'd grabbed her hands or pulled her to him roughly, the spell of the moment would have broken. If he had taken it as his due, instead of asking, the tentative connection between them would've fractured. She would've regained the little common sense she possessed.

But he didn't.

Massimo didn't do anything that she expected of him. And when he did the unexpected, he stole away the ground from under her.

As if she were the most precious possession to come into his hands, his fingers landed on her wrists softly. Turning one, he raised it to his mouth. The first press of his lips against the sensitive skin sent tremors of longing through her. He didn't let her look away, either. The flick of his tongue over the plump vein, the stubble surrounding his mouth scraping in contrast, the sight of his arrogant head bent to her wrist…everything conspired and coalesced into a temptation neither her body nor her mind could resist.

Knees trembling, she let out a soft gasp, an erotic sound that deepened the gray fire in his eyes. When he pulled her toward him, she went, desperately needing more. And he delivered, his fingers digging into her shoulders, moving lower, touching every inch of her. The first, barely there slide of her breasts against his chest was a sensation she'd remember forever. Breath punched out of her on a long hiss, the strength of his powerful thighs a teasing caress against her own.

He let his fingers splay on her back. The tips reached the

dip of her waist, spanned it and then moved back up. The rough hitch of his breath was music to her ears, bringing the knowledge to her ensnared senses that he wanted her just as much as she did him. When he moved his hands up from her waist, just a couple of tempting inches, the tips barely even grazing the sides of her breasts, she stiffened, tried to move away and stumbled until her hip bumped against his front and her thigh was caught between his.

Electricity zinged through her veins. He was so solidly masculine around her, both a haven of warmth and demanding need. Fingers on her shoulders held her rigid as he bent that mouth finally. A kiss from that mouth at her cheek, at her temple, the tip of her nose—like wings of a butterfly. And then he brushed his mouth against hers. "From the moment I realized you were the hacker who'd haunted my days and nights…all I could think of was doing this."

Nat jerked in his embrace, the sensations generated by the contact so delicious. So hot. If not for the heat in her veins, she'd have laughed for he did it with that scientific precision, as if an inch of her couldn't be left unexplored. Tired of waiting for him, she followed his lips with her own, seeking the heat and promise.

Sensations jerked through her at the hard contact. She licked his lower lip, pressed herself into his warmth.

She heard the soft curse he left on her lips, saw shock and something indefinable widen his eyes. As if he, too, had been unprepared for the spark to turn into a full-blown fire. And then he was repeating the torment all over again. For a hard, lean man, he had the most incredibly soft lips. And his beard, oh, it was such a contrasting scrape against the softness of his kisses, a pleading moan pushed out of her own mouth.

"You taste sweet and tart, *cara mia*," he said huskily, as lost as she was.

Kissing her all over, his long fingers climbing up her back, sliding around the nape of her neck, sneaking into her hair. And then, suddenly, his grip tightened there. When he pulled, her face tilted back, an offering she willingly gave.

Desire stamped out everything else from his arrogant features—the casual humor, the ambitious billionaire—leaving a starkness to him.

Gaze locked on her own, this time, when he bent that mouth to hers, there was no exploration. No entreating. He nipped at her lower lip, and blew warm breath over the hurt. Licked and plundered. A continuous assault that made tingles spread out. He took, and yet gave, such indescribable pleasure. The stroke of his tongue was a caress that had her gasping into his mouth. He licked into hers with an erotic hunger that had her rising up to her toes, burrowing into him to get even closer, clinging to his solid shoulders with shallow breaths. The scent of him, so familiarly male already, coated every inch of her.

Her own hands wandered restlessly, from the scrape of his beard to his neck and into his hair, pulling, tugging, wanting more of him. Desperate to keep the madness going. She moved them over his chest, loving the sinew, thanking the stars that he'd taken off the jacket. His shirt was no barrier against the heat he radiated. Air was something he granted her amid the hungry kisses.

"*Altro*, Natalie *mia*. I need more." His heated whisper inflamed her with its honesty. The differences between them melted away under the heat of their touch.

Tongues dueled, teeth banged, as the kiss lost its finesse and became nothing but hunger. A gateway to something much more.

Her back was bowed, his hands at her waist pulling her up, his fingers digging painfully into her hips. Her breasts crushed against his chest. Natalie could do nothing but drown in the avalanche of sensations. Revel in the pleasure coursing through her.

With a growly moan, Natalie pushed away at his hands, and thrust her hips into his. Driven by instinct, desperate for more. Not wanting the moment to end.

The slight graze of his erection against her soft belly before he pushed her firmly back jolted her out of the feral need pumping through her veins. His curse was loud and harsh in the slumbering silence of the night all around them.

She stared into the piercing gaze, stunned, mouth stinging. His breath was harsher than her own, his pupils dilated. The lean chest falling and rising in a rhythm her own matched. Her hands fell away from him, empty. Slowly, softly, their surroundings—the air redolent with the scent of flowers, their audience, more than one set of eyes devouring them—began to filter through her consciousness. Yet, nothing could penetrate fully the haze of pleasure the kiss had left in her mind. Her limbs, her belly, her breasts... she felt like she was swimming in honey. Naked.

"That went farther than I anticipated." He spoke slowly, as if each word had to be pulled out. Hoarse. His English thickly accented for the first time. "To go any further, *cara mia*, we'll have to revisit our—"

"I'm not sleeping with you," Nat somehow managed to whisper, her pulse still zigzagging all over the place. Desperate to cut off whatever asinine, calculating announcement he'd have made. It was bad enough she had crawled all over him, in front of his family and friends, no less. Had lost herself in that kiss, completely.

She couldn't let him insult her, too, by offering to pay for more services rendered or some such.

The kiss and the intensity of it had thrown him, too. As inexperienced as she was with arrogant, confounding men who kissed like fantasies given life, she could see the contradiction in his eyes, the tension in his brow. He'd expected it to be a pleasant diversion, for both himself and his bloody audience, a game of kissing the criminal, but it had slipped out of his control and morphed into something much more.

But for her, it had been her first kiss. A memory to be cherished.

For once in her life, she'd been allowed to be selfish. Given the sex-god incarnate staring at her, she was allowed to be foolish and flighty. Once. But no more.

"Why not?" he taunted back.

"Now you sound like that pretty, rich boy denied his new toy."

Color flooded his cheeks. "You can't deny the connection between us. From that first moment. It's already messing with my rationality."

She fisted her hands at her sides. Better than running them over her trembling lips. "Because we're not equals, Mr. Brunetti." He scowled at her use of his formal name. "How can I be sure what your motives are? How would I know if you're doing it because you want to try the novelty of having the hacker who bested you catering to your desires, under your control, in your bed—" she purposely made her words crude, for her own benefit "—or because you're arrogant enough to believe that you're such a good lay that I'll spill all my secrets to you in gratitude?"

He tilted her chin up, mouth tensed. "I know my own mind, *cara mia*. I want you, Natalie." His gaze touched her lips with such possessiveness that contradicted the logical, rational man she glimpsed in him. "I've never been attracted to a woman so much that I want to own both her body and mind."

His jaw tightened, the raw honesty of his words a revelation to both of them.

She wanted to believe him so desperately. Wished she had that innocence, those rose-tinted glasses she'd lost so long ago, to see all of this as some fantastic fairy tale. That all of it could have a happy ending.

Even for a short affair where she could live, be herself for a small capsule of time. But she wasn't built to have casual, torrid affairs with complex men.

"It doesn't have to complicate matters."

"Could you be so arrogant to think I'll fall at your feet?"

"Arrogance has nothing to do with it. That kiss speaks for itself."

"You've turned my world upside down in the matter of a few hours. You hold my fate in your hands.

"If I sleep with you, can you ever be sure if I was doing it because I wanted to persuade you to let me go or because I really wanted to have sex with you?" She wiped the taste of him from her mouth, feeling a sudden dejection. "All the power is in your hands, Massimo. Which means neither of us could ever be sure of our motives."

He didn't quite flinch. A vein jumped in his temple, and he sighed. "Even having been on the other side once, power and privilege are still hard to separate from yourself."

Just like that, he shredded all the defenses she'd propped up against him into mere dust. She'd have been less scared if he'd been less understanding, less kind, less… *Massimo*.

No man, she had a feeling, was close to the complexity of Massimo Brunetti.

And if he grew up amid this, how could he know what it meant to be powerless?

He took her hand in his and laced their fingers. When she shivered, he pulled her to his side with an arm around her shoulders. Even fighting it, Natalie couldn't help leaning on him, stealing his warmth for herself.

When he propelled her forward, she went, like a puppet whose strings he held with those elegant fingers.

The logic she'd sprouted sounded so right.

Now if only she could get her body to stop fixating on the taste and warmth of Massimo's kiss and treat this whole thing…as a job. A job on which her entire future depended.

CHAPTER FIVE

THE THEME OF elegant affluence continued indoors including the wide steps and the portico. More fool her if she expected anything less. Even the remnants of his kiss couldn't numb her to the decadent elegance of his home.

The large marble foyer had a wraparound marble staircase with beautifully dressed men and women drifting around it. A large Venetian chandelier hung from the high ceiling with hand-painted frescoes that she had to crane her neck to look at. Her entire apartment could fit into the front lounge. A dark red Persian rug covered a small area and beautiful, original works of art hung on the wall.

Natalie could feel so many sets of eyes on her and Massimo and soft whispers across the room as if the cicadas had drifted inside. She was suddenly glad Massimo had vetoed her request to leave. Prolonging this moment wouldn't change the reality of who she was.

A large, rectangular, gold-edged mirror hung on one cream wall. One passing glance at it as Massimo tugged her with him told Natalie she stood out like a sore thumb in this crowd. She grabbed a champagne flute from a uniformed waiter and threw it back as if it were cheap, boxed wine.

Massimo cast her a wry look. "You're not getting drunk on me, *cara mia*."

"Why not? It's not as if I can contribute anything important to the conversation around me."

He rubbed a finger over a drop lingering on her upper

lip. The heat from the pad of his thumb tingled her skin. "Maybe not to them, *si*? But to me, you're the most interesting person in this room." A lock of hair fell forward onto his forehead as he leaned down to whisper. His eyes shone with a roguish glint, his mouth tilting up on one side. "Take pity on me, *bella mia*. Only you here with me is making this evening bearable."

Her pulse raced. The villa, the grounds, nothing could equal the effortless magic he weaved with his words. "You're even more dangerous when you set out to be charming." She pushed the lock of hair away from his face, and then snatched her hand back when he leaned into her touch. How could his face, his body, his expressions, feel so familiar already to her? Granted, it was hard to maintain animosity toward a man who kissed like it was the single most fascinating experience of his life. "You want me to believe you're not part of this crowd?"

"I was the stereotypical geek growing up. Socially awkward, sick far too often, hiding behind the escape that computers provided. Trying to persuade myself that I didn't need my father's or this crowd's approval."

She could do nothing but stare.

My father is a bully. Suddenly, his words, the tension in him before coming in, made all the sense.

"Ah… I've rendered you mute with my sad story, *si*?"

She shook her head, something she'd long buried searching for voice now. Longing to be shared with a man who was from a different world and yet, somehow, she knew would understand. "The loneliness was the hardest for me. For all their rationality, computers don't offer warmth. Or a kind word, when needed."

His jaw tight, his eyes searched hers. "Now you pity me."

She grabbed his hand and pulled him to her. The stubble on his jaw pricked her palm, his sharp breaths stroked her skin, and still she couldn't pull away. Couldn't get her heart to disengage. "I'm just having difficulty imagining this…hot, sexy, gorgeous man in front of me as an awkward, pimply, pasty geek."

"I never said pimply or pasty," he said, before he took her mouth in a savage kiss that knocked the breath out of her very lungs. The searing press of their lips lasted maybe a few seconds and yet it was hot, all-consuming, a synergy of more than just their mouths.

Hands on her shoulders, he pushed her back too soon. His eyes mesmerized with the heat in them. "If I apologize for that, I will not mean it."

She licked her lip, wanting to savor the lingering taste of him. "I…just…"

He grinned and she grinned back like a fool.

If nothing else, the fast and hard kiss made Natalie numb to every other dynamic and drama that played out over the next few hours. Numbed her toward the glittering butterflies sipping champagne ever so delicately and the men fawning over them.

Only her *bitchery* felt more than justified as she met an awful number of perfectly horrid people who stared at her as if she were an exhibit.

"Ooh, look at the low-class, unrefined American in her thrift-store clothes and shoes, pretending to belong on one of Milan's most wanted bachelors' arm," she whispered, sick of that feeling in her belly.

"You didn't tell me you speak Italian so well," he said, confirming her understanding of the looks cast her way. A pinprick of hurt flashed and she shrugged it away.

"I don't have to speak Italian. Elitist snobbery, apparently, transcends the boundaries of language."

His laughter was raucous, booming, shaking his body, translating the motion to her own as she was neatly wedged against his side. He looked breathtakingly gorgeous. Conversations around them came to a stunning halt, the silence left behind so loud that Natalie gazed around with wide eyes.

"You know what I like about you the most, *cara mia*?"

The stupid organ that was her heart went pitter-patter. "That I'm far cleverer than you are?"

His teeth flashed at her and she had the overwhelming urge to taste that smile again. To take the warmth of it into her. "That tart mouth and what comes out of it…" His voice dipped, turned huskier, his gaze riveted to her mouth. "How is it possible that it also tastes so incredibly sweet?"

Her cheeks heated. "Massimo, please don't—"

"How much longer must I wait before you introduce your latest toy to us, Massimo?"

This had to be Greta. Natalie cringed at having been caught staring at Massimo like a lovesick fool.

The older woman, clad in a white-and-black cocktail dress that went superbly well with her gray hair, speared her with a frosty look that made her disapproval apparent without words.

Massimo dutifully bent his cheek for his grandmother's kiss.

"Nonni, this is my fiancée, Natalie Crosetto—" the lie flowed smoothly from his lips "—the most interesting woman I've met in…forever—" turned into a truth that knocked the breath out of her lungs in the next second. He lifted their laced fingers to his mouth and pressed a kiss to the back of her hand. "She let me…*persuade* her to marry me."

He winked at her as she shook Greta's hand, answering her invasive questions about her life. About her family. About her past. For a wicked moment, she played with telling the woman all the details of her colorful past. But she had no wish to embarrass Massimo or herself. She nodded like a dutiful child while Greta, with a voice that sounded like a boom box and with heavily accented English, told her what a privilege it was to land the scion of the Brunetti clan.

Natalie had had enough when Greta started rattling on and on about pedigree. "Is your grandson a fish to be caught, Mrs. Giovanni?" she said, tongue-in-cheek.

"You would offend your relationship with Giuseppe Fiore for this nobody, Massimo?" Greta said, loudly enough for everyone to hear her. "Reject an heiress like Gisela, who would make you the perfect bride?"

"I offer insult to no one, Nonni," Massimo replied in an equally steely tone, before he tucked Natalie into his side protectively. The smile bestowed on Natalie was warm, his embrace too honest and too possessive. So dangerous that even she wanted to buy in to their pretense.

He placed another kiss on the underside of her wrist.

Natalie shivered, struggling against falling into his spell again. Neither did she miss the presence of the petite woman, her voluptuous curves dressed in a green silk that was the height of sophistication, her pretty face artfully made up to accentuate the dark black eyes and the scarlet painted mouth, hanging a few steps back, listening to their conversation as if her life depended on it.

"I fell in love with a woman with whom I have a world of things in common," Massimo said in a husky voice, his eyes holding hers. "She's nothing like anyone I've ever met. Even I didn't expect it. Giuseppe or you or any other person has nothing to do with this."

With that he pivoted them away in another direction without waiting for Greta's reply.

Nat swallowed the thanks that rose to her lips. She was damned if she was going to thank him for rescuing her from a situation he'd put her in in the first place. She managed to flit through the guests at his side for the next two hours without running away screaming.

All through it, Nat was aware of the tall, dark, striking man who watched her every move like a hawk.

Leonardo Brunetti, the only other person there who knew what she was. The cold hauteur in his eyes, the distaste in his expression as he noted Massimo's arm around her waist, said more than enough.

Massimo seemed to be saving the best for last, *yippee*.

"Silence and the four walls of a jail cell don't sound like such a bad prospect right now," she said as he pulled her in yet another direction. "What do you think is the market rate for enduring emotional trauma these days?"

Massimo smiled down at her. She tried to ignore that it lit up his whole face. The reassurance in the way he squeezed her fingers. Devil or angel, she didn't know what to make of this man. "Ahh…but I would miss you, *cara mia*." She stiffened when he tugged her tight against him, his mouth buried at her temple. "Don't let Leonardo scare you, *sì*? My brother's bark is much worse than his bite."

Natalie nodded, not at all surprised that he'd noted her reaction to his older brother. He was far too perceptive. Barely two days since they'd met and he'd already tripped her up far too many times.

The only person who would actually meet her eyes, despite the confusion in her own when Massimo introduced her, was his grandmother's stepdaughter, Alessandra Giovanni. Who turned out to be *the famous supermodel* Alessandra Giovanni, naturally. Almost six feet tall, the woman had a stunning face that photographers over the world loved, with a bombshell body that would fire any red-blooded man's fantasy. *And* she'd grown up with Massimo and Leonardo after coming to live with Greta and her father when she'd been twelve.

Any twinge of jealousy Natalie was foolish enough to feel that this gorgeous creature knew Massimo intimately died at the genuine affection in her smile. "Love and you, Massimo? Has the world turned upside down?" she said in an American accent that warmed Nat.

"She's a hacker who can take down the best security systems in the world," Massimo whispered in outraged mockery that made Nat roll her eyes. "She took me down, Alex. Me!"

"Ah…" Alessandra said, her twinkling gaze studying them both. "Now that makes perfect sense." Then the woman colored. "Not that you're not lovely enough for Massimo to want beyond that. You're just…so not his type." She grimaced and covered her face with a groan. Natalie liked her a lot for that imperfection. "I'm making an utter ass of myself, aren't I? What I mean is you have to be extraordinarily special for Massimo to have not only fallen in love with you so quickly but to have even considered forever… Nothing, and I mean nothing, comes before his tech empire for Massimo."

"Let's just say Massimo couldn't bear it that I might be better than him," Nat replied. "And in a strategy of if you can't beat them join them, he locked me down in a contract I couldn't resist."

Alessandra laughed at that. A lovely, genuine smile that was like a beacon of light amid the artificial glitter around them. "Oh, I like you, Natalie. Please feel free to come to me if you need ammunition against him."

Her smile dimming, Natalie nodded. She would've loved to have a friend like Alessandra for real. But this wasn't her life. This incredibly sophisticated woman wouldn't say hello to Natalie if she knew all the things she'd done to survive.

None of these people would, even Massimo.

This was a virtual reality program she was projecting herself into.

By the time they reached the two gentlemen—she used that word for lack of a better term, for they both studied her from top to toe with an invasive and at the same time dismissive curiosity that raised all her hackles—Massimo had saved for the last, Nat couldn't give a damn.

Leonardo Brunetti, like Massimo, dominated the space he occupied. Like his brother, he was lean but broad-shouldered, his face more rugged and brutish than sharp like Massimo's, cynicism and disdain all but set into the planes. An aura of power clung to him like a second skin. Unlike Massimo, who she'd realized possessed a devilish sense of humor, there was nothing gentle or merciful about the curve of his mouth or the icy blue gaze he leveled at her.

Here was a man who was determined to be pleased by nothing and no one. At least, not just her.

The second man, Silvio, was as tall as his sons and a mixture of both. Hair gray at the temples, his face only retained a vestige of the handsome youth he must have been. His features seemed as if they'd been smudged and distorted by years of alcohol. Puffy bags sagged under his eyes while his mouth seemed to be curled into a permanent sneer.

Next to his powerful, dominating sons, he was a pale imitation, in both stature and presence. And yet, having been a recipient of it far too many times, Natalie could see the casual cruelty he was capable of in his rough features, in the sneer he directed at her, could imagine him as a rough brute bullying a young, innocent boy.

Massimo's arm around her waist tightened. Nat leaned into his weight, seeking and giving comfort automatically. As if they were together against the whole world. Not that he noticed. He was too caught up in whatever mind game ensued between his father and him.

"Massimo?" She nudged him, needing for the long day to be over.

"Natalie, this is my father, Silvio Brunetti, and my brother, Leonardo. This is Natalie Crosetto, my fiancée."

"What do you do, Ms. Crosetto?" Silvio shot at her without a preamble, his gaze utterly dismissive of her attire.

"I'm a clerk at a loan office, Mr. Brunetti," Natalie answered, refusing to let another snotty man make her feel ashamed.

"Your family—"

"My family is no one, since my father walked out one night and left me to fend for myself. If not for a conscientious social worker, I wouldn't have known he had fathered a son with a different woman who he also abandoned."

She felt Massimo's surprise at her side, his frown.

It wasn't as if he wasn't going to find out soon, anyway. And really, having met his snotty family, she felt as if she had nothing to be ashamed of. Even her deadbeat dad.

"Ah…at least you've saved us the bother of a background check," Silvio finished simply.

Natalie couldn't even muster outrage. Massimo could be called Prince Charming if this was the role model he'd grown up with.

His gaze swung to Massimo's. "You should be careful, Massimo, or you'll lose more than Giuseppe's contract. Empires are not built on weaknesses." Something oily smirked from his eyes. "You do not need to marry the girl to enjoy her."

"I don't need your advice," Massimo ground out through gritted teeth. Fury cast a dark shadow on his features. "On empires or weaknesses. Or how to treat women for that matter, *si*?"

"You were always the weak link in our family," Silvio said, a cruel sneer to his mouth that disturbed her on so many levels.

Was this what Massimo had had to put up with, growing up?

Silvio bent toward Massimo. "Leo tells me the security system you've built has been breached. I knew you shouldn't be trusted, not in the long term. I warned your brother to not tie Brunetti Finances with you. Don't let the little success you've enjoyed thanks to your older brother's benevolence go to—"

"Basta!" With one arm casually extended, Leonardo stopped Massimo from launching at their father, while with his softly delivered command, he shut his father up. Thankfully, most of the guests had already ventured into the next room when dinner had been announced.

"It is not your company anymore, Silvio. Do not forget that you come out of the clinic for one week per year at my discretion. *Mine.*" Leonardo's warning packed no punches. "One word from Massimo and you'll not even see that little freedom."

Silvio left without another word, a little sliver of fear in his puffed-up eyes.

Natalie wondered at how the older man cowered in front of his eldest. Leonardo reminded her of a predator—one who would cock his head and look at you in one breath and then pounce in the next.

But it was the fury on Massimo's face as he turned toward Leonardo that had her chest tight with pressure.

"You told him about a small breach after everything I've done for that blasted company and this family?" he said, his jaw so tight that it seemed to be cast in stone. Pain and anger swirled like shadows in his eyes. "You enabled him for years, you let him abuse…" Massimo turned away, his lean frame vibrating with contained tension.

A whiteness emerged around Leonardo's mouth. Neither had Nat missed his flinch when Massimo had turned on him. "I had to tell him, Massimo. He's the biggest shareholder after you and me. I need…*we* need his help to manage the old cronies on the board if I have to tell them about the breach. You're supposed to be fixing it. Instead…" Leonardo's gaze swung to Natalie.

There was no overt hostility in his dark eyes but she felt like scum on the underside of a rock.

A challenge dawned in Massimo's eyes as he pushed himself into Leonardo's personal space, shuffling Natalie behind his broad shoulders. She fought against the warmth that curled in her chest. If she wasn't careful, Massimo was going to tie her up in knots, swinging from one emotion to the other.

"Would you like to finish that sentence, Leonardo?"

Her heart pumped so hard that Natalie felt it like an ache in her chest.

"Do you know what you're doing, Massimo?"

Massimo didn't back down. "Do you not trust me now?"

The space of a heartbeat, filled with so much tension, before Leonardo said, "Of course I do. I have never trusted anyone more than I do you."

Massimo walked away. Without another word.

If Massimo could be influenced by Leonardo, if things didn't get fixed soon… She shivered at the consequences. Would Massimo ever let it happen?

She turned to Leonardo, her throat strangely achy. "Aren't you going after him?"

Leonardo's head jerked toward her. He'd forgotten about her. And suddenly, she wished she'd just quietly disappeared. "Excuse me?"

She tried to spot Massimo through the crowd. "He's clearly…distressed. Shouldn't you see that he's okay?"

"Massimo is not a child."

"No, but it's clear that he still resents you for what you failed to do when *he was a* child, isn't it?"

The barb pricked the hard face. The all-powerful Leonardo Brunetti flinched again. "Stay out of our family's matters, Ms. Crosetto. If your fate were up to me—"

"But, notwithstanding your father's assumptions, it's not up to you, Leonardo." He raised a brow at her familiarity with his name. She found she didn't care. "It's up to Massimo.

"Save your threats for someone who hasn't seen the skeletons in your family's prestigious closet."

He studied her with such an intensity that her cheeks burned. "Ah… I see it now."

Nat folded her hands, feeling as small as a bug under a microscope. Her cheap clothes, her untamed hair, even her shoes—nothing was missed by his gaze. "See what?"

"The draw you hold for him. You're obviously talented since you bypassed his design. You're bold, even when cornered, and from that conveniently sad backstory, you're quite the damsel in distress, *si*?"

"My brother—" again that flash of concern sat oddly on that ruthless face "—has a weakness for the unfortunate. You're a novelty, Ms. Crosetto. Once that wears off, once he realizes what a liability you are against his ambition, he'll send you where you belong.

"Massimo has an unending thirst, a relentless ambition, to be the master of the world."

"You get your kicks by scaring people who can't defend themselves?"

"I saw that kiss. I saw the way you look at him already, the flash of concern in your eyes when my father spewed his usual poison. This will not end well for you, even if not in jail.

"Tell him the truth and get out of our lives while you still can."

He bowed his head and walked away, leaving Natalie reeling. She'd have ignored his threats if not for the ring of truth in his words. That was two people who were close to him that had warned her about Massimo's ambition.

Suddenly, she felt as lost as she'd felt the morning she'd woken up to discover her father had walked out on her. Wanting to trust and hope that things would right themselves and then being crushed by that hope. Learning to lean on no one but herself. Learning to look out for herself in the big, bad world.

Leonardo Brunetti was right.

Getting out of here without sinking farther into the pit she'd dug herself was the most important thing. She couldn't afford to risk getting closer to Massimo, not even to save herself. She'd no idea how long his leniency toward her would last.

She had to forget that kiss, had to forget Massimo's laughter, the way his eyes glowed when they shared a joke, the sense of challenge he issued to her. She needed to forget the shadows of pain in his eyes when he'd spoken to his father.

She needed to remember that gorgeous, complex man had only looked at her because she had thrown herself into his path by recklessly posing a threat to the most important thing to him—his company.

CHAPTER SIX

IT TOOK A few hours before Massimo emerged from the dark mood a confrontation with his father always left him in. From the quick but ugly jaunt into childhood memories.

He navigated the unlit corridors from his wing to the new guest suites with his rescue dogs, Lila and Hero, limping along by his side, without encountering any more of his family members or their unending drama. On a given day, he could only stomach so much of Greta's relentless carping about the Brunetti dynasty, the increasingly frequent glimpses of loneliness in Alessandra's eyes, Silvio's penchant for spewing poison—a whole year's worth, in a week—and Leonardo's cynicism.

Dios mio, he should be immune to his father's taunts by now.

Instead, he reverted to that emotional, always sick *runt* Silvio used to call him, would still call him if he weren't so terrified of Leonardo.

The boy who'd been heartbroken and unable to protect her when his mother had put up with Silvio's emotional taunts for so long just to be near him, the teenager who'd had to contend with the four walls of his home instead of the outside world and friends, the young adult who'd been terrified that each vicious asthma attack would be the last one.

Only thanks to a miracle drug in his teens had he started getting better, started seeing that he had a future.

The tech world lauded his genius, praised his innovative

apabilities that had designed an e-commerce tool worth
illions by his nineteenth birthday…and yet, the shadows
f that boy still echoed within him.

Computers and the rationality they brought to his tu-
nultuous life, the control and power they'd brought to his
ands in a powerless situation, had been his lifeline. An
scape from his father's constant verbal abuse away from
ne eyes of Greta or Leonardo.

That he'd left Natalie to the pack of wolves that was his
amily had fractured his mood. For all of Silvio's crude
emarks, it was Leonardo who was the most dangerous
f them.

He grinned, remembering Natalie had no problem stand-
ng up to him. No doubt the little minx could hold her own
gainst them. This protectiveness he felt for her…was ri-
iculous. Unnecessary.

But he couldn't arrest the pulse of excitement as he
nocked on the door to her suite. Twice. He was about to
nock for the third time when a muffled curse made him
rin.

The door opened wide with her leaning against it, eyes
ussed with sleep and dark shadows under. Her hair was
n such a wild disarray that it was a cloud around her deli-
ate face. The overhead lights she'd switched on outlined
er body in caressing lines. A loose T-shirt fell inches
bove her knees, the neckline baring the delicate crook
f her neck.

Innocence and wildness combined together, she made
im want to pick her up and crawl into the bed behind her,
o drown himself in all that rumpled warmth, to bury his
nouth at that pulse at her neck, to discover every rise and
ip…

"All the power is in your hands, Massimo."

An uncomfortable sensation skittered in his chest.

She was right. They were not equals.

He wasn't the kind of man who preyed on the weak. He'
never be another Silvio, not even in thought. He couldn'
kiss that luscious mouth of hers until he didn't hold he
freedom in his hands.

It was imperative that he get to the bottom of the truth
And not just so they could explore this…thing between
them. At leisure. No, he needed this threat to dissolve be
fore they could continue talks with Giuseppe Fiore.

But it didn't mean he couldn't enjoy the delectable sigh
she made. Or rile her up. Or pit his smarts against hers. O
needle her. To give him the truth and more. Natalie was th
first woman who challenged him on every level.

He leaned against the archway and smiled at the confu
sion in her eyes. *"Buongiorno, cara mia."*

"Massimo?" She thrust her fingers through her messy
hair, which thrust her breasts up and revealed a little mor
of her toned thighs. Devoid of makeup or that intractabl
expression she wore like an armor, he was reminded of how
painfully young she really was.

Twenty-two, the report had said. *Cristo*, he'd hate send
ing her to jail.

"What time is it?"

He grinned. "Four-ten."

"Four-ten when?" she said, grumpy and cute and sexy

"In the morning."

She looked behind her, peeked into the corridor, the
back up at him. Her hand went to the neckline of her T
shirt and tugged it up. Her knees bumped, color climbin
up her cheek. "What do you want? I went to bed barely
few hours ago."

"We need to get to work."

"Now?"

"Sì."

"Are you mad? You flew to New York, you barely slept t my apartment, didn't even nod off on the flight and ow... Massimo, don't you need sleep?"

He shrugged.

"Well, normal mortals like me do. And that bed is... eaven."

He kept his gaze on hers. "I'll allow you an early night o that you can enjoy the bed some more."

She shook her head. "I'm messed up thanks to jet lag. I arely survived that vicious attack by your family. I don't ave enough brain cells to rub together much less—"

"*Sì*, you will, *cara mia*. Keeping you out of a jail cell epends on your performance in my lab, every day. Your reedom needs to be earned. Starting now. I'll give you iumbprint access to my lab and—"

"Your lab?" Her eyes widened. "You're letting me near computer?"

"I got your financials back."

She folded her arms and leaned against the door. "And?"

"You have a lot of debt."

White teeth dug into her bottom lip. "Do you believe ie now?"

"That you didn't do it for personal gain? *Sì*." He ran a and over his neck. "I paid it off."

"What?"

"I paid off your debts."

She moved closer to him, unaware of her movements, ie heat from her body licking against his. The skin of her heeks looked so soft he had to fist his hands. "You paid iem off...nine thousand dollars...you paid it off..." She vayed against the door and righted herself. "Why?"

"It was no more than a little change for me. And if it eeps your loyalties directed away from—"

"You think you can buy my loyalty?"

"I'm taking away reasons for you to do something s
stupid again. To decouple yourself from a person who le
you into jeopardizing your future."

"You didn't pay it off because you felt sorry for me?"

"I'm a businessman first and foremost, Natalie. I'll d
anything to protect an asset."

"Not even a little bit relieved that your instincts wer
right about me?"

He frowned. "I took a calculated risk by bringing yo
here, whether you took money for the job or not. But trus
ing some vague instinct, no."

"Does a cold report with numbers make so much of
difference?"

"Of course it does. Numbers don't lie, numbers don
make you lose objectivity. And those numbers will shut u
Leonardo's questions about whether I'm sane to be bringin
you into the biggest contract we've ever courted.

"Numbers over everything else, *bella mia*, over emo
tions, over instinct, over weaknesses. Always."

Her face fell. And the question hurtled out of his mouth
"Why does it matter to you that I trust instincts and fee
ings?"

"What if I can't always provide concrete proof for m
innocence?"

Her question came at him like an invisible punch. Re
minding him that she stayed a step ahead of him. That fo
all that innocence in her kiss, she was always thinking c
her own survival. That she was just as ruthless about pro
tecting herself and her lies as he was with his company.

"Then I suggest that you don't get involved in anythin
that might require you to prove your innocence, *cara mia*.
He pushed her into the room, before he was tempted to gri
her about the truth, and kiss her when she lied. "Chang
and meet me outside. I'll show you my bat cave."

                    * * *

e was debt free—like, completely debt free. For the first
ne in her life.

Unless Massimo was playing games with her...

Wrapping her arms around herself, Natalie stared at the
an walking in front of her, taking in the wet gleam of his
-black hair, the thick cable sweater lovingly caressing his
oulders and the light blue denim doing wonders to his
hind and... God, where was she?

No, Massimo had no reason to trick her. And, she knew,
ere was no point in arguing with him about paying him
ck.

Dawn swept into the long corridor through the exqui-
ely designed arches in ever increasing curtains across the
eam marble floor, creeping up and up, slowly illuminat-
g the even more exquisitely detailed murals on the other
ll that reached up toward the colorful frescoes upon the
med ceilings.

Every arch and crevice spoke of elegant wealth, of sub-
power.

Like he'd said, it was mere change for him.

But for her, suddenly, the world felt like it had opened
into infinite possibilities.

She reached for him as they turned the corner into an-
er hallway. "Thanks, Massimo. I just... You've no idea
at it means to me to be debt free."

He tightened his fingers over hers, pulling her to his
e. "Tell me."

Surprised, she searched his eyes. "Digging for infor-
ation?"

"You never stop looking for hidden meanings and agen-
s, do you?" Exasperation coated his words.

"I'm sorry. It comes with never having had anyone to
y on for so long."

His gaze held hers, understanding and curiosity and so much more in it. "Forgetting your crime and my blackmailing you and all these lies…you're a mystery to me, Natali I never could resist one."

She looked away at the beautiful gardens awash in so pink light. "It means I can start saving instead of just paying interest on my loans. It means I can get out of that ding studio and maybe find a two-bedroom apartment in a muc nicer neighborhood so that Frankie can go to a good publ school. It means that I can adopt him much sooner than had planned. Much, much sooner."

"So you didn't make him up?" he said, a tenderness his eyes.

She laughed and punched his bicep. "Of course I didn When you return my cell to me, I'll show you a pic of him

"When did you learn about him?"

"About…three years ago." Just the memory of the d put a lump in her throat. "I grew up thinking I was all alon in the world. Apparently, my father, after walking out me, went and did the same to another woman and her chil This social worker who'd known me when I was in the sy tem…she contacted me when he entered the system.

"I went to see him and Frankie—he was six and scared. When I held him, I felt as if the universe had do something right in my life for the first time. He…is th adorable, funny, cute little guy. I told him right there th one day he'd come live with me.

"Until then, I'd just drifted from minimum wage job job. I took out a loan the next day, enrolled in a couple classes at the community college and…realized it wasn going to be as easy as I'd thought it would be."

"You had no one to help you?"

She hesitated. The tightening of his jaw told her she betrayed herself. The last thing she'd needed after Vincen had already loaned her money to get her off the streets when she'd turned eighteen was to beg him for another loan so that she could get a degree.

"No. I didn't. But now…when I get out of this mess, I… So, yeah, thank you." She looked away from him at the wall in front of her.

The wall stretched out far in both directions, reaching up into the domed ceiling. There were murals detailed on the wall, tall, aristocratic figures looking down their long noses—shared by both Massimo and Leonardo—brows drawn together, almost as if sneering at a mere mortal like her walking their hallowed hallways.

Her frown deepened as she spied someone who resembled Leonardo, then Silvio and then Leonardo himself. But no Massimo.

"You're not here," she mumbled, searching for his familiar face among the stern, boorish ones.

"I hadn't earned my place with them when Leonardo invited the artist."

"And now?"

He didn't turn but she saw the tightening of his shoulders just as they reached a building separated from the main villa.

She kept thinking he was part of all this…this dynastic family of his, this alien world that dined on caviar and champagne. But the tension between him and Leonardo, Silvio's thoughtless comments… What if his childhood had been just as awful as hers had been, even in this magnificent home? Even surrounded by family?

The odds he must have had to overcome to build something like BCS when he'd been so sick, when he'd been constantly told he wouldn't amount to much…

She rubbed her face—all traces of sleep gone, confusion roiling through her. Even knowing that Vincenzo hadn't really asked her to steal anything, she didn't want to give up his name. Not after he'd helped her get out of a destructive spiral that would've ruined her life.

Not when he'd never asked for anything in return. Not when he'd been keeping an eye on Frankie's foster situation in the past two years.

Her loyalties, as they were, did belong to Vincenzo.

The very thought while she stood here thanking Massimo for his generosity made her faintly nauseous.

A huge metal door with an electronic thumbprint-access console guarded a huge stone structure that seemed to be built with pure mountain rock. Natalie watched with wide eyes as Massimo pressed her thumb against the console and pushed the door open.

They stood on a ledge with stairs leading down. A thick scent of…grapes lingered in the air as Natalie followed him down. "It smells like…oak and grapes and—"

"It used to be a wine cellar," Massimo said, before he pushed open another glass door. "Leonardo had it designed for my exact specifications. We took out the old stone fireplace, added temperature control and left the original stone structure intact."

Her mouth fell open as Natalie took in the glory of Massimo Brunetti's tech lab. The rock structure provided a magnificent contrast to the high-tech servers stored to the left, while more than three stations on her right housed state-of-the-art supercomputers and glossy monitors she'd only dreamed about. Because of the dark background provided by the rocks, the light from the overhead fixtures gave the whole lab a golden glow.

On the other wall stood a gigantic whiteboard with a leather couch, a snowy white cashmere throw hanging on it and a stand with tech magazines thrown haphazardly

Through the narrow corridor, she saw a small kitchenette with a refrigerator and a small wine rack.

"Wow, this really is your…bat cave. Like the hub of your tech genius."

Teeth digging into his lip, hands tucked into his pockets, he somehow managed to look painfully gorgeous and adorable like a little boy showing off his biggest toys. "You could say that."

"I did wonder at the strangeness of you living at the villa, with your family," she said, laughing. "Doesn't it put a damper on your…extracurricular activities?"

He burst out laughing. "How is that you can strip a layer off even Leonardo but can't speak plainly about sex?"

She hoped the soft light hid her blush. "I'm a complex modern woman."

"That you are.

"I have a flat in Navigli that I use for my…extracurricular activities. Bringing a woman to the villa would only confuse matters."

"Ah…what with the expiry dates and all?"

He shrugged. "I did consider moving out almost a decade ago. When my tech was released and turned into a billion-dollar revenue generator, I had been on a high, raw, so full of myself. I partied so hard," he said with a smile, and she couldn't help but get swept away by his energy. "Very keen to cut my association with my father and Leo and just…the whole lot. But Leo convinced me otherwise. Also, since he was the one who brought in the capital to scale it up in the first place, he had ownership of the IP, too.

"Keeping BCS under the umbrella of Brunetti Finances, Inc. was imperative for Leonardo."

She heard that faint whisper of resentment in his words, the whisper of a boy who'd been measured and found wanting against his older brother. Was he even aware of it?

"Is that when you transformed from gawky geek to sexy stud?" she said, wanting to make him smile.

"Probably, *sì*." Color scored his sharp cheekbones. "I don't think I've ever been complimented in such a... straightforward way." His gaze warmed and he pushed away from the wall. "It provokes me into wanting to return the compliment in the way I know best."

She took a step back, her pulse racing so fast that she felt dizzy. "You could just say I look good, too," she somehow whispered.

"Only you can make an oversize sweater look so sexy. There. But I also believe in giving one thousand percent ROI, *cara mia*."

She looked away from that irresistibly wicked light in his eyes, the grooves digging in his cheeks. "I'm going to need to carry an oxygen tank with me soon if you continue to look at me like that." She stopped his stride with her palm. A huge mistake. His abdomen was like a slab of rock that surrounded them, and yet somehow warm. "You'll fry my circuits if you kiss me again and I'll be of no use to you."

He laughed and she shivered at the joy and warmth of that sound.

"So this lab...it's a fantasy or what? Those servers, Massimo, I'm salivating at the thought of getting my hands on it."

He switched one on, and yet, his gaze never left hers. "Hard for a man's ego when he has to compete with a machine, *cara mia*. I'd give anything to star in your fantasy. Why is it such a big deal that we both want each other?"

All that rough masculinity leveled at her...her skin prickled with heat. With need.

Still smiling, he leaned against the wall, ankles crossed. Hips slightly thrust up. Denim pulling tight against those ock-hard thighs. His eyes looked blue in this light. Twin-ling. Full of naughtiness.

Hair-dusted arms folded at his belly beckoned her. Wet, lue-back hair piled high, gleamed. She had the most over-vhelming urge to walk up to him, and kiss that curling nouth. To lean her breasts against those corded arms. To ress her hips against his. To tunnel her fingers through is thick hair and pull his head down to her until she could iss that smiling mouth. To make those laughing eyes turn ark with slumbering desire.

To meet him as his equal, to trust him so fully that she ould give herself to him beyond any misgiving or doubt. o live like a normal twenty-two-year-old for once.

She shook her head to rid herself of the stupid long-ag. They were going to be working here for who knew ow long.

"You're a fantasy all right," she said, her words coming ut soft and husky. His nostrils flared. "When you look t me like that, when you laugh at things I say, when you uch me, when you…kiss me, it feels as if I was the center f your world. As if you couldn't get enough."

"I can't. Even knowing that you'll run at the first chance, nat you'll betray me for some twisted notion of loyalty, nat this will only get complicated even more if I do touch ou… I still can't stop." He ran a hand over his nape, his oice husky.

Take a step toward me, then, his eyes seemed to say vithout saying.

She cleared her throat. "But fantasies don't become re-lity. That's their very nature. Even if you and I had met vithout my little attack onto your system…we're too dif-rent, Massimo. For you that kiss was a pretense. A chal-nge. A pleasant diversion. A case of kissing the criminal. or me…" She bit her lip, wondering at how easy he made

it to be vulnerable with him when all she'd been her whol
life was tough.

He had this...insidious way of getting past her de
fenses.

She couldn't leave her fate to him, yes. But in this, i
this, the only way to protect herself was by showing hir
her weakness. Trust him to do the right thing. Because a
she wanted to do was ask him to make those erotic word
into vivid reality. "It was my first kiss."

He came away from the door. "You've never had...
He considered his words, as if this moment was impor
tant to him, as if she were important. "You've never bee
with a man?"

She shook her head, heat crawling up her neck at hi
prolonged silence.

"Why?"

Again, that feeling of warmth filled her. He never as
sumed. Massimo always asked.

"It's hard for me trust anyone. Hard for me to let peopl
close. I... I grew up in foster care, got shuffled from hom
to home. At a young age, I realized that I couldn't cour
on anyone, that people can bully, berate, be unkind for n
reason other than that they have the power to do so." A not
of defensiveness crept into her tone, daring him to moc
her background, like his family had done.

But all Massimo did was watch her with that intensit
"To give over my security, my feelings, into someone else
power is hard for me. I have friends, of course, but non
too close.

"I don't trust easily," she said, wondering if he unde
stood what she wasn't saying.

He did. "And when you give it, it's been earned. Neith
will you betray it so easily."

He'd already earned her trust that he'd never harm h

hysically, but… She nodded, bracing herself for his anger, or his temper.

"Then it is up to me to make sure you trust me and do vhat is right for both you and me, *sì*? You better believe t, *bella*, I can be very persuasive."

With a wink, he pulled out one of the chairs for her and nelped her get settled. Joined her at the next station. Natalie smiled.

"Now, let's forget the outside world, *sì*? Show me what you're really made of, Natalie. You have free rein."

She logged into the system, and looked at his network nfrastructure. Anticipation built like an inflating balloon n her chest, electrifying her very limbs. "What…what do you want me to do?"

"I want you to mount an attack and show me any more security holes you can find. In BCS and BFI."

"You're not joking."

"No."

"I need a lot of tools and I use open source tech. And get this…some twisted, creative genius named it after a Hindu demon hunter. I need Wi-Fi adaptors that can go nto monitor mode and inject packets for penetration testing, a Bluetooth device to monitor traffic, a separate device to install—"

"I have everything you need. If you dare, take me on, Natalie?"

On a wild impulse, Natalie threw her arms around him and took his mouth in a rough kiss. God, he tasted like sunshine and warmth and rationality and wildness, and in two seconds, he turned her awkward fumbling into a knee-bending kiss that stole the very breath from her lungs. His tongue danced sinuously in her mouth, chasing and rolling around hers, his deep groan sending reverberations to the wet place between her thighs.

And it was he that broke it off and settled her back into her seat. "Thank God you did that," he said, rubbing his lower lip with his tongue.

She smiled. "What do you mean?"

"I'm an Italian man in his prime, *bella*," he drawled, thickening his accent. "I cannot have the woman I want panting over some technology more than she does over me. I would have kissed you if you hadn't." He took a deep breath until his chest expanded and his brows were drawn into a leer. "How else would I validate my masculinity?"

Laughter rushed out of her like a firestorm, burning her stomach, bursting through her chest. His gaze filled with laughter, he was the most beautiful man she'd ever seen.

Blushing, Natalie kept her gaze on the screen while the rogue whistled a merry tune as if he'd already won the battle between them.

CHAPTER SEVEN

MASSIMO CAME TO a standstill as he located Natalie in the oval pool, a nightly routine she religiously followed for the past ten days once he called a halt to their workday.

Soft lights illuminated the entire area, including the figure swimming laps in the pool in a blur of yellow. Giant trees artistically grown around the pool gave it privacy and made a paradise that he'd never appreciated fully, before tonight.

Moonlight followed her in splashes of silver on her bare skin, sometimes the dip of shoulder or a toned calf, sometimes that dainty curve of that waist that fascinated him.

All the steam that had built up while Leo had told him of the latest problem he'd come upon with the Brunetti Finances board hissed out of him, all thoughts of business and schemes of revenge and throttling little hackers who lied through their teeth, evaporating like mist.

He'd been so angry with Leo for extending Silvio's stay. But the master strategist that Leo was, he'd expected this situation. Whatever their internal quarrels, it had been essential to present a united front of their family—with Massimo and Leonardo's stalwart presence behind their father's back. The trio of them a force to be reckoned with for any board members with delusions of grandeur.

But that it had come to that…this was on Massimo.

This was on his obsession with the little hacker.

Every day he spent with her, he was beginning to lose

his mind. Was losing his path a little. And they hadn't ever
kissed again, not since the last time.

There was such strength, such force, to her personality that he found the fragility of her physical form an endlessly alluring contrast. Ordering Lila and Hero to heel, he
settled onto the closest lounger to her, his legs stretched in
front of him.

The *swish-swish* of the water and the occasional whisper of a cicada were the only sounds surrounding them. He
noticed her focus falter for a few seconds as she noted his
presence and his silent scrutiny. Her head went under the
water, her arms flailing ungracefully. He pounced to his
feet, ready to jump into the pool when she surfaced, spluttering and choking, followed by a litany of inventive curses
that chased away the tightness in his throat.

He grabbed a towel and waited while she swam to the
edge of the pool. Pushing her hair out of her face, she pulled
herself up above the water supported by her forearms over
the ledge. Brown eyes shot daggers at him. Kissed by the
water, her skin looked so silky smooth that he wanted to
run his fingers all over. "You almost made me drown."

"You shouldn't be in the pool if you don't know how to
swim, *cara mia*."

"Of course I know how to swim," she said, a note of defensiveness creeping into her tone. "You're watching me
without a word and…" He raised a brow and she sighed. "I
only learned how to swim recently and haven't perfected
my strokes. I was doing perfectly fine until you showed up.
You're not good for my focus, Massimo."

That irreverence, that honest but baffled admission…she
disarmed him so effortlessly. "You didn't learn as a child?"

"Swimming lessons weren't really a priority for a foster kid." She blew at a wayward curl that was already dry
and framed her face. Hair plastered to her scalp, there was

a stark simplicity to her face, a soft beauty that was utterly without artifice. "Not when you're shuffled from home to home. I started taking classes at the local Y. When I get out of here, I want to bring Frankie to a beach."

She'd hate it if he felt sorry for her, he knew that instinctively. "The local Y?"

"Y is the YMCA. The lessons are free, for the most part."

A tremble in the slender line of her shoulders made him say, "Get out of the pool."

"Help me up."

He put his hands under her shoulders and pulled her out of the water. The T-shirt and jeans he'd changed into splashed with water but he couldn't give a damn.

Desire fisted low in his belly, rising through him as quickly as the rivulets of water running down her silky bare skin. The yellow two-piece bikini clung to curves he'd dismissed as meager, only held together by a flimsy string at the nape of her neck. The two triangles of the top held her high breasts like a lover's hands. He could imagine his own hands there, holding them, pushing them up to be savored by his mouth. Could imagine her throwing her neck back, her body arching as he ran his tongue over that rigid nipple pushing against the flimsy fabric. Her thighs were corded with lean muscle, yet somehow so sexy.

Cristo, how could he be so fascinated by her?

He released her hands suddenly. She squealed, her upper body bowing back, her feet slipping on the smooth tiles.

With a curse, he grabbed her. The motion brought her into his body, plastering her to him, from breast to thigh… Time seemed to thunder down to a halt. As if to better equip him to process the amazing sensation of her warm, soft body clinging to his.

"Where did you get the bikini?" he asked hoarsely.

Wide brown eyes gazed at him with liquid longing as he lifted his hands to her shoulders. Rubbed at a drop of water lingering teasingly at the juncture to her neck.

"Alessandra. I didn't pack for a vacation."

"Oversight on my part, *sì*. I'll arrange for a wardrobe for you." Polite words to drown the sounds of their harsh breaths.

Her own hands stayed on his chest, his heart thundering like a wild horse under her palm. "No. This pretense that I'm your fiancée…works if they believe I'm different. From my background to my cheap clothes." She swallowed. "That I'm a novelty to you."

Water drops shimmered on her hair like silver lights, spraying him on his face. She was silk under his hands, warmth and feminine hunger.

"And yet… I've never wanted to do all the things I want to do to you, right now. Even knowing that you're probably colluding with an enemy, that you're as complicated as they come." His gaze, with a mind of its own, followed other drops of water running down the valley between those breasts, down the dip and rise of belly and into the bikini bottom. "All I want is to sink to my knees, follow that drop of water across your silky skin. Trail it all the way to the seam of your bikini. To dip my tongue into—"

Her palm on his mouth cut his words off.

He took a long breath, cursing himself for having so little control around her. Tried to push her away from him. But she didn't let go, her arms going tighter around his waist. "Massimo, we agreed we wouldn't do this."

He sighed, the feel of her body molded to his, conversely taking the edge off. Fingers under her chin, he tilted her face up to his. "No, we shouldn't. You're right. Not when you'll hate me when you hear what I have to say."

She stepped back from his hold, fear swirling in the brown depths. "What? What's happened?"

Right and wrong had never been so blurry. Desire and ambition had never been so muddied together. This needed to be resolved before he did anything he would regret later. In his business life and his personal life.

Natalie shivered even though the glass-enclosed pool was balmy. A luxuriously soft towel instantly covered her shoulders.

He took her willing hands in his. The rough pads of his fingers—another riddle for her to solve—traced the plump veins on the back of her hands. Mesmerizing. Soothing. Arousing. She tugged her hands away. "Massimo, you're scaring me. Just tell me what it is."

"I've given you time. Let you understand that I pose no threat. But I don't have the choice anymore."

"I told you. No one put me—"

"Stop, Natalie!" He stared at her for so long with such intensity that Natalie felt stripped to the bone. After what felt like eternity, he sighed. Resolve tightened the soft curve of his lips. He let go of her hands and she felt the loss so acutely that she had to hide them behind her.

"Would your answer change if I told you the security breach is not an isolated incident?"

Shock made her reaction come in slow, horrifying sweeps. Her stomach plummeted. "What? There were other attacks into BCS's security design?"

"No, that was all you. Only you," he said with a grim smile. Even then, easily acknowledging her brilliance when more than one man scoffed at it. Interestingly, Vincenzo and he had that much in common—an easy acceptance of her talents. "But there have been other things happening at both BCS and its parent company, our finance giant Brunetti Finances, Inc."

She could almost hear the rapid tattoo of her heart. "Like what?"

"Three deals that we had in our pocket fell through. Silvio's colorful, abusive past keeps being recycled by the media and the press. Dragging all of us into the news cycles. Alessandra's personal life, her past, her family in the US, keep getting news time, which, in turn, makes Greta crabbier than usual."

"Your grandmother and Alessandra are close?" she asked, surprised that the crotchety old woman liked and approved of anyone.

"She's not a complete dragon. Nonni was devoted to her second husband. Alessandra's father. Carlo was a good man—he tried to be a good role model to me and Leonardo."

"Didn't quite take?" she said, being drawn into his life. Despite the feeling of a sword hanging over her head. How much had Vincenzo orchestrated? What did he want of the Brunetti family?

Instead of being offended, Massimo regarded it seriously. "He made a world of difference to me. Made Greta and Leo realize what a toxic man my father is. I think...all our lives changed for the better thanks to Carlo. Alessandra shuttled back and forth between her mother in the US and here, and Greta made a lot of effort to make her feel welcome when she finally moved here. For a long time, she even hoped, I think, that either Leo or I would..."

Natalie's heart kicked against her rib cage. "Would what?"

He shrugged. "Would maybe welcome her into the family officially."

"And?" Natalie said, aware of the demand in her tone

and unable to quell it. She could even see it from Greta's view. Alessandra would be the perfect bride for one of her grandsons—sophisticated and beautiful and intelligent.

Massimo smiled, his teeth gleaming in the near darkness. Whether at her or the idea of Alessandra with him, she had no clue. "Leo and I like Alex too much to saddle her with us romantically, I think."

Because Alessandra was too good to be played with. Because Alessandra was the kind of woman he respected. The kind of woman to not trifle with.

Whereas Natalie was perfect for an affair.

She felt as if he'd kicked her in the chest. That he was unaware of how awful he sounded didn't help.

Damn it, why did she keep hoping that he'd see her as something more than novelty? Men like Vincenzo and Massimo only had certain uses for women like her, was that it? Another commonality he shared with the man he was hunting.

"So, yes," he went on, unaware of her confusion. "Alex getting dragged into this mess riled Greta, interestingly, even more than the Brunetti name being muddied.

"Anyway, resources for planned projects have been falling through at the last minute.

"And the day before yesterday, there's been a new development. It's why Leonardo kept Silvio here for this long when he knows I loathe it. He had a feeling this was coming."

Natalie had come to hate Silvio's presence, too. The very look in his eyes made her remember all the stuff she was hiding from Massimo. "What new development?"

More than fear gnawing at her insides, Nat hated the doubt in his eyes.

"Massimo, you have to tell me."

"Should I, *cara mia*?"

"You can't think I've got anything to do with it. You've got me locked up here, cut off from the rest of the world."

"Someone leaked about the breach to one of the board members. Forcing our hand to come clean to the entire board. You can imagine how that went down. That our clients' information wasn't stolen becomes irrelevant, do you see?"

"It can't be anyone else?"

"The board member who accused Leonardo of hiding this from them, this is not the first time he's tried to cause trouble for Leo, not the first time he's strategized to oust him from the board. He's not going to give up his source, either. But don't you think it's a little too convenient that of all the board members, Mario Fenelli was the one who's been told about the breach? The only people who knew were me, Leo, Silvio, you and the person who leaked it."

Dread so complete enveloped Nat's limbs that she felt frozen. "Wait, you think someone is sitting there strategizing all this?"

"Yes."

Jesus, what was Vincenzo doing? It wasn't bad enough that he'd dragged her into the middle of this, now he'd gone ahead and leaked the news about the...breach?

Massimo's gray gaze stayed far too calm. Far too intense on hers. "It's too much of a coincidence to think otherwise. So far, nothing has been so bad as to bring us down. Not too much of a financial hit for BCS or Brunetti Finances. Until now, with the breach so cleverly exposed where it could do maximum damage to Leo. It feels almost as if—" he frowned, clearly struggling with something "—someone is trying to figure out—" his intense gray gaze pinned her, leaving her no way to escape "—what would hurt us the most."

The truth of his statement hit her like a lash. He ran a

thumb up and down her cheek. She sank into the feather-light touch, desperate for the warmth of it, despite the tension surrounding them. Despite the lines she'd drawn between them. "Maybe you didn't know what you were getting into. I will allow for that. Maybe you were never meant to know more about this. But now it's up to you to make the right choice."

He was not quite the stranger from the first night again—cold, powerful and a little bit frightening. But neither was he the man who had laughed with her, the man who had kissed her as if she were the only anchor in his storm.

Was Vincenzo behind the other attacks, too? Why? Why was he targeting Massimo and Leo? How could he involve Nat in something so underhanded knowing how precious Frankie was to her? How could she give him up to Massimo when she owed him so much over the years?

"You have a week, Natalie. I need a name. I need this to end."

"Or else what, Massimo?" she demanded, a shiver in her very words.

"Or else I will let Leo handle the situation. I would let him do the dirty work of sending you to prison, let him be the villain. See, I'm no one's hero, *bella mia*. In fact, I'm even worse than Leo. Because Leo accepts the reality of what he is.

"I...on the other hand, like to pretend, as long as it's convenient and easy to do, that I'm better than him. That I'm better than my father."

CHAPTER EIGHT

HEART THUMPING AGAINST her chest like a bird trapped in a cage, Natalie pressed her thumb against the electronic access panel. The soft *ping-ping* of the panel as it turned green had the same effect on her as a meteor hitting the earth might have. Her belly swooped and her sweaty palms slipped as she pulled the door to the lab open.

Just thinking about the gray gaze looking at her as if she were an unknown criminal, someone not deserving of even the little consideration he'd shown her, she shivered, even in the thick woolen sweater she had borrowed from him on that first day. Walking to the terminal he'd set up for her, she pulled the loose neckline by stretching it and buried her nose in the soft wool.

The scent of Massimo seeped into her breath, into her blood, calming the panic in her muscles. An almost hysterical laugh bounded out of her mouth, echoing in the huge space. How strange that here she was planning to betray his trust again and it was the scent of him that calmed her.

She watched her reflection in the huge monitor as the system booted. Two days and countless conversations in her head hadn't made this decision easier or given her a different solution.

Yes, Vincenzo was a sneak and a master strategist and he was completely in the wrong for doing what he was against the Brunettis and for putting her in the middle of it. And no, she still couldn't betray him. Which meant she had to look out for herself.

Thoughts jumbled, tangled, piled and raced through her head while her fingers raced over the keyboard, creating the bot program that would search all of Massimo's cyber infrastructure for the proof against her. For the record he'd diligently put together to track her and nail her.

When her program found it, it would destroy the proof that he could use to send her to jail. Come tomorrow morning, Massimo would have nothing on her.

Except pure hatred.

Sweat gathered on the nape of her neck, the lab suddenly feeling like a jail itself, taunting her for what she intended to do.

God, she couldn't bear to see the disgust and the shock of betrayal in his eyes, couldn't bear for him to see the reality of what she was.

If she did this, there was no going back. He wouldn't trust her ever again; he wouldn't smile at her, wouldn't laugh with her, wouldn't kiss her ever again.

She buried her face in her hands and groaned.

And yet, to leave her security to the whims of a man, even if the man had shown her kindness and generosity, a man who prized his ambition over everything else…it went against every grain of instinct that had helped her survive for so long.

God, she was tired of fighting, so tired of being tough.

All she wanted, desperately needed, was to leave this lab, this place, this man who threatened her security on so many levels.

She had to.

The soft chirrup from his wristwatch grabbed Massimo's attention as he waited in the foyer for everyone to arrive.

An alert from the access log for his lab.

He frowned, but pushed the notification away with a swipe of his finger. Right now, he had more important things on his mind. Already, he was far too distracted and excited about the prospect of seeing Natalie. Eerily, it was the sensation he remembered from being a skinny geek, hoping the girl he liked would notice him at university.

Wait till you see her tonight.

The pithy text from Alex almost two hours ago while he'd been finishing his workout had filled him with all kinds of anticipation. He had trouble enough to focus when Natalie was close even when she wore her usual skinny jeans and any old T-shirt. Even now, he could recall the sight of her pulling on his thick sweater, flashing him her belly, by simply closing his eyes. Oversized, hanging off-shoulder, it should have looked anything but sexy on her. And yet, when he'd spied her burying her nose in the fabric, a smile playing around her lips, he had gone hard as stone.

Cristo, she revved him up so quick just by being present. Who knew what she would do to him if she actually dressed up for him.

Tonight was the night of the annual charity gala that the Brunettis hosted at the Galleria Vittorio Emanuele II. The one evening that Leo and Greta insisted they present a united front to Milan and the world at large. Much as Massimo preferred to toil in his lab over playing political games with the most powerful families of Milan, tonight was one night even he didn't dare buck tradition.

Giuseppe Fiore would be there, and Massimo wanted to see him in a setting away from the usual meetings. Without being surrounded by all his yes-men with their own agendas to push.

The man was an incisively clever businessman, noncommittal to the last moment, and Massimo needed to see if the news of the security breach had reached Giuseppe's ears. If it had, he would have to do damage control. Both on the business front and the personal. And having Natalie on his arm, he hoped, would smooth over any drama with Gisela.

No one who could see them together could doubt he had only eyes for her. The decision of what to do with her—on so many levels—had begun to give him sleepless nights.

"Keeping an eye on her is one thing, Massimo," Leo said. "Scratching an itch is one more indulgence. But letting her access your security designs for the Fiore contract… isn't that a bit much?"

Massimo had expected this confrontation the same evening that he'd introduced Natalie to his family. That Leo had waited a whole two weeks when his ruthless brother never hesitated to cut anyone, whether personal or business.

He frowned. Was Natalie right?

Had Leo kept away because of Massimo's harsh words? Was it possible that his accusations had hurt his brother?

"Stay out of this, Leo."

"I stayed out of your lab, literally, for ten days, Massimo. Left you to indulge in whatever you…want with her. Hasn't that been enough?"

"Do not speak of her that way," Massimo gritted through his teeth, the very idea of Natalie as some kind of toy to be used disturbing him on multiple levels. Even though that's what he'd always used women for. Meaningless, casual affairs so that nothing could distract him, nothing could become an obstacle to his ambition. "She's been working around the clock with me to fortify the security of BCS. She's brilliant. If I can get her to commit to us, she'll be an asset to us on the Fiore banking project."

"Despite the fact that what she did might jeopardize our

chance to get the contract? Before we clear up the problem she created, Massimo?" Leo set his perceptive gaze on Massimo. "She committed a crime. She refuses to tell you why or the name of the man responsible. You conveniently set all that aside because you want her.

"It's a little too close to Silvio's behavior—"

"Natalie isn't like any other woman you or I know."

Leo's eyes widened. "You like her."

The words washed over Massimo.

He did like her. For the first time in his life, it went beyond physical attraction. He'd threatened her that he would turn her over into Leo's hands, but could he, really?

Protecting a woman who was determined to keep her secrets over sound business decisions… For the first time in his life, Massimo wondered at the weakness that Silvio had always said resided in him. Was this it? Was this… unwillingness to threaten everything she held precious a weakness in him?

No! It couldn't be.

Leo pushed his fingers through his hair as if he'd discovered a bigger problem to solve. "I never thought you would be a fool for a woman."

"I'm not marrying her, Leonardo. I just refuse to take advantage of her."

"You really can't believe that act of innocence."

No, he didn't think Natalie was unaware of her own culpability. Or that she would ever stop looking after her own interests first.

But her shock when he'd told her about the other attacks had been genuine.

They'd spent days fortifying BCS's security design, patching up flaws that Natalie found with an incisively brilliant mind. He'd seen her brilliance with security design, her sheer joy in playing with it. He'd also seen her struggle with what he'd told her. She'd asked him questions again and again, sifting through detail, trying to connect the dots. He could almost see the picture emerge in her head last evening. See the conflict in her brown eyes, eyes that had never been able to hide anything.

Leo turned his gaze to Massimo. There was still that wariness in his eyes. As if Massimo were a stranger. As if Massimo could attack again and possibly hurt him.

His brother—the powerful, cynical, ruthless Leonardo Brunetti—hurt by Massimo's words? If not for Natalie, he'd have never seen it.

"If she's poor, buy the truth from her," Leo said into the awkward silence. "We need to know who's behind all this. She's our only lead. Nothing else is panning out."

"Natalie is not the type to be bought." She was brilliant, and funny and naive and more than a little defensive about her background and a whole lot loyal. Discovering the complex depths to her only made her even more interesting to him. Made him to want to protect her. Made him wonder what a man had to do to earn that loyalty.

"How do you not see that's worse? It means her loyalty has already been given to another man."

"She'll tell me the truth."

"Why?"

"I don't know, okay? I'm putting all the pressure I can on her," Massimo said, hating that he had no better answer or way of getting it. Hating that he was acting weak. Was he being foolish enough to hope that she'd open up to him eventually? When did being fair turn into weakness? Why the hell didn't the woman just save her skin? "Leave it, Leonardo, *per favore*."

The words he really wanted to say to Leo lingered on his lips. He cleared his throat. "Have you considered it might be someone Silvio cheated or abused or plain pissed off? Both you and I know his sins are numerous. Against many."

"That's the first thing I thought of." His brother rubbed his face. "I'm looking into it."

"*Bene.* I thought you might have forgotten what kind of a man our father is."

"I tolerate him better than you do, *sì*. Does not mean I forget what he is capable of."

Massimo nodded. *Cristo*, emotions were hard to put into words. But he had never shied away from the truth, either. "I owe you an apology."

Leo jerked his head up.

"For blaming you for Silvio's actions. All these years."

Whiteness emerged around Leo's mouth. As if his biggest fear about their relationship had come true. "Massimo, you didn't... I have never held that against you."

"No?" He smiled at his brother's uncharacteristic lenience. "Then you should. You were just as much a child as I was. Just as much brainwashed as I was. When I see him, I only see the bully. The insecure, pathetic narcissist who made Mama's life hell.

"The face he showed you...it's much more dangerous— it's charming and loving and you had to see beyond and beneath all that. Until Natalie pointed it out to me, I... I didn't realize how much that resentment still festered. How easily I could believe that you would choose him over me."

Leo's eyes held a wealth of regret before he looked away. "I... I wish I had realized sooner. Massimo. I wish..."

Massimo rubbed his brother's shoulder. "It's in the past. And even knowing it, Mama had never been able to stop it. But that's the kind of woman Natalie is, do you see?

"I'm not saying she's not culpable. Even as you advise me to incarcerate her, knowing your opinion, she made me see how much resentment I still harbored toward you.

How much I pitted myself against you. How much it hurt you. Even knowing the both of us for so many years, can you see Greta doing anything like that? Calling me on it.

"As if I had to prove I was better than you. As if I were still in competition with you for his affections," he finished, disgusted with himself.

"You're a much better man than me, Massimo."

"I think I forgot that."

Leonardo raised a brow in mock arrogance, his mouth split into a smile. "Good to see you back on form."

Massimo laughed at this dry wit. How had he not seen that his brother showed this side of himself only to Massimo?

"No, that's not right. It's not a competition between you and me," Massimo corrected himself. "I'm my own man. There are, of course, shadows of Silvio in me, but Mama and Carlo tried their best to cancel that out, I think." He looked at Leonardo and realized how lucky he had been, in a way, that Silvio had shown his true colors from the beginning.

"Now I can sleep better, knowing that whoever is causing this at least won't come between you and me." Leo gestured between them.

Massimo nodded, ashamed that he had caused Leonardo that fear. "We'll find a way, Leo. Even if—"

His brother's gaze turned away from Massimo, a pithy curse flowing from his mouth. Massimo frowned and turned.

His own intake of breath sounded like a shout in the quiet lounge.

Dressed in a gold evening dress that left her slender shoulders bare, Natalie walked down the steps. The bodice of the dress was two wide strips of silky gold fabric that roped up from her midriff, crisscrossing, to cover her breasts, like a lover's demanding hands, before the ends tied behind her graceful neck. Under the bright lights of the crystal chandelier overhead, the valley between her breasts shimmered, drawing his gaze.

Desire made his muscles tight. He had the most over-whelming urge to run the tip of his tongue there, before uncovering the plumpness of her flesh. The dress, designed to make men salivate, left the sides of her midriff bare, showcasing more bare silky skin, the sexy dip of her waist flaring into her hip.

Her glorious hair was tied into a knot at the back of her head, unruly, wavy tendrils falling forward to frame her jawline. Her eyes shimmered with a false brightness while her mouth, painted a wild red, curved into a tremulous smile. The pulse at her neck fluttered rapidly.

The slinky fabric fell to her ankles, shimmering with every step, the thigh-high slit in it revealing glimpses of a toned thigh. Three-inch heels finished her outfit. One hand anchored on the banister while she pressed the other palm into her belly.

She'd never be sensationally beautiful like Gisela or Alessandra. But her beauty was more than skin-deep. It lured with those intelligent eyes, made him laugh with that beguiling mouth, stripped him to the core by peeling off her own layers. But in that dress that highlighted the innate sensuality of her slim figure, delicate cheekbones carefully highlighted by clever makeup, she looked incredibly fragile, wild. As if one touch from him would mar her innocence.

She came to a halt at the last step, her gaze holding his, inviting and teasing and alluring. Lust spread through his limbs like drugged honey.

She had chosen the dress with him in mind. Her expressive eyes said as much without coyness, without artifice. She let him see the desire in her eyes, demanded he do the same. Never had a woman continually stunned and stripped Massimo to his core like Natalie did.

"Do you still believe her innocent?" Leo's voice at his back sounded eerily like his own beneath the desire drumming through his veins. "She stands there like a Christmas present waiting to be unwrapped by you. She's incredibly bold, such a tempting challenge, *sì*. What man can resist such open invitation? If this is not an attempt to seduce you into granting her freedom just when you tell me you're tightening the screws on her…then I will never speak against her again."

Massimo tightened his jaw, fighting the atavistic urge to punch his older brother, to hide Natalie away from his gaze.

She was dressed to draw a man's gaze and keep it.

Why was she into him now when nothing had changed, if not to seduce him into granting her freedom? Was he a fool to have trusted her this far?

CHAPTER NINE

NATALIE STARED AROUND her openmouthed, even after two hours, at the opulent grandeur that was Galleria Vittorio Emanuele II. The two iron-and-glass-covered walkways met at a central piazza below the grand, wide glass dome. The mosaic on the floor, depicting so many patriotic symbols of Italy, glittered under the bright lights.

Large circular tables covered with snowy white linen and adorned with beautiful floral arrangements that combined white orchids with bamboo were placed along the four branches of the gallery, welcoming eight guests on each. Each table, she'd been informed by Greta, cost five thousand euros, which would then be donated to a charity project offering meals to people in need throughout Milan.

There were designers from world-famous fashions labels, tech business leaders and even the mayor of Milan in attendance.

Massimo's subdued mood, something she couldn't get a handle on since she'd arrived at the lounge where he'd been waiting with his family, couldn't take away her attention for too long. The glorious setting and the dazzling gala felt like a stay on an execution that would come tonight.

But even the fear of where this night would end couldn't rob her appreciation of the setting. It was as if she had entered a different era—a different world. As the formal seated dinner finished, Massimo silently studying her responses all through it, the guests started wandering. Scents of the bitter coffee and decadent chocolate lingered in the air. A pianist sat in a corner, his fingers flying over the ivory keys, Beethoven's Sonata filling the air.

The Galleria, she'd been educated by a smiling Gisela in halting English, was the very heart of the city that married an intricate and complex historical period of Milan with technical, engineering and industrial accelerations. She wished she had her cell phone so that she could capture the glittering night and share it with Frankie later. To look secretly at night when she wished she was part of this world again.

Only families like the Brunettis—power and connections built into their very blood—could indulge the idea of using the Galleria, a cornerstone of Milan's history, for a private charity dinner.

During the day it was the site of the much-lauded Milanese luxury shopping, with many prestigious labels and brand shops. Even without any money to spare, Natalie wished she'd seen the place during the day. Wished she'd begged Massimo to bring her out for a trip to see the city.

They both needed a break, anyway—from being cooped up in the lab for seventeen-hour days and from the tension that seemed to corkscrew around them every time they looked at each other. Damn Vincenzo, the man was like an apparition between them, choking the air around them.

Natalie stole the chance to wander away from the Brunettis. She could already more than tolerate or ignore Greta's snide commentary, which almost seemed to be by rote. She laughed, surprised at the thought that Alessandra might have had a word with the old woman before she had left this morning after she'd seen Natalie crawl out of the lab like a thief, tense and shaking. Tongue-in-cheek, Natalie had attributed it toward nervousness for this party.

She was about to make her escape when Massimo

clasped her arm, and coiled it through his own. The tight cast of his jaw silenced her protest. "I want you to meet Giuseppe Fiore and his CTO."

She nodded, her heart beating rapidly at the frost in his eyes. Had he already discovered what she'd done this morning? How? She hadn't triggered the program to start until this evening. Even before she'd tweaked it again.

She let out a soft gasp when his thigh pressed against hers, the heat from his body a warm caress. His chest pressed into the side of hers, grazing her breast, setting nerve endings on fire. His fingers landed on her bare skin at her waist to steady her, searing her skin. Neither did he stop. He spread his palm out, maximizing the contact, his fingertips digging into her skin, the gesture utterly possessive. Breath coming out shallow, she raised her eyes to his. "Massimo?"

"You're playing with fire, *bella*. Are you prepared to burn?"

She could do nothing but stare into the desire he didn't hide.

Even seeing the beautiful Gisela on her father's arm, in a striking emerald creation, completely in her element as they joined them, commenting about casual acquaintances that Natalie would never know, sharing inside jokes, falling into rapid Italian that Nat had no way in hell of following—even that went over her head in contrast to the all-consuming possessiveness of Massimo's hold.

After all, her job tonight had been to hang on to Massimo with a doe-eyed adoring look that telegraphed to everyone that he was taken. For his part, Massimo was perfect in playing the adoring fiancé role.

Neither did she miss the way Gisela sidled to his side every chance she got, the way she put her hand over Massimo's chest, the way she leaned into him. While he didn't encourage Gisela, neither did Massimo look troubled by the way Gisela touched him without his consent. As if he were Gisela's property just because he was doing business with her father.

Natalie stayed by his side as more guests joined them and with effortless charm he soothed ruffled feathers about the continuing threats to Brunetti Finances. For a technical genius, he didn't talk down to any of them or dismiss the questions that Giuseppe's CTO raised as inconsequential. She couldn't help but admire the clear, concise way he explained the security breach—her hacking attack.

Natalie stiffened when he introduced her to them, expounding on her brilliance with cyber security design to the older man, surprising both him and Natalie.

When Giuseppe had asked for Natalie's experience and qualifications, Massimo smoothly slipped it in that it was Natalie that had launched the attack on BCS but very cleverly left it in the air for Giuseppe to think that she had done so at Massimo's behest and somehow the news had leaked of his own measures to tighten the security.

It was a brilliant business move—using mostly the truth, he calmed Giuseppe's fears about the security attack and yet proved that he had everything under control with Natalie at his side. Massimo might detest the business side of things, but it didn't mean he was any less of an astute businessman than Leonardo. She saw the flash of shock and admiration in Leo's eyes as Giuseppe bought it all.

The older businessman was much more gracious than his daughter for he wished Natalie well, congratulating her on landing "a most brilliant young man."

Once Giuseppe seemed to be satisfied, Natalie pushed away from Massimo and he let her go. She drifted from group to group, slowly making her way toward the bank of elevators a uniformed waiter directed her to.

She had held up her end of the pretense for tonight. Now, she waited for the ax to drop.

Voices thinned and drifted into soft whispers as Natalie made her way toward a smaller corridor that held the elevators to the HighLine. She'd heard walking on the HighLine over the Galleria would be like touching the sky. And right now, she couldn't bear to be around a man whose opinion was coming to matter too much to her.

The elevator car opened and Natalie stepped in. Before the doors closed, a handmade Italian leather shoe stopped them. His broad shoulders pushing the doors open, Massimo stepped into the car. Natalie pressed her hands against the cool metal, to puncture the tension filling the enclosed space instantaneously. Her belly swooped, more to do with him than the car rushing up.

"Running away, *cara mia*?"

"I just wanted to look around," she whispered. And then hating the quaver in her voice, she straightened her shoulders. "To get away from the woman fawning over you. That's allowed, isn't it?"

When he punched the button to stop it, she swallowed. "Then it's also allowed that I follow my errant fiancée, *si*? At least to make sure she's not meeting another man in secret?"

Natalie paled. "You can't seriously think I've arranged to meet someone when you've cut me off from everyone. You...don't think like that. Did Leonardo plant that in your head?"

His jaw tightened. "Leave my brother out of this."

"Massimo, why are you so angry? You've been in a foul mood all night."

"Why did you dress up tonight—" his gaze roamed over her chest, and then pulled up, a banked fire in it "—when it took me three days to convince you that I need you here at the gala at all?"

That's what this was about?

"I didn't want to embarrass you or you to be ashamed of me. Even if it's all a sham, I didn't want you to realize I was beneath all those women. I wanted…"

To appear to be worthy of you. The words stuck in her throat.

How had he become so important to her that looking out for herself felt like a betrayal to him?

"You wanted what?"

God, she was sick and tired of being twisted by her own feelings.

She clasped his jaw, tugging his head down to meet her eyes. Never in her life had she felt so vulnerable, so willingly weak. Only this man did that to her. He made her wish for things that would always be out of her reach. He made her wish she was…different. And that was the worst sort of thing to do to herself. "I wanted to look like I belonged on your arm."

The rough stubble in his skin sent longing unfurling through her stomach. She dipped her face, burying it in the crook of his neck. The scent of his skin seeped into her very breath. Her hands crawled up from his waist, to his chest, touching him, exploring him.

His heart thudded under her palms, his harsh breaths feathering through her hair. Need and fear drove her to do things she wouldn't have dreamed of. Instinct spurred her on. Pressing her chest to his, she vined her arms around his lean waist. Inched her legs to be cradled between his.

Gray eyes darkened into the color of the sky during a storm. His breath came slow and shallow. Burrowing her-

self into him, she felt the stirrings of his erection against
her belly. Hardness and heat.

She met his gaze, then stroked the tip of her tongue at
the seam of his lips. "Kiss me. Please, Massimo."

"Why?"

She laughed. The soft sound filled the small space.
"After all the teasing and taunting of the last two weeks,
now, when I ask you…"

A vein in his temple throbbed. "Why the sudden change
in mind, then?"

"Because when you kiss me, I forget everything else. I
forget the whole damned world and what is right and what
is wrong. When you kiss me, I'm not so tightly wound anymore. I'm not scared." She sent her hands seeking into his
hair, and tugged his head down. Pressing her mouth to the
sides of his, she drowned herself in him. With the tip of
her tongue, she licked at the soft lower lip, stroked it along
the carved line, from this end to the other until the taste
of him was embedded in her blood. "Don't ask questions,
Massimo. Please. Just for now. Just for a few moments.

"Imagine that the outside world—your company, your
family, your ambition—none of those exist. Imagine you
met me that first night in the cyber club and we connected.
Imagine that I came to you willingly, desperate for the pleasure you could give.

"What would you do with me if I were all yours?"

What would you do with me if I were all yours?

Natalie's question unlocked all the desires Massimo had
been struggling to bury since he'd set eyes on her. The
press of her mouth against his, hungry and soft, seeking
and searching, innocent and mind-numbingly addictive, destroyed the anger that had been brewing at her conniving intentions tonight. Right and wrong had never been so blurry.

Cristo, he was such a cliché of a man.

The slide of her body against his, his chest crushing her breasts, her long legs tangling with his, the way her soft belly grazed his thickening erection—it was heaven and hell. His hands crawled into her hair, tugging and pulling.

Yes, she thought to seduce him with a motive, with a goal.

Who said she would attain her goal?

Who said she would win in this game she'd started between them?

Who said he was going to grant her her freedom?

And not just because keeping Natalie around was good for BCS, even for the hundred-billion Fiore contract. Not because she still was the only lead they had in discovering the mastermind that was strategizing all this.

He wasn't going to let Natalie go, not for a long while yet. Because he wanted her brilliant mind around. Because he wanted to explore this thing between them, see this through to the end.

Acknowledging that freed him from his own guilt. From his own restrictions.

He pressed his mouth to her shoulder, dragged it to the tender nook of her neck, licked the pulse hammering away madly. Desire was a deafening drumbeat pulsing through his body. He opened his mouth, planting a wet kiss before sinking his teeth into the supple flesh, tugging it and releasing it until she was squirming against him. Burrowing into him as if she meant to reside under his skin. She tasted sweet and salty and soft and silky. Curling his fingers at her neck, he jerked her head back, until her spine curved, until he was all she could see.

Brown eyes muddied with desire stared up at him. Her glorious hair was coming away, rumpling all that innocence. Her chest rose and fell shakily, her nipples tight points poking against the slinky fabric. "Are you sure you want this, *bella mia*?" he said, desire deepening his tone, struggling to hold on to the last thread of sanity.

"Of all the rights and wrongs between us, this is the only thing I'm sure of, Massimo."

Pulling her up, Massimo took her mouth like a drowning man. Dove into the soft cavern of her mouth like a starving man. With rough movements, he turned them around, until her back was against the wall and her front was plastered to him.

She came into the kiss with a groan that pulled at his control, that reverberated inside him like a bloody gong going off. As if schemes and seductions were nothing compared to her hunger for him. Her voracious mouth. Her kisses tasted like honesty and passion and innocence and everything that aroused him, that tied him up in knots, about his little hacker.

"Anything, Massimo. Tonight, anything for you," she whispered in a litany, sinking into his kiss, sinking those misaligned teeth into his lower lip. Hard. Pain flashed at the edges of his consciousness, crystallizing the pleasure she drew from him even more. A feral groan ripped from his mouth as she swiped that tart tongue over the hurt she gave him.

He licked and nipped at her bottom lip, before thrusting his tongue inside. She was sweet, and hot, and *Cristo*, she was a quick learner the way she pressed her tongue against his when he went seeking. His hands continued their own foray, cupping her buttocks, squeezing her hips, learning every dip and swell, tracing the contours of her back before returning to her bottom again.

With his mouth, he trailed the silky softness of her cheek, her neck, licked at the pulse again before sucking it into his mouth. He was being rough, rougher than he'd ever been with a woman on their first time, rougher with a woman who'd so bravely admitted that his kiss had been her first.

Her little pants and mewls were like beacons guiding him, giving him a map to her body, a key to driving her as mindless as him. When he snuck his hand under the slit and cupped her bare buttock, she moaned.

When he buried his mouth in her neck and sucked at her skin, she pushed herself into his touch.

When he shifted the flimsy fabric of her dress away to reveal the globe of her breast that had been playing peekaboo with him all evening, she shuddered in his hold.

When he rubbed the pad of his thumb over the plump pink tip he discovered, she sank her fingers into his hair and tugged.

When he licked the knotted tip begging for his caress, she ground her belly against his erection. When he swirled his tongue over and over around the pink peak, she let loose a string of curses that were music to his ears.

When he took her nipple into his mouth and caressed it with press of his tongue, when he closed his mouth around the peak and pulled, she came away from the wall, a litany of cries falling from her lips.

For every small action of his, she reacted like the sky lighting up, like thunder that shook the ground. With explosive passion. With unbound enthusiasm. When he moved his hand from her rounded bottom that filled his hand oh-so-perfectly to the line of her hip and tugged at the string of her thong, she stilled.

"Massimo?" she whispered, a wealth of desire and a flicker of doubt in it.

He covered the mound of her sex with his palm, the raspy brush of hair, the warmth of her stinging him like electric current. *Dios mio*, he didn't remember a time when he'd been more turned on. He lifted his head and kissed her. Softly, this time, slowly, letting their mouths dance to the tune their bodies demanded, willing her to trust him. In and out, he plunged his tongue, in a rhythm his erection desperately needed. "You're so responsive, *cara mia*. I want to kiss, lick and touch you everywhere."

Eyes so wide that he could drown in them filled with sudden shyness. "Here? Shouldn't we go home?"

He smiled, the sight of her swollen lips, lipstick all smudged, the dilated pupils, her hair in a wild disarray, her pulse fluttering—a visual feast he'd never be able to forget.

A sight that made every possessive instinct in him flare into life. The thought of any other man seeing her like this, knowing this intimacy with Natalie, being the recipient of her smiles and her joy and her brilliant mind… *Cristo*, where was this possessive instinct coming from? Why was he muddying sex with emotion?

"Massimo?" she said, prodding him softly. Kissing him, dueling her tongue with his, just as he'd taught her mere minutes ago.

"Here, Natalie," he said, resolve filling his very blood. She would be his, only his. Somehow, he'd make it happen. "I can't f—" He tempered his words, now, today.

Another day, another night, when he showed her how it could be between them, when she reveled in this heat between them, when she realized she couldn't live without him inside her, again and again, when she understood the power she could have over him and he over her, then he wouldn't curb his language. Then he would use the filthiest words he wanted and take her every which way.

But for now, this trust she gave him that was so hard for her to do was a gift. A gift he intended to prize above all else.

"I can't be inside you here. Not without protection." She

colored so innocently that he took her bruised mouth again in a rough kiss. "But I'm desperate to see you come, to hear the sounds you make when you do. When we walk out of here, and the boring monotony of that party makes me want to pluck my eyes out, the sounds and scent of your orgasm will be my strength to get to the other side."

She smiled, desire lighting up her eyes into a thousand colorful beams. A little naughty. A lot willing. Her hands trembled as she straightened his jacket. "Beneath all that ambition, you're a wicked man."

She was laughing when he took her mouth again in a kiss—a sound that seemed to burrow into his veins, and it was the most joyous, arousing thing Massimo had ever heard in his life.

Her mouth matched his this time, hungrily licking and nipping, teeth banging, tongues tangling. As if he and his kisses and caresses weren't just to meet the needs of her body but to fill her soul, as well. As if it were a challenge she was laying down at him, to meet her fully.

He ravaged her mouth roughly all the while pulling her up, until his hand lodged under her thigh, tugging her leg up, opening her center up for him, until his cock was pressed into the hot V between her thighs.

Goaded by instinct, he rocked his hips into the welcoming groove. Pleasure burst over his skin like a million little charges had burst into life. Their mingled groans filled the air with an erotic thrum.

Cristo, he wanted to be inside her now. Without protection. Without caution. Need was like a thousand needles under his skin, stealing away rationality, urging him toward making promises to her. Promises that would chain her to him.

Promises that would have given him nightmares a mere month ago.

Promises of a future he'd never once in his life even considered as an option.

Instead, he sent his fingers seeking her wet heat. Anticipation had nothing on reality when he pushed her thong to the side and found her sex. *Cristo*, she was willing and wanton. For him. Only for him.

Moaning, she threw her head back when he found her clit. Jerked as if a lightning storm had hit her when he rubbed her moisture at her entrance, when he slowly penetrated her with one finger.

She was a wet, hot sheath, and every inch of him tightened, imagining how she good she would be around his cock. Sweat beaded on his forehead, restless heat clamping every muscle. "*Merda*, you're tight, so ready, *cara mia*. Look at me, Natalie. Tell me how it feels."

Eyes glazed, she looked down, her two front teeth buried in her lower lip. Her hands descended to his shoulders, her forehead pressed into his shoulder. "It feels…new, strange. Achy, Massimo. Like there's a fever inside me. Please…don't stop."

"That's my brave little hacker," Massimo whispered against her mouth while he pushed another finger into her and stretched her slowly. Every inch of his body corkscrewed with tension, crying for release. He kept his thumb pressed against her clit while working a slow rhythm with his fingers. "Move over my fingers, *cara mia*. Tell me what feels good, learn what sets your body on fire."

She came up and away from him, her body tense and shaking, soundless cries falling from her lips. He used his other hand to cup her breast, loving the stiff poke of her nipple at his palm. Color filling her cheeks, hands clinging to his shoulders, she caught on to the rhythm of his fingers. He plumped and petted one breast after the other, rubbing and rolling her nipples, watching her—fascinated, hungry, obsessed with how sinuously she moved, how quickly she learned what made it good for her, how greedily she demanded he move the heel of his palm to exert counterpoint pressure to the slick movements of his fingers.

Panting and moaning, writhing against his fingers, release came upon her, sending her slender body into spasms. Her skin shimmered with a damp sheen, her eyes heavy-lidded. She opened her eyes and held his gaze with such crystal clarity, such a possessive light, tossing them both up into the intensity of the moment.

Dios mio, would he ever have enough of this?

He helped her ride out her climax, her pleasure feeding his, until she arrested his wrist, and flopped onto him like a spent storm. Arms cradling her, he held her while she clung, whispering inanities, telling her what a beautifully wild creature she was.

He leaned his forehead into her shoulder, the musky scent of her arousal filling his very breath. This was not him. This man blinded by lust, egged on by the need for possession.

BCS was his life, his goal, his everything. He never had, *didn't* have, time for relationships. He definitely didn't have what it took to keep a woman like her. Innocent and fragile, complex and defensive. He couldn't let her mess him up like this, couldn't let her—

The stinging peal of his watch fractured the moment with the same effect of a hammer swinging at the closed walls. He pulled himself away from the welcoming warmth of her body, frowning.

Natalie stiffened just as he clicked on the warning trigger he'd programmed into his cyber infrastructure.

The alert he'd put in himself took a few seconds to sink in.

A rogue bot program was loose in his network. Scouring every nook and cranny. Searching for something.

He looked up.

Guilt screamed from Natalie's stiff posture. She looked sexy and wrung out, mouth swollen, a pink mark on her neck courtesy of his teeth, dress rumpled.

"A rogue bot program is scouring through my personal security network, destroying each level of encryption like a deck of cards. I'm assuming that is you?"

That was why she'd been so restless and nervous all evening? Why she had…

He cursed so filthily that the air should have turned blue. "Was that—" he pointed to her disheveled dress, his mouth twisting "—to pacify me when I discovered what you'd been up to?"

Whatever color had filled her cheeks mere minutes ago fled, leaving her pale and shivering under the glare of the lights. But she bucked up, tilting her chin up, gathering that toughness she wore like an armor all around her again. Shutting him out. "Don't be nasty, Massimo. It doesn't come naturally to you."

He flinched. "Then what the hell am I supposed to think?"

Her arms went around her midriff. She looked lost, defensive, utterly enchanting. "I… I didn't exactly plan for… to throw myself at you tonight. I've been wound up all day, wondering where it would end. After that evening of—" her arm trembled as she pointed to the outside world "—pretending to be everything I'm not, of being near you and wanting you and not knowing what the hell is right and wrong—" she bit her lip and groaned "—something snapped inside me. I wanted to be reckless, and daring and just take what I wanted. You… God—" she pushed her hands through her hair "—only you do this to me.

"Really, if you use that incisive mind of yours, you'll

realize that I don't have either the experience or the confidence to turn…this thing between us to my advantage. A pity that, because then I could've gotten myself out of this mess the moment you caught me."

His watch emitted another beep, jerking his attention back to the pressing matter. This time, it was an alert he'd programmed to go off when anything accessed a particular directory. The one that had files pinning Natalie to the security breach. This time, he wasn't surprised. He knew where her bot program was going.

"When did you go into the lab?" he asked, trying to sift through the anger and outrage and so many other emotions.

"This morning, when you were meeting with Leonardo. And just before we left, again." Sweat beaded over her upper lip, a faint tension vibrating through her body. "That second alert means my program found those files, doesn't it? I saw the layers of encryption around that directory."

"You planned to destroy the proof?"

"Yes. Then I'd have my freedom."

"Brilliant as always."

She laughed, the sound edging into hysteria. Her fingers crept into her hair, tugged, and then she dropped them with a soft gasp. "All day, all night… I've been going crazy. When you said you'd let Leonardo handle the situation, I wondered…"

"What?"

"I wondered how long it'd be before you decided you'd been lenient enough with me. I was just waiting for him to turn me in." She swallowed and looked away. "I was terrified. I felt as if I'd lost everything all over again," she said, fear turning those beautiful eyes into wide pools. "I was determined to destroy all the files you have on me."

"What did you intend to do once you destroyed the files?" he said, something building in his chest.

"I was going to beg Greta's help and run far away from here. From you. She'd have helped me. She hates me."

"You had everything planned, didn't you?" He'd been expecting something like this from her. "The sheer nerve of you to hack into my network and let something like that loose…while you kiss me at the same time…"

"Sheer nerve? How about desperation? I'm sinking, Massimo. I don't know which man to trust and protect and which man to betray…terrified that I'll make the wrong decision."

"It's not hard to stay away from the man who's doing illegal things. Not hard to stay on the right side."

"Only a man born to privilege can be so absolute about right and wrong. A man who's never known hunger. A man who's never had to worry where he would sleep that night. I don't know why he's doing this, but he's not a monster.

"He saved me from a bully, from a bastard of a foster brother. He saved me from going to juvenile detention. He…he…for years, he looked out for me. He…caught me trying to steal his wallet and fed me a meal when I was starving.

"He found me a place to live, gave me money to get my own place. All these years, he never asked me for anything. He only gave, Massimo. He…said he saw something of himself in me. Years and years of favors.

"And when he asked me to do this one small thing of taking down BCS, wrapped it in lies I could swallow, I bought it willingly. I did him the favor. I… The second time, when he asked again, I could have said no. He wouldn't have pushed me. But I'd been caught in my own hubris, lured by the challenge of taking you on.

"So, no, I can't betray him. Even if I hate that he threw me into the middle of some awful vengeance scheme he's been cooking for who knows how long. Even if I hate that

e's causing you…this much trouble. And I don't even hate
im fully for involving me in this, because how could I?

"If not for him, I wouldn't have met you. If not for him,
wouldn't have known what it was to want a man so much
hat I can't breathe. Can you imagine how twisted up I am
n all of it?" She wiped the lone tear off her cheek, her chin
etting into that stubborn tilt. "So the only rational thing
knew to do was to try to steal that proof before you sent
ne to jail.

"But… I couldn't. I just couldn't. All evening, I've been
vondering if I've gone insane. Wondering if I'm really los-
ng it."

Massimo felt as if she'd hit him in the solar plexus.
'unch after punch solidly connecting, knocking the breath
ut of him. "What do you mean you couldn't?" Another
amned peal from his watch.

"That bot program is only meant to locate my files. I…
couldn't bear it if you hated me. I couldn't bear to break
our trust.

"But I had to break this impasse. So I went back and I
weaked the program to just locate the files. I meant to show
ou that I'm capable of saving myself, of betraying you,
gain, but I choose to not do it. To show you that I… I would
ever break your trust again, Massimo. Just please don't
sk me anything more. Don't ask me for what I can't give."

So much she held on to, so fully, so completely she
ave of her loyalty even under the harshest conditions. It
vouldn't have cost her anything to give this man up. To look
ut for herself. And yet, she wouldn't… He didn't know
vhether to kiss her for her guts or to banish her out of his
ife for making everything so complicated.

He thought he knew her.

Dios mio, she'd told him enough about her background.
Ie knew enough to understand that to survive in a harsh

world, she'd become tough, and that she hated to be vul
nerable in any way, that she was a wild thing that wrappe
herself in layers of armor to protect herself...but this, fo
her to be willingly vulnerable to him, for her to give ove
her freedom, her security, into his hands, trusting that he'
do the right thing—the devastating result of that was in he
eyes wild with fear, in her mouth that didn't stop trembling
in her body vibrating with tension.

This was ravaging her.

And yet, she'd done it.

To gain his trust.

The weight of her admission humbled Massimo, th
emotional expectation beneath that decision...did he eve
deserve it? Did he want it?

She rubbed her eyes, smudging the mascara, ruinin
the makeup that he hadn't, leaving her still breathtakingl
lovely, starkly beautiful. Eyes that had glazed over durin
her release filled with alarming tears. "I hate that you mak
me so weak. But I'm done fighting it."

The *swish-swish* of the elevator doors behind him re
vealed the stunned faces of Leonardo, and Greta. With Gisel
and her father behind them. They'd been gone too long
Maledizione, the last thing he needed was the whole worl
to hear that his fake fiancée had been ready to leave him.

And still, Massimo couldn't find a mask to pull. Couldn
dig deep enough to care.

Let them think it was a lovers' quarrel. Let them se
how crazy Natalie could drive him.

He pushed his hands through his hair and went to her
not wanting the world to see her like that. Not wanting any
one to see the vulnerability in her posture. Clasping he
jaw, he tilted her face up to him. "What shall I do with you
cara mia?" Laughter burst through him and she stared a
him, as if he'd lost his mind.

Had he? Would she leave with him with not even a semblance of control? It felt as if he had crossed some hith-
rto invisible line, had left safety and sanity behind. She'd
ragged him into a new place, a place where he didn't know
ho he was anymore. Where emotions barreled through
im.

He struggled under the weight of tenderness, of posses-
veness, of deflated outrage. God, this woman…she stole
e very breath from him. "You'll drive me insane before
ou're through with me," he said, before he kissed her hurt
outh. His lungs seemed to fill with air, his limbs infused
ith energy again, as she sank into the contact. He tasted
er tears, her soft admission, her vulnerability. He held her
ght, wanting to capture the essence of her.

"I… I'm tired, Massimo." She clung to him like a rag
oll. All the fight and fury had deserted her. Her breath
hispered over his jaw, her hands roving over his chest.
'm tired of being tough. I'm tired of being pulled apart.
m tired of worrying about my brother, about you, about
e man who started all this. About everyone else when
l I want is to…"

"You…you're shredding me into so many pieces." Her
ngers traced the bridge of his nose, his mouth, his chin,
ven the small scar on his temple.

The look in her eyes, longing and something more, ar-
sted him. "With your kindness, and your charm, your
ughter and your warnings. Your second chances. Your
nate goodness. Your kisses. Your…" She looked down,
ashing her gaze away. "But remember this, Massimo.
When I could've freed myself from this dangerous game,
hen I could've protected myself—the only thing I know
ow to do—I chose instead to keep your trust.

"When I could've, *should've*, escaped, I chose to stay.
ith you."

CHAPTER TEN

MASSIMO STOOD IN the study that he and Leo used some
times, a drink in his hand, his mind drifting from thought
thought, landing on the woman in the guest suite upstairs

What would you do with me if I were all yours?

Maledizione, he couldn't forget that line or the vulner
ability in her face when she'd said it. Still couldn't wra
his mind around what she'd done tonight.

He verbalized his frustrations into a pithy curse as h
heard the door open and close behind him, knowing wh
it was.

Leo's laughter had such a shocking mirth to it that h
turned. "I'm glad you think this is funny."

"I was just remembering Giuseppe's and Gisela's ex
pressions earlier. I think you erased any doubt as to wher
your…interests lie, back in that elevator."

"And you've come to congratulate me about it?"

"Are congratulations in order? That didn't look like
fake engagement."

He scowled. "Cut to the chase, Leonardo."

"The way you spun it with Giuseppe—that the hack
ing attack and the security breach was something you ha
planned to find flaws in the system, that you brought he
on for that express purpose—Silvio and I can use that sam
logic successfully to calm the board's considerable doubt
and questions at the gala. Thanks to your quick thinking
we're in a good place.

"But it is imperative that we do something aggressive about stopping this…man, Massimo. Before we sign on with Giuseppe Fiore. Even a whiff of scandal like this again—"

"Could ruin that project before it even begins," Massimo finished, giving voice to his greatest fear.

Relief filled Leo's eyes and Massimo laughed. "You think I do not see the risks? You think I'm that far gone?"

Leo shrugged. "Women, and relationships for that matter, this family, this legacy, have never been an important part of your life before, Massimo. Even with your mama, you hardened yourself, letting her go so completely. You… simply decided Silvio had tortured her enough, decided that you were a weakness dragging her down. I'm not quite sure I'd have been able to do that. You decided you'd focus on your career, your ambition, you decided you would conquer whatever demons you had, and you did it. For a decade, I've watched you work crazy hours, go from strength to strength."

Massimo frowned. He had never looked at it quite that way.

"But with Natalie, you went rogue, completely off script, from the minute you met her.

"Honestly, I don't know what to think. I can't help but think maybe you've lost your edge for…this."

His brother's perceptiveness rendered Massimo so shocked that he could barely muster a response. "I haven't."

"And maybe you need to be told that it's not a—"

"Leonardo! All I will say is that yes, Natalie disarms me like no one else."

"I have to admit that to prove to you that she could steal it but not actually do it… I still don't feel comfortable that she could so easily ruin everything you're working toward, but I have to admire her guts. I can admit to seeing the lure she holds for you."

Massimo's problem was that he was beginning to admire a lot more than just her guts. Was beginning to lose his control, his path. "The Fiore contract is still my first priority, Leo."

"Bene." Leo nodded. And his vote of confidence meant something to Massimo. "I will not waste time and energy worrying over you, then. Greta and Silvio are far too much already. What did you find out from her?"

Massimo looked away. He'd never been so conflicted in his life. And he didn't like it one bit that she did this to him.

He walked across the study, taking in the expansive room that had been the seat of his father's power when he had ruled most of Milan as the CEO of Brunetti Finances.

Usually, he preferred to not step foot inside here, since all the memories he had of this room were of being summoned by Silvio at all hours while he was recovering from another asthma attack or a fright induced by an approaching one or when he had failed to exhibit great athleticism or when he saved a kitten. There had been countless things, and then being shouted at that he needed to let go of his mama and grow up and be a man.

That she was coddling him too much. That she was making him soft and spoiled.

That he would never be man enough or strong enough or ruthless enough like Leonardo. Never good enough to be a Brunetti.

Today it seemed like the two parts of him—one with an unending thirst to prove himself to Silvio and Leo, the entire world and to himself, and the second, the weak boy whose mother had tried so hard to teach him right from wrong, who had told him to define himself in a different way, his own way, who tried to negate the harmful narrative his father had perpetuated in the house for so long—clashed violently.

Dios mio, his mother had put up with Silvio for so long for Massimo's sake. She had tried so hard to stop Massimo from thinking that he had to be cruel and ruthless to be powerful and successful. In the end, she'd found love with another man, forced to choose between a new life and Massimo.

Massimo had bid her goodbye happily at the age of fifteen, desperate for her to find a little happiness, desperate for her to stop sacrificing herself for him. But there had been selfishness on his part, too. He'd been determined to prove that he could survive without her shielding him from reality.

And he had succeeded beyond his wildest dreams.

He had carved his own path, found his own empire. His cyber security business had infused much needed capital into other branches of Brunetti Finances, a dynastic multigenerational financial institution, when it had been limping along on its last leg. His brainchild, BCS, was the only reason they stood irresolute and unshakable today when most of Europe—and Italy, in particular—were floundering and falling into financial crises.

And when they signed this hundred-billion-euro contract with Giuseppe Fiore…there would be no looking back.

Yes, Leonardo was right that they still needed to find the man who was targeting them. But no, he didn't need to hold Natalie's freedom over her head to achieve it.

It was not a weakness to grant her her freedom. Not a weakness to achieve his goal, realize his ambition without crushing the one powerless person in all this. Not a weakness to grant her that desperate sense of control she needed over her life.

I chose you, Massimo.

That constant knot in his gut slowly relented, a sense of rightness settling his breath.

He saw the study with new eyes. Leonardo had decided to redecorate the space. The transformation had been fantastic—it had gone from a cloying, ghastly room with so-called precious antiques to an open space with contemporary art and clean lines.

Greta had put up a dirty, vicious fight carping on about legacies and dynasties but Leo had shut her up. But it had been a new direction for Brunetti Finances, and even better, it had been a new direction for the Brunetti brothers to take the company, their legacy.

"She told me enough about this man to give us a trail to follow. A money trail. He transferred her money when she turned eighteen so that she could get off the streets. I'll dig down to the exact dates once I get out of here. All we need is to trace her bank account to see where the deposits came from."

"And his name?" Leo prompted, clearly not satisfied with what Massimo gave him.

"There isn't one."

"Massimo, you have to make her tell you—"

"*Nessuno!* I will not," he said softly, "coerce her or threaten her with imprisonment. That's my final decision. She has too much stake in this now, Leo. I need her by my side to keep Gisela in line, with Giuseppe so close to signing. I need her to work by my side on the security designs. You saw how impressed Giuseppe's CTO was with her tonight."

"You're basing a lot of important things—things we've worked years for—on the fact that you trust her. Her loyalty—"

"Is not something that can be bought or forced. The way

Silvio got things done, we swore we would be different. We swore we'd build our fortunes the right way.

"Natalie will be an incredible asset to not just BCS but Brunetti Finances in the long run.

"It's plain, pure business sense."

Leo finally nodded. "*Bene.* As long as you're sure that's our guiding principle, I will follow your lead."

"It is. It has to be," Massimo reiterated to an empty room long after Leonardo left.

Natalie let the stylist use her like a fashion doll. She let the makeup artist pull and prick her scalp, straighten her hair to an inch of its life, probably burning away most of it, in the process of making her good enough to be the fake fiancée of the Brunetti scion.

A week since the disastrous and most spectacular night of her life, Massimo hadn't decided her fate. Still. Despite her throwing herself at his mercy. Despite puking her guts about how much he was coming to mean to her. Worse, her emotional outburst seemed to have only pushed him away. Filled the space between them with an awkward kind of tension she couldn't disrupt.

Excusing themselves to a curious audience, he had dragged her home that night. Warning her to do nothing for once, if she knew what was good for her. Closeted himself in the lab. The next morning, he'd shown up at her door again at the crack of dawn, like clockwork. For a whole foolish minute, she'd hoped he'd come for…personal reasons.

Nope, the workaholic that he was, it had been back to business. At least he hadn't revoked her electronic access to his lab. He had made her sign what felt like a hundred contracts, officially bringing her on the payroll for the Fiore

contract, including confidentiality agreements and waiv-
ers and whatnot.

Making it clear that she wasn't going anywhere, anytime soon.

Once she'd started thinking straight again and not out o
a desperation born of lust and longing, she realized Massimo couldn't simply tell the world that his fiancée was a
criminal or send her to jail.

There was the little matter of their fake engagement
She couldn't contest the fact that he needed her—at leas
as his fiancée—to keep Gisela in line. Especially since i
looked like Giuseppe had been more than impressed witl
Massimo's initial design and, with his reassurance abou
bringing Natalie on, more than ready to sign off the contract to BCS.

Now, he had officially tied her to that contract, too, by
bringing her on as a consultant. Her future was secure
Not just secure. Better than ever before. Because Massimo
Brunetti was a generous employer. She could put away so
much for Frankie's college. She could save for a future.

He'd even let her Skype with Frankie. More than once
Forced her to introduce him, too, since he kept hanging
around during the call.

He hadn't asked her a single question again about Vin
cenzo.

All this generosity was beginning to choke her since he
didn't even…really look at her anymore. She much pre
ferred his accusation that she'd been trying to distract him
while she deceived him rather than this polite distance, thi
courteous withdrawal. He didn't laugh with her, he shared
no horrible hacker jokes that he found on the internet, he
didn't tease her into kissing him.

A week since that night—the night her body had come
alive in his hands so violently that when she went to bed

every night, she closed her eyes and touched herself, trying to recall his warmth and scent and his desire. But her fingers were poor substitutes to his wickedly clever ones. So she tossed and turned, feeling a restless hunger after being cooped up with him in the lab for the whole day. Being near him, touching him accidentally, breathing the scent of him until he was a part of her.

And now this engagement party… It wasn't too much of a reach to think Greta was doing this to punish her.

She sighed when the stylist finally finished with her hair and the two too-cheerful assistants plonked a full-length mirror in front of her.

Despite her glum mood, Natalie's attention stirred.

Her hair straightened into a silky curtain fell past her shoulder, giving her the sleek sophistication she'd always wished she possessed. The white strapless gown that had been chosen for her fell a few inches past her knees, its beauty lying in the clean, classic A-line cut. It hugged her small breasts, clinging to the dip and rise of her waist and hips, ending in a big ruffle at the end, a beautiful feminine touch to contrast the severe cut of the bodice.

Pale gold powder accentuated her cheekbones and brow, and a glossy pink lipstick subtly enhanced her lush mouth. This look was night and day different from the one last week. Of course, that afternoon, she'd explicitly asked Alessandra for the kind of look that arrested Massimo's gaze, in her desperation to be worthy of him.

Tonight, about to be presented to Milan's Who's Who on the Lake Como estate, which was the home turf for the Brunettis, the stylists seemed to have been instructed that she needed to look classy, elegant. Instead of resenting the high-handed approach, Natalie decided to embrace it. Really, she had disadvantages enough when it came to Massimo without falling into a pit of insecurities about how she looked.

She'd just pushed her feet into bright pink pumps the stylist said would add a pop of color to her outfit when Massimo walked in.

His gaze swept over her, a soft smile playing around his mouth. The first one in a week. "You look…beautiful, *bella*."

In a black tux that highlighted his wide shoulders and lean waist, he looked absolutely gorgeous. Divine. "You look good enough to eat," she retorted, and he laughed.

"Well, it's the truth."

"I'm glad the true you hasn't been buried beneath all the primping, *cara mia*."

And just like that, her heart fell right into his clutches. God, she was really tired of the impasse between them. "Massimo, can we please not…"

She closed her mouth when he pulled out a small velvet box. Without asking her, he reached for her hand and pushed the princess-cut diamond ring in white gold onto her ring finger. "I… I have been remiss about that. Appearances must be maintained, *sì*?"

Natalie folded her lips inward, stalling the pinch of hurt. "Of course," she added, pasting on a fake smile. This was getting harder day by day. "Appearances are the most important. Even for fake Brunettis," she couldn't help adding.

He smiled, as if he were delighted by her snark. "Your bot program was brilliant. I didn't think you could take down the encryption around that directory, truly."

"Your ego is not dented?"

His mouth twitched. "You know me better than that, Natalie. I've never asked you to hide what you are capable of, from me. I never would."

Feeling like a fake of the worst kind, she nodded. What

ould he do, however, if he knew the extent to which she'd
sed those capabilities to survive her life, she wanted to
ay. She swallowed the question, struggled to push away
he niggle of shame. Her past was just that. The past.

And then he was pulling out something else from his
ocket, and Natalie's breath stuttered in her chest. Palm
p with it in the center, he looked at her. "I went the old-
chool route. I saved it on a flash drive. And the directory
ou found... I've scrubbed it permanently."

Her knees threatened to buckle from under her. "What?"

"The files are gone. The trail is scrubbed. This is the
nly remaining copy of everything I put together to find
ou."

"You're giving it to me," she finished lamely, her throat
ching, tears gathering like a storm.

Only a nod.

"With no conditions?"

"*Sì.* You'll never have to worry about ending up in jail.
s long as you don't do anything criminal again, that is,"
e said, the corner of his mouth tilted up, a glimmer of that
easing Massimo in his eyes.

She swallowed, but the boulder-size lump in her throat
ouldn't budge. She wanted to grab the flash drive and
un away. Far from this man she couldn't seem to dislodge
rom under her skin. Far, far away from her own heart's
tupid longings.

"Why are you doing this?"

"I'm trusting you. Isn't that what that stunt was about?"

"It is. And I'm glad. But...where do you and I stand,
Massimo?"

The warmth disappeared from his eyes. "We still have
n agreement. You're clever enough to understand that you
an't just up and leave. Not now when you're an official
mployee of BCS. Not when Giuseppe is ready to sign on

the dotted line. Having heard of her unstable reputation, shouldn't have messed with Gisela. Even if she knew the rules of the game. I'm afraid she's fixated on me."

She nodded, agreeing completely. "I won't let you down, I promise. I'll play the part of your perfect fiancée as if was born for this role. I'll be nice and sweet to your family and in public—"

He laughed so loudly that his brother and Greta looked up from the foyer where the first guests were beginning to arrive. "Do you know the meaning of the words *nice* and *sweet*, Natalie?"

"I do," she replied, basking in the warmth of his laughter. She loved it when he was like this—smiles and teasing—and…she loved that he understood her so well, and that he…

A wave of shock rolled over her.

No, she didn't.

She couldn't love him.

How could she, when she didn't even know what it meant? When all she'd ever known was survival?

No.

She was mistaking gratitude for a deeper emotion. It couldn't be love—could it?—when the very prospect of it terrified her to her soul. When the very idea of giving him so much power over her threatened to break her out in hives. She trusted him more than she did anyone in the world and she wanted him. That was it.

"Leonardo thinks I'm foolish to take such a gamble on you again. Don't make me lose face with him, *sì*?"

"*Sì.*" When he turned to leave, she grabbed his arm. "Wait, Massimo."

He folded his hands. *"Sì?"*

She turned the engagement ring over and over, feeling its weight on her soul. "What about you and me?"

"There is no you and me. There should never have been, ou were right.

"I'm still recovering from a stupid mistake I made by angling with Gisela. Even knowing that I was going to do usiness with her father, even knowing that she...had the eputation of being wild and unstable.

"And you—" his gaze drank her face in "—you've never ven been with a man before. The last thing I need is to nake another misstep like that, with you of all people. ou're far too—"

"If you say I'm innocent, I'll hate you. Don't take away he power of my choice from me."

"We belong in different worlds. Want different things n life. I will not do anything that will rock the boat now, ow that BCS is going to handle a hundred-billion-euro ontract any day. Now that you're an important, moving art of the company.

"I can't afford to blur the lines in this relationship."

If he had thrown her into jail, Natalie would have been ess shocked. A sense of falling, with no safety net, claimed er chest.

"Shall we go?" he said, offering his hand, and she nod-led. Her other hand closed over the flash drive.

She was free, finally. For once in her life, she was get-ing a break. More than she deserved. And yet, freedom ad never felt so costly to her emotions.

Tears stung at the back of her eyes but she held them back. Just. A cold that was absolute took hold over her.

He'd given her everything she'd asked for and more.

Gave her back her freedom.

Given her a secure future.

And yet, this...this distance he imposed, this calcula-ion in his eyes that she was a weakness he couldn't afford, this was a rejection. Like he'd given her everything and ye[t] taken away the most important thing from her.

Him.

He'd taken himself away. From her.

For a woman who'd built her whole life being self-su[f]ficient, trusting no one, why did it feel like such an achin[g] loss? Why did it hurt so much?

And was she prepared to let him do it? She'd always ha[d] to fight for what she had, worked hard just to keep her hea[d] above water. Now when she was faced with losing some[-]thing truly important, was she prepared to let it go so eas[-]ily? Was she really going to let Massimo push her away?

No. No she wasn't.

She wanted Massimo. And she was going to fight fo[r] him.

CHAPTER ELEVEN

PREDAWN PITCH-BLACKNESS WAS a thick blanket Natalie had to wade through as she made her way to Massimo's room.

She was done living in caution, done safeguarding her heart. She wanted, craved, that excitement. She wanted whatever pleasure Massimo could give her. She wanted, even if only for a few days, a few months, whatever time, to be the woman who brought out the wicked, wild side of the tech billionaire.

Except from the moment he had put the ring on her finger and dealt her that rejection several days ago, he hadn't looked at her once with that desire in his eyes. Not once had he been tempted among all the evenings they'd spent in each other's company. Not once had his polite mask slipped.

Enough was enough!

The marble was smooth and cold under her bare feet. Having learned his punishing schedule by rote—billionaires really worked the longest hours—she'd decided to just…show up at his door. She heard a sound from within just as she raised her hand to knock and decided against it.

Why give him a chance to reject her again?

Slowly, she turned the knob and stepped into the lounge. A small lamp at his desk illuminated the sprawling sofas and the contemporary art on the walls. She rubbed her feet on a thick rug, relishing the warmth of it. The sound came again—a cross between a moan and a growl, sending shivers down her spine. A thousand thoughts flashed through her mind—did he have a woman in there? Had he already moved on? God, was he *refueling*? If he was, she'd...throttle him, the unfeeling brute!

She didn't even have to barge into his bedroom for he had left the door open. Tugging the cashmere shawl she'd wrapped around her shoulders tighter, she stepped in.

The massive golden shaded lamps on both sides of the even more massive bed emitted a soft yellow light. Papers and electronic devices lay scattered on the nightstand. A gray suede headboard framed most of the wall. Dark gray bedcovers were rolled away. A white towel dangled off the end of the bed. And at the foot of the bed, leaning against it, stood Massimo.

Stark naked.

Head thrown back.

Breath coming out in harsh inhales and exhales.

Neck muscles corded tight.

Defined chest muscles gleaming with dampness. Falling and rising.

Abdomen so tightly packed that she wanted to run her tongue along it and see if he was really that tight.

Thighs rock hard and clenched, dotted with hair.

And his hand wrapped around his...erection. Even from the distance she could see the corded tightness of his wrist, fingers wrapped tight, and the head of his erection visible above his fist every time he moved his grip up and down with a grunt that seemed to claw up from his chest.

Heat licked up every inch of her stinging skin instantly. Every inch of her body reacted to the gloriously aroused naked man in front of her, reveling in sexual abandon. Her breasts turned achy and heavy, nipples knotted points rubbing against her T-shirt. And there was that wetness at her sex, readying her for him. Her skin felt as if it were two sizes too small for her feverish muscles.

Her breath left her lungs in an audible gush like a balloon deflating. And then she struggled to get more air in because there was none left in the room. She gasped under the overload of sensation.

Massimo's head jerked down, breath shallow. His gray gaze pinned hers to the spot, pupils dilated. He frowned, his hand coming away from his erection, which bobbed up against his taut belly. With shaking fingers, he rubbed his face with his other hand. And then looked at her again with an intensity that seared her. Twin slashes of color climbed up under his olive skin.

Had he realized she was there, not in his imagination? Oh, God, please let it be her that he'd been imagining...

"You shouldn't be here, *cara mia*," he said, husky desire making his voice low and raspy. Even his words seemed to ping on her skin, overheating her.

"Did I ever give you the impression that I'd abide by your rules?"

"No," he said, leaning that tight butt against the bed, jutting those lean hips up, so confident and comfortable in his nudity. So utterly, irresistibly male. "If you did, it would solve a lot of problems for me."

"I want to be here. All week, I've been trying to muster the courage to walk in here. All evening, I readied myself for you. I've plucked and waxed and bleached and shaved and peeled and massaged..."

He cursed. Then laughed. Then shoved his fingers through his hair. "You don't have to change yourself, in any way. I want you just the way you are, with an insanity that for the first time in my life even work won't do it for me. I think of you all the time...which is hard enough because you're there by my side 24/7."

Simple truth. No games. "Then why pull away from me?"

His gaze swept over her face, her neck, her sleeveless

tee and her shorts, her thighs, her legs. "I swore to mysel
a long time ago, even if I forget it from time to time, that
would never be the kind of man who hurts…fragile things
You're…breakable, Natalie. I'll use you, and then breal
you, before I discard you. I couldn't face myself then."

She'd never seen him like this—so desperately hungry
such stark need in his eyes. So much desire that her firs
instinct was that he would drown her in it, make her los
herself, and running away was probably the best thing. Bu
she refused to listen to that flight instinct. No, she woul
stay. She wanted to stay. She wanted to drown in him. "
don't need you to save me from you or from myself, Mas
simo. I don't want a hero. I've never asked for one. I've al
ways saved myself. Found another way, another path.

"I want a man to show me all the stuff I've missed ou
on because I was so afraid for so long. I want a man whe
will help me live, experience, feel. For however long we
want it to be.

"I want you, flesh and blood, like this, desperate for me
Out of control. Stripped to the core. Because that's how
stand before you."

Each second of the silence that ensued let panic loose
in her head. He was too honorable, too much of a protec
tor, to take her. Not unless she drove him to it. She needec
to be the aggressor, at least until he got his hands on her
Then all bets were off. She knew. She knew how desper
ately he wanted her.

She took a few steps toward him, not quite touching dis
tance. The jut of his shoulders, those rock-hard thighs—
every muscle in him clenched tight.

"Were you thinking of me?" she asked, licking her
tongue, wondering why her mouth felt so dry. "Please tel
me you were thinking of me and not another woman. Be
cause I'd have to hunt her down and kill her."

A dark smile split his mouth, a beacon of light in the darkness. A flash of that wicked, wild Massimo that she adored. A glimpse of the man she was falling for, fast. But there was only exhilaration right now in her veins. Only anticipation, excitement.

"Morning, noon and night, I think of you. I go to bed thinking of you. I wake up hard thinking of you. You in that gold dress, a goddess teasing and taunting me. You in that yellow bikini, like a sunflower in a field of frost. You in that white cocktail gown looking so demure and classy and calm and nice and sweet."

"Are you insinuating I'm not classy?" She pouted, taking another step. She was walking into a lion's den, she had no doubt. A willing sacrifice. And yet, she'd never felt so alive. So present. So in touch with herself. All of her.

His gaze swept over her with a warmth that was just as arousing as the desire. That made her feel safe. Secure. That made her want to throw herself headlong into this. "You're tart, and down to earth and loud and snarky and wild and...you're a summer storm, *mia Natalie*."

Happiness was a fountain spurting in her chest, overflowing to every empty space within her, filling her with warmth she always felt when she thought of him. She touched him with her gaze—that high forehead, sharp cheekbones, aristocratic nose, carved mouth, the tendons in his neck, the sparse sprinkling of hair on his pectorals, the defined lines of his abdomen, and his...his erection thickened and lengthened under her gaze, and her panties were soaked. A growl fell from his mouth, filling her veins.

She rubbed a hand over her nape and then over her breasts, aching all over. "Did it work?"

"What, *cara mia*?"

"Thinking of me, and doing that...did it relieve your... ache?"

Thick lashes flickered down and then up again. His shrug brought her gaze back to the jut of his shoulders. Tense. Taut. Really, his body was like a treasure, and she didn't know where to look or what to touch. "*Sì*. For short periods of time."

"It didn't for me."

A rough thrust of his fingers through his hair. An infinitesimal tremble of his chest. Her words were getting to him. A jolt of power filled her. "What?" he breathed.

"I…tried it, too. Touching myself, trying to find relief.

"After that night when you made me…" She swallowed at the devilish cast to his features. The need he couldn't hide. "Every night, when I go to bed after spending all day with you, I feel so restless. As if I were a prisoner in my own skin. I'd shower, remembering your smiles and your teasing and your hunger that night, and the strokes of your fingers… By the time I got out of the shower, I'd be thrumming with need. I'd get into bed and touch myself.

"One hand cupping my breast and one hand, delving into my… On and on… I'd be wet and I tried to… But I… just ended up making it worse." She swept a hand over her breasts and belly and his gaze followed her movements like a hungry hawk circling. "I… If you're not going to take me to bed, at least maybe you can give me some pointers?" She bit her lower lip and took another step. Another soft growl from his chest.

He didn't look like the suave, charming tech billionaire that had people eating out of his hands. No, he looked savage and rough, like the lowest denominator of himself.

"You want me to show you how to get yourself off?" Disbelief couldn't puncture the desperation.

She shrugged.

He cursed and laughed and cursed again. His powerfu

body rumbled with the force of it. "*Cristo*, you were sent to torture me."

"You look like you've had a lot of practice. I could just—" she turned around and saw the chaise longue "—sit there, y'know, and you could stand there, and we could—"

"Only since you came into my life, I've felt this madness, this constant fever. I'm like…a goddamned teenager, needing to jerk off every few hours."

"I've never been so jealous of a damn hand. That hand."

She pressed her palm onto his abdomen and he growled, arresting her wrist in his hand. He was like a slab of damp heat and delicious hardness under her fingers and all she wanted to do was roll around in his heat, in his scent, until he was imprinted on her very skin.

"*Dio en cielo*, Natalie. If I do this, one night won't be enough."

Lifting her gaze, she held his. Saw the last thin thread of control separating them. "Who said anything about one night?" One more push and he would be hers. She pulled her hand away from his grip, and ran a finger over his length and moaned softly. How could he get even harder and bigger? "Shall I go down on my knees?"

His eyes gleamed. With need. Danced at her offer. He was tempted. *Hallelujah!* "You've got guts, bluffing your way through this, daring me with your tempting offers. How do you know you'll like it?"

"Will *you* like it?"

"*Sì.* It's all I can think of when I want to shut you up. When you argue with me. When you use your damned loyalty against me."

"Then I'm sure I'll like it, too."

When he simply gazed at her, she gave voice to her innermost desire. Pressing her forehead to his chest, she licked his skin. Tasted the essence of the man. Salt and musk and pure Massimo. "Please, Massimo.

"I… I want to be here, Massimo. Only here. With you, in that bed. Under you. Over you. Any which way you want. I can't sleep, I can't think straight…even my dreams are restless and leave me aching and wanting. You're the only man that has ever made me want to live. Live for myself. Experience everything life has to give. Risk myself. To laugh, cry, howl, plead."

To love with such abandon that would have terrified her before… She didn't say it.

It was the simple, incredible truth. Like the sky was blue and the earth was green and the world was a harsh and lonely place but also joyful and full of wonders if only one had the courage to step out and reach for them.

Love and its demands and its constrictions and its expectations had no place here tonight. Or maybe ever, with Massimo. And that was a price she was more than willing to pay to own a part of this incredible man, even if for a little time.

His fingers sank into her hair, and he tugged so hard that her scalp prickled. That, too, added to the surfeit of sensations beating her down. She felt his mouth at her temple, his other hand running in mesmerizing circles over her back and buttocks and hips, and he was tugging her T-shirt up, up and away, over her head, and pulling her into him, and suddenly, her bare breasts were pressed against his damp chest, her nipples dragging against the wall of his muscles, and they were both sinking and drowning and gasping at how good it felt.

Her hand slid back to his solid erection.

"No," he said abruptly, practically screaming the word into the darkness that enveloped them. As if he needed to control and corral this boundless want between them. "No, you can't touch me, not yet, *cara mia*. Not tonight. If you do, it will be over before we even begin and there's so many things I want to do with you before I'm pounding into you. So, no, no touching me. Get it?"

Natalie could barely form coherent thought, her brain too busy processing the deluge of novel sensations pouring into her. All she could do was press her mouth into his shoulder and dig her teeth in. Holding on to him.

Rough hands on her buttocks picked her up, pushing her thighs shamelessly wide, her feet on top of his buttocks, his hip bones digging into her fleshy thighs, until her sex was notched oh-so-snugly against his shaft.

"*Merda*, you're dripping wet. Is this for me, *cara mia*?"

"All for you. All I…feel is for you, Massimo," she whispered, and then she took his mouth the way she wanted to. Thrusting her tongue into the warm cavern of his mouth. Pressing it against his, retreating when he tried to catch her, sucking on his tip, tugging at his lip with her teeth, drawing blood, licking at that spot, until he was shuddering and shaking and pulling her down, down, down into a vortex of sensation that swallowed her up.

And then he was turning them and rocking her into that massive bed, giving her the friction she needed exactly where she needed it. His shaft pressed and slid and glided and rubbed against her clit and she caught on to his rhythm and was pushing herself into him just as he rocked his hips… Her swollen nipples scraped against the rough hair on his chest, his mouth buried in her neck told her in explicit terms how he was going to take her bold offer one day and put his shaft in the warmth of her mouth, and Natalie was drowning as pinpricks of sensation poured out from her neck, her mouth, her breasts, her belly, pulling and tightening and building into concentric circles in her lower belly, and she was sobbing, clawing her nails into his damp back, demanding he give her more…

Instead, he pulled away. Brought her down shaking from the cusp of pleasure and Natalie railed at him with her fists. Afraid that he'd leave her unfulfilled. Afraid that this was another dream she was going to wake up from. Afraid that she'd go through her entire life and not know his touch.

"Shh…*tesoro*," he whispered at her temple. "Look at me, Natalie. I'm going nowhere. I couldn't even if a thousand hands tried to rip me away. I couldn't leave if my breath depended on it."

Her bottom met a cloud of soft sheets, and when she opened her eyes, he was looming over her, sweat coating his skin, smelling like man and heat and sex and belonging. He kissed her bruised lips, so softly, so sweetly, so tenderly. "You trust me, *sì*?"

"I do. Like I never have another man. I…" She rubbed her fingers over his swollen lip, the tiny cut she'd given him. She searched for something light to puncture the dam of emotion building up in her chest. "I took a risk on you, Massimo. Pay it up, *per favore, caro mio*."

He nodded, a wicked light in his gray eyes. "Put your hands above your head. Clutch the sheets if you need to. But don't touch me, *sì*?"

She nodded, biting her lower lip. And watched him. Anticipation built up slowly this time. His mouth drew down on the pulse at her neck, while his hands plumped her breasts, readying her. She arched like a bow when he tugged a nipple into his mouth and suckled, a little roughly, building that fever in her veins. That tension in her pelvis again. "*Cristo*, you will come like this if I continue, won't you?"

She nodded, and of course he released her breast. "And you're going to be thorough and detail-oriented, aren't you?"

With a roguish smile, he continued the foray of his mouth down her body. Licked maddening circles around her belly button. Natalie was panting again, gasping for breath as he separated the folds of her sex with his fingers.

She felt him pulling in a deep breath, pulling the scent of her arousal into him. Heard his pithy, foul curse breathe into her skin. Felt the tremble in his shoulders. And then his fingers were at her clit again. Stroking, swiping.

"Is this what you did?" he whispered against the crease of her thigh. "Is this how you pleasured yourself?"

She opened her mouth and swallowed air. Somehow she managed to say, "But it's nothing like when you touch me." God, nothing and no one in the entire world was going to feel like Massimo ever again.

Then his mouth replaced his fingers and his fingers were inside her and all her fears vanished under the onslaught of the sharp sensations. "Like this?" he whispered, weaving some new magic.

"Or like this," while he explored her, learning, and gave her the key to her own body.

And he was licking at her tight bundle and hooking his finger until he touched some magical spot that sparked fierce pleasure in her pelvis. On and on, again and again, until she was nothing but pure sensation. And when he pulled his mouth and fingers up and away from her, Natalie followed him with her hips, sobbing and begging. And then he tugged at her clit with his teeth.

Pleasure threw her apart into so many pieces, fracturing her, tossing her, and he continued crooning against her sex and she kept coming, tears flowing out of her eyes, and she dug her fingers into his hair, because she was afraid he had broken her apart and she would fly away. She writhed on the sheets as the waves slowed and ebbed, whispering his name over and over again.

She was lost in a sea of pleasure. She was lost to this man, forever.

When he climbed onto the bed and he pulled her into his arms, his thighs cradling her hips, she folded like a deck of cards, shivering and shaking. He was a fortress of warmth and safety at her back. She rubbed her nose in his bicep, loving the smell of him. When he stretched his arm to reach into the nightstand, she stopped him. Looked at him over her shoulder.

"I'm on the pill. Alessandra took me to a pharmacy."

He raised a brow, the ghost of a smile shimmering around his mouth, and she blushed. How could she blush when he'd put her body and her emotions through a ringer?

"I wanted to be prepared." She kissed his chin. Nipped it with her teeth. Felt his erection like a hot brand against her. She wriggled in his lap and his fingers dug into her hips with a curse, hard enough to leave bruises. So she did it more. And he groaned. "I was going to have you, come what may. If you didn't know already, I'm a determined woman."

"That you are," he said, turning her to face him. "I'm clean." A flash of white teeth. "You can tunnel into my network and see the medical certificate."

She shook her head, smiling. If only she could somehow tunnel her way into his heart, too… She pushed damp tendrils of hair away from his face, burying fear deep inside. "I don't have to."

"It will hurt," he said, his features severe. His strokes on her face gentle. "I… I've never made love to a virgin so you need to tell me if it's too much. If it hurts too much. If you just want a breather or want to stop completely. I'll stop, *cara mia*. Anytime."

"I want this, with you. Only you."

He touched his forehead to hers, and gave her the softest, sweetest kiss. Even inexperienced about men, Natalie had a feeling he was bracing himself for it. Gathering his control. Because she knew him. She knew he'd never forgive himself if he hurt her.

Muscles that seemed to have turned into so much blubber firmed up as he pulled her up into his lap, pushing her thighs indecently wider. His kisses shut rational thought away, going from soft and tender to hungry and urgent in a matter of seconds.

She felt his erection hard and demanding against her belly. Threw her head back as his hands plumped her breasts, rolled her nipples. He whispered endearments into her skin, tasted every dip and rise. Told her how much he'd dreamed of her like this—completely his.

Slowly, with infinite patience, with skillful touches, he aroused her spent body until she was shivering again, and there was wetness at her sex. His clever, wicked fingers played with her, working her over, building her to a fine fever, cranking her on and on. Already he knew her body so well. Better than she did. And she wanted to chase that mindless high again. Fall down hard from it into his solid arms. Again and again, until she didn't know where she began and he ended.

And then he lifted her, murmuring soothing, soft words, and she looked down, refusing to miss anything, and he took his shaft in hand and drenched himself in her wetness and then he was there at the entrance to her body and his hands on her shoulders were pushing her down, and with one smooth, hard thrust, he was inside her.

She cried at the sharp, unending pinch of pain, tugging at his hair while he buried his face in her neck. His breathing was loud and hot and his big body was so tight as if he were spending an enormous amount of control to stay still.

"*Merda*, you're like a glove. So good, so…" He looked at her and cursed. "I'm hurting you, *sì*?"

She nodded. And he kissed her softly. Butterfly kisses at her cheekbone. The tip of her nose. The corner of her mouth. Beneath her ear. At the juncture where her neck met her shoulders. "It's okay, *cara mia*. Just…just hold on. We'll stay like this. As long as you need. Or I'll pull out and we'll try again some—"

"No." He was like a hot, hard poker inside her and she never wanted to move or let go. And he was frozen like one of those marble statues littered all over his damned estate, so rigid and hard and taut and tense around her. Inside her.

Natalie pushed back with her fingers on the jut of his shoulders and gasped when even the small movement sent a sharp pinch through her pelvis again but she desperately wanted to look into his eyes, at this man who had stolen her heart. The invasion of his shaft and the pain of their joining, and the comedown from her orgasm—everything was conspiring, pushing her toward tears, pushing her toward hiding away from this moment, toward an emotional climax just as powerful and even more dangerous.

For the one thing she couldn't do was throw herself open even more. Not when she wanted a lot more of this intimacy with him.

So, she kissed his temple, tasted the sweat of his skin. She wrapped her arms around his shoulders, needing the glide of his bare skin against hers, needing the closeness. Needing the scent of him deep inside her. "Tell me, please, tell me what to do. I want this to be good for you. I want…"

He caught the tear falling down her cheek, and kissed her temple as if she were the most precious thing he'd ever held. "Good, *cara mia*? If it got any better, I'd die from the overload."

He rotated his hips slightly, softly, and Natalie gasped. Laughing. "That wasn't so bad."

When he laughed, she bit his lip.

"No, that was fantastic. Great. Do it again. Please, Massimo."

Massimo thought he'd die if he didn't start moving soon. Pressure knotted up in his balls, tingled in his lower spine. And yet, he'd rather die than hurt her. "Are you sure?"

"Yes. Hundred percent. Move. Now."

And she demanded that he move inside her like she demanded everything else of him. Boldly. Honestly. Courageously.

Holding her hips, Massimo pulled her up a little. And brought her down just as he thrust his hips. The friction was amazing. The pleasure she gave him indescribable. Another thrust. Another stroke. He stilled to delay his climax rushing at him. "Listen to our bodies, *cara mia*," he whispered, laughing, when she bumped into him on a downward stroke. "Listen to your instincts. Try swiveling your hips, moving this way and that. Just…find your rhythm with me."

"So less bumping and grinding, and color by numbers and more instinct, Massimo?"

"Yes, more instinct. Less numbers. Especially when it is this good," he said, giving her a wink.

She laughed, pushing her hair away from her face, thrusting her breasts in his face. This time, she met him thrust to thrust, in perfect synchronicity, creating magic.

Cheeks pink, brow dampened, hair a wild cloud around her face, eyes glazed with passion, mouth swollen, she was the most breathtakingly beautiful thing he'd ever seen. She was passion and enthusiasm and joy and he felt as if he was drowning in her.

He pushed her onto the bed and covered her, increasing

the tempo of his thrusts, all but mindless in the pursuit of his own climax. Picking her up by the hips, he angled her so that his abdomen rubbed over the top of her sex every time he retreated and she was sobbing again, writhing and digging her teeth into his bicep as she splintered, and Massimo followed her.

Two hard, swift thrusts and he came in a rush of heat and lightning. Afterward, laughter followed, for only his brave little hacker could make him laugh in such a moment by shouting, "Hell, yeah, that was awesome, Massimo. How soon can you go again?"

He let his hard body cover hers completely for a few seconds, needing this closeness with his lover for the first time in his life. Needing to steal away something from her, for himself.

Maybe he wouldn't ever be able to offer her what she deserved from a man. But he was determined to never hurt her, to never dull the spark that fired up his brave, little hacker.

CHAPTER TWELVE

"How much longer are you going to avoid me?"

"What?" Massimo said, loosening the knot of his tie. He shrugged off his suit jacket and leaned against his bed, just…drinking in the sight of her.

A weak spring sun dappled her in golden light as Natalie stood in front of the French windows that framed his bedroom. She'd given up fighting to subdue her hair today apparently because it was loosely tied in a ponytail at her nape.

Today, she wore a pristine white sleeveless shirt that showcased her toned arms and flowy pants that sat low on her waist, leaving a slash of that taut abdomen he had licked just last night, on his way to other important things, bare for his gaze. The diamond pendant on a delicate gold chain he'd bought for her gleamed on her skin.

It had taken him three arguments, two days and one… session of persuading her with his fingers and mouth and tongue before she'd accepted the gift. Before confiding that it was the only piece of jewelry she'd ever owned.

And then, of course, being the extremely competitive woman that she was, she had proceeded to pay him back in return for his wicked persuasion. Her hair tickling his thighs, her mouth laughing and licking and wrapped around his arousal, she'd driven him to the most powerful climax of his life. Leaving him stripped to the soul.

Just thinking of it, of her, of her unflinching, unending desire to know all of him, to learn all of him—he was turned on simply by looking at her, his arousal a throbbing need in his trousers.

"Something's wrong, Massimo. You and I both know it."

He willed his body to focus on her words. His mind to maneuver the minefield of confrontation that they'd both been pushing away, desperate to not test this...thing between them just yet. Or was he the only one who thought like that? "I'm not used to sharing every small thing that occupies my mind," he bluffed.

Something was wrong with him, *sì*. But he didn't know what or how to fix it.

Her chin fell and she nodded. "But this is important enough that you distanced yourself from me. You do that when you have a design problem, did you know that?

"You swim endlessly...you box in the gym...you avoid looking at the problem until it works itself out in your head. I know you, Massimo. Better than you think."

Three and a half weeks since the night she'd snuck into his room and proceeded to blow his mind. His hunger for her only seemed to increase the more he touched her, the more he kissed her, the more he basked in her laughter and her quick wit and her affection.

She brought out the best in him, and yet, she brought out the worst in him, too.

He wouldn't have realized how seamlessly she seemed to work herself into his life until that meeting that had wrecked the bliss of long, drawn-out nights amid silky sheets and the exhilarating rush of pitting his mind against hers during the day.

Natalie was a woman unlike any he'd ever known, for he had a feeling he would never know all of her. Possess all of her. Just when he thought he did...another facet of her was revealed.

Even at a recent meeting with Giuseppe Fiore's CTO, his first instinct had been to defend her, to protect her from even a whiff of accusation, to storm out of that meeting until he could process it on his own.

"Your fiancée is a common thief."

"That association could cost you, Massimo, your reputation at least, if not this contract, if it gets out."

Since Giuseppe's CTO was a friend of his, Massimo had convinced him to put it aside. Massimo had used an invaluable business connection to vouch for Natalie. Created a debt for himself in a cutthroat business world.

A small thing but an unprecedented thing. A fissure in the line he drew between his ambitions and his feelings. Blurring the lines between what he wanted to be and what he was.

Dios mio, she complicated everything with her truths, and her lies and her dares and her kisses, and he needed to get a handle on this and her. Fast.

He'd screwed the chance of keeping things between them separate—professional and personal. He'd blurred all the lines between them from the moment he'd seen her walk out of that club.

When he'd decided she would be the perfect foil to discourage Gisela Fiore.

When he'd decided she would be an asset to BCS. When he'd brought her on board to work on the Fiore project. He'd lost his mind from moment one. Lost all caution and discretion and common sense that had made him such a world-renowned success before thirty.

She'd fought him from the beginning, on every arrogant assumption of his, at every decree he had laid down, even his short-lived honor. She'd told him clearly, point-blank, that she didn't give her trust easily. She'd told him, again and again, that her loyalty had to be earned and couldn't be bought. That her heart, she'd lived with it under lock and key for so long.

So, this was on him. And yet, he also wanted to blame her. To use this as a reason to push her away. To...stop this madness before it deepened and someone really got hurt.

Her—she would be the one who was hurt in the end.

"I've been busy," he fibbed. "This project is taking everything I have."

"I know you're busy. I'm in there with you most of the time. But this is not just work stress. This is not you tuning everything else out to untangle an analytical problem.

"You've been freezing me out for a week. I don't know why or what I did. You won't...look at me. You won't smile. You...don't talk to me in the lab. You...come to me in the middle of the night and make love to me, but by morning... you're back to behaving the same way again.

"It's almost as if you're...ashamed to converse with me outside of bed."

"You're being ridiculous," he said, an inane response to her perceptive gauntlet.

"No, I'm not. You didn't even tell me how exceptionally clever my design was for the bank's interactive portals. If nothing else, I count on you to tell me how brilliant I am on a regular basis, Massimo."

That irreverence, that honest but baffled admission—it was a balm to his masculine ego. Which the woman had the disconcerting knack of knocking off balance with a regularity. At least she was in this madness as much as he was.

"Are you done with me, with us, Massimo? Is that it? Do you want to move on?" Vulnerability in her voice even as she stubbornly tilted her chin up. "Because if you are, just...tell me."

"Nessuno," Massimo answered automatically, speaking his instinct before even processing that question.

"I can take it. I told you I don't need—"

"Fiore's CTO, Franco, summoned me last week to tell me he'd discovered that you had a juvenile record. As part of the routine background checks they do on every member of this team.

"For a *financial crime*, Natalie!

"Do you realize what that does to BCS's image? After everything we've had to put up with over the last few months? After all the fires I've been putting out? Now, when we're so close to that contract?

"*Cristo*, Natalie, is it true?"

All color fled her cheeks. She looked down at her hands and then up at him, her heart in her eyes.

Something in his chest deflated, as if he'd been expecting her to deny it. Call it just an accusation. Demand that he listen to the truth. What a coward he was that he couldn't face her truth. Couldn't face the power she already had over him.

"Yes, it was when I was fourteen."

His curse rang in the room.

But she didn't flinch. "I transferred some money from my foster father's bank account to his daughter's. He was a bully and she offered me two hundred dollars for it…" She shrugged, as if it didn't matter. "I had already learned how to break most security designs. I… The cyber investigator—it took him forever to pin me down for it. The judge sentenced me to community service, and a warning, and sealed those records. Those should have been sealed records. It was a juvenile offense. Before I met *him*. Before he persuaded me that I couldn't continue like that… I didn't know right from wrong, Massimo. All I knew was survival."

Tears filled her eyes and she looked away from him. Her body bowed as she stared out the window, and all he wanted was to pull her into his arms and hold her tight. To tell her that no one would ever push her to that ever again. That she'd never be so alone in the world.

Instead, he stayed where he was, watching her, willing this desperate need inside him to calm, willing rationality to take over again.

How had he picked the one woman who with every breath, every word, jeopardized his goals? Why didn't he just push her away, now that he knew the truth? Why couldn't he say yes, this association was too costly for him?

Why didn't he just draw the line here, now?

Every rational instinct he possessed urged him to do it. Better late than never. They could just be colleagues and still live under the same roof. He'd done it so many times before.

And yet, he stood, every muscle frozen.

Slowly, her shoulders straightened. He saw her dash away the tears with a rough gesture.

"You should have told me."

She turned back to him, her eyes shining with pride. "I didn't realize I was supposed to tell you every part of my unsavory life."

He rubbed a hand over his forehead, hating that he made her so defensive. "This is a hundred-billion-euro security project for a finance empire. All of us will come under the microscope. I can't keep covering for you. You should—"

She pushed away from the wall. "Did it ever occur to you that I was too ashamed to tell you? Or that it's not a part of my life I want to advertise to you when I'm begging you to not send me to jail? Or should I tell you when you already think I'm deceitful and low class and—"

He pulled her into his arms, incapable of not touching her.

She didn't come easily. Her fists came at his chest, her

ody shuddered; she jerked in his embrace, but he held fast.
Willing her to trust him. Consigning the war between his
mind and his heart to hell.

"Let me go, Massimo."

"Calm down, *cara mia*. I just…"

"You what?" She pushed her hair away from her face,
brown eyes shooting daggers at him. "You are ashamed of
associating with me. You're already calculating damage
control. You're…"

He flicked his lashes down, afraid of what else she'd discover that he didn't even know himself. Those eyes taunted
him before she laughed. A sad sound filled with bitterness
and pain. Pain he was causing her. Doing the one thing he
swore he wouldn't do.

"Wow, you're no better than one of those supercomputers of yours, calculating gains and losses per transaction,
per every interaction you have with me, huh?"

"Stop, Natalie. I told you to give me space. I was going
to work it out. You're the one who pushed me into this…
discussion.

"I've already asked the project manager to take you off
the team for now. You just need to lay low until Fiore signs,
that's all. It won't go any higher up than this. His CTO will
arrest it there. Especially since those are sealed records.

"But we can't risk you being on the project. We can't…
f there's anything else I should know…"

"How about I sleep separately for a while, too? How
about you come back to me when this is done?

"Is that what you've been finding so hard to say? Too
bad you tied yourself to me in front of your whole bloody
world, *sì*? Too bad you can't just throw me out of your life
as easily as you can cut me out of the project?"

"Natalie, you know what this project means to me."

"You… My past, who I've been, who I am, is a liability

to you. You…you weigh everything in life to see whether it serves your ambition or not. You weigh people around you in terms of assets and liabilities.

"I'm a liability. I'll always be a liability to you.

"But I refuse to be ashamed of who I am and what I've done in the past to survive."

Natalie let the hot water pound at her, washing away the sweat and grime of her workout. Wash away the tears that should have dried up a long time ago.

With a groan, she pressed her head into the cold tile. The worst part was that, despite her defiant words to him, she did feel ashamed. Wished she could change things she couldn't undo now.

And even worse was the feeling that she wasn't good for him. Good for his image. Good for the Massimo Brunetti who was going to take not only Milan but Italy by a storm with his innovative cyber security design for Fiore Worldwide Banks.

That she would never be good enough.

She rinsed off the soap, lethargy and tiredness crawling into her muscles. And she felt him standing outside the shower before she heard him, the scent of him calling her.

"Can I come in?" he asked softly, though he was already partly inside the open gap in the marble-tiled shower, his hair catching on water drops, the front of his unbuttoned shirt more than half-damp.

She turned, angling her body away from his gaze. She wasn't really a shy person but she couldn't brazen it out, either. Neither did it stop her skin from tingling in a million places. Waiting for his touch. For her body to tighten and clench and loosen in anticipation of the drugging pleasure he could give. And gave frequently and generously and at every chance they got.

God, he'd even persuaded her onto the table in his lab while they'd been working late one night. Dropped to his knees and tucked his head between her thighs and now she couldn't walk into that lab without blushing and heating up.

And here she was again, after that argument, standing there naked, letting him look her over, going weak at her knees wondering where he would take this… If she wasn't a pushover, she didn't know one. "I'm almost done."

A small smile played around his lips. "I don't really want to be in there if you get out." He leaned against the wall, pulled up his knee and watched her. As if his goal in life was to watch her bathe. "You have a little soap you need to wash off. There. Under your right breast. Where you have that mole. Where you…"

Her breasts were heavier, her nipples tight buds begging for his attention, her sex wet and willing by the time Natalie mustered enough senses to understand his game. "It's not fair. We had a fight and sex doesn't fix it. Even the fantastic sex you give."

His smile vanished, though the warmth of his gaze didn't. "*Sì*. We did have a fight. And maybe you could've been more honest—" he raised his hands in surrender when she opened her mouth "—if I had been more thorough about the scope and reach of this project. If I hadn't backed you into a corner.

"I brought you on, so the mistake is mine.

"But it doesn't mean, never did it mean, that I don't want you here. In my room. In my lab. In my life.

"I'm trying to make this work, *cara mia*. And no, I've not been and never will be ashamed of what you had to do to survive. You're right. I can't imagine what it must have been like to be that girl who had no one, the girl who had to make herself so tough." He cupped her cheek, his thumb pushing away the tears that trailed down them, his voice so infinitely tender. His lips were warm and familiar against hers. "Meet me halfway, *tesoro*. Just…let me get through this milestone. I need you here. I want you here."

And just like that, with easy charm and sincere words he made mincemeat of her anger and her hurt and her defenses. He hadn't apologized, really, for putting that contract above her. He didn't even think of it that way.

He was far from admitting, even to himself, how much he cared about her, much less to her.

But he made accommodations for her in his life. And he let her know how much he wanted her. It was more than Natalie had expected of him, entering into this relationship. God, he'd never lied to her where his priorities lay.

She pushed her wet hair away from her face and nodded.

He inclined his head.

The antagonism in the air shimmered away, instantly replaced by hunger and heat.

"I missed you," he said, his head completely in the water now. "Yesterday. In my bed. I didn't sleep well."

She was tempted to say she had slept soundly. But they didn't play games with each other. Not when it came to this. Here, there was only truth. Utter truth. "I didn't, either."

"Say no if you don't want to do it in the shower, *cara mia*."

"Can I say yes?" she said, reaching for his shirt and pulling it out, seeking the hard, warm male skin.

He smiled and pulled her to him. And took her with a devouring hunger that filled all the empty places inside of her. He told her with his kiss, his touch, his hard, hungry caresses what he would never say in words. His arms caged her, as if he meant to never let her go, his belt buckle digging into her belly. "I want to be inside you, now. Please Natalie."

"Now is good. Now is always good with you. Take what you need, Massimo," she said, and somehow, they managed o undo his trousers, push the wet fabric past his lean hips, and she wrapped her legs around him, and he rubbed at her clit to check she was ready and then he was inside her.

Natalie threw her head back, feeling him all over inside her, in this position. He was in her breath and in her blood and in her heart. And any fear that she was heading for a heartbreak of epic proportions melted away under the onslaught of sensation when he flicked his tongue over her nipple.

She rocked into his thrust when he turned her to the wall and swirled his hips. Her breasts bounced and scraped against his chest, and she felt the tension coiling in her belly and when he pressed her against the cold tile and brought her hand to her clit and smiled wickedly, she massaged the swollen bundle.

And when he took her mouth, hard and fast, all the while rocking into her with short, swift thrusts, Natalie let go of all the fears and doubts and let herself be washed in him, in the pleasure he wrought in her, in the magic they created together.

A week later, Natalie clicked on the encrypted email that was sitting at the top of her in-box on the tablet Massimo let her use, her heart racing, threatening to rip out of her chest. She'd instinctively reached for her tablet, wanting to see if Frankie had replied to the stupid meme she'd sent him about cats.

Massimo lay on his chest with his arm over her midriff, still asleep.

Meet me tomorrow. One p.m. at Piazza del Duomo. V.

Her heart thumped, her pulse racing with fear. She exited out of the program quickly, spending two more minutes to clear out the history, erasing every inch of her account from the hard drive itself.

Vincenzo was here? In Milan? What did he want with her?

She wanted to throw up at the very idea of lying to Massimo again. At the very thought of deceiving him.

If she told him, he would forbid her to go. He would… tell Leonardo, and God knows what Leo would do.

But how could she just…not go?

What if this was her chance to convince Vincenzo to stop this crazy agenda? To find out why he was doing this in the first place? What if she could solve this problem, once and for all, for Massimo and effect some kind of peace between him, Leonardo and Vincenzo?

Then she would be more than a liability. Then she'd be worthy of his respect; she'd maybe even be worthy of him.

CHAPTER THIRTEEN

PIAZZA DEL DUOMO, Milan's main, spacious city square, was bursting to the brim with tourists and locals as Natalie walked in on Tuesday afternoon. Pausing, she looked up at the massive facade of the Cathedral of Milan. The architecture was magnificent and she desperately wished she could have a carefree day with Massimo.

On the other side was the world famous La Scala Theater he'd promised to take her to soon.

The cobblestones clicked beneath her black pumps, the air filled with the decadent scents of chocolate and coffee, friends and lovers calling out to each other, buzzing with energy. The constant knot in her belly she'd been walking around with since yesterday tightened when she spotted the dark head, sitting at a table outside a café.

Palm flat on her belly, she walked toward the table just as Vincenzo looked up. Almost severe in their sharpness, his features lent him an austere beauty that arrested more than one woman walking by. Dressed in a blue dress shirt and black tailored trousers, he was the epitome of masculine appeal.

"Come, Natalie," he said in that deep, bass voice she had known for so long. When she didn't move, except to stare at his outstretched hand, a dark smile played around his lips. "Come, little cat," he said again cajolingly, using that little moniker he'd always used. "I won't bite, *cara mia*. You know that."

Natalie shook her head and took his hand. He clutched her shoulders and studied her face. Bent his head and kissed her cheek. And slowly, his arm wrapped around her shoulders, pulling her to him. He was the same man who had done her a thousand favors, the same man who had kept her safe, helped her make a life for herself.

Natalie went into his arms, even though she felt as if she was betraying the man who'd again and again given her his trust, his loyalty, and earned hers in return.

There was something so familiar about Vincenzo—the scent of the cigar and his aqua cologne—that she calmed. "You're well?" he breathed the question over her head. "You weren't mistreated?"

She felt the tension in him dissolve when she nodded. He wasn't a monster. Not the man who worried about an orphan he'd saved years ago. "You know I can watch out for myself."

"I had to remind myself of your strength every day. There was no way to get in touch with you. I went to see Frankie and he said you'd called him and told him you were leaving the country for a friend's wedding. He was super excited for you."

Natalie's heart crawled up to her chest. "You saw him? He's good?"

"He's doing great."

"Thank you," she whispered.

"How are you doing?"

"I'm fine, Vincenzo. I've been…good, too."

He stared at her questioningly, but nodded.

He pulled a chair for her and then settled into the next one. When the waiter inquired, he ordered two coffees for them, telling the waiter to make hers extra sweet and extra milky, with a distasteful scrunch of his nose. Natalie laughed, and tucked an errant curl away.

His gaze arrested on the diamond on her finger, and she hastily dropped her hand.

"What I heard through the grapevine is true?" The warmth didn't quite leave his eyes but there was something else.

Natalie opened her mouth and then closed it. She wanted to ask him so many questions: how long had he been in Milan, in Italy, what was he planning and why. But she curbed her curiosity. She didn't want to get in the middle of this. Not after today. Also from everything she'd learned in the last two months, he was a master chess player, moving pieces back and forth, ten moves ahead of everyone else. "It's a fake engagement. Too convoluted to explain."

"Massimo shouldn't be trusted. None of them should be. Using people is in their blood—"

"You're the last man who should lecture about using others. You—"

"I never forced you. You could have said no at any time."

"You knew I wouldn't. You manipulated me... I could've gone to jail."

"I trusted you to look after yourself. I would have been here, within the hour. You know that."

Natalie wanted to say no, she didn't. But seeing him again like this, she couldn't. How could she convey all the complex emotion twisted around this man to Massimo? How could she convince him that Massimo didn't deserve what he was doing? "This is such a...mess. Please, tell me you're done."

He shook his head and her heart dropped. "Stay out of it, *cara mia*."

"You dropped me in the middle of it."

"You shouldn't have gotten caught. You're supposed to be brilliant."

"I got caught because Massimo's just as brilliant as I

am. But he's also kind, and funny and charming and… He
could have sent me to jail and he didn't, even when I re
fused to give him your name."

"I wouldn't have held it against you. You're a survivor
Natalie, just like I am."

"Loyalty means something to me. Massimo's a good
man, Vincenzo." She reached for his hands, as he'd don
to her long ago. Hoping to get through. Hoping to stop thi
before more people got hurt. "Whatever you're doing, he
doesn't deserve your hatred."

He studied her slender hands in his, squeezed them and
then slowly released each finger. Slowly but surely shut
ting the door in her face. When he looked up at her, ther
was such dark emotion swirling in the depths of his gray
eyes. "This started long before Massimo became the finan
cial force behind Brunetti Finances, Inc. But he's a part o
it. They all are. For years, they perpetuated what…" He
looked away, as if to control himself. "This won't stop be
cause you like him. This won't stop until…"

He stood up, and Natalie's hopes dashed into dust.

She looked up at him in his black suit jacket and tailore
trousers and expensive haircut, and the way he stood…he
heart ached for whatever drove him to this. "Until wha
Vincenzo? How much more hurt will you cause befor
you stop?"

He offered her his hand and Natalie stood up, their cof
fees untouched.

Suddenly, he felt like a stranger. Like he'd never show
her his true self. She wanted to run back to Massimo, and beg
him to fix the whole sorry mess. And he would, she knew it

He would at least listen.

Vincenzo took her elbow as they stepped away from th
table. "Return with me. My jet's waiting."

Natalie stared back, stunned. "With you? What? Where?

"I don't want to leave you here, with them. Not after today, and not after… I want you far from here. Back in the States. Safe."

His words pelted Natalie's skin like small cold stones. She pushed away from his touch. "Vincenzo, please, put an end to this."

"This doesn't involve you. I'd hate to hurt you any more."

"It involves the man I trust and if you do this… I can't keep you a secret anymore. I won't. He's earned my loyalty. I work for BCS now. On a dollar-huge project for Fiore Worldwide Banks. I—"

"He won't win that contract."

Natalie felt as if he had punched her in the gut, as easily as he smiled at her. "Yes, he will. I designed it with him. I won't let you steal this away from him. I won't let you hurt him."

And it would, she knew for sure.

Massimo prized that contract above his relationships. Above everything else.

"Massimo Brunetti is a genius who treats women no better than his father did. In the end, he is his father's son. Prestige, family name, power, that's all that matters to them. He will delete you as he does yesterday's technology as soon as you become irrelevant. Come away, Natalie. I don't want this on my soul."

"Do you have a soul?" she whispered at him, and he flinched. "You can't escape the consequences." Tears filled her eyes. "I thought I could fix this, appeal to you. But I don't know who you are.

"Don't contact me. Don't try to save me. Just…stay away, Vincenzo."

The *tap-tap* of her pumps on the marble floor cranked up the panic running through her as Natalie walked into the

sitting lounge. She came to a stumbling halt as four set
of gazes swiveled to her with a wide range of expression:

The Brunettis were out in force.

She took a few more steps into the lounge, her hear
beating so fast that she was afraid it would rip out of he
chest. Massimo stood all the way at the back of the va:
room, his back to her, the tension in his shoulders makin
her own tighter.

Her belly somersaulted with fear.

Did he know she'd gone to meet Vincenzo? How?

Leonardo seemed the most relaxed, sitting in an arm
chair, Italian-loafered ankle crossed over the other kne∈
swiping something on his cell phone. There wasn't the usu:
cynical amusement or contempt in his dark gaze. Just plai
curiosity. As if he were a predator deciding whether h
wanted to rip her apart now or later.

She walked past him to where Massimo stood with hi
back to her.

"Massimo? What happened?"

He turned, and the fury in those eyes stopped Natali
in her tracks. The dark emotion touched all of him—thos
perceptive eyes, the bridge of his nose, that mouth tha
could curve with such wicked laughter—making him loo
so severe, so much like one of those portraits she'd seen i
that long hall, contemptuous and arrogant.

The Brunetti aristocracy of so many generations that h
thought he didn't belong with. Men steeped in power an
prestige and cruelty.

Dread knotted in her chest that she had to force herse
to breathe first, but it was centered on what Vincenzo ha
let loose this time. "Massimo, why are you guys still here
I thought you were meeting the Fiore team for the offici:
signing—"

"I canceled the meeting."

"You canceled the meeting? Why?"

"Our security design for FWB was stolen from the network server and published on the Dark Net. A half hour before our meeting." His body bristled with unspent fury. A year's worth of work out there for any hacker to go through, to target the banks. Thousands of customers' financial information would have been in jeopardy. I had to disclose the hacking attack to them.

"The intricately detailed triggers you executed... I knew the plans were being stolen the minute someone tunneled in."

"Wait? I don't understand. That design was brilliant. The security layers literally incorruptible. You saw what I built...you went over that design with me with a fine-tooth comb. It can't just—"

"I thought so, too. But then it's not so hard if you handed over the blueprints to all the layers, is it? Or, say, if you logged into the server and created a tunnel for them to access it?"

Natalie stared at him, her mouth opening with an inaudible gasp, her brain processing his accusation over and over again. Because he couldn't be saying what he was saying, could he? "You're blaming this on me?" Her throat was achy and full of tears and she looked around as if she could gather strength from something or someone, but instead only saw the accusation now in their eyes.

"You think I... I gave them access to the server? I let them in? I helped steal plans I toiled over with you for the last few weeks?"

"It happened when you returned from your secret meeting and accessed the server for the plans."

Vincenzo had played her so well. "You can't... I did log into it. I accessed the plans, yes, but only to make sure the

security layer was tight. Something he said made me reali;
they might not be as safe as we thought. You can't think—

"Something he said? Or something he asked you to d(
Is it that much of a stretch for me to believe that you fo
lowed the instructions the man gave you when you m
him this afternoon?"

Accusation after accusation and Natalie had nothir
to fight them with. She'd been so foolish. God, if on
she hadn't gone to meet Vincenzo this afternoon, if on
she…

"Massimo, I didn't. I didn't betray you. I know how th
looks, okay? But I—"

"Who did you meet this afternoon?" he finally sai
As if she were a stranger. As if he hadn't made love to h
this morning.

"Vincenzo. His name is Vincenzo Cavalli." His nan
dropped into the silence with the same effect as if a mete
had crashed through the roof, into the room. Natalie sa
Leo coming alert, clicking away on his phone, but not!
ing could tear her gaze away from the cynicism in Ma
simo's own gaze.

"There, I said his name."

Massimo smirked, and she hated everything about
"Did he give you permission now that he has done irrev(
cable damage to us?"

"He sent me an encrypted email, asking me to me
him, and I—"

"Then why didn't you tell me? Cristo, you were in b(
with me when you got that email, weren't you? You smil(
at me, you kissed me, and you lied to my face. You pron
ised your loyalty was mine. You promised…" He thru(
his fingers through his hair roughly, shaking. "You cou
have told me he contacted you. You could have told n
where to find him. You could have solved this problem f

s. But no…instead, you decided to protect him. Instead, ou chose him.

"I trusted you. I let myself feel…but in the end you icked him. You jeopardized everything I've worked for, ll these years. Leave, Natalie."

"Don't say that. Please, Massimo, I want to help you fix his. I can help—"

"Get out. Get out before I—"

"Before what, Massimo?" she shouted back, tired of is accusations, tired of being afraid. Tired of…the emp-iness that waited if he kicked her out. "What would you o to me?"

"Call the *polizia* on you. Have you arrested for corporate spionage, for breaking a hundred confidentiality agree-nents, for selling your loyalty. I don't think you stopped eing a thief."

If he had slapped her, Natalie would've been less hocked. Less hurt. Pain came at her in huge, rollicking vaves, twisting her belly, knocking her out at her knees. How… That's so unfair. You can't… I can't believe you vould throw that at me? Knowing why I did it. Knowing… trusted you to understand. To…"

He searched her face, studied the tears running down er cheeks. Maybe, for a second, he even softened. Natalie aw the familiar Massimo, the Massimo she loved with her vhole heart, in his eyes before he shut it down. Before he hut that part down. Or maybe it was all her foolish hope. Ier blinders still on when it came to him. "You didn't trust ne with it, either, *cara mia*. You hid it. And you defended ourself, as you always do, when it came to my notice."

"Massimo, think it through before—" Leo chimed in.

"Now you support her, Leo?" Massimo's voice was cut-ng, so full of bitterness. "When all along you've been ask-ng me to throw her out? When she's proved you and Silvio

right? When my allowing her into all this, when my trust
ing her, trusting my emotions, is what brought us to this?"

With one last look at her, Leonardo walked out.

Massimo tucked his hands into his pockets, every inch
that ruthless, powerful stranger who had cornered her tha
first night. "This is my fault. All mine.

"From the moment you came into my life, you neve
told me the truth.

"Why should I not believe that you engineered this'
Why should I not believe that when I realized you were a
liability…you jumped back to his side, you looked out fo
yourself once again?"

It was over, Natalie knew then. He wouldn't believe her
He had decided to not believe her. He had decided to fin
ish this.

He had decided, maybe even before this, that she wasn'
good for him, that he was done. And nothing she said woul
change his mind.

Her tears, her begging, nothing would dent that resolv
she saw in his eyes.

Nothing… She wiped away her tears, anger rescuing
her from the pit of self-pity and pain. Anger made he
straighten her shoulders. Anger made her aggressive, se
clearly. Anger made her realize how worthless she'd though
of herself when it came to him.

Anger made her realize how she'd strived to becom
worthy of him, how she'd foolishly assumed that he'd lov
her if she wasn't a liability anymore. She was done. God
she was so done with him, with thinking that she was les
than him. "This is so convenient for you, isn't it?"

"Convenient?" he said, sneering. "You ruined a projec
that I've been working toward for a decade. You ruine
my chance to—"

"To what? To prove to your father that you're not th

ick rùnt he calls you still? To prove that you're better than
Leonardo? To join those heartless, arrogant, bloated with
power ancestors that are hanging on that damned wall?

"Your chance to prove to yourself that you're a Brunetti
through and through—cruel and power-hungry and looking
or any excuse to push away anyone who cares about you?"

"You've no idea."

"Of course I do. This project means everything to you.
was there. But…it is also such a good reason to push me
way, too.

"Look in your heart and tell me you truly believe that I
old you out to him? This is not about me. This is about you.

"Because you feel something for me, too. A weakness
hat could weigh you down. Because I was becoming a li-
bility to your goddamned reputation, your pursuit of bil-
ons, your ambition with my petty theft record. A liability
o what you think Massimo Brunetti should be.

"Anything's better than examining what you feel for me.
Anything's better than letting yourself love me. Anything's
etter than becoming what your father thinks you are.

"Because Brunetti men don't have weaknesses. Because
Brunetti men are monsters.

"You act like you're better than them all but…you're
he worst of them. You know better and you still cling to
. There's a little good in you and you kill it every chance
ou get.

"I fell in love with you. I was twisting myself up in knots
hat I wasn't good enough for you…but you're the one who
oesn't deserve me. You're not the man I thought you were.

"Congratulations, Massimo. At least there will never
e a doubt in your mind that you're a Brunetti, after all."

CHAPTER FOURTEEN

MASSIMO STARED OUT the window of his office at Brunet Towers in the financial district of Milan, not really seein the noisy crowds of tourists and locals.

The city's financial pulse—something he had alway felt so strongly, something he'd strived to be part of for s many years, left him feeling nothing but emptiness. Th villa, his flat in Navigli, even his lab—his lab, which ha always been his sanctuary… Guilt haunted him, consume him, ate through him.

Leo had probed and pushed and, in the end, given up It wasn't as if BCS would die without him at the helm fo a week. Vincenzo Cavalli could raze BCS to the groun for all Massimo cared.

He hadn't eaten or worked or slept in so many days. I the two weeks since he had thrown his dirty accusation at Natalie.

She'd been right.

He'd behaved worse than his father or Leonardo. He ha always thought himself as better, prided himself that h mother raised him with different values, had assumed tha when the right woman came along—someone with clas and sophistication, and someone who understood that he place would always be second to his ambition—he woul treat her well.

For all his arrogance and ambition, instead he'd found

oman who was fire and passion and love. When push had
ome to shove, he had proven himself to be worse.

The first day when he'd discovered that Vincenzo had
ired a consortium of hackers to leak the security designs,
sing Natalie's past hacker activity as the key, he'd made a
undred excuses for his behavior.

She had been the gateway for them to steal the plans.
e had never been taught how to process his feelings for
woman, especially such a complex one. She had come
to his life at the wrong time. Part of it was her fault be-
ause she had gone to see Vincenzo behind his back…on
d on and on.

He had prioritized the wrong thing in life. Looking for
ays to end the one thing that made him look deep into
mself, to reach for something he might not be capable of.

He was a Brunetti man who courted power, prestige and
llions because he'd been terrified that if he wasn't the
ost powerful of them all, then he was nothing.

And yet, she had found something in him to like. To
ve, even.

"I fell in love with you," she had thrown at him, so full
pain, her eyes big and bright, bowed by his cruel words.
ut not broken.

Because she was right. He was the worst of the Brunet-
s, after all. He was the one not worthy of her.

She had survived with her heart whole, and courageous.

And if it took him the rest of his life, he'd spend it mak-
g himself worthy of her.

fter numerous calls from his secretary and Leonardo pok-
g his head into his office all of four times for an urgent
eeting, Massimo forced himself to move.

He owed Giuseppe the courtesy of showing his face,

even if the association they had both sought was a pile
ash. Pushing his gray suit jacket on, he ran a hand ov
his jaw.

Cristo, he must look like he'd been living under th
green moss under the crappiest rock after his trip to Ne
York and back to Milan in the space of thirty-six hours. E
hausted, he couldn't sleep because he hadn't found her. He
even made a trip to see her little brother but Frankie hadr
heard from her except the usual, weekly check-in call.

Where the hell was she? Had she gone back to Vincenz
knowing now that Massimo didn't deserve her?

Nauseated by his thoughts, he walked into the confe
ence room and grabbed a bottle of water.

Giuseppe and Leo sat on the opposite sides of the lor
conference table with Franco next to Giuseppe and... *Na*
alie next to Leo.

His heart thumped so hard against his rib cage th
Massimo dropped the bottle of water. It hit the carpete
floor with a soft thump, rolling away with a swish. An
he had the most ridiculous notion that it was his heart an
he wanted to groan and laugh and share it with her, but I
had hurt her with his cruel words.

Perversely, he'd never been so cruel to anyone else
his life, only the woman he loved. If that didn't tell hi
everything that was wrong with him...

He wanted to tell her he had all the time in the world
listen to her now but only silence was left. She'd taken jo
and light with her.

Dressed in a white dress shirt that hugged her slend
frame and black trousers, and hair—*Dios mio*, that wav
thick hair, bunched into a sophisticated knot at the top
her head—she looked like composure, and sophisticatio
and brilliance and beauty and heart, all combined into
complex woman.

The woman he adored with every breath in him. The woman he'd go down on his knees for. The woman who could strip him to his soul with one look, one word, one kiss.

The woman who refused to shift her gaze from the laptop screen in front of her and spare him a look. The woman who was even now digging those misaligned front teeth into her lower lip.

"Massimo, take your seat," Leo said. Massimo covered the distance to Natalie, his chest such a tight knot that it was a miracle he could breathe. The scent of her, so familiar, made him shake.

Somehow, he kept his head as Leo began the meeting and Franco asked questions about the recent leak of the security designs while he made copious notes, and in between, there was Natalie, pulling up schematics for a new multilayer security design on the projector, addressing Giuseppe's and Franco's questions, and Massimo went from dumb disbelief to utter amazement.

She had come up with a new set of security designs? She'd been working with Leonardo? Giuseppe—who apparently appreciated Massimo's proactive backing out of the contract because of the security leak, whose CTO had been smart enough to recognize Natalie's unusual talent—had persuaded his board to give BCS another chance.

Natalie's frantic, almost feverish movements in collecting her laptop, her handbag.

He moved his body into her space and she stilled. "I've been to New York to see you. I've seen Frankie." When she turned her stunned gaze at him, he nodded. "He's good. He's excited to see you soon."

"Thanks, but I'll see him in a day. I've tried to repay any damage I've done to the project. You have it, Massimo, everything you ever wanted."

She hitched her bag over her shoulder, calmly dismisse Massimo and moved to Leonardo. There was no spark i her, no fight, no laughter, no joy. Just a...pale imitation.

"Thank you for letting me fix this. I'd prefer to wor from home if you still want me on it. If you arrange for ride to the airport—"

"You're not going anywhere," Massimo bit out.

"Massimo—"

Fury burned through him as he met Leo's gaze. "Yo know I've been going mad trying to find her."

Leo shrugged. "That day, you weren't in a place whe you'd hear a word I said. No chance for rational talk. Yo persuaded me that she was brilliant. I saw no reason to n use her. Later, after I convinced her to fix it, her conditio was that I not tell you."

Had she written him off completely? Had he lost he before he had realized what he'd had?

Leo closed the door behind him. When Natalie move to follow his brother, Massimo waylaid her, trapping he between the table and his body.

"Let me go."

"*No!* Tell me why you helped." He wanted to touch he so desperately, more than he needed his next breath.

"Because that project meant something to me. Bein on a team that created cutting-edge technology, being on team with you and Leonardo and all those men and wome discussing strategies with you, building something real ou of all those years of dreams...it meant something to me.

"More than money. More than the power or prestige it. More than..." She looked away. "All my life, I've neve been a part of a community like that. I wanted to finis what I'd started."

"Then stay. See it through."

"I can't stay near you."

He placed his hands over her shoulders, bracing himself
against the waves of pain crashing through him. "Natalie
mia, will you please look at me?"

He fell for her all over again when she leveled those
beautiful eyes at him and gazed steadily.

"Where do I start, *cara mia*?"

"There's nothing to start, Massimo. Nothing to say…"

He clasped her jaw with his hand, his heart bursting with
all the things he wanted to say. "First, I beg for your forgive-
ness, *tesoro*. Please, Natalie, if you ever thought that there
was something worth knowing in me, loving in me, please,
cara mia, you will stay a minute and you will listen, *sì*?"

She looked up at him then, meeting him square in the
eye. Gaze filled with tears. "You shamed me. You… You
gave me everything…everything I never asked for, everything I never expected to have in life. Everything I had
ever even dreamed of…and in one moment, one moment,
you took it all away, Massimo.

"I've never felt so alone. More alone than that night
when my dad didn't return. To not have known you would
have been okay.

"But to know you and love you and love the best of you
and then…" She looked down, and her tears poured onto
her chest, dampening her white shirt. Massimo pulled her
into his arms, unable to bear her pain, hating that he'd done
this to her. "You made me doubt myself. As if I was less. As
if I didn't deserve you. I only went to him to talk about—"

"No, look at me, Natalie! I don't care why you went. I
don't give a goddamn about him. *Cara mia*, all I care about
is you. About you and nothing else in the world." He tilted
her chin up to look at him and the pain there skewered him.
Cristo, you're the most wonderful thing that has ever come
into my life. The most joyful thing. The thing that Mama
hoped I would find and nurture."

He kissed her soft cheek slowly, softly, breathing in th
scent of her. Looking for courage in the tension that swep
through her body. "Forgive me for all the dirty accusations
A kiss at her temple. "Forgive me for not listening." A kis
on the tip of her nose. "Forgive me for putting the blood
contract before you." A kiss on her forehead. "Forgive m
for not trusting you."

He dropped to his knees, anchoring his hands aroun
her hips, burying his face in her belly. Pressed countles
kisses to every inch of her he could touch and feel. He wa
shaking and he couldn't stop himself because he was sti
afraid he would never hold her like this.

He let the fear and the joy and the warmth gush throug
him, let himself breathe it in. Because this was what lov
ing Natalie meant.

Embracing this…emotional storm. Embracing the fea
Embracing the fact that she'd make him weak and stron
but better for it. And he let her see all the things he couldn
put into words in his eyes. "Forgive me, the most, for no
trusting myself. Forgive me for not listening to the part o
me that is worthy of you.

"Forgive me, *cara mia*, for not saying that I love yo
Forgive me for being an arrogant bastard who couldn't se
love when it kissed him on the mouth and held him in th
night and told him there was a hero inside waiting to ge
out. *Ti amo*, Natalie. You make me a better man, *cara mia*
If you were with me I'd be the best of them all. The be
Brunetti of all. And I'd maybe start a new trend of what
means to be a Brunetti, *sì*?"

Natalie fell into Massimo's waiting arms, the sob she'
been trying to bury bursting out of her chest. "I love you
too, Massimo, so much that it terrifies me. I… I've neve
loved anyone like that. I…want to trust this but—"

"Shh…*cara mia*. No, there's no place for fear or doub

etween us. There's no place for anything but love." And
en he was kissing her mouth, so softly, so tenderly, and
atalie fell into the kiss. His desperation, his relief, his
armth, his love—his kiss spoke of a thousand things and
e took it all in. "Say you'll believe me, Natalie."

He had believed her when he had no reason to. Given
r a chance to prove herself. She would give him a mil-
on chances, she realized, shaking with alarm, but what-
ver fear and doubts came at them, Natalie wanted to face it
ith him. Together. "I do believe you. I'm all in, Massimo."

"We'll bring Frankie here immediately. We'll build a
ome for ourselves. We'll start fresh, *cara mia*, with no
adows. And when you marry me—"

And just like that, Natalie fell in love a little more.
What?" Her heart thudded in her chest.

His eyes shining, Massimo slid his lips over hers in a
lky caress. "When you marry me, we'll start our own
rood of Brunettis and the first thing and the only thing
e will teach them is—"

"How to be courageous in love," she finished, her eyes
ll of tears.

His teeth dug into his lower lip and he nodded. "So you
ill, *sì*?"

"*Sì*. You're my hero." He was so solid and warm and
ard around her. "And you're all mine," she said, and he
odded, and when he pulled her into his lap and buried
is hands under her shirt, looking for warm skin, she gave
erself over to it.

He was her hero. Her man. Her entire life.

EPILOGUE

IF SOMEONE HAD told Natalie a few months ago, or even
few weeks ago, that she'd be walking down a beautiful
manicured path with elegant trees and boxwood and wi
teria on either side, while her little brother walked in fro
of her, toward a stunning vista of lakefronts and mou
tains in an ivory designer gown that supermodel Alessand
Giovanni had requested personally of a designer friend wh
never did private commissions, toward the tech billionai
Massimo Brunetti to make her wedding vows, she'd hav
laughed hysterically.

She'd have rolled on the floor, laughing her ass off.

No woman was so lucky to have a wedding at such
stunning location with the elements behaving perfectly a
if they'd conspired to give her their best on her most im
portant day.

No woman could be so selfish as to demand a design
gown that was yards and yards of lace and tulle that mad
even skinny little hackers look like a princess.

No woman would hope to have a kind, sexy, absolute
wonderful man waiting for her at the end, his heart in h
eyes, looking knee-meltingly gorgeous in a black tuxed

No one in their right mind would at least guess that all
the above could happen to an orphan who'd never thoug
she was worthy of anything so wonderful.

But it was happening. Alessandra and Greta looked stu
ning on one side and Silvio and Leonardo on the other sid

e latter with a warm smile for her that still stunned Nata-
e even after a month since she'd saved the Fiore project.

And then she was there, close to the man she adored
ith all her heart.

As she reached Massimo and he took his hands in hers
d tugged her closer with a little too much enthusiasm
at had the small, intimate crowd laughing, Natalie was
embling, sheer terror that it was all a dream that would
sappear taking hold of her.

His fingers tight around hers, his breath whispering
ainst her temple, Massimo said, "I have you, *cara mia*.
ou're the most beautiful woman I've ever seen and I love
ou so much, and whatever comes our way, we'll face it
gether, *sì*?"

"I'm scared, Massimo. I love you so much and it robs the
ry breath from me when I think of our future and with—"

His finger covered her lips, the warmth of his body a
mforting cocoon. "But I shall never, ever let you go. If
ou fall, I will always catch you. We will build our em-
re or take down someone else's if that's what you pre-
r, *sì*?" he whispered, and Natalie laughed because this
an knew her so well and each day he showed her what
e meant to him.

She licked her lips, knowing that everyone was waiting.
ut God, she didn't want to start their life together with lies
d shadows. "I wanted to tell you but I was afraid. Afraid
at it would hurt you," she added quickly when she saw
e light dim in his eyes. "This…this tiara—" she touched
e exquisitely delicate diamond tiara wrought in the finest
hite gold that had been delivered three days ago sitting on
p of the elaborate coif that her hair had been beaten into
—I… I didn't borrow it from Alessandra. I lied. Because
was worried you wouldn't understand.

"He…he sent it to me."

"I knew it, *bella*."

"What?"

"From the moment you opened the package and tried t hide the packing material and then burst into tears whe you saw the card."

"Please don't be mad, Massimo. I've cut my associatic with him but he was still a big part of my life. He'll alway be a big part of my past and I can't change it and I hate th I hid this from you—"

"I have long decided to forgive him, *cara mia*," he sai stealing the ground from under her. "I will help Leo fir him, and stop him from causing further havoc in our live but how do I stay angry with a man who protected you whe you were alone in the world? How long do I hate a ma who gave me the most wondrous, beautiful gift of you? amo, Natalie. Your past and your present, your stubbor but loyal heart, your fire and your flaws, I adore everythir about you, *cara mia*."

Her tears plopped down her cheeks and Natalie didn give a damn if her makeup was ruined. "I love you, to Massimo. Now, hurry up," she whispered against his mout "so that we can start building that empire and a brood Brunettis."

His eyes glittered with wicked warmth and then th priest was admonishing them and Alessandra sighed ar Frankie asked Leo in a loud whisper if they were going kiss so frequently and then in the midst of the chaos ar the love and the laughter, suddenly, she was now Natal Brunetti.

And when Massimo took her mouth in a soft, tender kis she lost her heart all over again.

* * * * *

JOIN US ON SOCIAL MEDIA!

Stay up to date with our latest releases, author news and gossip, special offers and discounts, and all the behind-the-scenes action from Mills & Boon...

 @millsandboon

 @millsandboonuk

 facebook.com/millsandboon

 @millsandboonuk

It might just be true love...